D0581150

GLASS

GLASS

PATRICK WILMOT

JACARANDA
London

First published in Great Britain 2014 by
Jacaranda Books Art Music Ltd
98b Sumatra Road
West Hampstead
London NW6 1PP
www.jacarandabooksartmusic.co.uk

A CIP catalogue record for this book is available from the British Library.

Typeset by James Nunn.

Printed and bound in Great Britain by CPI Group (UK) Ltd, Croydon, CR0 4YY.

ISBN: 978 1 909762 01 5

The paper this book is printed on is certified by the (c) 1996 Forest Stewardship
Council A.C. (FSC). It is ancient-forest friendly. The printer holds FSC chain of
custody SGS-COC-2061.

MIX
Paper from
responsible sources
FSC
www.fsc.org
FSC® C013604

To the memories of:

Nicolai, my son

and Tajudeen,
my friend, student and comrade

The darkness drops again; but now I know
That twenty centuries of stony sleep
Were vexed to nightmare by a rocking cradle,
And what rough beast, it's hour come round at last,
Slouches toward Bethlehem to be born?

WB Yeats, *The Second Coming*

CHAPTER ONE

The empty water glass skidded on the small wooden table as I jumped when the phone rang. It's not every day you get a call from the Prime Minister of your country, sounding like your bosom buddy, asking you to write his biography. I had been listening to Radio 4 and was switching to the World Service as the ringing filled the room. I must tell you right now I have the worst phone manners in the world, finding myself easily distracted by the TV, or the radio. Sometimes I do crosswords, but mainly I just wander about inside my head, like a fucking vagrant, all while apparently carrying on a conversation with someone. I admit I was paying attention to this phone call, completely unforeseen as it was. Eddy Haddad, Prime Minister of the Caribbean island of Woodwater, was on the phone, his voice high and excited, regaling me with tales from back home, how we were in high school together and offering mostly salacious details to convince me he was not making it up. I'd not been to Woodwater for what seemed a lifetime but am pathologically curious and regularly check the online newspapers to see what my troublesome fellow citizens are up to. 'It's a long time you haven't been home, Prof., not since you wrote the book about Joseph.' When he said 'home' I felt a chill all over and when he called me 'Prof.' I got fine goosebumps on my skin.

'Prof.' was the schoolboy nickname bestowed on me, as the youngest in my class, by a monster of a football player who'd taken it from a rather nasty comic book. The comic featured a scientist with an outsized brain who thought up convoluted experiments with which he threatened to destroy the world. The salvation of our planet was left to his harassed wife, a scarecrow of a woman with mounds of frizzy hair who managed to pull the plug just before we all went ka-boom! The comic was translated from German, and when I studied that language I learnt the 'Prof.'s' literal title was 'Mr Professor Dr. Big Head Full of Shit.'

Years ago I'd written a book about a poor local boy who'd contracted polio as a kid and later overcame it to become a world champion athlete. At the time there was little interest in the story at home; people in poor countries prefer bread to paper. But a clever publisher reprinted it in the UK and it sold. 'You know we're a poor country, Prof.', Haddad continued, 'but the changes of the past few years back home have been spectacular.' His voice, I realised then, sounded odd to me. My dis-ease with the call could partially be explained by the fact that I could understand Eddy clearly. His pronunciation was clipped and precise and it appeared that he must have been coached since our native patois can be so crude, sometimes even I find it tough going. The realisation served to remind me I was speaking to a politician.

'We should get together, Prof.,' said Eddy, 'chew the fat about St Dunstan's, get up to date about what we have done since graduating and,' he paused, 'work out how we can go about writing my biography. In Woodwater we see you all the time on television, now we get *Deutschewelle* and *Al-Jazeera*. You're a real shining star!' Like hell, I thought. He thought he'd manoeuvred me into something I hadn't agreed on; a typical politician's trick to put you in a place where 'No' was not an option. Wrestlers did this when they pinned you in hold to submission – so did rapists. Although I had a favourable impression from the fact we were graduates of the same school, he was still a politician and I knew politics had nothing to do with being nice – especially from the part of the world from which he operated.

'We have to arrange a meet, Prof.,' Eddy prattled on in a thunderstorm of words, repeating himself about how good friends we were as boys. The phone call was becoming tiresome and my mind wandered terribly. The predictable mess that was Radio 6 played *No Regrets* by a singer I wasn't familiar with and my mind immediately latched on to it. As a graduate student I'd gone out to Berkeley, California to present a paper on a play by Hoffmanstahl and got to know a final year student who was possibly the most intelligent woman I ever met. Originally from Japan, she was also fluent in Mandarin, Swahili and six European languages. She had a quiet but determined way and soon we were spending languid hours on the floor of her tiny living room listening to music. She had a CD collection of songs by Tom Rush and Richie Havens but she would always play *No Regrets* and I noticed when we listened to the song how her body went stiff and small raised bumps would form like the opalescent peaks of a tiny mountain range all along her arms and legs. Nothing happened when we listened to other songs but *No Regrets* brought up something frozen from deep inside.

I suspect she'd had some inappropriate relationship, some idiot who jilted her after he had his way. Smart people are often foolish in love; perhaps she believed him when he said he would love her forever. Still, the way she shook when she held on to me seemed to tell a tale of even deeper horror, something, perhaps, truly awful.

'I have a little place on Eaton Square, Prof., and I'll be here another three days. We must get together.' Haddad did not really have a question in his tone, more of a command and there were no 'little places' in that part of the city. I knew. Years ago I had been in that part of London looking for the Instituto Cervantes for a book launch. The book was on the conquest of Spain by the Moors. I saw the mansions that lined the streets there, reined in by shining black wrought iron gates I remember the place, the night, vividly. I had broken a wine glass in my hand when the book's bespectacled author joked to the crowded room about drug dealers beheading opponents in Mexico, and I found myself attempting to share the joke with a German billionaire whose face I only recognised from having seen it splashed across one of the tabloids. I wish I had paid more attention to his story. The frustration rose as my mind went there anyway, desperate to recall why I had seen the images of this man, his face highlighted by the flashing bulbs of the paparazzi, and again as a still image over the shoulder of the poker-faced news reader. I inadvertently clamped down on the glass in my hand and it fell away, shattering into crystalline spears that first seemed to float about us in the air and then stopped abruptly as they made contact with the hardwood floors.

'You give us a time, Prof., although as our Jesuit Fathers always said, "no time like the present"!'

The irony of a man in a gigantic, possibly thirty-million pound house suggesting I set the day and time of our meeting prompted me to want to play hard to get and Eddy continued the charade when we lobbed dates and times at each other, each proclaiming that *no the other was busy, couldn't make it then, sorry.* Finally I grew bored and I told him the day after tomorrow would be fine if he was free. The sigh of relief from him was so fulsome I felt as if the receiver in my hand had begun to inflate.

'Thank you Prof., you don't know how relieved I am you didn't say tomorrow! I have a meeting with the PM, and after that there's a reception I'm expected to attend at the Embassy on Belgrave Square, and then there's dinner at the Palace. I was afraid I wouldn't get the chance to spend quality time with an old friend and distinguished graduate of our old school!'

The other staple of the politician is to flatter, so you lose perspective. I knew this but I was so puffed up thinking of myself in a queue behind the PM, Queen and Duke of Edinburgh, I allowed my Prof.'s Head Full of Shit to swell even larger. My wandering mind took over again as I imagined myself and my new best friend cavorting and consorting with the most beautiful and powerful people, in the best hotels and world-class venues. Then I came to, hearing all the sounds of the surrounding city; the oppressively loud police and ambulance sirens infiltrated the room and competed with the banal clatter of the radio and all the negative energy it brought swelled over me, dark and heavy in my small room. Dimly heard, Eddy's voice chattered on.

My flat on the small leafy Green in west London (surely among the busiest places on earth) is not the best for conversation. I'm on the fifth floor and even when I keep my windows closed traffic sounds like what you'd expect to hear close to a beehive, but heat rises so the windows are mostly open, even in winter and there's no escaping the clatter. It's only a one bedroom flat and I have difficulty throwing things out. The former owner had built a few shelves but those were filled up immediately with the books I'd moved in with and since I don't have a relish for DIY, those I bought since are scattered about on the carpet, chairs, tables and bed. Haddad, reminding me of my comic book namesake, got me thinking I could use a wife to tidy up my mess as while not on the scale of world destruction, the place still looks fucking bad. Listening to my mate Eddy, I surveyed the works of Mankell, Larsson, Nesbo, Nesser and all the others I could not fit next to Chandler, Greene, Achebe, Ngugi and Hemingway. When my confined space pressed in on me, and I started to yearn for open space I checked out Google Earth, looking at locations along the Thames, from Putney Bridge up to Walton-upon-Thames where the loony killed that poor little girl. I was obsessed with the glasshouse between Kingston and Hampton Court and longed for a place like that if ever I had the coin.

The previous owner of my flat had been a slob. When I arrived the grey carpet was so worn I could see the black slab flooring coming through the open pile. And I couldn't decide whether the grey painted walls had begun life that way, or if out of sheer neglect over the years whatever optimistically pale hue they once were had given way to the putrid, deadening colour they had become. Since I hated all forms of DIY and repairs, I found a Trinidadian chap who cheerfully replaced the old grey carpet with a thick new navy one and painted the depressing grey walls a brilliant sky blue. Eddy's voice, along with the blue walls made me recall my island home in vivid colour. I was seeing our fabled blue sea and sky, our rare butterflies, hummingbirds of dazzling brilliance and speed and was filled with a growing nostalgia. Even though I had no truck with politicians, still, I was curious. As a small child I couldn't avoid turning off on any branch of road as I was walking wanting to know where it led, what it might reveal. And despite my intellectual mantra that we 'bring truth to power', I was fascinated with the money and influence represented by a man like Eddy. Unsure and unknowing I found myself agreeing to meet Eddy in London and to return to Woodwater with him. The latter left a knot of apprehension and excitement in the pit of my belly. I was going back home.

CHAPTER TWO

The voice on the intercom announcing the drive to the PM's 'little place' possessed my hometown accent but his was distinctly overlaid with what must have been years of elocution. As I made my way down the five flights of stairs to the waiting car I tried to imagine what the speaker looked like. None of my imaginings came close.

'I'm Donovan, sir. I went to St Dunstan's; I remember you from your photos. You were always pictured with medals from track or certificates in exams'. He smiled me into the car.

Donovan was a bit taller than me, not that much younger but far superior in looks and build, with a handsomely square face and soft but intelligent large brown eyes. He was immaculately (and expensively) dressed. I admit I was surprised a driver could afford to wear an Ermenegildo Zegna suit or that he had been able to afford St Dunstan's fees, which usually produced recruits for the Professions, business and politics. I was even more surprised to see the stretch limousine and two motorcycle cops, whose flashing lights seemed to compete with the garishly effusive Christmas lights running the length of the high road and across all the shops, whether they were internet cafes owned by Somalis, or the grocery stores run by bearded men from Iran, Iraq and Afghanistan.

We moved through the traffic, the car expertly guided by Donovan's manicured hand. I took note of the silent tower blocks across the Green, the shabby displays at the Christmas Fair, the bare trees and anonymous crowds, some who had gathered to stare at the limo as if Christ had made the Second Coming and was ushering them into Paradise. On the Green dahlias were emerging even though it was only December. The Somali-owned mobile phone shop displayed wilted yellow flowers, reminding me of an old Tennessee Williams film where a wizened old hag sold flowers. But I couldn't remember her chants as she dragged herself along the decaying alleyways of New Orleans.

When I tired of the food I usually bought at the Caribbean takeaways littered along the high street, I went along the Uxbridge Road to buy pitta bread, houmous, falafel, goat's cheese, yogurt and spices at one of the Arab shops with Christmas trees. Just above the falafel shop, advertising boards displayed vast portraits of Beyoncé and Rita Ora, looking down suggestively and invitingly on the long lines of pimply youths waiting for one of their screeching hip-hop heroes to go on stage at the famous O2 Empire and indulge them in fantasies of cosmetic sex, synthetic violence, plastic feelings and disposable emotions. Admittedly at the sight of the giant hyper-sexed images of the women, I felt a twinge in my groin and it wasn't because of rumours Jay-Z was nailing Rita – that must be a lie; the Prince doesn't poke the frog when he's already got a fucking superstar Princess in his bed.

We sped on alongside the giant glass-sided mall, which loomed up, dominating the landscape where once there was grass and small houses. Once the mall was built, the cops were more diligent about escorting druggies and alkies away as their presence was deemed incompatible with the big money the mall owners saw coming. From the car, there were no more people visible only the glass of the building and the concrete of the road.

'We'll be there in fifteen minutes, Sir.'

'You don't need to call me sir, Donovan. I'm not that old.'

'Yes, sir.'

His suit may have been expensive, his hands manicured and heavily moisturized, but his thinking we could get to Eaton Square in fifteen minutes was crap. More sirens blared as two cop cars and an ambulance cut through the traffic like Moses parting the Red Sea.

'A drink, sir?'

I looked at the bar, at bottles you couldn't get in any shop – including Harrods.

'I'll take an Armagnac, Donovan.' I said, reaching into the nest of miniature bottles. To save my liver and pocket I normally drank only on weekends but one should never disregard free booze.

On the seat beside me were three Duchamp shirts along with three Armani ties. I imagined Eddy changing between Number 10, the High Commission and Palace. Donovan's Hermes lemon scent wasn't strong enough to mask the odour of musk, fine leather and exquisite brandy now filling the car. Settling back into the soft sweet-smelling leather seat an old Don Drummond number played softly in the background and I was sure I'd hear Bob Marley's 'No *Woman, no Cry* before we arrived. Deep inside me some memory of Eddy from our schooldays was rising like mist in a graveyard. With the police escort we were making rapid progress and the usual paranoia I felt on buses, when stressed for time we'd hit every red light, under Donovan's expert driving and the police escort, turned into a swift ride through the streets of London. We flowed along like celebrities, royalty. In the limousine the houses around Sloane Square didn't look as intimidating as when I was searching for the Instituto Cervantes on foot. I supressed a smile when cracking open the car window as we pulled up to Eaton Square, a woman who could have played a body double for Camilla Parker-Bowles, bumped the latest Jay-Z – Kanye West hit from her small Audi. The waves of sound reverberating throughout was what I would have expected from a young brother who the *Mail* and *Telegraph* would swear was on his way to a hit or drug deal.

'Welcome, sir.' Donovan, the richest smelling lemon I had ever met smiled his welcome to me over the open car door. I surveyed my surroundings, the huge white columns flanking the heavy, shiny, black front door, its brass knocker and numbers gleaming in the night. Above my head were six floors of money, in the street in front of my parked car were two black Bentleys and a maroon Maserati Quattroporte. I looked at my fake Omega which now felt extra cheap and my silent stare congratulated Donovan's prescience: we'd arrived in twelve minutes.

'Watch your step, sir.' He smiled again.

I was a bit rocky after the Armagnac and my eyes were fixed on the expensive cars guarded by two huge cops with Heckler and Koch submachine guns. The cars had no diplomatic plates, and there was no flag above the house. I assumed this must be the private property of Eddy Haddad. I marvelled at the apparent wealth of his people. I knew a lot of people with names like Haddad who had made it big since migrating from the Middle East and who'd made the Caribbean their home. Many of them had been in school with me. I shook my head to clear it from the slightly alcoholic haze I was in and followed Donovan who was leading me through a six-inch thick black door, that alone must have cost more than my whole garret, towards a cloakroom smelling of the same musk as the car. I didn't need it as I hadn't worn an overcoat. Somehow in mid-December I thought it would appeal to the macho in my PM, coming from a country which prided itself on its national virility. Donovan hadn't bothered with a coat either.

'Through here, sir.'

He opened another thick black interior door and I tried to stifle my gasp, hanging from the ceiling were six enormous crystal chandeliers, centred above four low, very fine, tan leather couches. Beneath the chandeliers were thick gleaming glass tables and the smell of wealth and power, the very mixture from the car of musk and hide, citrus and alcohol, in this room became overpowering. Over a cavernous marble fireplace, a forty-inch plasma television played a DVD showing oil rigs scattered across an expanse of cobalt blue sea. Around the room Eddy had placed paintings of scenes from the Caribbean and though beautiful they seemed entirely out of context in the environs; the colours too intense, the styles too *avant-garde* for Eaton Square. There were metres of dark leather-bound books with gold lettering. Uniform in size, they seemed to have been chosen and arranged purely for decoration. Most of the floor was marble, but in places thick blue and gold carpet was laid. In the corner was the largest indoor Christmas tree possible, heavy with silver, ruby, gold and blue ornaments. Underneath it were brilliantly wrapped presents, alongside a large beautifully crafted wooden hamper containing bottles of a world-renowned 25 year old rum West Indian, small hessian bags of the finest Caribbean coffee (the kind the Japanese bought in bulk) and a Patek Phillipe watch in a gilt gift box. This was an Aladdin's cave replete with the treasures of the world. But the best treasure of all was the bronze statuette Eddy retained of the island's greatest male sprinter, made by the Caribbean's finest sculptor, the incomparable Gamboe Botbhi. Gamboe took his name from the ancient woodman of the Baole region of Cote D'Ivoire whose statues, plundered by French conquistadors and housed in the Museum of Man in Paris, became the inspiration for Braque, Giacometti and Brancusi. There was also a brilliant glass figurine of the island's greatest female athlete. Lalique had created ten exclusives of athletes, three of which were owned by two of the world's wealthiest billionaires and Eddy Haddad.

I approached the bookshelf, wanting to check the beautifully bound titles, and found myself nonsensically comparing the shelves to my own dilapidated, overflowing ones at home, but Donovan appeared in front of me, slightly preceded by the sound the movement of his arm made against the expensive fabric of his suit. He guided me into a pristine lift that did not appear to have ever been used.

CHAPTER THREE

The lift door opened revealing it's innards, it was lined with the same soft tan leather as the drawing room chairs. There were eight buttons, six for the ground and upper floors, one for lower ground, and another for lower-lower ground. There was the clinging leftover odour of feminine perfume starkly contrasting the more masculine scents I had been enveloped in since getting into the car behind Donovan. We ascended in silence, me thinking about the invisible woman, (probably a heartbreaker, who snuck away in the night leaving only the hint of a vapour as a reminder of the body). Feeling no sensation of us having moved at all, we arrived at our floor and the solid metal door opened soundlessly onto another heavily carpeted hallway. Off this there was another cloakroom, with racks of men's thick, blue overcoats, and hung apart, a woman's smaller, lighter red one.

'In here, sir.'

When he opened the door I did not see the identical exquisitely handmade chandeliers, leather couches, Christmas tree, or more metres of books. Nor did I see the plasma television showing more oil platforms in an even deeper cobalt blue to that of the television downstairs. I only saw her. She wore a white silk blouse, against which her long, black hair lay seductively, black wool slacks hid long, long legs, and I assumed the bright red coat in the cloakroom was hers. The feminine perfume from the lift hung in the air and I wondered if it meant she was a young woman with taste for old-style lovemaking. The stiffness in my briefs reminded me of how horny I was. I couldn't remember the last time I was with a woman. I'd recently seen a set of sexy red lingerie in the Style section of the Sunday newspaper, the colour so intense I had to don my sunglasses. I imagined her in them now and felt for the big hankie in my pocket I would use to blindfold myself when my cock slid into her and the crimson spurted a million miles into the air like a fucking solar flare.

'I'm Maria, Prof.; Eddy will soon be with you. Welcome.'

When I was about twelve I attended the finals of a debating contest presided over by a beauty queen who'd attended the girls' Academy twinned with St Dunstan's. It was an annual affair and that year St Dunstan's had won. The beauty queen's hair was dark recalling a thick forest above her face, which itself might have been carved in heaven. I was the smallest boy in the room, along with my friend Chin. She kept looking at me and smiling, and by the time the debate finished I was convinced she was in love with me. How jealous I'd felt when she presented the winning trophy to my classmate and kissed him on the cheek.

When she was leaving she detoured to stoop and kiss me on the cheek (she *was* in love with me!) and all the boys and girls screamed at me, 'Lover Man!' From her look I could tell she thought I was affecting some kind of curtsey but even then my cock was like an electric pole and I had to bend low to hide it from her and Chin (who was snickering and pointing at it). She became the standard against which I judged beauty in all women, my version of the Platonic Form of the ideal woman. As if she had been poured into her low-cut white dress, she'd bent over to kiss me and I saw the tops of her breasts bursting against the blue silk of her lace bra. Her perfume had been distilled from all the flowers in the Garden of Eden before Adam and Eve fucked up. I was only twelve but had to think of ice blocks to steady the rise in my pants, which would have drawn even more raucous cheers from the mob of screaming children.

Maria, now standing before me in Eddy's luxurious house did not have as spellbinding an effect on me as my childhood beauty queen, but the way I was feeling toward her was not far from it and I inwardly thanked Eddy for providing me with such a gift. Maria beckoned me to a spot next to her on the couch. I sat there eagerly, but made sure I left just enough space between us to show I was not desperate, and therefore non-threatening, but enough to slide into if things started heating up. I thought at first I had to be careful, that Maria might be Eddy's girl or fiancé. But the way she looked at me suggested otherwise. Her eyes told me that she was ready, willing and able, perhaps even that she was mine for the night. You might have figured out by now that I'm emotionally disadvantaged when it comes to women. Although I'm a very intelligent guy, I'm a Speedy Gonzalez when it comes to love – as soon as I see a nice face I fall in love, and should just even the tips of our fingers touch my mind goes overboard creating searingly pornographic images of innocent women I have just met.

Donovan appeared suddenly, bringing with him a bottle of 1980 Chateauneuf-du-Pape and two very large, elegant red wine glasses.

'Sir, this is Miss Maria's favourite.' The smile again.

Either Donovan was being cute, saying it was Maria's favourite, or there was something else that joined her with me besides our potential mutual desire to screw. At my university on Sunday's when parents visited, they would serve us the very same wine along with fourteen-inch sirloin steaks, so the wealthy parents would think their children were eating as well as they did at home and that the exorbitant fees were worth it. Eddy's attention to detail (it takes some sort of ability to become PM at his age), must have been the reason behind why the wine was being served now and then there was the *Patek Phillipe* watch, superb coffee and grand old rum he'd put under the Christmas trees. If you had read my work over the years, all of these items would have been mentioned as the ideals of perfection I'd buy when and if finally I had the bread to do so.

'Cheers,' Maria said, as we clinked our glasses. 'Eddy had such a bitch of a day, he's sorry to keep you waiting. He so wanted to see his old schoolmate – these people just won't let him rest!' She sounded very close to Eddy, and was clearly concerned about his welfare. I began, reluctantly, to have second thoughts about us, but the look in her eyes and the way she licked the wine from her lips, assured me we were still on the road to a very beautiful friendship. The wine was excellent as usual, bringing back so many memories, but I swore to slow down, not let it push me into a place where I could be accused of boorish conduct. Alcohol messed up my judgement and if I'd known I'd meet a stunner like Maria I wouldn't have had the mediocre South African

Shiraz from the supermart. I sipped the Chateauneuf, looked deep into her eyes and imagined myself back in my small flat, with her in my arms, pushing the books from my single bed making space for what we were longing for now.

'Eddy said you were a fantastic distance runner, that you won a lot of races.' She leaned in toward me to speak and I could feel her breath on the side of my face.

'Not that good, Maria.' I said, feigning humility. 'Eddy's a politician – you know how they like to exaggerate!'

Was she saying she knew I had stamina, like the girls from the Academy who used to approach me after I'd run some exhausting race, when I couldn't have done anything even if they pulled me on top of themselves and tied me up?

I did have stamina and a talent for running, but I'd been introduced to athletics as punishment and practice was always pure torture. As a child I would run fast, as if I was running away from a bogeyman who was chasing me, threatening to chew me up if he caught me. My PE master, Father Reinhardt, was an ex-Green Beret studying to be a Jesuit and we all had nightmares of him as the master torturer. His ruddy skin and pale blonde crew-cut conjured images of Nazi's and the SS, especially when we saw the sneer he always seemed to have on his face as he watched us working out, sweating in the harsh October Caribbean sun.

One particularly hot afternoon, feeling extremely thirsty, I drank some water on my way to practice. This of course meant I was late. When I arrived the master torturer ordered me to run the water out. To do this I had to run for what seemed like hours until he was satisfied that all the sweat leaving my body was somehow equivalent to the amount of water I had dared to ingest without his permission. I ran and ran becoming increasingly disoriented and looking much the worse for wear until I couldn't see or hear anyone or anything, least of all him. I couldn't hear when he shouted to me to stop, his face red and contorted in concern and I certainly didn't see his ugly face as he screamed his commands at me. I kept running until I collapsed on the track and all my schoolmates rushed forward sure that I had succumbed. I hadn't and ironically surviving this event made me something of a star at school. When I got out of the sick bay the athletics coach sent for me and I became the star of our track and field team. Scarred by my experience however, I refused to train. No amount of threats could get me back in the field without spectators and supporters lining the tracks. That season I never lost a race. I kept winning though I refused to train and the coaches had no choice but to field me each time. Many years later I searched online for Father Reinhardt and discovered his had finally vented his masochistic spleen in South America. He then truly found religion after being involved in the massacre of an entire village in El Salvador. Glancing over at Maria's profile in the dim light I gave her a look I hope conveyed that I was hers tonight, for as long as she desired.

Ever the dutiful and expert employee, Donovan interrupted us again. 'The PM's sorry, Prof.,' Donovan said, 'he was coming over when he received a call from the President. He said he hopes Miss Maria's taking care of you. More wine?' He picked up the bottle and saw there was still some.

'No, Donovan, thank you. Miss Maria and I are ok.'

CHAPTER FOUR

'**P**rof.!' Eddy's voice shattered the sensuous quiet in the room sending fireworks off in my head. The magic man had arrived. I didn't know how I had managed to forget him – his voice was so far beyond forgetting. He was tall, with the upper body, shoulders and arms of a boxer but there was not an ounce of fat on him as he moved towards us, shaking off his jacket which Donovan expertly caught. In his tailored Duchamp shirt, with one arm outstretched, his fingers splayed in anticipation of the grip he was about to give my waiting, outstretched hand, he continued, as if to the entire room, 'Prof. was my inspiration for all those races you watched me run at Florida State, Maria.'

I jumped to my feet, feeling thankful that, yet again, my education had trained me to at least know the proper form when greeting people.

'You won everything from 1,500 to 10,000 metres, if I recall, Eddy. You were such a talent. The star, Maria!'

Instead of a handshake Eddy suddenly moved both arms upwards and grabbed me by my shoulders, encircling me. He was squeezing the life out of me. 'And I owe it all to this man!' I tried not to notice that my feet while in his embrace had left the ground. He then let me go, grinning widely and I attempted to sit back down on the couch with a modicum of grace.

Donovan put the jacket on the chair next to our couch, the label conveniently exposed. It was vicuna, a relative of the alpaca, only ten times more expensive. We settled down to talk, the silence feeling slightly awkward now that Eddy's booming voice was stilled. Maria sat between us exuding a sexiness that was deeply distracting. Finally Eddy broke the silence. 'Maria's Cuban, Prof. Her grandfather was a comrade of Fidel's till *El Commandante* became a colossus. You know not all men can breathe the same air as the Almighty! The old man now lives in Miami and Maria's father is a state senator there. He's being considered for VP on the Republican ticket.' I nodded along as he spoke. So Maria had pedigree, she wasn't some woman he'd picked up online to keep me happy for the night after all. Donovan delivered a ceramic bottle of Stolichkaya vodka, (apparently the same kind was made for Vladimir Putin), together with small white dishes containing brown sugar, slices of lime, nutmeg and ice.

Maria didn't seem to want the conversation focussed on her, she brought it back to the only topic we'd talked of all evening: the athletic prowess of our schoolboy days.

'I thought you boys were sprinters, Eddy, including the gifted one who had polio, the one Prof. wrote about.'

Eddy nodded in agreement. 'But Prof. was the master, Maria. You know he never ever practiced? He would just turn up and run like the blazes, but he never practiced a day'.

'You played some football, didn't you, Eddy?' I ventured

hesitantly, not sure I wanted him to know yet how much I had researched him since our initial phone call. One article revealed he had been a kicker for the football team at Florida State. 'You have such a memory, Prof.! I was a right back on the team, but that was after you had already left for America.'

Maria then asked if I had played football in America, to which Eddy let out a roar of booming laughter. I admit I almost did too. 'I couldn't make the football team, Maria. That would've required practice and a better build than I had,' I said, recalling I was so small opponents could have punted me down the field along with the ball.

'You know that book he wrote was about a boy in my constituency, Maria. After the exceptional success of it, I got many, many votes when people heard I was in school with Prof.' Flattery will get you everywhere I thought.

'I cried when I read it, Ed'. Maria seemed genuinely moved. 'They should make it into a film. A boy with polio who becomes an Olympic sprinter is pure Hollywood.'

'Indeed, Maria'. Eddy tried to not sound dismissive. 'You know they called Prof. 'Lover Man' in school? He was a real lady killer back then!'

I had problems interpreting Maria's look; her eyes were so deeply guarded I couldn't tell if it was fear in them or admiration for the man she would fuck tonight, though he was a committed philanderer. But the smell of her perfume and the way she licked the wine from her lips staring fixedly it seemed, at my groin gave me the assurance I needed. Then through the doorway emerged a ghost from both our pasts and a chill ran through me.

CHAPTER FIVE

Elizabeth Cairncross was the preternaturally mature and beautiful scion of one of Woodwater's oldest and wealthiest families. Growing up on the island the Cairncross name was as synonymous with our country as the blue water, and sugar cane. The Cairncross family ancestors were among the early invaders who conquered Woodwater. And John Cairncross, though he was a devout Catholic, was one of the biggest slave owners. He had at one time, the largest plantation in the Caribbean. An ally of the early pirates, Henry Morgan and Francis Drake and a distant relation to Queen Elizabeth II, John Cairncross also had a passion for architecture. He had designed many of the immense old plantation houses and developed the island into one of the Caribbean's most valuable colonies. Back then and to this day the Cairncross's ran everything. A Cairncross was captain of the national cricket team, several were among our champion polo players, their grand ladies opened all the new schools, banks, churches, stadiums, and their name was on many boulevards and fine buildings. So prolific were their men that as much as up to ten per cent of the island's population were named Cairncross.

Like her forebears Elizabeth Cairncross made her mark on the world at an early age. Elizabeth's sport at school was target shooting and the newspapers the family owned often published pictures of her as a child posing with her father's hunting guns, or successfully competing in competitions all over the island. When I graduated from university at eighteen, I saw her picture on the front page of the *New York Times*, smiling her dazzling smile, looking confidently, maybe even a little defiantly into the camera. They had captioned the picture 'Ice Queen' her name unofficially, because of how steady her hands were and how beautiful yet attainable she appeared to be.

She had just competed at a tournament in Madison Square Gardens, where she made perfect scores. She was sixteen years old. The newspaper article was all focused on the surety of her gold medal at the coming Olympics (one of only two our little island could expect that year) and listed all the princes, professors, sportsmen, playboys and tycoons who were either lusting after her or wanted to marry her. She seemed to have the world in the palm of her hand. But then almost overnight everything changed for her. The papers began running stories of her falling apart. Pictures of her in a notorious dive in Harlem, in the arms of a horrendously muscled popular musician, whose hands were buried in areas they had no right to be. Another showed her in the same musician's seedy apartment, eyes bloodshot looking dishevelled and completely stoned, the weed smoke in the room not thick enough to hide the tranches of cocaine on their table.

When she attempted to return to the tournament at her family's insistence and with their characteristic determination to distort reality, no amount of make-up could conceal the bruises on her cheeks and around her eyes and the scandal then became not so much about her behaviour, but focussed on her family's apparent lack of care, since they insisted she carry on competing instead of getting the help she desperately needed. She dropped out of the tournament, didn't make the Olympics, and the newspapers in which her family were major shareholders ran no more stories making mention of her.

Seeing her before me now, she looked like a beggar from the street. She had aged badly, wore a tatty, faded black tee-shirt and torn denim jeans that showed off her thin frame. Despite it being December, she wore an old pair of flip-flops so worn down on one side her toes splayed out in order to keep them on her feet. She was an addict for sure. I saw the marks like jiggers between her toes, as if she had run out of veins for shooting up her daily syringes of heroin and coke. Unlike all of the people I had spoken to up until now, ironically, Elizabeth Cairncross, the most well-bred and educated of them all, had adopted the accent of the yard or ghetto.

Eddy went over to her, it momentarily made for a sad strange picture of extremes: great wealth and great loss. 'Lizzie, my dear friend, this is Prof. Remember I told you about him? He's the writer of the book about the Olympian.'

'Me know him. After you people make all that noise about him book me read some of it, about that poor disable boy. His parent's old house not far from ours on the hill.'

I couldn't seem to take my eyes off Elizabeth, even as I barely understood what she was saying. My mind wandered back to the image of her as a young and beautiful island girl so full of potential. 'Me go down their house one time', she flicked her head in my direction. 'Window dem all board up, all the door open but nobody go inside to take a thing. Me go in and cook, tell me father me enter where devil fear to tread.' Elizabeth looked weary.

'Prof. don't know about the house, Liz. His grandma who lived downtown bring him up,' Eddie spoke as if to a confused child.

No matter what drugs she was on, Elizabeth could hear the warning in his voice. The room began to get warm and my head started to feel light. Eddy looked sharply at me as I began to slump toward Maria. I'd been too shattered to tell Donovan 'no' when he'd brought more wine and clearly I'd had too much to drink. I could hear them talking, see their images stark and clear like cartoon characters but I wasn't there anymore. I was in my grandmother's house and there was a hurricane raging outside.

My grandmother was a kind woman, what Boll said of Robert Faehmel's mother would have fit her as well as her signature blue headtie: *full of compassion the eternal heart.* Her house was the only sturdy one in the quarter and my grandma was a kind of local celebrity. It was she who gathered all the poor ones in to take shelter, singing about Jesus spreading his wings over his precious little ones. But the devil was at work also.

Outside the hurricane winds blew above the low-lying dwellings of the poor tearing the roofs from their reinforced concrete houses, denying refuge to the occupants. The rain water poured down on us in great sheets. Enemies who hadn't spoken to each other for years embraced, spoke of their love for each other, born of desperation, and begged for their Lord's forgiveness and a dry skies. The Lord replied with atomic rolls of thunder so powerful it sent the people back on their knees in supplication, a state perhaps more pleasing to the Almighty. As if He really gave a shit.

CHAPTER SIX

P rof. had a nap, Maria! You know these big brains work so
hard they need a rest to cool!' Eddy chuckled. Shaking off
my drunken inertia I looked over at Maria to see if she
was disappointed I seemed to lack stamina after all. There was
alarm in her face but I didn't think a woman like her would get
so upset at not being fucked energetically this night. There was
humour in Eddy's voice but not enough to hide the mockery at
my frailty. Schoolmates or not, politicians thought intellectuals
were pussies. I checked my watch to see how long I was out,
saw it was less than a quarter of an hour though it seemed
embarrassingly longer than that. I looked for Elizabeth who
I blamed for my condition, stirring up memories I obviously
wasn't equipped to handle. But she had left in a hurry apparently,
leaving behind, like two black rubber turds, on the gold and
blue carpet her worn out flip-flops. My eardrums pounded as
if the thunder from the perpetual storm that raged over my
grandmother's house in my dream had followed me to Eaton
Square. I saw a look of horror on Maria's face and followed her
gaze to the sight of a man like a moving mountain making his

way across from the DVD player in the corner of the room over to where we sat.

Rhino was a political thug turned dancehall star, who earned his name because of the shape of his sloped and ridged head and his behaviour, as wild and deadly as the common rhino. When under attack Rhino preferred to defend and even kill with a vicious head-butt rather than a typical gangster choice of weapon – an M16 rifle. I watched with deep unease as he approached Maria and pulled her into his arms in greeting. The bulk he possessed appeared to be crushing poor Maria and although I didn't think he could take her from me, I was afraid his voice might overwhelm her, causing agonising confusion. His thick black dreadlocks hung from his head like colossal vines and smelt of stale weed and old incense. His eyes were hidden behind gigantic shades whose mirrored lenses reflected us back to ourselves and in them we looked like miniature actors in a staged set piece. Around his neck lavish gold chains were ostentatiously layered and he wore a Gaultier coat of many colours beneath which hung an Alexander McQueen silk smock. At his wrist a classic gold Rolex shone and a multitude of giant gems and ornate gold rings bedecked each thick, fat finger. A sheen of sweat covered him like swamp-water over bog-land. Rhino was also Elizabeth Cairncross' lover. The one whose giant fists had tattooed the bruises I saw on her earlier, some faded and sepia toned, others fresh, red and raw. The one who introduced ghetto life to her, the life she now seemed unable to turn away from. Now I understood why she had disappeared so suddenly.

'Clive', Eddy's tone caused Rhino to release Maria from his grasp. 'Prof. is the man who's writing the book about us in the party'. This caused the big man to finally throw a disdainful look in my direction. Prof., this is Clive, I'm sure you know who he is.' I struggled to make eye contact with him. Clive didn't give a shit about some nobody who wasn't a dancehall musician, drug smuggler, or mass killer. He had already returned his attention to Maria and was busy telling her about the new mansion he'd just bought in Florida, where the main radio station played his chart-topping singles continuously. A shiny green board with red neon stars logged his hits everytime they reached number one. He continued to tell of how in his honour they'd made a replica of the waterfalls near the village he was born in. But he was a real ghetto youth, his patois unapologetically dense, his attitude crass and careless. Maria's face, contorted in barely hidden revulsion, said it all.

'Clive house near your father own, Maria. I'm sure the old man enjoy Clive song!' Eddy said.

I stifled a laugh. I'm sure Maria's father called the cops 24/7 to tell them how much he dug the hallucinatory noise of the gigantic cock-sucking *Negro*. Right-wing Cubans were known racists, that's the reason they hated Fidel and loved Reagan, the Bushes and Romney. Eddy continued in the same vein, but I was focused on Rhino and his past antics. I wondered how he got back into the country. Last time he was here he sang his hit song 'Kill all Battyman' at the Brixton Academy, middle-class Brits applauded – they didn't understand his words. But when a BBC Radio 1 presenter who worshipped Caribbean music showed up, dancing wildly as he shouted, 'show them your big horn, Rhino!' Clive stood on stage and singling out the BBC presenter, denounced him as a 'battyman' and incited his followers to attack. They swarmed the young man, kicked him to the ground, beat him unconscious with bicycle chains and gun butts, then stabbed him. Clive was castigated in the press, the Home Secretary signed an immediate deportation order and declared him *persona non grata* for as long as he lived.

'So how did you get back into the country?' Astonished, I turned in the direction of Maria's voice as she dared to ask what I had been thinking. I held my breath, absorbed by the girth of Rhino's upper body, unnerved by the fact that we had not yet seen his eyes. They remained camouflaged behind his mirrored sunglasses. Maria drew her hand through her dark hair. The move was suggestive just enough to entice Rhino to loosen his tongue. His voice sounded harsh, overworked and abused by too many cigarettes, blunts and alcohol, he nonetheless, with great willingness launched into an animated account.

We all listened in silence as he detailed how he had escaped the deportation order, calling on friends and the odd acquaintance and finally scoring a lift on a private jet belonging to some oil executives who were celebrating having found a colossal oil field off the south coast of the island. Once he'd escaped back to Woodwater it wasn't long before his criminal tendencies found an outlet and he was back drug dealing and gun running, even as his records climbed the charts and his popularity surged along with his increasing notoriety. Here the story became vague, Rhino used his raucous laugh more than actual words and I struggled to follow what he was saying. Eddy, looking pleased and uneasy all at once seemed to be willing Rhino to shut up. I concluded Rhino was only in this room, his massive hands all over *my* beautiful girl, his irritating voice over-bearing, at Eddy's bequest and that there must be money involved. Eddy wasn't above showing those dependent on his favours that he was boss and could do what the fuck he wanted. Rhino continued, now complaining about his cousin and dancehall rival, Cabal, who had just been jailed for twenty-three years in Miami-Dade County, Florida, for a list of at least thirty-five offences many of which would have earned a less well-connected criminal several life sentences.

'I tell you, Eddy, them put Cabal in solitary because him is a black man and come from a island where man is man and don't like battyman.'

I'd read about A.B Cabal, how he had been caught by Federal agents travelling on a private Falcon jet chartered by a big oil company with fifty kilos of coke from Ciudad Juarez. He carried five enormous bales of Jamaican marijuana, seven AK47s, five M16s, six Uzis and eight thousand rounds of ammunition. He was also in possession of the .45 Colt used to kill seven decapitated opponents of his gang. While they were processing him they discovered the thirteen-year-old whom Cabal was promoting as the new dancehall queen, was pregnant with his child. Not even the plea by his expensive lawyers of his diplomatic immunity – a letter of invitation from the oil company CEO who was Honorary Consul of his country – cut water with the prosecuting authority, especially when they found he had twenty-seven million dollars in various accounts and a notebook listing the top ten leaders of the notorious Bathtub Posse, who had killed almost fifteen hundred people in the US and Canada. 'We got to do something 'bout the boy, Eddy. Me grow up with him, we go a school together, play football, make music, and do the ting with plenty girl. Him going crazy in that isolation cell in Miami,' the Rhino said.

'I tell you be patient, Clive. This is diplomacy, not dancehall. In diplomacy you got to be patient, star, you can't rush t'ing like you do in music. All day me meet with executive from here and America. Me tell these people we can't give them no oil if them keep we boy political prisoner. Just before you come, me on the phone with the President, me tell him when me come a Washington me going make him know the problem we having.' Instead of exchanging sweet nothings with Maria, I was listening to this statesman explain in *patois* to a psychopathic killer how he would use diplomacy to free a mass murderer, drug baron, and child molester from his maximum security prison cell.

'Me tell you, Eddy, me going get a bunch of boy from town and go down there and bust him out. Me nah play-play battyman, you know, star.'

I could see some alarm on Eddy's face, 'I tell you, Clydie – no busting out, no violence, no gunman high on ganja smoke. This time we got to give Diplomacy a chance, star. You know what you Rastaman say – peace and love, brotherman, peace and love!'

There was total incomprehension on Rhino's face. For him, dancehall, drug-dealing, extortion and mass murder were violence in its natural state. Elizabeth had not only been his lover but had begun to manage his career. She had brokered the deal resulting in his recording contract from which he made his millions, and I'd seen the thanks his fists and forehead had wrought on her body. He didn't dislike her but his love of violence demanded it. Sitting where she was she must have seen his locks and shades on the CCTV when he pressed the bell and she'd left to get some respite: it was written in scripture that God never gave you more shit than you could bear.

Then suddenly there was a shift in atmosphere in the room. A relaxed calm descended on all the faces in the room. An impossible transformation came over Rhino as if he had been shot up with a tanker load of muscle relaxant and he was now in favour of Eddy's 'Diplomacy'. And the sun appeared to rise in Eddy's eyes when Donovan rushed in and whispered 'Mr Brett is here, PM.' When I saw Mr Brett's face I wondered what magic this miracle man was wielding over my companions.

CHAPTER SEVEN

His blonde hair cascaded like a waterfall just above his shoulders, which themselves were broad, comfortingly so, as if imagined by Hollywood. He was tall enough to play basketball alongside Lebron James. His navy turtleneck jersey and light blue jeans looked as if they had been spray painted on his body and when he removed his Ray Bans I saw his eyes were colour-coded with his clothes. Maria, the woman I thought Eddy had procured for me, shouted 'Honey!!!' then leapt into Brett's arms and locked him into an open-mouthed kiss, looking as if she was attempting to swallow him, her tongue flopping about his face. She was dangling at least a foot off the floor, his arms wrapped around her tiny torso and together they were an ode to Popeye and Olive.

When on the political trail, Eddy usually fired up his ghetto followers with shouts of 'crazy baldheads' and blamed the ills of the ghetto on 'White Leeches' and 'Cuban Communists' but now confronted with Brett's blonde-haired, blue-eyed version of beauty, was so excited he looked like he wanted to replace Maria in Brett's comforting arms. Clive, one of whose songs I had deciphered to mean 'White men are battymen' and 'their women need black cock to make them real women', could have been on his knees, or prostrate on the carpet, his intimidating bravado diminished by the presence of Brett's real deal machismo. Against Brett's sleek physical prowess, it was clear who didn't need to be brutish to show power. Seemingly out of deference to Mr Brett, the Rhino had removed his shades, his squinted eyes suggesting he was near-sighted, like his animal namesake. Without his dark, prescription glasses, and in relation to Brett, Rhino seemed to shrink in form and attitude, even Brett's bright blue eyes out-sparkled Rhino's glittering gold teeth.

'Brett,' Eddy sighed, 'O, Brett,' then slapped his forehead in mortification and grabbed my hand to introduce me to his All-American Hero.

'This is Brett Farnham, Prof., a classmate and close personal friend. Brett, this is the Prof. I told you so much about.' My hand disappeared into his, a small brown bird covered by a hawk's giant wings.

'I feel I know you already, Prof., my big brother John D told me about you, how you were this brilliant youngster from the same island where we have a little place on the beach. He said you came into the school looking a bit lost, but he tried to help you adjust to our cold climate and impersonal people.' Back then Brett's brother John D, was the real star of that family. He could have become quarterback for a top team in the NFL or gone to Harvard Law or Business School, but chose the Navy Seals then the CIA, and was now Deputy Director (Plans). He had been featured in the latest *Alumni Magazine* for having made a $30-million dollar donation to refurbish our old college.

The 'little beach place' Brett made sound like a three-bedroomed semi rented to families from Hoboken, was in fact a sprawling family estate on a stretch of beach that had been declared private and off-limits to locals. The estate had its own chapel, police station and post office and was protected from the rest of the island community by a high concrete wall, which gave the place the look of a huge prison or mental hospital. The wall went on down to the beach where it extended into the sea and was guarded by uniformed men in top speed patrol boats with artillery guns as big as cannons. Being schoolboys we found ways of climbing on top of the wall and we thought we'd found the Heaven we were promised if we did everything the priests told us as we saw wonders of a huge, stylish compound of many houses, cars of every expensive make, sleek speedboats, and the kinds of golden suntanned bodies only found in glossy magazines.

'Hello, Mr Brett …' Rhino's roar, now reduced, sounded like a little girl pleading for her doll.

'Rhino Man! A wha a gwan, star?' Brett pumped Rhino's hand, genuinely impressed, his blue eyes seeming to sparkle in the dimly-lit room. He was good: he could have survived in Clive's ghetto, speaking like his killer friends, eating like a local, fucking like a man was supposed to. 'I'm political officer based in Baghdad; we listen to your records all the time, man. I was out in Fallujah – all the Iraqis sing your songs, though they don't know a word of English!'

Brett's brother though he mentioned me, hadn't mentored me. We hardly spent any time together, he was too senior and too great a chasm existed between us. He was captain of the football and Lacrosse teams, always on the Dean's list, was sports correspondent for the school *Daily* and girls from

Smith, Holyoke and Vassar would cut their heads off for him to fuck them. When he heard about me, the young boy from the island, he probably expected a muscle bound thug in a string vest with dreadlocks like ship's ropes, barking expletives no one could understand. Instead in me he found a miserable weed, so shy he stuttered, and who couldn't make eye contact – even if he stood on a ladder. While at the school I looked John-D up in *Who's Who,* found the Farnham's – who's name had the most pages – but it took some time to find him among all the many John-D's. It was a shock to discover that one of the Farnham ancestor's had been the same American Civil War General who'd declared 'the only way to end the war is to make it terrible beyond endurance' and who had orchestrated the scorched earth policy to burn all, rape women, kill old men and children, till the Confederacy accepted that going to war was not stroking pussy.

I don't know if Brett went into the Navy Seals like his brother but his job as Political Officer meant he called Iraqi community leaders 'Sir', with the same unctuous tones he called me 'Prof.' before summoning huge black choppers to fire Hellfire missiles up their asses. 'When I finished at Andover I thought I'd get into your school, Prof. but now you have to be from Malawi or Tonga! Somehow I ended up at Florida State.' I saw the regret on his face as soon as he realized the insult to his classmates. He squeezed Maria around her waist and waved to Eddy like a penitent altar boy. 'For which I have absolutely no regrets – I wouldn't have met Eddy and Maria!'

'Brett was linebacker, Prof. I was kicker on the football team. He used to help me and Elizabeth get visas for the musicians we invited up for concerts.'

'It was a splendid time, we had a ball.' Maria was curled up inside his arms, like an infant marsupial in its mother's pouch. Brett's enormous body squeezed her in closer. 'A real royal feast, 24/7.'

'There was never a dull moment, Prof., if you'll pardon the cliché! You're a famous writer, I know how writers hate clichés!' Eddy was still ecstatic at the presence of his superhero friend.

'John-D told me about your old school, the good college days. Attendance there was a family tradition from the day the school started in 1702. But Florida State was something new, that's what everyone wanted to hear about at family reunions. Sometimes I think John-D was jealous!'

I felt the need to say something: 'It was an experience for me, meeting people like your brother and so many other fascinating guys. I think I was the first person from Woodwater to make it there.' Maria peeped out of her pouch, still friendly, but showed no regrets she wouldn't fuck me tonight.

'I read your book after Eddy recommended it; I was impressed a boy from the island could write so well. You know it's almost our second home!' That was saying much – they had homes in New York, Rhode Island, Aspen, California, Paris – on Avenue Foch near Mobutu's old pad – and that street off Pall Mall, near the Anglo-American building and the home of the Hindu billionaires. During Prohibition they built an estate in the hills on Cairncross land where aristos, gangsters, sportsmen and showgirls could drink all the rum they wanted, and all the whisky smuggled in Joseph Kennedy's ships.

'Bo Baker did a film on our last campaign, Prof. It made a big impression at Republican gatherings in the South and Midwest. Brett thinks he could make a docu-drama from your book,'

Eddy said.

'The book contains many themes to make a big hit on the Republican circuit – how a poor, disabled boy climbed out of poverty without revolution, violence or godless communism,' Brett said.

'We put quotes on big posters in the constituencies: *There's no mountain too high to climb, no obstacle that cannot be overcome; you can always find hope, and keep hope alive*,' Eddy said.

'We need themes like the schools in America, to reduce the number of young people who graduate to prison from high school. We gave copies to some senators and hope they can put it on reading lists throughout the country.' I felt my near empty pocket and imagined royalties flooding in from right-wing billionaires with brains like a pit full of rattlesnakes.

'That's why I want him to do his next book on our party, Brett, so poor countries can have a formula to get out of poverty without regard to the foolishness of Castro and Chavez.'

'You're still young, Prof., but you have a heavy burden to help the world's poor. When you get down to Woodwater you won't recognize the place – I hear you haven't been there for a while.'

'Eddy has done an extraordinary piece of work,' Brett said. Maria seemed to be in the land of sweet dreams in her warm pouch; I didn't feel any resentment that I wouldn't get any tonight and hoped she realized she had to stay on top when they slept so the magnificent Mr Brett wouldn't stifle her. Brett was a pro, he drank slowly, but now he took a deep draw from his Jim Beam on the rocks. Pussy like Maria's did wild things to a man and I took a sniff of the *First* he'd been inhaling all night. When I shook his hand I noticed there was no smell of aftershave or deodorant: apparently real men controlled their sweat and BO, and perfume was made for women and girly men.

'The family has interests in studios in California and Florida, Prof., I'm sure they'd want to look at your book on Eddy.'

When I was in school I was too immature, too skittish to know what power was, even though many of my classmates would be in *Who's Who* and occupy positions of influence all over the world. Sitting here now on the same couch one of them, holding the woman I dreamt of fucking, I knew that power meant you got what you dreamt of, but there was no difference between want and fulfilment. I had no power so I could only dream of fucking and go home and sleep alone, whereas Brett would stay fucked, even if he didn't dream of it. He just had to say they would make a film of my book and I could taste the coke and begin munching the popcorn. The wine had done its job, mellowed me, chilled me out, put me in a cosy place where I felt relaxed. All the bullshit Brett and Eddy put out about my book meant they thought I was too naive to decipher their game. At this time of the morning I admit I couldn't, but frankly I couldn't fucking care. They were both right-wing fucks, a politician and a spy, and lying was their game. Did they think I was an Obama freak, trying to butter me up with the idea they thought crime and violence were products of social circumstances? Or were they edging from the Right after they kept losing elections, so some GOP cocksucker like Rubio could replace the Tea Party and a brain dead cracker in the next political road show?

Dreaming of Maria, flickering Christmas lights, dimmed chandeliers, and the snow job conversations of Brett and Eddy had made me forget all about Rhino Man, so when he spoke I felt as if he had just sprung from some gigantic pile of shit, with lights flooding from his gold teeth.

'Maybe the Prof. can write a book about we poor musicians, Eddy.' My eyes opened so wide I feared they might pop out and splat against his ebony skin. I looked at his jewellery, expensive apparel, and calculated I could work a year and not have enough coin to dry clean one of his shirt sleeves.

'Why not, Clive?' Eddy asked. ' I'm a simple man and it not going take him long to do a book on me! Then he can do one on you dancehall persons, the really important somebodies in our home country!'

I'd always admired our people for being so concrete and positive, saying 'persons' instead of the abstract 'people'. Clive appeared pumped up by Eddy's fake endorsement, like a big teddy bear, he now had the confidence to speak in front of Mr Brett. The one thousand four hundred and forty people it was estimated Clive's gang slaughtered in North America paled in comparison with the hundreds of thousands Brett's people wiped out in Iraq, Yemen, Syria and Libya. Clive, thus enervated from his bashful silence, attempted to speak in what for him approximated English.

'Eddy tell me what you doing to help me cousin get out of jail in Miami, Mr Brett.'

'You're an old friend, Clive. Eddy and Liz know you a long time; you have a big following in your country – and all over the world! Anything for an old friend, Clive. Anything at all.'

Rhino Man knew when he mentioned Elizabeth, it was Brett who had got her sprung when she was caught at Miami airport with three customized Louis Vuitton suitcases packed with ninety-six kilos of 100 per cent cocaine from the Ciudad Juarez cartel. I'd read about it in a left-wing blog.

'Thank you so much, Mr Brett. You know how much poor

man like me and me cousin, Cabal, appreciate when a big man like you have time to help.'

'I can't take all the credit, Clive. You know how our friend Eddy worked his ass off with all those oil company CEO's and even the President himself. You must thank him, Clive.' Clive thanked Eddy to show he didn't think less highly of him, just because he wasn't two metres tall, had three hundred million dollars in trust, could kill any number of Afghans, and had a dreaming Maria pressed into his groin. I was thinking it was time to be going home. Without Maria I didn't want to struggle up five flights and didn't want to fall asleep here again. I'd seen the Rhino's key card for the Savoy and was sure Elizabeth's company had arranged a limo to take him home with an escort from Oxbridge or one of the London universities. Maria and Brett were close personal friends and could stay here with Eddy, on any of the eight floors. They could go to the house off Pall Mall – all they had to do was call the butler. Or they could sleep at the Ambassador's in Regent's Park – Brett was his first cousin.

'I have to go, Eddy, I'm sure you have a full day tomorrow.' When I stood up I confirmed we were being watched – Donovan rushed in, looking bright as the first light of morning.

'Goodnight, Brett. It was nice meeting you. Tell Maria when she wakes up. Goodnight, Clive.' He was so tamed by Brett's power that he stood up to bid me good night.

'Good night, Eddy, and thanks for everything. Don't bother seeing me off, you have guests.' I said.

'Nonsense, Prof., this is like home to Brett, Maria and Clive.' He held me by the elbow, and steered me to the lift where Donovan stood waiting. The elevator door slid open and we all got in.

'This is too much, Eddy. You don't need to come down.'

As Donovan walked to the limo, next to Rhino's stretch with the student asleep inside, Eddy embraced me. He obviously thought I believed all the crap he and his friend Brett had frothed about me.

'Tell Donovan your plans to travel home, Prof. This was a nice evening, you met my real friends.'

There was no car waiting for Brett – when you're a Farnham you don't need limos or sports cars to boost your ego, taxis or rentals would do just nicely. Besides, Eddy had other drives.

'A little nightcap, Prof.?' Donovan asked, lifting the cognac flask.

'No, Donovan, I still have to climb five flights of stairs!'

With a slight shrug he handed me a large brown envelope and, even if it only contained a bunch of five pound notes, it would still be more money than I had ever held.

'Eddy paid for your ticket and anything else you need for your journey, Prof. Just let me know when you decide the time is right.' He gave me a bottle of wine 'for a nightcap, Prof.' I didn't get Maria but the packet I held was certainly heavy enough for another kind of horny.

CHAPTER EIGHT

I was so eager to see how much money was in the envelope and what a first-class airplane ticket looked like, that my hand moved to open it as soon as the limo drove off. But I'd always suspected pushers, whores and hitmen peopled my building on the grittier side of west London and I didn't want to risk the possibility of having to surrender my bounty before I'd had a chance to enjoy it. It made for a much different ride home than the one going out there. I was awash with conflicting emotions and a feeling that regardless of what happened, something new and exciting was already underway. When I finally got inside my little flat, my head spinning from the wine and the potential of the situation, I tore into the envelope, my fingers trembling more than they would have if I were ripping the clothes off Maria.

The first-class airline ticket was not printed on gold but the price was such it could have been. I started calculating all the things I could do with that kind of money and my imagination was only limited by how low my expectations about ever having that kind of money had sunk. In the end I settled with being able to put down a deposit on a much better place. For some reason Oprah Winfrey in her thinner form appeared to me screaming, 'Dream big, dream bigger'. The money was still in plastic covers, the notes crisp and new, and there were eight packets, each containing two thousand five hundred in fifty pound notes. I opened just one and counted each note, relishing the touch and scent of unearned virgin money; they were so new I thought they would smudge. I was still unsure of what Eddy wanted from me, but he was clearly willing to pay well for it.

Later that day I went to Harrods to buy some linen slacks, polo shirts and shoes. I wasn't put off by all the Maseratis, Ferraris, Bugattis and Lamborghinis, parked outside like taxis in a Lagos motor park. The Arabs didn't have Brett's subtlety and wanted to show off their shit. I went inside and though I liked the smells and girls in tight skirts, I refused to spend £300 of Eddy's money on trousers. I went up Brompton Road and found an Italian place where linen slacks were seventy quid. I'd read *Gomorrah* by Roberto Saviano, about how the mob controlled the Italian fashion industry and I decided to test the olive-skinned guy behind the counter by asking for a twenty percent discount if I paid cash. He agreed and when I said I'd take the slacks in four colours but had only two hundred, he grabbed my money before I could change my mind.

Eddy called the next day to say how much he enjoyed our little get-together, how impressed Brett and Maria were with his gifted schoolmate and how much he looked forward to our working together. I made sounds like I enjoyed his spiel, though I didn't know yet what shit he wanted. He said he was leaving early next morning for Germany and France. I thanked him for the money and ticket and he reacted with the feigned modesty of a hot slut telling you not to thank her for the sex. He handed me over to Donovan who then apologised that he had to accompany the PM but that Patrick, whose number he would text me, would take care of me. I was so unused to apologies my cheeks felt as if I was blushing at a nun who flipped out her tits for a quick suck. Patrick called before I got Donovan's text and apologetically told me that he would have to come around – he had something for me from Eddy.

It was strange how apologies sprouted like weeds when you entered the magic circle. I felt concerned that perhaps my 'thank you' to Eddy might not have sounded effusive enough, so he was sending another packet. But when Patrick arrived, he instead came carrying electronics. Out of a large expensive brown leather case he pulled the thinnest laptop I had ever seen and then began droning on about the extraordinarily extensive memory (over five hundred gigabytes and equipped with latest Celeron technology for lightning speed connectivity). I could not imagine even that level of advanced software was any match for the generators that were still used in over half of the island where I was headed. Eddy clearly had this all under control because then Patrick handed me a mobile phone unlike any I had ever seen. Neither item had any branding and when I went to set them up everything was initially in some indigenous Chinese language. I learned then too what is meant when people say something is priceless.

Patrick looked like a clone of Donovan. Eddy seemed to insist on employing good-looking, athletic young men, about his height of just under six feet, and dressing them in expensive high design suits costing ridiculous sums of money. Looking at Patrick I wanted to read his labels. I didn't know who designed the beauty he was wearing, it wasn't Zegna but in that class and it seemed to give him the added confidence he needed, when right now he wore his tech hat as he taught me how to work the sophisticated gear. I could only imagine the kinds of work he had been asked to undertake working for Eddy. Up until then I'd congratulated myself on having a mobile phone without a camera and a laptop I lovingly called 'the snail'. But when Patrick showed me all the features that were now available and these were free, I felt like an idiot for staying so long thinking it was cool living in the Stone Age.

Like Donovan, Patrick had taken elocution lessons and his accent might not have been cut-glass but was just as mellow and rich sounding, like the twenty-five-year old rum our country boasted about producing. He asked about my travel plans and I told him the date I'd chosen to leave for the island and that I'd need a few weeks to check the archives at Kew. He said no problem, he'd sort it out with BA. Then he was gone, leaving me to wonder just what the hell was going on in my life. This much I knew, I was being vetted and feted by some very powerful people, who were prepared to spend exceptional sums of money on me, that they were going to great lengths to keep me happy and all I needed to do, was the one thing I would do anyway, had been doing anyway and for embarrassingly low recompense: write. I shook off any uneasiness I was feeling and lay on the couch, moving through the radio dial. The latent scent and idea of Maria invaded the entire room making my heart light, while the thought of Eddy anchored it all with something altogether heavier and more sinister.

Patrick came at 7AM, exactly four weeks later and three hours before my flight from Gatwick, said it would take forty-five minutes to get there and that I would have time to chill out before they took me to the plane. We drove in a brand new Mercedes 500 and this time there was no need for outriders as there was no traffic and Eddy wasn't around. Without Eddy present the government didn't have to butter him up by providing security for his friends. I wasn't complaining however. The car we drove in was still a much more luxurious form of transport for me than anything else I was accustomed to.

That time of morning the little towns we went through were quiet as cemeteries and probably more boring, this wasn't the Green. We arrived at the airport in record time and again the absence of people, pressure and noise was a little unnerving. There were no queues, only a good looking girl in a sharp navy blue British Airways suit waiting at the check-in desk. She smiled up at me in prefect plastic precision. She was so good I actually believed her when she wished me a good morning. She checked my suitcases in and swiped my ticket advising me of the usual guff about gates and departures, all the while smiling and directly looking into my eyes. The next thing I knew I was sitting in an airport lounge I never knew existed, where she handed me over to another precise, plastic beauty. I refused the champagne they offered at first, remembering my embarrassment with Maria but after half an hour, thinking of the nine hours in transit, I asked the plastic beauty for a flute and the relief on her face was so pronounced I felt a tremor in my crotch. I wondered what she'd do if I suggested she accompany me to the head.

First class was so trouble free the flight didn't feel like nine hours. Patrick must have requested a special diet – they served food the island was famous for – stewed oxtail, rice and peas, sweet potato pudding, and I had to ration my intake of really good rum punch so they wouldn't take me off on a stretcher. I was feeling so mellow I didn't even realise we'd landed till the captain's voice interrupted my sleep, advising that we had and wishing us all a safe and happy trip. Another beauty retrieved my hand luggage and unique and expensive laptop from wherever they had stashed it and after an immigration official took my passport they led us to a customs man standing with my luggage near the exit. He delivered me to a patiently waiting, immaculately turned out, Donovan.

'Welcome home, Prof.,' Donovan said, thanking the stewardess for taking good care of 'our guest'. Donovan's linen suit was more Hugo Boss than Zegna but his cologne was still Hermes. 'Here's our car, Prof.' Another handsome young man in a sky blue linen suit and striped blue tie held open the door of a Lincoln town car and I could feel the air-conditioning roaring like the latest hurricane, though this one was of the Arctic variety. 'I'm Delroy, Prof.,' this driver said.

As I stooped to get in I recalled my last trip back home, when the shit advance from my publisher meant I had to pick up a local cab from a rank, all of which looked like beat-up hearses. It had taken an hour to get off the 747, the air-conditioning in Arrivals had broken down, so I was drowning in sweat before I got to the endless queues at immigration and the carousel kept stopping causing the luggage to pile up. When we finally got out I felt like breaking down. I'd just read a story online where taxi drivers collected strangers at the airport, robbed then killed them and 'disappeared' their bodies in the surrounding hills. Another article mentioned that beheading was a speciality of the dominant Ciudad Juarez cartel, which smuggled dope through Woodwater. I had recurring nightmares of a huge man swinging my severed head like a toy. Luckily, back then I had seen, looking earnestly about him, a man in a white linen suit and Panama hat, who appeared as if he belonged in a Graham Greene novel set in Port au Prince during the time of Papa Doc. He had smiled at me to come over, said he was an old boy of St Dunstan's and asked if I had a lift. He had said his name was Stephen Walters, that he'd watched me race when he visited school track meets as an old boy and knew of the big scholarship I won – which none of the 'fucking Chinese or Syrians' could. Walters was the name of one of the seven families who had run the country since slavery, so I wasn't surprised when his uniformed driver led us over to an enormous Mercedes SUV with freezing AC. That was the only thing to have elevated my last visit home but this time was different. This time Eddy's money and power had raised me to that level, and inside the Lincoln town car I felt puffed up and, finally, important.

Before I'd inserted myself into the luxurious car Donovan had seen me ogling the enormous structure going up next to the old airport. It was an attempt at futurism in architecture and whoever the hell was building this beauty had jump started to the future, with glass panels that sparkled like a thousand alien suns. Neither the Gherkin nor even The Shard conveyed the future promise of this monster. 'The Chinese,' Donovan offered. 'They're building a new airport; should be finished in under three months. When the new one's ready they'll tear down the old and build a cargo terminal to export stuff to the US and Latin America. That's what Eddy was telling you about, Prof.' Remembering now I had the new phone with camera I quickly took it from my bag and took shots of the slinky beauty. The old airport I recalled was ramshackle and unsafe, the Chinese now overlaid it with sparkling glass and chrome construction.

Brought in as indentured labourers, historically the Chinese were almost as badly off as the slaves who worked the old plantations, but they had carved out a position at the top through a bit of hard work and a lot of favouritism. Most of them ended up being schooled at St Dunstan's. Those graduates were now big in business and must have been key to the perceived Chinese invasion of the country. Unlike people like Donovan and Patrick, the Chinese graduates didn't need Eddy to afford their designer suits.

We were on a superhighway now, and from the pristine condition of the road alone, could have been driving anywhere in Europe, America or China. Looking out below I could see the old airport road I'd taken on my last trip. Back then the Mercedes SUV had bumped along over, around and through the many potholes and I kept cursing the left-wing government, blaming them for the mess in the country. When I had left for America there were beautiful flowers lining the road, in every colour of the rainbow, planted by a madwoman who must have thought flowers could calm our brute instincts. But the new government had let them die. They said *flowers are for the bourgeoisie.* Equally made to die out were the old dwellings that lined the road. I saw none of the shacks now, or the people lounging like skeletons in ragged clothes. Instead I saw Chinese men directing construction crews repairing the old road, which now bypassed the airport and led to the town called Gomorrah, which lay at the end of the peninsula where once upon a time pirates ruled. Its destruction by earthquake was deemed to be the 'punishment of God' by local zealots.

'The Chinese covering the whole island with first class roads, Prof.' Donovan sounded proprietorial when he spoke of their achievements. 'See the exits leading to the government offices which Eddy keeps downtown to remain close to the people.'

I strained to see as the car sped on the straight, flat road. I identified some of the places where the exits led but most of the slums we passed last time had been replaced by tower blocks and new ones appeared to be rising before my eyes. Donovan offered me drink and I refused. He then asked if I wasn't thirsty, 'How about some cold water?' I really wasn't, besides I couldn't be in the artificial cold inside the car drinking what would feel like equally cold water, but didn't want to give him the idea I was 'refusenik'. I tried to focus my attention outside of the car.

When we started up the hill I couldn't recognize anything: pine and royal palm were planted along all the broad avenues where ultra-modern glass-clad houses with pools and gazebos were spread out, as if in an exterior shot for a Hollywood blockbuster movie. When I was a kid these hills were bare or covered with scrub, with shacks made entirely of driftwood, cardboard and plastic sheets where criminals and outcast Rastamen squatted. Sometimes when I felt down I would sneak out of my grandmother's house and run up here, with a feeling I was in outer space, as in the science fiction books I borrowed from the library. Now, Eddy and his Chinese friends had torn down whatever shacks there were, cleared the scrub and replaced them with mansions that would sell for millions in the UK. They were still at it, further up the hill, where Chinese surveyors were marking out even bigger plots than those further down. This was a staple in our country – the further up the hill you lived, the grander you were, just as in the time of slavery when the masters built their great houses on the highest hill, to simultaneously look down on the people they were screwing and feel nearer to their God.

'This is your home, Prof.,' Donovan said, as we stopped before an automatic gate which opened slowly to reveal a house with enormous glass windows, sliding doors and a high, triangular roof covered with green tiles. It could have been a ski mansion in Aspen, Colorado, Switzerland or France. The flower-beds of yellow, purple, blue and red would have been at home at the Chelsea Flower Show or Hampton Court Palace. I wasn't an expert but recognized anthurium, heliconia, philodendron, polianthes, azalea, anemone, hydrangea and roses. There were also beds of irises, aloe vera and bougainvillea of varying colours, some young fruit trees – oranges, mangoes and dwarf coconuts. All seemed placed at random but deep inside I was sensing patterns, perhaps designed by the Chinese. A woman with smart glasses and a white coat came through the automatic glass door.

'This the Prof. I told you was coming, Miss Robotham.' So Eddy hadn't told him my 'Prof.' was from a cartoon character with enormous head full of shit and he clearly thought I was a real Professor.

'Welcome, sir, we hope to serve you well and that you will enjoy your stay.' She spoke with such formality it felt awkward, even wrong. I imagined her reading from a gilt-edged script lined with images of tropical flowers.

'You don't have to call me 'sir', Ma'am. I'm young enough to be your son!'

'Certainly, sir.' An old man in a green khaki uniform suddenly appeared and took my suitcases from the boot of the car, carrying them into the house while Delroy took my laptop and hand luggage.

Inside it was mortuary cold and I couldn't wait for them to

leave so I could find the fucking thermostat and turn it way the hell up. I'd switch on the heat in my flat when it got to fifteen degrees and this was much colder.

'I've set up Wi-Fi for you in your study, Prof., and we can test your laptop.' The room was bigger than my cell back in London, there was a steel desk with a big, semi-circular glass top, a Steelcase Straffor desk chair like the one I'd had at Oxford and three very expensive looking leather chairs. There were several classy looking blue glass bookshelves, filled with atlases, guide books and histories of Caribbean countries. 'This is our menu for the day, sir,' Miss Robotham said. 'If you don't like the set meals, you can order á la carte.' There were local dishes, things I liked despite all the places I'd been – curried goat, escoveitch fish and oxtail. 'This looks beautiful, Ma'am. I'm not hungry now but after I've had a rest and wash, I'll most definitely be ready to eat.'

'Just let me know, sir. And have a nice rest. The intercoms are here, in the bedroom and the parlour.' Donovan led me into a cavernous bedroom with a massive bed, huge walk-in closets, more tan leather chairs and a marble jacuzzi with gold taps in the ensuite bathroom, which itself was lined with bottles of cosmetics and perfume.

'Hope everything you need is here, Prof. You can call me or talk to Miss Robotham if there is anything not to your liking.'

'I'm sure there's more than I need, Donovan. And I have your number and Delroy's.'

'Then have a nice rest, Prof. We'll talk later.'

When he left I immediately found the thermostat. It was at fourteen degrees and I turned it to twenty-five then looked around. The couches were long, low, of the same fine leather as those in the study and bedroom. The leather and style looked Italian but the Scandinavians made modern stuff like this too and they were probably all manufactured in China. The floors were brilliantly polished mahogany, light tan to set off the dark of the leather, tables were glass and steel, the paintings were done in the same style as those in Eaton Square, with lines stark to the point of harshness and colours of sickening intensity. I tapped on the glass and saw it was thick and hard; it must be bullet proof and if it wasn't for the air-conditioning the place would boil. It was certainly a hot house.

Somehow I'd never thought of glass as hard and protective, my idea of it was more like the delicate *Lalique* figurines, which looked like they would shatter if you sneezed. I was still feeling a bit cold, the thermostat hadn't yet done its work and the cold made me feel lonely and vulnerable. From what I'd seen of Miss Robotham's path when she left I knew she and her people stayed far away, on the other side of the house. And she wouldn't come around except at mealtimes or for cleaning, and if I were in she would call to warn me first. So I was as lonely here as I was high up above the Green in London, browsing Google Earth and reading crime fiction from the coldest regions of the Scandinavian North.

I felt like a brandy but didn't want to use the intercom, so I walked over and found a large swanky kitchen with elegant, shining fittings. Outside, Miss Robotham, with two young, very pretty girls, also in white smocks, were pulling up weeds in a little garden and I could smell the thyme, dill, oregano, peppers and scallion. I slapped myself hard when I felt my cock stiffen at the sight of the girls, who could not be more than sixteen, and realized how horny not fucking Maria made me. When the pain made the feeling go from my crotch to my head, I started to appreciate the depth of colours of the flowers, flowing into me like torrents of blood.

CHAPTER NINE

O ur first session was a press conference at the Palace of the People, followed by a reception for the cabinet where I was introduced as the Prodigal Son who had gone to distant shores, only to return to chronicle the achievements of my people. I therefore deserved the fatted calf served up in trough loads inside the minimally decorated great halls, filled with Scandinavian and Italian furniture. The leather chairs had obviously been made by the same factory which manufactured those in my guest house. The 'Palace' was a gift of the Chinese to our own persons, and had been constructed in record time to celebrate Independence Day. It flaunted the same spotless glass facades of so many of the new buildings on the island but the steel was painted bright green, which I learnt was the colour of Eddy's political party, The People's Mandate. The great man himself wore a matching green Lacoste shirt and smart linen trousers, while members of his cabinet wore Nike clothes of the same, so tame they could have been drafted by partymen. It was ironic to find the *NYT*, CCTV, BBC and France 24 sounding like our *Chronicle*, but I guess they too were owned by people who wanted a share of our pirate treasure.

'This is our dear Prof., a graduate of glorious St Dunstan's, like me and most of my cabinet. You know the love of discipline and order the Jesuits drilled into us.' The soft questions they asked allowed Eddy to stretch the limits of the truth. He told how the economy was growing almost as fast as China's, how the free education system his great party introduced meant that children of the rich now had no advantage over the poor, how new oil blocs were coming on stream, and production would double in three years.

Then the reporters were led into another ferociously air-conditioned hall where drinks and canapés were served, while Donovan and a bevy of other expensively clad, athletic young men mingled, to ensure Eddy, his party, and the country got the best possible coverage. I followed Eddy as he led me and his cabinet into a more dimly lit room where good-looking young women were serving local delicacies and a strong rum punch to wash them down. I still felt the hangover of Maria's rejection, and when I saw how well the women's asses fit their tight green skirts my mouth became dry like the Sahara, I felt tiny volcanoes erupt at the base of my cock and had to imagine icebergs bigger than the one that felled the Titanic to prevent my embarrassment showing. I was self-conscious in my light blue polo shirt and navy linen slacks but consoled myself with being able to afford linen now.

I didn't recognize any of my schoolmates but they told me how much they enjoyed my book, looked tearful as they talked of Joseph's miraculous achievements and how grateful they were I'd brought his suffering to their attention. I recognized the Foreign Minister, Colin Shepherd, who I'd seen on TV with Eddy when he gave that press conference outside No. 10 with Cameron, Osborne and Hague. I'd wondered why he seemed to keep to himself, constantly rubbing his nose as if to stop sneezing and concluded he probably had hay fever. He hadn't found medicine for it I noticed, as he was still rubbing away at his nose, and just pecked at his canapés. He didn't look like the men our people usually admired but I suppose he was good for foreigners, since he might be the only man in our country who wouldn't exude testosterone with every drop of sweat.

'I expect you all to give full co-operation to the Prof.; he's sacrificing his valuable time and energy to help put his country on the map.' So while in my mind I was still the cartoon character – Prof. – those not in the know were clearly thinking 'Prof.' was an academic title. I did not object to the deceit and sipped at the rum punch I had been offered which served to make me feel even more puffed up so that when Eddy spoke of my 'sacrifice' and 'excellence' and went on about how lucky they were to have me there, I began to believe him and the words 'don't believe the hype' took on a new tenure. I blithely hoped in future my sacrifice would be as lucrative as it had been so far.

Unlike me, the rum seemed to have no effect on Eddy or most of his people and I knew constant indulgence meant these people would be sober even if they downed it all day. The Finance Minister took one sip then held his glass at some distance, looking at it like it was a piece of snot on a napkin. While Eddy was recounting my feats at St Dunstan's I got a text from my agent saying Gutenberg had paid a fifty-thousand pound advance for my book. Unfortunately, not even the rum could make me feel a sense of achievement at this. While Eddy was still in the UK I'd read online that the company had signed a multi-million pound contract to supply textbooks to the Ministry of Education and the publisher owned the Independent oil company that had been awarded promising oil blocs off the islands South Coast, not far from Cuban waters. Eddy didn't seem to be in any hurry to leave for our next assignment, to open a school in his constituency. He did the rounds, introducing me to his people, telling me what each achieved at St Dunstan's, and when we got to the FM he slapped him on the back, laughed and said: 'Perk up, Cousin, we'll soon be with the little girls!' Shepherd smiled weakly, shrunk further into himself, and took another sip as if to show Eddy he wasn't teetotal or anything.

The road to the school was new, there was construction all the way and a sense of how things might have been during the height of slavery came over me. Only here the Chinese overseers had clipboards and measuring instruments, not whips and straw hats, and there was yellow skin and muscle shuddering above jackhammers. The foundations were being laid for a new hotel, the sign above the scaffold proclaimed that at forty stories it would be the tallest in the Caribbean. Bemused, I thought proneness to earthquakes and hurricanes ruled out skyscrapers here but then I wasn't Chinese.

Driving along the road all the traffic lights were green. When we got near the school there were lines of children in green uniforms sweating in the sun, some taking shade in the shadow of the huge USAID signs outside the community centre at the entrance of the Estate where the school was located. I'd thought Eddy was a compassionate guy when he spoke of his mother but he didn't seem concerned about these little kids broiling in the sun, waving signs emblazoned with 'Redeemer!' or 'Behold the Redeemer Cometh!' There were huge American signs above the tiny community centre they had built, yet there was hardly a line praising the massive achievements of the Chinese. This struck me as odd. I jolted when I saw one of the children fall and the others screamed as they rushed to pick her up. I took a snap on my phone. The school was located just beyond a series of tower blocks, constructed just before Eddy's first victory. The blocks were modern and stylish, with none of the Brutalist architecture of British and American public housing. As usual here were the ubiquitous glass facades, but the brick or stone corners were rounded, and there were swings, sandpits and fishponds among very beautiful multiply-hued flowerbeds. The story I kept hearing was of an architect who insisted on lots of glass usage in construction, apparently to take advantage of sunlight, the only thing in abundance in our poor countries. That explained the glass in all the private and public buildings I'd seen since my arrival and prepared me for what I now faced at the new school.

Children were packed into the assembly square, located in the middle of the building as at St Dunstan's. When the kid's lining the road came back and tried to join, there was jostling, till some muscle in green t-shirts and tight black trousers viciously shouted for the excited children to stop, though they refrained from smashing any heads with their short, fat black clubs. The Foreign Minister's wife, Cordelia, had been a long-jumper and discus thrower at the Academy and had represented the country at international athletic meets. She looked like Will. I. Am but without the beard. At the Palace she hadn't gone near her husband, but stood with a bunch of her friends looking over at him, making googly-eyes, and laughing. That was the sort of thing to turn a man's cock to tomato paste. She'd left the meeting at the Palace early. Now she led the teachers shouting 'WELCOME EDDY!!!' and 'BEHOLD THE REDEEMER COMETH!!!!' as Eddy and his people hopped from their limos and leapt onto the stage, the PM clasping his hands above his head like a prize fighter, shouting 'WORK HARD AND YOU'LL SUCCEED!!!' The slogan was repeated on a painted banner above the stage, and the kids were prompted to join in with shouts of 'BEHOLD THE REDEEMER COMETH!!!' Another kid fainted and her mates took her into the building. Eddy didn't react, and I didn't take a picture this time but other kids did. The headmaster introduced Eddy as the miracle worker who had made education free for the poor, gave fine housing to their parents, and built them this fantastic school. (Applause.) Eddy was a natural mimic, could easily copy any accent and at this time if I closed my eyes, I could hear a very good impersonation of Martin Luther King, rousing the kids to heights of patriotic fervour as they rushed to thank him and his party for the gifts they brought. He sounded drastically different from the man I heard in Eaton Square, his voice rising and falling tremulously in the thick afternoon air. 'Children of St Elizabeth's High, when we were growing up we didn't have the opportunities you have today, of free education, inspiring teachers and this wonderfully constructed school building you're seeing here. Children, you should know these are gifts of God and our Party, not of Pharaohs with beards, in green khaki uniforms!!' (Sustained applause).

Donovan handed Eddy caricatures of a Pharaoh and Fidel Castro and he theatrically held them up, to hilarious applause from the stage. 'Ancient and modern pharaohs loved their beards – even women pharaohs had to wear beards!' Donovan handed him the poster of a big busted pharaoh with an artificial beard and I saw the FM's wife touch her moustache, as if to remind them she was no Pharaoh; she was a woman who had no beard. Her husband had put on the blackest shades I'd seen since Rhino Man's and now he was rubbing his nose as if something had roused his allergies.

'In ancient times God rescued the children of Israel from Egypt by making a covenant through Moses, so that persons would be free and remain free, if they obeyed His Commandments. But Moses despaired when persons transgressed, he went against the will of the Most High, he could not hold the faith or keep hope alive. So God excluded him from entering the Promised Land.'

The FM's wife, Cordelia, forgot about the female pharaohs, ignored her moustache, raised her muscular arms as if to indicate she wouldn't make the errors of Moses, and her shouts of 'BEHOLD THE REDEEMER COMETH!!!' were so intense, her husband who seemed to lift up from his chair, released his nostrils, and his glasses almost flew off. To the side, another child fell.

'Our time has no use for a Moses who cannot hold on to faith, keep hope alive, be loyal and obedient, disciplined and constructive. God will have no patience with a modern Moses, the way He kept the original Moses alive, despite his disobedience and disloyalty. Our time is a harsh one; the Promised Land is not for prima donnas and the disloyal; only our loyal, disciplined, organized party, the People's Mandate, can lead us to the Promised Land. Looking at this wonderful building, at these promising young children, you can see we're at the gate already!!!!' (Prolonged applause).

'UP OUR PARTY OF THE PEOPLE'S MANDATE!' Now he was roaring and Cordelia led the audience echoing his words 'UP OUR PARTY OF THE PEOPLE'S MANDATE! BEHOLD THE REDEEMER COMETH!' Even her husband applauded, hesitating at first then gently clapping his small, delicate hands.

When the left-wing government was in power the Americans spent billions undermining them and in the proxy war with the Soviet Union thousands were killed. To protect themselves from the trauma the people became more religious and when Catholicism proved inadequate, Pentecostal churches made inroads. Some were Millenarian and I wondered if there was one against Moses, which would explain Eddy's outbursts against the Prophet. Eddy again clasped his hands above his head, shouted some more slogans then jumped from the stage, followed by his acolytes, and led by Cordelia. As the children surged forward to lay hands on their Redeemer, the muscle men at the sides of the square moved forward and joined hands, pushing them back. Then women in green aprons approached, pushing green handcarts. I smelled meat pies. The children surged forward but men with raised whips and clubs pushed toward them. The children started to scream but then the men began to hand out local hundred-dollar bills out of cardboard boxes taken from the Security Minister's car boot at which the children began to cheer. The men with whips were still there sweating in the noonday sun, and they raised them to those who tried to take more than one bill. The now orderly children, took the money and marched over to the serving women to collect brown paper bags containing meat pies and cans of warm Pepsi.

The next stop for us was the church. It was less than five hundred metres away but we drove there, our convoy roaring down the narrow road and it seemed as if we were getting out of the cars almost as soon as we left. It was a five-sided church with a mixture of architectural styles. Above a wooden spire reached skyward and contrasted with the modern glass walls through which was revealed row after row of long pews covered in green cloth. It was Pentecostal, the congregation almost all women dressed in green gowns, singing party hymns adapted from the Psalms and popular folk tunes by the nation's very tall, thin poet laureate who waited at the top of the steps at the front door of the church with the pastor and his flock. When the left-wing party was in power the laureate had written a hymn comparing the achievements of its Leader to the Heroic Actions of Kim Jong-Il. He was a cautious man, he didn't join in with the women as they tried to submerge Eddy with affection. When they were pushed back by Eddy's black clad Death's Head Commando, he swerved out of their way. But Eddy was still so pumped up by the adoration of the swelling crowd and the congregation that he ordered his security to part, the crowd. Armed with his rod, he ploughed into the multitude, allowing them to lay hands on him, like groupies being blessed with the touch of their favourite rock star. The pastor who in a show of loyalty to Eddy, wore a green gown as elaborate as that of a Fulani Emir threw his arms open to receive Eddy as he would Jesus when He returns to save humankind. 'WELCOME TO OUR HUMBLE HOUSE, REDEEMER!!!!' He thundered.

Cordelia took charge of the women who returned his exhortations with shouts of 'BEHOLD THE REDEEMER COMETH!!!!' Then I saw Eddy signal to his commandos and they immediately linked arms to push back the crowd without smashing them with the butts of their guns. Eddy bounded up the aisle, leapt into the pulpit and shouted 'JESUS BLESS YOU ALL, SISTREN AND BRETHREN!!!' The women shouted 'REDEEMER! REDEEMER!', each time more intense, till Colin Shepherd's sweaty face was streaming like a waterfall.

Welcome, Sistren; may God, Jesus and His Holy Mother bless you with the riches of their hearts!' There were flecks of foam around Cordelia's mouth as she shouted 'GOD BLESS YOU, REDEEMER!!!!'

Eddy repeated, word for word, what he had said to the school-children about the pharaohs, Moses, the Children of Israel, the Promised Land and received equally enthusiastic applause, modulated and punctuated by the response from the crowd. But now Eddy's intonation was different, as he was speaking to religious women, not hungry children.

'My dear mother taught me to respect women, Sistren!' At the mention of his mother, they erupted into exuberant applause, so raucous and loud I saw fingers of the men in black tighten on the cold blue steel triggers of their Heckler & Koch machine guns.

'Our women are the foundations of our new party and country, Sistren. Without you we would never have outlived slavery and colonialism, never survived in our modern world. We would not resist the chicanery of white devils, not be here today, celebrating the goodness of the Most High!' The women looked so roused they seemed about to jump the Hero and smother him with love. The Commandos looked at their leader, as if to ask – should they suppress the Danger – *now*. 'Look around you, Sistren, all of you are women, only your pastor is a man. Your men are out drinking rum, smoking weed, rubbing up their baby mothers while you're here singing God's praises!'

They'd heard enough, were possessed with the Spirit, started swaying and hopping, foaming at the mouth, before storming up the aisle, just below the pulpit, and falling to the floor writhing in ecstasy. Cordelia looked uncertain at first then stroked her moustache and joined them, her arms flailing like a swimmer struggling against the tide. I saw Eddy's commando approach from the side, surround him like the Red Sea enveloped pharaoh's host, then spirited him away from his adoring acolytes. As I tried to follow, in company of his ministers, I heard the women rise from the floor and we sped up so they wouldn't smother us. But they were not after us.

I smelt food and by the time we got through the door there were two catering vans parked and more young men in green bringing out loaded trays of oxtail stew, ackee and saltfish, pig's tail, jerk chicken and pork, escoveitched fish, rice and peas, fried rice, boiled green bananas and fried dumplings. The women were now more aroused than when possessed by the spirit and the commando did nothing to restrain them when they reached for the fruits of Paradise. Eddy was safe, he called me over, and I saw him and Donovan looking at a newspaper, *the London Independent*, with a lurid front page about a group of Eddy's boys who had massacred seven people on a rival estate, including a ninety-year-old woman and three kids under five. Donovan was showing Eddy the YouTube video on his Samsung smart phone.

Four men in shiny black uniforms, with black balaclavas covering their faces, were firing M16s into a pink house so fragile it must have been constructed by a squatter. A few shots came from the house at first but long after they stopped, the firing continued till the wood began to decompose and the house to fall. Then, as smoke rose as from a cauldron, and a boy of about fifteen, in bright orange overall and Yankees baseball cap rushed in with a Scorpion machine pistol, its 850 rounds per minute flaring the same orange as his uniform. Donovan had lost his elocution accent and his *patois* could have been mistaken for the dancehall magic of Rhino Man. He asked, 'Is what we going do bout Winston, PM?' Eddy didn't think a boy like me, who had gone to America and Britain, should be exposed to such lack of elocution. His face was at first thunderous, but now subsided into something more statesman like. 'You see what I mean, Prof., you see the problem we have out here? What you mean *do* bout Winston', Donovan? You know we have freedom of speech now, not like the time of those communists. Winston has a right to say what he wants. We won't *do* anything to him!' I knew this was for me and I was still giving Eddy the benefit of the doubt, despite what I'd seen today – fainting children, hysterical women.

I had money in my pocket, more in the bank, and this restrains your judgement when needing to knock the source of your good fortune. Eddy told Delroy to drive back to the house and invited me to ride with him in his Obama-style five-ton armour-plated Lincoln. He wanted to know what I thought of the day's events and I wanted to be diplomatic. I couldn't tell him what I truly thought and he was smart enough to know if I was just schmoozing. So I praised his delivery and eloquence, how he tailored his speech to the expectations of his audiences, and how viscerally the people responded to him. But I said I'd spent too much time in the US and Europe to appreciate the antics of the FM's wife, throwing herself on the floor with those women. I have sensitive antennae, and picked up that he didn't think much of the FM and his athletic wife, so this was criticism that wouldn't hurt me.

Earlier I'd asked Delroy about Joseph, I was keen to see him again after all these years. Delroy appeared disconcerted with the question and hesitated before he told me Joseph was coaching kids on the North Coast. When I asked if he could take me to see him sometime he said I had to clear it with Eddy. So now in the confines of his luxurious car, with the success of the day probably ringing in his ears, I asked Eddy. For a man of such self-assurance I was surprised he looked so taken aback and I immediately knew he was lying when he stuttered, slapping his forehead with his palm, 'I'm sorry, Prof., I forgot to tell you. You see what it's like running a backward country like this! I was so impressed with your book I gave him a scholarship to the University here.'

'Delroy said you could tell me when we can go see him, Eddy.'

'Of course, Prof. I'll tell him when.'

I'd never seen Eddy so quiet, I thought it impossible for Superman to be at a loss for words. I didn't say another word till we got to the house where Miss Robotham and her troupe came out to greet their PM, as sirens wailed and the automatic gates closed behind us.

CHAPTER TEN

I t rained all night, the thunder boomed like artillery, and as I slept with my door open I could see the lightning-fractured sky beyond it. I couldn't turn off the air-conditioning but kept it low so I could sleep without getting up to piss. I liked the sound of the rain falling on the roof but it was nights like this when I used to have the horrors, when my grandmother woke me up screaming and hushed me as she wiped the sweat from my trembling body. I never found out what triggered my nightmares but she would wait till I slept again and I would find her on a chair watching me when I woke at dawn. By then the rain would have stopped, the sun out bright as if to welcome the morning and it was as if it had been dry all night. As a kid I remembered running on my secret forays from home, when it would be raining darkly on one side of the path and bright as steel on the other. When the priests taught us of good and evil at St Dunstan's, I thought of this invisible line between sun and rain.

Miss Robotham called on the intercom to ask if I was ready for breakfast and I told her I had an early interview with the PM.

She always served me herself. Sometimes I'd see one of the girls gathering herbs in the garden, or a man driving the little red mower which reminded me of the horse I rode on the merry-go-round at the Christmas fair. Miss R, as I had taken to calling her, was married and she had grandchildren, but we called her Miss, because so many of the other mothers were unmarried and it felt more polite. I could have had an English breakfast, it was on the menu but I wanted ackee and salt fish, boiled bananas and fried dumplings, plus freshly squeezed orange juice and our brilliant home-grown coffee, from plantations I later learnt had been bought by the Chinese. Miss R seemed happy I preferred our food even though I had a British passport and so warmed to me she started calling me Prof. instead of sir. As I looked at her happy face I tried to shake the true association of the name 'Prof.' and the German cartoon character.

Then I got a call from Donovan to say Eddy was tied up, so our interview was postponed but Delroy would take me where I wanted. When he came, Delroy looked gloomy. I didn't think a handsome, well connected young man like him could be having woman trouble in a country with 3:1 ratio of men to women and as he wasn't a woman I couldn't blame it on his time of month! 'I brought the papers, sir.' There were local ones, some pro-Eddy, others violently against, plus the overseas edition of *the Guardian*.

In the car I struggled to engage with Delroy, he was clearly disturbed in some way.

'We aren't going to Eddy's office Delroy; I have stuff to check out at the National Archives,.'

'I know, sir.' It seemed whatever caused the postponement might have had something to do with his glumness. As the car moved off I began looking through the newspapers Delroy had thoughtfully supplied. There was nothing to read in *the Guardian*, I wasn't interested in the Arab 'Awakening', coups in Africa, the idiocy and anarchy of the political scene in America and Europe, the chaos and criminality of Russia or the control freakery in China. The pro-Eddy papers had splashes of us on front pages, focused on me in my linen shirt, a blue island in a sea of green. Some highlighted the athleticism of Cordelia as she overshadowed her husband who cringed in his chair while rubbing his nose. Then I got to the anti-Eddy lot, I saw the ragged sheets of *the Independent* with the bold headline *The Making of Eddy Haddad*, written by Winston Pinnock. The day before Pinnock had published the article with an accompanying video he'd posted on YouTube. Both proved to be very upsetting for Eddy, the one dark spot in his otherwise unblemished, triumphant day. Unfortunately, we were already at the archives so I would have to read the piece later.

'You can go, Delroy, do whatever you want. I should be here till about lunchtime. I'll call you.'

'I can wait here, sir, I have no plans.'

'No need, Delroy. Just go, take the time to see your girl!' Whatever was bothering him was so bad even thoughts of his girl did nothing for his gloom. I left him sitting slightly hunched forward over the wheel, the picture of dejection and defeat.

At the archives I requested files on the founding of Eddy's party and tried to focus on the trade unionists, lawyers and drug dealers, but all I could see were headlines from Pinnock's article and soon I found myself reading the same paragraph over and over. Finally I asked for files on the foreign minister and his wife and managed to concentrate for a while. Apparently the minister was Eddy's first cousin, son of his mother's older sister. He had come first in the national exams and won a scholarship to Cambridge where he got a First in Linguistics. He spoke six languages and was considered a good foreign minister, despite the fact he was a man of few words. He had been a year or two ahead of me at school. I remembered him vaguely, as a boy who wore thick glasses, did no sports, was considered a brain and swot, did not like girls, and kept to himself. I guess a guy so bright must have looked into the depths of hell and emerged a wreck.

His wife, the daughter of a politician close to the Haddad family, gloried in her athleticism, and was a champion tennis player in addition to her long-jumping and discus-throwing. I forced myself to continue reading about quite possibly two of the world's most uninteresting people, but then I gave up. I was getting a headache trying to concentrate while the Pinnock article was at the top of my mind. I could not stop thinking about what he might have written. I called Delroy and he arrived quickly, but was still looking grim and as I picked up the paper I was sure everyone in the country except me was reading.

Pinnock started out his article with a look back through Eddy's childhood, detailing Eddy's birth into a middle-class family. His mother Miss Violet, was a teacher at the cademy, and his father Eddy senior, a successful real estate agent. There was no explanation as to why he'd entered St Dunstan's so late. He revealed Eddy was a good but not brilliant student, his performances erratic, but in athletics he excelled, running all the long distances, as well as being a good centre back on the football team. He won an athletic scholarship to Florida State. It was there that he teamed up with Elizabeth to promote the musicians who would later put the country on the map. Elizabeth became close to his mother, her teacher and protector at the academy. Although she had the Cairncross fortune, she became involved with the dealings of shady musicians who smuggled coke from the Ciudad Juarez cartel in their equipment, aided by Eddy, who in turn exploited his American connections to expand and protect their trade. Drugs and music became integral to the making of Eddy Haddad.

Left-wingers trying to copy the Cuban model, while lacking the vision or discipline of Fidel and Raoul, dominated Woodwater at the time. The Americans introduced terrifying destabilization to stamp out the Cuban-Soviet menace and Eddy became a central part of their strategy. They facilitated his drug dealings with the cartel, helped promote his and Elizabeth's musicians, and lay the foundation for his rise in the most crime-ridden ghettoes, as well as among the right-wing middle classes. Just then I noticed the car slowing and Delroy sitting awkwardly over the wheel. I looked up and saw a man and woman trading punches.

Their clothes were torn and hanging, the woman was biting the man who kept hitting her while a crowd egged them on, many filming on their smartphones. The woman looked like a tall Alexandra Burke, with the smooth ebony skin and out-thrust cheek bones of the Ashanti. In the course of the fight the man had ripped off her blouse, one tit hung out of her torn red bra and she held her head bent forward as if she were sucking her own nipple. The man rained blows on the back of her bent head, punching her head down relentlessly and then I saw she had actually been biting him and now, as she drew her head back and her teeth from his body, his blood spurted over her bare back in thick globs, like bright crimson grapes. She then seemed to drop to the ground but it was soon clear she was trying to tear through his trousers to bite off his cock. Somehow Delroy managed to keep control of the vehicle although we were both absorbed in the graphic violence displayed as if on a wide screen through the car windows. We turned on a side road but immediately had to turn again as a mob of people running, all with phones to their ears, descended down the road towards us.

'Persons at the fight call their friends to join them, sir. Others upload images on YouTube and Facebook.' Delroy almost absent-mindedly relayed the action of the street as if I was on a tour of the back country and he, my guide, had operated the tour one time too many.

Then came the sirens and three Land Rovers with heavily armed paramilitary police and soldiers sped down the new road into which we had just turned. Delroy slowed, but still tried to drive as far away from them as possible and sighed with relief when they passed. 'Shouldn't we have tried to help that woman, Delroy? She was taking a bad beating.' Delroy whipped his face toward me with such speed, I was afraid he'd drive us into the lamp post and the look he gave me would not have been more incredulous if I'd said Eddy, the Pope, the American President and his grandmother were child molesters and fucked blind goats on Good Fridays at noon. 'For person like that all person like us in car are enemy, sir, especially government car. If we do anything, that woman will lead the mob to attack us then burn the car. If we survive, when police arrive they start shooting, they don't look who's who. It won't matter you the PM friend, sir. They don't expect you in place like that, with hooligan and other bad person.' As with

Donovan his elocution lessons had failed him under pressure. I'd been feeling a twinge of moral cowardice, knowing a lot of such fights ended in serious injury or death, especially if that woman got hold of the man's cock and bit it off. But Delroy's explanation soothed my qualms, and I went back to reading Pinnock's piece with only a slightly less murkily guilty conscience. Pinnock said that while all parties financed their activities and enriched their supporters with drug money, Haddad's party did so on an industrial scale, aided by the CIA's Air America and others who helped in recruiting mules. All parties worked with criminals but his People's Mandate used police and soldiers for unimaginable crimes. The leader of the biggest crime syndicate in the country, aided by the Americans and right-wing Europeans, was instrumental in driving out the leftists and installing the People's Mandate. Violence was an integral part of all political activities in Woodwater and Eddy had access to all the arms markets of America, Europe, Russia and China. While most political leaders were stupid and incompetent, Eddy was a superb strategist and tactician. In other stories the paper showed Eddy's goons in green uniforms caning weeping children. The pictures were poor but clear enough to show me wearing a blue linen shirt and Ray Bans thus identifying me as the exiled artist and author, imported to polish the image of the Prime Minister in a new book.

Another grainy photo showed church-women in torn gowns throwing punches over pieces of escoveitched fish with Scotch bonnet peppers and fried bammy. Upon reading the entire article I knew without doubt Eddy would be particularly upset. And to think, Winston was an alumnus of St Dunstan's too.

Thankfully, due to Delroy's skill at the wheel we had already put some distance between us and the growing unrest. We passed the site where the Chinese were building the hotel and saw they were now on the second floor and soon after that we were walking up the flower-lined road back to where I was staying. I almost looked forward to seeing Miss R. As the gates opened Delroy quietly asked if I wanted him to return later and if not, what time should he come for me tomorrow. I could not answer, could see nothing because standing in front of the door, chatting with Miss Robotham, was a dream, my perfect woman.

CHAPTER TEN

S he was the impossible dream you could imagine but never realise. Plato's Idea of Beauty, the one he knew he would never behold, the secret heroine of every work of art. I heard screams for her inside my groin. 'Hello, Sharon,' Delroy said, 'you come already.'

'You have a visitor, Prof.,' Miss Robotham said, 'I got to supervise some lunch.'

I couldn't hear Miss R or see Delroy handing me the newspapers, my laptop and mobile. Sharon told me her name again but my mouth agape I couldn't hear, and when I told her mine she must have thought I said 'Mr Magoo'. I signalled like a zombie for her to go through the door, pointed to the living room, and heard the echo of Delroy saying he could see I was busy. She was at least five ten, her legs seemed to hang from the sky; her tits, ass, waist and hips fit together so perfectly you couldn't single out any one of them from the whole. I no longer had an ideal of woman to aim for, I had found her.

'I went to the academy but it must have been after you left for that American university', she said. I was still suffering from selective mutism. I couldn't answer her though my eyes were glued to her so tight C4 couldn't blow them off. She wore light blue linen trousers like me, a red silk blouse – surprisingly ,buttoned up to the top. They must have told her to wear Russell and Bromley loafers since they knew I didn't play in the NBA: If she was wearing Christian Louboutin *Aborina veau velours* pumps I would have had to climb a six foot ladder to mount her.

The house stocked South African, Australian, and Chilean reds of a slightly higher price range than those I bought at Morrison's. Miss R also showed me the Chateauneuf and Lafitte of early 2000 vintages which she told me were for special visitors, and she knew I preferred the local red rum with Coke. She came with two big glasses and bottles of Chateauneuf.

'You young people need something special, dears. Which one, Sharon?' Everyone must have been told I loved Chateauneuf: Sharon pointed to it and helped Miss R pour.

'Just something light, Ma'am. You know I had a heavy breakfast.'

'I'm not so hungry either, Miss R.' Now I'd got my tongue back I looked at Sharon's impossibly beautiful face. I had to look away quickly; I felt my eyes and crotch exploding.

'What did you study? You look like someone who took English or French literature.'

'After the Academy I did political science at the University. I saw your pictures at St Dunstan's, winning medals in running and prizes in the sciences and literature. I also read your book on Joseph.' I should have taken the opportunity to ask her about Joseph but Eddy and Delroy had lied about Joseph and this early in our relationship I didn't want her to have to lie to me too. I was looking at those legs and thinking of Merlene Ottey or Jessica Ennis and a thousand female sprinters who powered down the track – cameramen always focused on their groins – and I imagined them having orgasms each time their feet hit dirt. Now I had one such woman in front of me and was intellectualizing instead of actually dragging her into bed and fucking her. I imagined how colour co-ordinated she'd look with my navy bedspread, red sheets and pillowcases. I couldn't see a milligram of fat on her legs, with those stretches of beauty she must have been a demon in sprints, breasting the tape with her divine tits.

'Cheers,' she said, we clinked glasses and I felt we were wed after a courtship of a thousand years. But I was angry at Eddy for sending her without warning, knowing the shock of seeing her would cause me to make a fool of myself, as I'd done with Maria. I was also surprised that a man of such impressive calculating ability would send me a woman of quality, who would rouse not just sexual but intellectual desire. The ideal woman for his purpose would have tits, ass and lips so out of proportion I'd drag her into bed after thirty seconds, let her fuck me comatose, then fuck me more if I revived. Then I'd write the shit he expected. Yet here I was, with the perfect woman, Hamlet-like, thinking 'To fuck, or not to fuck...' Now I remembered how I despised characters like Frasier and Seinfeld who had pussy on the plate but spoilt it by talking. I'm no racist but always thought only white men were neurotic about pussy.

Sharon was telling me about her plans for graduate school, how she'd studied French and German to make her more competitive in her application for international studies at an Ivy League school or Oxbridge. 'You'd need a big scholarship. Unless your father's rich you can't afford graduate studies at these schools today.' My eyes were sympathetic but my head was saying 'I'm sure Eddy will give you the money if you fuck me right.'

'I'm working hard to do well on the GRE and the admissions people said my work in the foreign ministry would count as work experience.' Miss R came in with jerk pork, salad and patties, and I thought this was light enough if I decided to take her into the bedroom after. I was sure she wore blue or red lace underneath and once I got inside her I would not stop. But after eating, my anger at Eddy's presumption in sending her unannounced boiled up and I decided to play hard to get.

'I don't know what to do, Sharon, Eddy cancelled an interview and I don't know when he'll call again.' She looked at me as if I were a child who couldn't figure what people do in the adult world.

'Eddy's working on a strategy to counter what Winston wrote in the *Independent*. It's also time for the cabinet to make work for their supporters' Christmas money. I doubt he'll be free today.'

'Then I'll go back to that estate – there were things I couldn't see when we went there before.' Her eyes widened and I saw two suns ignite in the heaven of her face.

'You can't go by yourself – Eddy won't like that.'

'No problem, he won't know. I'll call Delroy to take you back then take a taxi there.'

She looked even more alarmed. 'No!' she said, 'don't call him!' So she feared Delroy would report her failure to fuck me senseless. And I was confused, thinking of my fiasco with Maria.

CHAPTER ELEVEN

I could see disappointment in her eyes, less assurance and certainty as she looked at me. 'I don't want him to take me. Eddy would think you're going behind his back. I can call the taxi which took me here; he can drop me on the way.' She called, speaking our full dialect. I couldn't get it all, but understood her telling him to take us to her place and nothing after.

Her place wasn't far down the hill but the quality was different. Still, this was a gated community of two and three bedroom condos and a sign read 'No Taxis'. She must have been friendly with the guard – he raised the barrier. I knew she couldn't buy this house if she saved all her life, couldn't afford the rent even if she didn't eat, buy clothes or pay tax. The place was air-conditioned though not arctic, the floor covered in brilliantly glazed blue tiles, the pictures modern, though the lines were not as stark or colours as intense as in Eddy's houses. There was a big picture on the wall facing the door, she saw me looking at it with surprise. 'My classmate, Elena ,' she said, 'we grew up together.' The girl was good looking, if Eddy had sent her to me instead of Sharon, I would still think she was way above my pay grade. But it wasn't her picture alone I found surprising: Colin Shepherd stood next to her. 'She's the FM's cousin, she works in his ministry.' The cousin wasn't standing next to him the way a cousin would, her stance said ownership, with plans to make it permanent, and I could imagine the muscular arms of the FM's athletic wife smashing the picture over her husband's head. In the picture they were wearing gowns of *ase oke*, a very expensive hand woven cloth from Yoruba land in Nigeria and Benin; she wore the headtie and he the cap of the same material. I went out with a Yoruba girl once in London. She said if a man gave you *ase oke* it meant he was serious; he had the bread to take care of you, and you could open your legs for him. 'He taught Yoruba at Ibadan University before Eddy made him minister.' They were also wearing heavy necklaces of red stone, an Ibo speciality, which shouldn't be worn with *ase oke*. But nobody was perfect.

When we entered the house the forty inch Bravia was silent. *Valley of the Dolls* playing in mute. I was sure it wasn't Sharon but her roommate Edna who watched such shit. She switched it off and put on a DVD with Otis Redding and some other old soul people, who looked flamboyant in their exotic costumes of earlier years. Elena must have put up the plastic Christmas tree in the corner too. It didn't look too cheap and had nice decorations but did nothing for me as I didn't do Christmas. I tried to hide my feelings but I saw the embarrassment on her face. Obviously the FM provided the house and wanted Sharon to keep Edna company when her 'cousin' was with his fucking wrestler of a wife.

'I soon come,' Sharon said and I smiled as I recalled what the expression meant in our country, 'you may never see me again, certainly not for another five hours!' I thought she'd gone to piss after drinking cold water at my place but when she came back my eyes almost popped out, as did what I had in my Hom boxer shorts. I was sitting in one of the double seat rattan chairs, probably from Thailand or China, and when she sat it didn't leave much space between us. She'd opened the top two buttons of her blouse. I could see her blue lace bra and the top of her tits. It was a push up, she'd obviously raised it, and to anyone but a neurotic it said 'Come!' When I first shook her hand I'd sniffed for her perfume but couldn't smell any, and even Miss Robotham's Avon had a more powerful signature. Now she'd splashed on Boucheron perfume and it was coming off her like a storm. When we were at my place up the hill I was so hard I was hurting and had to think of island sized icebergs to chill myself just to get up. Now she was looking a thousand times as hot, I felt I was about to explode and had to will the whole Antarctic to prevent me moving across, as Otis trilled *Sitting at the Dock of the Bay.*

'Excuse me,' she said again, went to the kitchen and came back with a tray holding our island aged rum and a 2005 Merlot. 'You can have any of these – we don't have a huge selection.'

'I had too much wine at lunch, Sharon. Maybe a small glass of this.' Either she liked me a lot and wanted me to take her by the hand and drag her into her bedroom, or she was trying hard to do the job Eddy had given her. I even tried to figure what hold Eddy had on her, what he'd threatened or promised, how fear or hope could put a woman in the state she was in. Then I figured that even if she was doing it for Eddy, from what I saw of her that's not what I wanted. She was beautiful, intelligent, warm, and with her gifts she would have had a much bigger house if she were willing to fuck a 'cousin.' I'd never had a girl like her, I'd met beauties that were hot, fucked the first time, kept fucking till we woke one morning and found we'd fucked out. A purely sexual relationship was not what I wanted from a girl as wonderful and I felt I had to leave even if she took her clothes off.

'It's getting late, Sharon. I want to go to the estate now, so I can leave before it gets dark.' I could see the hurt, her body seemed to implode, and I felt so cold my cock shrank, becoming like a little red gunga bean, the one we use for rice and peas. Her voice was down, as if announcing the death of a favourite aunt. 'I'll call that driver, he comes from an estate not far from there. I'll also call a friend.'

I wanted to kiss her, tell her we were still friends, that we could do what we felt like doing later, when we knew each other better. But I felt like a fool when we heard the taxi and I simply waved goodbye. My New Year's resolution had been never to refuse a fuck when offered and now I'd blown it, for God's sake. 'Delroy gave me your number. I'll call so you'll have mine.'

CHAPTER TWELVE

The driver's face had the look of a man who returns to his house to find it's been flattened by a hurricane. It said I was crazy to leave what I had, to go to a place peopled by brutal, testosterone maddened men. No sane man, or real man, left a woman of such quality behind. When he dropped her he must have assumed she went to be fucked; a woman so beautiful could not go to discuss works of J.D. Salinger or Derek Walcott. When she called he must have been mildly surprised but reassured when he saw us going to her house to resume where we left off. Now he had to come back for me I could see the horror in his eyes. Even if Sharon was not as beautiful, even if she didn't surpass the quality of every movie star or pop idol who ever existed, he'd expect her to fuck me so hard I had to be collected by an ambulance after a week, not his fucking taxi. He looked suspiciously at my linen slacks, Swiss cotton shirt, and smart loafers – this was not the fashion for a beat up taxi but for a Mercedes Sports. He looked alarmed when I sat in front but chilled when he heard I was foreign. 'This isn't the way we went last time, Bunny.'

'This way shorter, sir, the other way only through government control area.' We drove on and slowly the kept yards gave way to haphazard bush, stony roads strewn with piles of garbage every few feet. This was more like the ghettoes I was used to seeing on my last visit here. There were broken hovels made of zinc, cardboard or plastic, huts with shattered windows covered with papers. There were few walls or fences, where these survived they were fractured and hanging. The asphalt was scraped from most of the roads and Bunny swerved to get round potholes that would break his axle. I had to hold on to avoid bumping into him. I failed, possibly confirming his suspicions that I was a man who liked men. The street was full of men who were not at work. Some were drinking from quarter bottles of over-proof rum and others played dominoes. Overweight women shouted loudly as they sold yams or bananas on sidewalks or quarrelled on verandas, threatening to 'tear each other's pussies out'. These people had remained in opposition, believed that being left-wing was good, and had not learnt the lesson that resistance was futile. So Eddy had not permitted his Chinese friends to do their magic and introduce them into history and commerce.

There were roadblocks manned by young men with short-sleeved sports shirts left hanging outside their trousers, guns hidden in their waistbands underneath the billowing fabrics. Some carried guns of such size and high calibre their shirt tails could not fully conceal them. I saw an emaciated boy who was probably twelve but looked eight. He was so small his .45 Colt seemed to be carrying him and he'd probably end up in orbit if he attempted to fire it. The strips of tee-shirt on his bones were Jean-Paul Gaultier lite, while his shredded trousers had the aura of John Galliano's craft. The only things with flesh on here were two vultures, weighing down the branches of a leafless mango tree. Red traffic lights were permanently on but Bunny drove through. 'Police can't come this side, sir. That's why your people take you the other way. I see you picture in *Independent*. I surprise when Sharon call me to take you here.'

All along the way were roadblocks manned by equally emaciated and raggedy boys who waved us through – taxis were regarded as neutral and they knew I was foreign – I sat in front and my face wasn't scarred with contempt. A man like me was expected to sit in back, tell the driver he was fucking stupid and his mother smelled of shit. Ahead I saw the towers and realized it had taken us about half the time of Eddy's convoy to get here, despite the outriders and Death's Head Commando's driving people off the roads with whips and gun butts, and all the traffic lights green for us. The entrance we'd taken was blocked off and Bunny stopped at another where a young man in black sunglasses stood smoking a joint. Bunny spoke to him in very low tones as the wind blew and I could smell the powerful aroma of the weed he had been dragging on, and the sunlight glinted off the grainy butt of the colossal 9mm Glock special like Christmas sparklers. 'Are you Trevor?' I interrupted.

'No, sir, I telling this driver how to get to him.' Black Sunglasses was inhaling as he spoke. I knew he couldn't be Trevor; Sharon had sounded close to the man when she spoke and I couldn't see her being close to a boy who smoked weed in public and wore an exposed gun. And he was a boy, though the vacuum in his eyes showed he'd probably been killing people a long time. As it turned out Trevor was waiting around the corner, in front of one of the tower blocks. I'd expected him to be muscle bound, square jawed, with a voice like a foghorn, the type to always get the girl when men got together to strut. But he was slender, with grey eyes, some freckles on either side of his nose, his voice so quiet you needed to lean into him to hear. Bunny jumped out of the car, they hugged then indulged in a complex handshake, directly copied from their Miami and LA idols. 'Thanks for bringing the Prof., Bunny. Sharon tell me it was you. Welcome again, sir. I see when you come with Eddy.'

'Thanks, Trevor, but you don't have to call me 'sir', I'm not that old!' It didn't surprise me I hadn't seen him, a man like him needn't stand out, didn't need muscles or a square jaw or shades to get the girls, or to kill. I suddenly felt hot, a pang of jealousy made my face tighten as I thought of him and Sharon. A girl as beautiful as her would start attracting attention from boys her age when she was five, older boys would try to force themselves on her when she was ten and by the time she was fifteen every adult male she came in touch with would want a piece of her. Trevor was a little older, he would treat her as a little sister, become her protector with fists, clubs, knives and then the Glock cannon now stuck down the back of his trousers. There would have come a time when she'd feel that if she gave it up to him she could get the men chasing her to leave her in peace. And though he probably felt for her like a little sister, what man could resist a girl like that without clothes on? All this thinking about her had got my cock hard and I tried distracting my thoughts to bring it down again – you can't have a hard-on like that in front of men here. They'd think you were after them; a capital offence. Trevor spoke, 'Wait here, Bunny. I'll show the Prof. round the place.'

My eyes stayed on the bulge of the gun under his green shirt feeling in the moment jealous of that too. I'm not a gun person by nature but sometimes I had the fantasy of firing into an enemy's forehead, feeling the power to annihilate another, though I'd probably collapse at the first bang. I was a fucking coward, if you want to know the truth, though I pretend to be Superman. Now here I was with a man who would kill without breaking sweat, and who had probably fucked the woman I was too cowardly to take when she offered herself to me.

'There is twelve blocks, sir. Each have over five hundred person, almost the whole Eddy constituency.' We were walking around, I didn't see any people outside, and only a few opened their curtains when we passed.

'People on vacation, Trevor? Place like this you expect crowds going about their business.'

'You know those bad boy come round and kill plenty person, sir. Everyone afraid.'

A group of young girls suddenly rushed from between two blocks. When they saw us they started shouting 'Trevor! Trevor!!' They were not afraid, they knew gunmen wouldn't shoot, not with them walking around braless in tiny tops and hot pants which revealed more than they concealed. Having noticed me, they began staring hungrily at me, at my expensive linen and shoes, Ray Bans, my old fake Omega with false alligator skin strap. The best looking one licked her lips and came closer, pushing out her tits as if in offering, her eyes smoking under her unkempt black hair. She couldn't have been even fifteen years old yet and I was beginning to feel nauseous. I wasn't a child molester. 'Go away, girl, is why you not in school? I showing the PM guest around.' The PM's name didn't affect them, the boldest one pressed even closer, her eyes telling me there was a spot behind the block where she could show me skin. 'Go away!' Trevor said, and this time there was an iron in his voice capable of making other killer's freeze. 'These children start early, sir. They missing school daily, next thing you know they is baby mother.'

I wasn't hearing him. I saw another one with wide eyes that seem to be brimming with tears about to overflow, hiding behind a raw concrete column. The one who offered herself to me could have been made of the same concrete, scarred and hard, nothing could touch her, but this one with the eyes, she was glass, so fragile the gentlest wind could shatter her like an exquisite Lalique statuette, leaving behind the quality craftsmanship in broken pieces of excellence. As she continued to look at us from behind her seemingly impenetrable facade, her dark eyes haunted and afraid, stayed steadily focused on mine making my flesh shiver even in the afternoon heat. She could have easily been a twelve-year-old Sharon, but this one was too timid to find a protector like Trevor, to whom she would offer herself before she began to bleed. I thought back, to the girl I had once held, when we were teenagers in university and considered ourselves old beyond our years.

She was daughter of a prominent Brahmin who promised her to the son of a friend in the warrior caste, predicted to become a billionaire before he was thirty. But the Brahmin was enlightened, he told his daughter she could live the life she wanted at the school when, like me, she had perfect scores in the SATS and won a full scholarship. We were inseparable for three years, she said she came to me because she felt she'd known me in another cycle of existence and I believed – I felt as close to her as an identical twin. Maybe she felt free after the prison of caste for thousands of years and something deep inside made me feel like a prisoner too. But after my last exam, when I looked for her to celebrate, she was gone, until I saw pictures of her wedding in *The New York Times* and *Newsweek*. Since that time I had felt as if an ocean had opened up inside and all the women after her were less than a teardrop; they were garbage bins in which I deposited waste. Until I met Sharon. I looked at Trevor again, happy that my shades hid the anger in my eyes. Then I looked at my little Lalique girl, still shivering like a new leaf in a storm. She didn't have five thousand years of Brahmin history, the Laws of Manu, a billion dollar husband nor friendships with Melinda Gates, Queen Rania of Jordan, or Angelina Jolie to protect her from the horror I was seeing in her eyes. And she didn't have a Trevor.

'Jesus Christ Almighty and all him angel!' I heard Trevor groan but the powerful roar of a car's engine and music so loud it made the glass in the windows shake drowned his voice out. Driving slowly towards us, the high shine of the metallic body and silver metal rims on the wheels, giving it the quality of some kind of exotic beast roaming the plains was a souped-up red 1964 Mustang. The man who jumped out of it was a slightly smaller version of the Rhino. He had the blackest skin, the likes of which I'd seen only once before in Dakar, Senegal. His skin of polished ebony was set off by his huge golden 'grill' which resembled closely Rhino Man's own. These grills, inspired by the wealthy hip hop stars of the day, were usually made of pure gold and diamonds and fit over the teeth giving the wearer a fearsomely wealthy appearance. I remembered him now, from an online feature on stars of the dancehall. He was an exponent of 'Blackism', a deeply underground sub-group advocating the killing of white men and fucking of white women.

'Is wha' happen, star?' he roared at Trevor who flinched at the tightness of his embrace. When he spoke I realized the tune almost shattering the glass was his – his song saluting his sixteen year old baby mother who had presented him with twins. 'This is the Prof., Lion Man, the one here from England to write that book on Eddy.' A red, gold and green bandana held down his locks, he wore a gold Rolex and rings on each finger. I could smell the weed and Brut between the sweat and he kept the butt of his .45 Magnum outside his shirt to show he was a man.

'We have a thing uptown, Trev, plenty young pussy. Is why you don't come with the Prof.?' Trevor sounded alarmed: 'Prof. here to work, star. Him don't have time to go up or downtown!'

The girls had been quiet, put off perhaps by my obvious lack of interest in them; I thought they'd gone away but when they heard the dreadlocked musicians voice they recognized it immediately and they rushed out again, shouting 'Lion Man! Lion Man!!' The one who had earlier offered herself to me now thrust her tits out even farther, almost took them out for the musician, and grabbed his arm as if to pull him onto her. I couldn't see his eyes behind his shades but imagined rage like swirls of a hurricane as his enormous hand with a trove of gold rings swung back, smashed her in the face, blood spurting as she fell. Her shriek was plaintive, like a young animal's, as her friends rushed, helping her to her feet and pulling her away. I felt Miss Robotham's lunch coming up and it took a huge act of will to keep it down. Trevor's gun hand clasped and unclasped the handle of his piece but he didn't draw, probably calculating that a girl who offered herself to men like this needed to be taught a direct lesson in pain they would remember, no point wasting a bullet then. Lines from his hit song, where he roared to a gut-wrenching beat about how to 'tear up pussy first time' assailed the night air, covering the still crying girl and the calming voices of those who tended to her.

Lion Man was smiling with satisfaction as he listened to it, then drawing himself away he growled, 'Excuse, Prof., me and Trev have a little 'ting to talk 'bout.'

'Make it quick, star, you no see me have a important visitor to take care of?' I could see the anger in Trevor's face as the musician pulled him away, and heard Lion Man voice buzz like a jackhammer, though I couldn't understand a word that came out. 'That ok,' Trevor said, 'now leave me so I can get back to the Prof.'

Before we could reconvene there came the chug of a cheap motorcycle and a smiling young man wearing a cap from Jay-Z's Brooklyn Nets and thick, clear glasses, rode up and stopped, shouting 'Where's, Trev?' Trevor was coming back with Lion Man only a few steps behind him, his face enraged apparently by Trevor's pleasure at seeing the newcomer.

'Is who let you in our place, Jayzee?' At this the two fell about laughing. I could understand the dread's upset. Jayzee rode a Jingchen, not a high-powered American car. His glasses had proper prescription lenses, and were fashionable but he wasn't wearing them purely for fashion. He had no gun tucked away down the back of his trousers, you could perfectly understand his English and he smiled easily and naturally. That being said, to Lion he still lacked the qualities of a real man. 'This is Jayzee, Prof. He real name Carter, he want to be big time rapper, and dream of doing the thing with Beyoncé!' Jayzee threw a fake punch at his head then said: 'I saw the Prof.'s snap in Winston's paper, Trev, and I've read his book about Joseph.' He handed me a demo DVD he probably made himself. Lion Man sucked his teeth, the height of impoliteness in our culture. 'I tell you I get a thing uptown, Trevor. I going go now. Enjoy writing you book on Eddy, Prof.'

The girls obviously hadn't learnt their lesson. As he got back into his wheels, gunning the engine they rushed out again, screaming as he waved them away, his rings flashing in the dark. The girl with the cut cheek, now covered by band aids, led the charge, shouting 'Come back soon to see we!'

He sucked his teeth in irritation. 'You gyal should go to school, not chase after gunman like that. Soon you going become baby mother.' He took a roll of thousand dollar bills from his back pocket and gave one to the leader girl. 'Go buy yourself something, Ri-Ri.' The girls grabbed the money and rushed off, singing the lyrics they'd just heard on Lion Man's giant Realistic speakers and I imagined them overtaking the 'Wall Mart' two blocks over in which the money would be spent so fast it would seem to disintegrate into thin air. I looked for my little Lalique girl, saw her blending into the background, chameleon-like, perhaps waiting until the danger passed. She made a slight move, as if to follow the others but then held back. Perhaps she was hungry but afraid, not just of us, but of all there was. When Jayzee initially came I thought I saw a smile on the face of my little girl made of glass and when she looked at Jayzee her fear distinctly diminished but not enough to draw her out.

Trevor motioned to me and we followed them to the shop. For where it stood, it was surprisingly large and clearly well-stocked, but in reality it was no Walmart. My face must have shown my consternation because Trevor offered, 'The owner is Eddy friend, Prof., him have a big mall uptown but come from round here and want him person to have the same as uptown person. But price here lower as we poor.' It turned out I needn't have worried. They could just as easily have called the shop 'The White House' or 'Obama Provision Store' for all Eddy cared.

'Unemployment very high, Trevor, how you people make it here?'

'We do this and that, Prof. Person from here who make it give us a money; the Party give us a work Easter and Christmas time. Sometime we go uptown and people give us something.' So they survived on hand outs, government made work, extortion, robbery and killing. I noticed the little girl had not stirred from behind the rough concrete as the others emerged shouting and laughing from 'Wall Mart' armed with patties, cakes, sweets and packets of banana chips. Eddy and Delroy had lied when I asked about Joseph and I wanted to test him, to see how creative he would be with his answer.

'You know how I can get in touch with Joseph, Trevor? You know what he's doing now?' He was a nice guy, I liked him and felt pity at the anguish I saw in his grey eyes, as if a flint-hearted boss had ordered him to get rid of a tight friend with a bullet between the eyes.

'Joseph have a grandmother in the country who sick, sir. He there taking care of her. He her first grandson.' Jayzee had been humming the tune from one of his numbers. I saw the look of incredulity on his face at what Trevor said of Joseph. I was reading some of the lyrics from the cover of the demo tape Jayzee gave me – they were first class, didn't mention tearing up young pussy or killing men. *'I saw your face in the morning, / shining, brighter than the moon, the sound of birds / echoing the passing of the night,/like the sun rising from beneath the sea / when the wind of summer blows from the west.'* If he'd been born in Europe or America he could have become another successful, Stevie Wonder. But here he had to be a thug like Lion Man and rape as many women as he killed men to make it. 'I have to go to a studio downtown, Trev. Nice to meet you, Prof. Good luck on your book.'

'Prof. is Sharon friend, Jayzee. Is she send him here.' I could see he thought I was fucking her and was happy for us.

'Nice to meet you, Jayzee. Good luck with Beyoncé! When I get back to London I'll show your DVD to some friends.'

'Thanks, Prof. It's nice meeting you too. And greet Sharon for me.' He waved as his machine chugged off, and I feared for him as I feared for the little girl behind the concrete pillar. 'Let me show you a thing before you go, Prof.' He took me to the big generator housed in front of one of the tower blocks. It would have made a nice villa for a middle-class family. 'One of them big American company get a contract for a power plant and Eddy insist they build a thing for person in his constituency, sir.' He opened the door and I saw how big the machine was, like a power station for a small town.

'Thank you very much, Trevor, I've got to go. I don't want the dark to catch me on the road.'

'The road safe, sir. But is alright if you want to go back to Sharon.' She'd called, asking when I was coming but I put her off again, saying I had to write up my notes. I wanted so much to see her but I wanted a long-term relationship. Still I felt that ocean of pain Indie left when she went without saying goodbye and I struggled with trusting my heart to another woman again. The wild girls had disappeared. I didn't know where they'd find a man to beat and fuck them. 'Come, Bunny!' Trevor shouted in his mobile and I waved my little girl goodbye. But not even her eyelids flickered in the shadow of the concrete.

CHAPTER THIRTEEN

I thought Eddy was in a hurry for me to finish his book but then he kept putting me off when I tried to arrange a time for interviewing him. The matter was complicated by virtue of us having difficulty fixing the venue as Eddy had a lot of government houses. Part of Eddy's first campaign manifesto was that he'd live in his own house, to save taxpayers' money and be closer to the people. The problem was that he had many houses and he couldn't decide which one he wanted to renovate. Instead many more were 'brought up to standard' in case he had to put up another important head of state there.

The first one he invited me to was set on a hill where once stood a historical great house that had been knocked down and his sprawling modern estate built to replace it. Another equally expansive model was built on the outskirts of the capital city with specialist Italian glass walls and Argentinian imported stone. On another occasion he arranged for us to meet in a smaller house that was an almost exact replica of the house in London on Eaton Square – mahogany floors, doors and furniture, hand-made crystal, chandeliers and enough of an assembly line of modern paintings to fill a museum. We got little done, visitors kept coming and as a 'man of the people' Eddy couldn't refuse them.

The same happened in the enormous compound he'd built next to the American Embassy. National prestige demanded it had to be twice the size than it's foreign neighbour. Each visit prompted more incredulity and fascination in me. It became difficult to not spout inanities. When Eddy's people caught me staring slack-jawed at one particularly excessive renovation project that had just been completed, they assured me the PM would reimburse the government when he left office. In my mind I saw Eddy handing over one cent to a yawning grey haired man at the treasury, with a wispy beard. I finally made progress with him at his palatial beach house, built by the Chinese, drawing on thousands of years experience of pleasing megalomaniac emperors and insane empresses. I couldn't even count all the rooms with walls of polished mahogany or cedar I went through, each reinforced to withstand hurricanes, earthquakes or bombs. Most had skylights, and flowers of every variety and colour filled the house with sweet perfume.

The Chinese were supposed to be scientific socialists and Eddy was a mathematician but the house was built in accordance with the principles of Feng Shui. Sharon explained it was based on Chinese superstitions about directionality, where to locate buildings, rooms within buildings, objects within rooms, all according to the positions of the compass and some complex numerology. The centrepiece of this construction was a courtyard where they had erected an immense water fountain in the middle of a flowing pond filled with giant carp – some said to be over a hundred years old – and surrounded by circular beds of red, white and yellow roses. There was an outlet to the sea but a fine mesh grille kept the fish in. Beyond the pond a stone patio overlooked the beach, its sparkling white sand like tiny diamonds leading down to the foaming cobalt sea and across to Cuba and Jamaica.

The house had just been completed by specially imported Chinese workers and Eddy appeared to be serious this time. No announcement had been made that we were there, he turned off his five Blackberries and two tablets and told Donovan he'd speak only to his mother, Elizabeth, Brett Farnham or Maria. Even the Chinese and American Presidents were to be told he would call back. I'd never seen Eddy so excited. He told me how wonderful his mother was, how much he loved her and from what he said of Miss Vie, Mother Theresa and Princess Diana were slags. Although his campaign literature and his autobiography made it seem he came from the ghetto and thus a man of the people, his father was a successful real-estate dealer and financier, his mother a teacher at the prestigious academy for girls (although she had also inherited wealth) and they lived in a grand house uptown, with a custom-made diamond shaped swimming pool on eleven acres of beautifully landscaped grounds. But in Eddy's mind he was brought up poor. His mother was concerned for those more unfortunate than herself. Money she would use to buy expensive clothes, supermarket food, take trips to Miami or New York, or to operate high powered SUVs like her cohorts, she used instead to buy clothes, food, school books, or religious pamphlets for the people downtown. Eddy played with children of his rich neighbours but most of his experience was with kids in the ghettoes, where he developed his affinity for dancehall musicians and the athletes who came from those parts. His mother arranged birthday and Christmas parties at their house but invited people from downtown, to the chagrin of neighbours who didn't want their kids to mix with such persons and soon stopped sending them over. But Miss Vie never got angry, she chose not to judge the parents and when the party was over brought over food, drinks and presents for children who didn't attend.

Eddy presented his father as a saint, a man who gave full support to his wife, did not scold her for spending his hard earned cash on poor persons and accompanied them on their trips downtown when he found time. As he praised his father as if he were a combination of Saints Joseph and Francis, I watched him closely to see if he showed any signs of discomfort that Eddy Senior couldn't be his biological father, that not even he was powerful enough to overcome the laws of genetics. His father was the perfect parent – Eddy Junior had an ideal childhood and all his political ideas about doing good for the people he inherited from his parents.

'So your ideas about the welfare of the people owe nothing to Marxism or Social Democracy, Eddy?'

'No, Prof.,' he replied, affecting the superior demeanour of the headmaster addressing a naive pupil. He was no longer the modest pupil of St. Dunstans, praising his superior schoolmate. 'My mother and father were good Catholics, they believed God took care of the weakest of his creatures, that we, as privileged ones, had the obligation to give the poor the opportunity to make good. You know what Ronald Reagan said, about not giving a person a fish, but teaching him to fish.' I didn't want to correct him about the saying of the B-movie actor. Mao, to whom it had been attributed, had probably stolen it from some Confucian scholar who lived a thousand years before. This was not my role.

I'd mistaken his actions toward me as warmth or generosity but when I saw how his people treated those children who collapsed in the sun, I realised his behaviour was an act. A lot of what he offered me came directly from my book, which he was treating as a script on how to please me. The wines he provided, the local foods I'd said I could never resist, despite rejecting just about everything else from my island culture. The rum, coffee and watch I admired. Even Sharon was the type of woman I had written was my ideal, though I questioned his judgement on not supplying me with a slut.

Eddy's descriptions of Florida State, given me in previous meetings, had features you'd be hard pushed to find in a state institution – pseudo-Gothic architecture, Nobel Prize Laureate Professors, beautiful girls with high IQs – were features of Ivy League and other elite private universities. But what surprised me was the emotional flatness he displayed when he spoke of his parents, who he wanted to impress on me as ideal. His account glorified the obvious and superficial and could have come from some *Readers Digest* puff piece, while I could sense something more intense underneath, like the nightmares I have of hurricanes, floods and earthquakes. As a politician he was tightly wound, personal feelings hidden, very controlled, defence so perfect no emotion could escape. The closest he came to openness, when I saw a crack in his armour and he showed vulnerability, was with Elizabeth, Brett and Maria in London. And when he lied about Joseph.

'You know of John Cairncross, Prof.? From the time of slavery his people ruled this place. Despite his wealth and power he treated his only daughter worse than most fathers in the ghettos.

When Miss Vie saw her arriving at the Academy she was like an orphan. She chewed her nails, burst into tears at the slightest provocation and even wet herself. My mother practically adopted her, sent for her father and censured him like one of her unruly pupils. This was a man who could have the President or Prime Minister sacked or killed if they displeased him but he sat humble and respectful as this poor woman lambasted him and his ways. If she'd demanded anything he'd give her, any of his properties, any amount of money, but she never accepted even the smallest present he sent through Elizabeth.' Eddy puffed up with pride at his mother's generosity and fortitude.

'Your party symbol's the cockerel, Eddy. I wondered about that. Are you appealing to our men's obsession with sex, promising endless orgasms, like fundamentalist imams? Mobutu gave himself a bizarre name, which meant 'the warrior who can never be defeated, the cock who leaves no hen unfucked'

'An excellent question, Prof. Actually the cockerel has nothing to do with sex. You know what Jesus said to Peter before they crucified him? "Before the cock crows twice, you'll deny me thrice." Loyalty is what the cock is all about, Prof. When people see the cock it reminds them of Jesus, the need not to betray their leader, their saviour and redeemer.'

I liked the way he fused his persona with Christ's. He dialled on the intercom, told someone to bring the photo albums, then smiled at me and said: 'Now you'll see what I looked like before I became the Eddy Haddad you know, Prof.!'

I'd always seen men like Donovan around him, athletically built, in very expensive, well-fitting designer suits and now I expected a clone wearing Hermes or Dunhill lime-scented cologne. But I was surprised when a wave of Carolina Herrera perfume swept over me and wondered how one of our super macho, homophobic men could risk wearing woman's scent. Then I saw her, she smelt overbearingly of perfume, as if she might have emptied a bottle over herself. Her mini dress clung to her so tightly it acted like a magnifying glass, revealing what she should keep hidden. Eddy didn't introduce her, she grunted at me perfunctorily and gave me a full stare when she bent over to hand the photograph albums to Eddy, showing me what she had on her chest was all hers, ready for stroking, squeezing and licking.

We have a mango tree here on the island which is short and whose huge, shiny fruit hang like ripe baubles, ready for sucking, and that is what her tits were saying. Her nipples stuck out like ballistic missiles, primed for take-off. She was brunette, cute though not beautiful, fabulously made up, spelling out S-E-X. I was surprised she was acting so boldly in front of Eddy and fantasised that if I reached out and raised her skirt she wouldn't resist. If I pulled her round the corner and bent her over she'd do the dog without protest, and if I lay her on the floor she'd open her legs, erupting like a volcano. If I hadn't met Sharon I'd tell Eddy I was going to piss, grabbed her and give it to her in the john. A girl like that needed no foreplay. He didn't tease me for giving her the look, showed no emotion when I watched her leaving, twisting her ass like a model on the catwalk, to show she wore nothing under that superfluous dress.

'My mother always said I was the most beautiful child she ever saw – I suppose all mothers say that!' Eddy flipped the pages of the first expensive leather album, they revealed him as a big boned baby in startling white lace, a clenched fist raised just as he did on lecterns today. Another album showed him as a young child, in white linen with lace collars. When he came to the albums of his time at St Dunstan's I saw in the pictures how he dwarfed his classmates, and tried as hard as I could to imagine seeing him as a boy in a lower form. Surely I'd remember a boy that big just entering the school? But I couldn't. 'Maybe you remember me now, Prof.? '

'Yes, Eddy, I told you I remembered you a long time ago but you know what time does to memory, even before you get old!' Lying was less stressful when you felt comfortable. He called again, the girl came, her eyes seeming to ask why she and I weren't getting it on, if I were scared of Eddy? The smell of her heavy perfume had remained behind like a misty, scented aroma from the sea and now she entered again like a skinny dipping bather. 'Tell the driver to come,' Eddy said. This time I didn't watch her, I was thinking of Sharon, and what this one was offering was being given too eagerly. 'I want to show you a little seaside village, Prof., not far from here. You'll see how our ordinary persons live!' Since we were going to see 'ordinary persons' the driver came in a brand new Mercedes 500 and a single policeman with a Heckler and Koch machine gun, rather than a convoy of Obama Lincolns and/or a string of Range Rovers with black clad commandos and an armoury of cannon. Eddy must have hired the drivers himself as this one too was a clone of Delroy and the one who took me to Gatwick. The village was less than fifteen minutes away, the driver was in no hurry and when we got there we were greeted by people of all sexes and ages wearing party colour tee-shirts and baseball caps, lined up in orderly rows by Eddy's party thugs and his ministers. They were drinking over-proof rum, rum punch, and the kids drank soft drinks. Huge cauldrons steamed by witches' on kitchen wood fires. The people had killed two cows, several pigs, goats, chickens and the day's catch of fish. Heads and limbs of all the animals were piled on sticks near the village school, and would be used to make soup if they were not satiated after eating the meat, rice, bananas, plantains, dumplings and yams. Or they would be chopped up and distributed to the villagers.

'You see how our poor persons live, Prof.'

'Yes, Eddy, I can see.' He walked over to greet a very old man struggling on a stick as he emerged from a small brick house. A very fat, shiny black woman held a big snapper in one hand and a rum punch in the other, 'other politician come here, they give us talk and foolishness.' She held up her fish and glass like a winning gladiator. 'See what Eddy bring? Miss Vie bring up that boy good, me tell you.' People cheered her name. After visiting the old man, Eddy moved among the people, his face a mask of concern as he pressed the flesh of men and women, children he picked up and threw in the air. If I didn't know better I'd think he really gave a shit, that this wasn't an act. But I was really thinking, how much better than Forest Whittaker Eddy would have played Idi Amin in *The Last King of Scotland*.

CHAPTER FOURTEEN

S haron kept calling and I kept putting her off, until I made up my mind to tell her about Indie and the effect her leaving had on me, why I had brief relationships which I ran away from when I started feeling affection, or the woman asked for commitment. There were legions of them, like migrating birds. I knew we were very young at the time but didn't want to use this as an excuse – we were very intelligent and Indie sometimes acted as if she were thousands of years old. Sharon was beautiful, a bit younger, but she understood, with the maturity and wisdom of a much older woman. 'I got the impression you were running away, afraid. Now you've said it we can go on.' I felt my eyes getting full but like my *Lalique* girl I couldn't let them overflow.

When we went out we were a couple and reactions of other people confirmed it. Sometimes, by accident, we wore the same colour linen trousers or Russell & Bromley loafers. We held hands, kept touching, had eyes only for each other or kissed. We were loved up, as teenagers now tweeted. Having discovered the power of my smart phone, I couldn't stop taking pictures of her, our fabulous animals and unforgettable plants. She took me to restaurants where I had the best food – at least since my grandmother's. One was in the living room of a single mother with four kids, whose cooking was so good all her children looked healthy, content and well behaved. As we ate they were sitting on stools, clean, well dressed, shiny, doing their homework. We went early and were alone, and the chef told us about her only love, the father of her four children. They knew each other from primary school, started living together at seventeen, and had their first child before they were twenty. After a tough life and four kids, her man got a break, a British passport from a cousin in Liverpool and he got into the country because immigration didn't pay attention to the match between him and the passport photo. She had been a dressmaker and started sewing wool clothes to survive the cruel winters. When he stopped writing she panicked, thinking he was dead. But after some time a cousin over there told her he brought over a younger woman, with whom he had a child in Woodwater. Looking at us she said she knew we'd never be parted like that, that I was a faithful and true man, a wonderful catch for Sharon. She gave us slices of sweet potato pudding and home-made ice cream, the best I ever tasted. Then I took pictures of her and her kids with Sharon and promised to send copies to her. She whispered to Sharon, thinking I could not hear, 'take good care of him, Sharon. He loves you very much.'

We went to a fish place in the town at the end of the peninsula near the airport where Captain Morgan did his imitation of Sodom. It was little more than a shack but they cooked the best fish in the Caribbean. They prepared it straight from the sea, kept live in a pool, so you chose your own dinner for the pot. I told

Sharon to choose one for me to prove her undying love. I was too cowardly to tell her I'd lose my appetite if I looked at the fish live, gazing into its eyes before they cut its throat. The manageress kept smiling at us and after a while she came over. She thought Sharon was a visitor too, 'you young people look so loving you must have learnt it over there.' She gave us very rich conch soup, which the locals thought was an aphrodisiac. She winked at Sharon as she whispered to her: 'this will make sure his eyes never stray!' There was a west wind blowing across the sea and Sharon was so wonderful I knew our love would last. I almost fucking cried.

The Chinese restaurant where they had twenty prawn dishes on offer was a real experience. It was divided in sections with cuisine from different provinces and big screens showed videos of the regional venues. The food was delicious and prices reasonable. Right next door was a gambling den where you went to lose money after the food cast its magic on your head and guts. The Chinese were buying up a lot of places and a young couple from Guangzhou owned this one. The woman was beautiful but looked harassed. I supposed she worked hard like all Chinese and was obviously impressed with us. She served us personally and kept giving us extras, like butterfly prawns. I knew she was drinking – I smelt the Mao Dai on her breath when she went into the kitchen and came out. She served us rum punch and after a while we noticed she was pissed off with her husband, who wore a smart leather jacket and Versace jeans and had slicked back his thick hair like an Italian pimp. She was saying things to him in Mandarin, quiet at first but louder as the drink filtered in. I knew a little Chinese from my best friend Chin in school and had taken a course for one semester in university. I couldn't understand all she said when her outburst rose to crescendo but it approximated, 'you're a donkey's cock that rotted for a year, you'd ram your whang in a diseased hedgehog, you undress crippled women with your eyes while looking at me like a crippled shadow, a fucking ghost. Why can't you treat me like that nice young man is treating his young woman? See how he's nibbling her ear, opening her zipper to stick his finger in. That young girl you ride like a kid rides a new pony could be your daughter'. I couldn't find the English for 'you're like that monster whose look turns everything to reinforced concrete mixed with shit.' I didn't tell Sharon what she said, nor thank her in Mandarin when she gave us lychees and truly wonderful Chinese sweets for free. The husband went out; before he left he slicked his hair with a comb from his pocket, doused himself with Armani perfume, and sprayed his mouth from a tube matching his Dunhill cigarette case and lighter. I took her picture with Sharon and when she saw the snaps she cried, burying her face in Sharon's shoulder. 'He's off to see her,' she said. She showed us the girl's picture on her phone. She was part African, part Indian and her eyes were Chinese. 'She's so young,' Su Ming said. 'So beautiful and sweet looking. But she's a devil; she gets money from other men. He used money from our business to buy her a Honda Sports car and pay the rent on her condo. He's such a child.' Her howling rose as she went on and Sharon was crying too, holding and hushing her. In my head I looked for a place to run and hide.

Whenever I went through duty free I always looked out for perfumes on offer. At Gatwick I'd picked up Ferragamo Incanto and Sharon loved it but complained she had to hide it as Elena was using it up and blaming her cousin, the FM for being so fucking unimaginative he couldn't get her anything but Boucheron. The first time we made love I told her most women wore clothes to hide their plainness, to deceive men into thinking they were Aphrodite. I'd burn her clothes so she would go around naked, showing us the perfection she was hiding! She said I was a flatterer and punched me in the stomach, a love tap which made the electricity run through my body, unlike Father O'Malley who hit me 'playfully' when I had a perfect score in the national exams. I had to kill the scream and hide the fact I was paralytic – he had been a Golden Glove boxer before entering the priesthood and thought constant pain the only thing to make a boy a man. I lost track of time but figured I must have been on Woodwater for about a month. I wasn't counting the days or wishing they'd never end.

Sharon promised to take me to see Eddy's mother, who she said was so simple and nice she would make me cry. We went to look for presents for her in the new mall they'd just built, one of the biggest in the Western hemisphere, with almost three hundred shops and sixty restaurants. We walked along the luxury section filled with Gucci, Prada, Versace, Dior, Wolford, Zillie, Miu Miu, Christian Louboutin, Louis Vuitton, and about every other boutique you'd find in New York, London, Rome or Shanghai. We found a little shop selling books by African writers like Achebe, N'gugi, Marechera and others – Heinrich Boll, Gunther Grass, Franz Kafka, James Joyce, T.S. Eliot, John Steinbeck – and a host of other literary stars.

'Guess who owns it?'

'Can't – only a madman would own such a place here, where people don't even read comic books.'

'It belongs to your old teacher, Bloom, and your friend, Stephen Walters, that notorious womaniser.' Bloom I wasn't surprised about, he'd introduced me to the classics of world literature which enabled me to appreciate the genius of Avram Berger, the Jew whose knowledge of German literature was so Prof.ound the grandchildren of Nazis had given him every honour they possessed. But Stephen was a champion sportsman, more than a champion playboy and gambler. The idea of him selling books by Marechera and Marquez was more incredible than if George Bush memorized Pablo Neruda and recited it to Dick Cheney on a turkey shoot. We went in and found bilingual editions of Rilke's *Duino Elegies* and Böll's *Nicht nur zur Weihnachtzeit.*

'This will help you with your German lessons.' I saw her eyes light up as she scanned the pages and began to mouth the words. Ten, fifteen years ago, they couldn't afford such a place here and, if they did, the mall would be full of Europeans, Americans and Japanese. Now most of the bearers of Gucci bags, Prada skirts and Louboutin pumps were Chinese and I quietly saluted the fleeting glory of the world shifting East. There was an enormous Christmas tree and I thought it was Norwegian until Sharon told me the Chinese had a plantation on one of the hills, with trees grown from seedlings they imported from near Stalin's birthplace in Georgia, Russia. The tree was decorated with goodies from the designer shops and it even had one of the latest bags from Louis Vuitton, the bag that had a waiting list of three months in New York and LA, according to *The New York Times* nestled in its foliage. There was a desk near the tree and the girl selling gifts knew she looked like Beyoncé and wore a skirt like Eddy's slut to show the cheeks of her ass.

'How long will it take to order a bag, Miss?' She'd been looking at us like beggars but her eyes lit up when I asked and we came close enough for her to see we wore linen and imported shoes.

'You pay now and collect it from the store, sir.'

'I don't want any Louis Vuitton,' said Sharon.

'Why not? I have the money.'

'I don't like designer ware, they have 'Louis Vuitton' splashed all over. You know I like simple things.'

'Like me', I said, winking at Beyoncé who tried to smile, almost cracking the foot of make up on her face. I ducked when Sharon swung, pinched her ass and she swung again, hitting me on the side of the head. Beyoncé smiled again: 'If you see anything else you like, Ma'am...'

'Please take care of my little girl, Miss. I soon come – I have to do what a man's gotta do.' We'd seen a La Senza store, Sharon said there were lingerie sets she liked but I told her they were cheaper in London and I'd get her some when I went back. Next to the shop there was a boutique with good linen slacks, as well as Victoria Secrets and La Perla. I ordered matching pairs of different coloured slacks and sets of Lingerie asked to have them wrapped in Christmas paper and said I'd collect them later. Then I went back, we said goodbye to Beyoncé and Sharon checked to see if I gave her the eye. We lined up to get patties and jerk pork to eat and drank some really thick soursop juice. Then we went to an M&S store to get stuff for Miss Vie.

'She won't take anything for herself; we have to get her stuff to give her people downtown,' said Sharon. We bought knickers, children's clothes, sweets, pencils and exercise books and when I took out my wad to pay she refused. While Sharon paid I found two nice pairs of red and black bra and knickers in the M&S Autograph range, bought these and hid them in my laptop bag. Being with Sharon in a place like this made me feel puffed up like a fucking duke.

Miss Vie lived in a house on a side street where the lower middle classes eked out a shadowy existence. 'When I interviewed him, Eddy said his parents lived uptown, on a landscaped acre with a manicured lawn and big swimming pool,' I said.

'When her husband died she said there was no need for it, sold it, bought this one and gave the rest of the money to the academy scholarship fund.'

'I bet Eddy exploded, like a Taliban IED.'

'He did but he spun it – one of his papers did a feature on Miss Vie giving up earthly treasures to take care of the destitute – you know: 'full of compassion the eternal heart'; 'Blessed are the poor' – that shit – you know?' Miss Vie's door was open, she was in the kitchen washing up and we went in when she called 'come in.' The furniture was the type you found in worker's homes, made by local carpenters. Perhaps the Chinese were putting them out of business but I got the impression Miss Vie would not abandon them. Sharon pulled her away from the sink and took over the washing up.

'So this is the young man you told me about, Sharon? He's better looking and nicer than you said!'

'You like teasing me, Miss Vie.'

'Sharon's a proud girl, Prof., she doesn't like taking things from anyone. Hope you know how to handle a girl like that.'

'I hope so, Miss Vie.'

She squeezed lemons and limes, made lemonade, put in ice and handed the glasses to us. 'Sharon said you had lunch. She does that – doesn't want an old lady to bother in the kitchen!'

If I hadn't seen the slight physical resemblance and already know she was his mother, I'd think Miss Vie and Eddy came from different planets. While he accumulated such excessive wealth and the trappings of wealth, always surrounded by an army of helpers, his mother had very little and even then gave away what little she had. Eddy put up a wall of defence around him so tight nothing could touch him, while his mother was open, like a fresh wound, exposed to all the good and the bad around her. She was fearless, seemed invincible and knew nothing could harm her, while Eddy, with his armies, was so paranoid he even feared the beggar who might refuse to wear the party colours.

Sharon came out of the kitchen drying her hands. 'Finished, Miss Vie. What next?'

'Have to do a little weeding, dear – the tomatoes started to flower. You and your young man can watch television. Some man whose daughter I helped at the academy insisted on giving me cable!'

'This man doesn't even know what tomato plants look like! He can sit and watch while we women work!'

'You see how cheeky this little girl is, Miss Vie? I have to teach her some heavy manners!' I removed my socks, put my shoes back on and followed them into the garden. I'd seen Eddy's mansions in Eaton Square, London and here, seen his acres of landscaped grounds, stylish furniture and rows of the most expensive cars in the world. But because of her goodness, this little piece of earth I now stood on with his mother, seemed more valuable than all the gold and diamonds I could imagine in Eddy's safes. While watching me weed Sharon was pointing at me and laughing and whispering to Miss Vie.

'He's trying, dear, nothing to mock about.'

She was real. That's why I'd wondered about Eddy, how he could have a mother like this and still feel so empty he wanted to possess the whole world, or fucking destroy it.

CHAPTER FIFTEEN

I accompanied Eddy to the 'Freedom for Cabal' concert, held in the supersized arena on the edge of the PM's constituency where the stars of Elizabeth's stable and those hoping to be battled during the week to be featured on weekends. The stars tonight were Rhino Man, Cabal's first cousin and the fourteen-year-old dancehall queen, heavy with the child Cabal thought was his. As this was a place where we would mingle with the people, the wheels consisted of Mercedes and BMW saloons and SUVs. Eddy insisted I ride with him in the 500 though I didn't like the freezing air-conditioning. I could hear the music from the time we left Eddy's office and this was some distance away. I'd heard stories of the Chinese using sonar technology to smash American tanks, and making speakers capable of bursting eardrums and tumbling walls in our country, where noise was a chief resource, was a good way to test it.

We started out early, at the Ministry of Sport, where the minister, a former beauty queen, introduced us to the latest sprint champions. My hero, Joseph, had been a star but now these boys were stars of such power the mind boggled. Just imagining them on track made me feel my head exploding. Then, about lunchtime, we were at the education ministry where there was a huge commotion as we ran into Miss Vie on an errand for her school. Eddy lost control of his people, they were all practically prostrating, saying in reverential tones 'Good morning, Miss Vie', or 'Hope all is well, Ma'am.' She spotted me, came over, and I was so confused I mumbled as I greeted her, like a little boy confronted by a dignitary too important to comprehend.

'Hope you're enjoying your vacation, young man.' I was still too confused by her simplicity to reply, when her son cut in.

'He's here to do that book on our people, Miss Vie. I told you.'

'He's a young man, Eddy, he's here to relax, have some fun.' She wasn't criticising Eddy, a woman like her didn't criticise, didn't judge, but I could see the frustration and shame in his face, like the small boy tapped gently on the head by a benign adult, who thought he should know better than to fart in front of the headmistress. Was he upset that his poor mother had such total control of these worshipful acolytes, which he could never achieve with all his power and money? Eddy was older than me but not by much, and I'm sure she often told him to chill.

When we finished our tour around five he said I could have dinner with him before we took off for the concert but I excused myself, saying I had a backlog of notes to write up. He instructed Delroy to pick me up from the house around ten, so we could proceed together around eleven. I went by a jerk joint, picked up chicken and pork, extra peppers, and when I got to Sharon's we ate the meat with hard dough bread and drank strong, very nice rum punch she said she made from her father's recipe. Elena seemed to be spending more time with her 'cousin' and I'd seen her only a few times. After supper we rested a while, Sharon slept off the lunch, I took a shower and was dressed by the time Delroy came. I didn't wake her but left a note, telling her how much I loved her, drawing a smiling face at the bottom. For me it was a strange experience regarding a woman with affection, without the prime objective of fucking her.

When the sound started bouncing the car off the road and I thought we were there, we still drove on, and I wondered why they hadn't given us earplugs. Sharon said she didn't want to come and when Delroy asked I said I wasn't sure it was a suitable place for a young woman like her. He looked at me strangely and I thought he meant Sharon grew up with people like those we were about to meet. But I understood when we finally drove into a glass and steel pavilion, through an entrance guarded by two APCs, three Range Rovers full of commandos and six paramilitary police with H & K machine guns, tear gas propellers, stun and smoke grenades and hi-tech Chinese radios.

Eddy's entire cabinet and top party officials were there; they rose when we got out of the cars, clapped till I thought their hands would bleed and burst into the latest party anthem fashioned by the lanky poet laureate. The pavilion was new, there was an illuminated portrait of Eddy with the Chinese PM and another of our Minister of Construction and leaders of the work team who had completed the project in record time. The roof was covered with small spotlights, which lit up when the PM arrived then dimmed. The glass must have been sound as well as bullet proof. The decibel level had been lowered to that inside an A380 engine. We could see the writhing multitude of dancehall aficionados outside, in lights kept bright in case they wanted to haul out their guns and start to celebrate. The public section was open, framed by steel pipes for the heavy tarps they would roll out in case of rain. I didn't know where to sit, I was looking at the heavy leather chairs at the end of the front row but Eddy pulled me over to sit next to him. I was happy his security was so tight I was unlikely to be shot and, since the glass kept out most of the sound, my head would not explode. Ensconced behind bulletproof glass, with air-conditioning, important people and all you could consume, I understood mingling with the people didn't mean you had to mix with them.

It seemed everyone outside had a joint, the smoke swirled up like geysers in the centre of hell. The warm-up musicians, after greeting their PM and thanking him for his efforts to free Cabal, started shouting out their latest hits. I didn't understand most of what they said; I had a small recorder in my pocket and Sharon would translate later but what I heard was all about 'killing battymen' or getting 'baby mothers in the way.' The women were of every age, from grandmothers to schoolgirls, every shape from obese to anorexic, and the rainbows of tops and hot pants, riding up and down with the music, spelt S-E-X. Fucking was not allowed on the dance floor – there were toilets for gents and ladies and some distance away, in the unisex area, men and women in need could mix it up. I watched a man in a brown felt hat and multi-coloured shirt plunge his hand down a fat woman's shorts, and it kept disappearing till I thought he reached his elbow. Then a spot brightened on a man with a pistol raised in the air, two cops grabbed his arms, removed the gun and led him out. They didn't shoot him, smash his head or shout at him, the PM and his guests were watching and there could even be foreign reporters present – our place was on the cyber map. In the light I saw Trevor without a joint, drink, or exposed cannon and was glad I hadn't brought Sharon. I didn't know what they did together but I didn't want to rub it in, make him think I had the right to fuck his woman because I wore linen, had money in my pocket and sat on the right hand of the PM behind sound and bullet proof glass. He looked lonely, confused, and the sport shirt outside his trousers didn't give him much protection from the deafening music. I'm sure he was part of Eddy's security and I hoped he didn't have an assignment to kill anybody this night. My sympathy with the lonely gunman was shattered when I heard the roar of thunder and thought the glass had broken, letting in the flood of naked dancehall sound. But it was only Rhino Man roaring to make his presence heard, together with the rotund dancehall queen. I hadn't seen them since we arrived tonight; they must have been in some side room and although the Rhino was a pro and wiped powder from his nostrils, his companion was still under fourteen and traces lined the drippings from her nose, like a child who plundered her mother's powdered milk.

'Clive!' Eddy shouted and his entourage echoed 'Rhino Man! Rhino Man!!'

'Respect, PM. His hand swallowed Eddy's, the 'queen' reached up to peck her PM on the cheek. 'Thank you, PM, for what you doing for Cabal, me baby father and me.' Cabal had been inside a year, she was three months pregnant when they arrested him a year ago, so this one, which must be at least six months gone, could not be his. Rhino Man must have been helping out his cousin and she could tell Cabal it was his when the Americans released and deported him in twenty-three years. The Rhino and Queen waved goodbye to their VVIP fans, then went back to their side room to reinforce themselves fucking or snorting.

They didn't need a concert to raise money for Cabal's legal fees, the dancehall star was receiving even more royalties now his draconian sentence attracted sympathy from his middle class fans in Europe and America. Rhino Man had just received two Grammy's, and a contract from Sony for five records and was boosted by the music press as 'revolutionary' and 'earth-shattering', they didn't understand his words and his rhythms caused brain aneurisms and curvature of the spine. The Feds, had seized twenty seven million dollars in cash and millions more in drugs from Cabal but there was a lot more where that came from. He and Rhino Man were members of the gang which smuggled tons of cocaine to the US through the Caribbean and continued to kill hundreds each year to maintain their power.

Now Eddy was respectable and couldn't afford the stigma of associating with drugs, all the profits went to his musician friends. But Eddy was a 'Pol', he needed to show the people he was 110 per cent behind their boy. I watched him now, puffed up with satisfaction as the MC announced the warm up artists had done their bit and we should now get ready for the FIRE!!!!! Suddenly I saw his body tense, his face flush and nostrils flare as Donovan whispered in his ear. His expression was the same as that from schooldays, when we prepared to smash the boy who had shouted 'your mother is a smelly whore!' He looked around in panic when Donovan pointed, to see the excrement causing him so much grief. Then he put on his actor's masque, looked at me, smiling. 'I want you to meet someone, Prof. A big party man.'

'Ok, Eddy.' The rum punch and noise should have knocked me out but being so close to power buoyed me up. As we passed ministers, party officials and business persons they all stood up, saluted Eddy and reached out their hands, some of which Eddy took. I saw some stunners, dressed in Prada or Chanel, who had swum four laps in Cartier perfume and said with their eyes and smiles they were wide open for big contracts. We got to a corner table where a man sat alone; there was barely enough light to see his bottle of white rum, bowl of sugar, fresh limes and goblet with ice. I couldn't see him clearly but what I saw reminded me of James Earl Jones. The first thing I noticed was this one didn't stand up, unlike all the others who jumped like rabbits when the great man blew his nose. He was built like a boxer and I shuddered as I remembered that priest in school, whose pat made my solar plexus feel like that of a gnat.

'Hello, Moses, Donovan tell me you here.'

'You don't need to bother, Eddy, you here to show support for Cabal.'

'I want you to meet the Prof., Moses, he here to write on our Party. You know his book on Joseph, the one everybody reading.' He stood up now, I could see his face widen, his eyes light up.

'You the one? Good to meet you, sir. Welcome home.'

'Thank you, sir. Glad to meet you too.'

'He'll need to speak to you about the book, Moses.'

'Eddy has my numbers, sir. Anytime.' Moses looked like an old man but his handshake reminded me of Father O'Malley's brutal grip. 'We got to go, Moses. Rhino Man and the dancehall queen ready.' He couldn't hide the resentment in his voice, at this man, built like him, who radiated so much power. 'See you soon, Prof. Eddy, remember you give him my number.'

When the stars began, their voices were so rough they seemed able to smash the glass. Rhino Man must have outweighed the queen about five to one but it was her voice I was hearing. She was barely a teenager but her voice sounded old, full of centuries of pain, longing and abandonment. As usual I didn't get it all and felt the Sony voice activated tape recorder whirring softly in my pocket. What I heard had to do with all white men being battymen; they had to punish black men to get their kicks; they locked up Cabal because they were jealous he fucked her so hard he put a stallion inside her. She was still shouting, echoed by the Rhino, when she bent over to show how she'd received him, and her hot pants slipped further down, revealing even more crack in her ass. Rhino Man got behind her to show how his cousin did it, humping harder and harder till the delirious audience climaxed and joined her in song: '*Fuck me! Fuck me!! Fuck me harder!!!! Harder!!!!!Harder!!!!!!*' Her writhing became so intense, her last scream so strident that I hardly heard the first bullet discharge. I looked at Eddy – there was no alarm, even he was caught up in ecstasy of a fourteen to two-hundred-year old woman lamenting her man who was lost.

I figured she was about the same age as the little girl chewing her nails in the estate, but this one would take no shit from anyone and would last longer than the crocodile. For over three-hundred years the Europeans taught us their languages; fortunate ones like me had become as proficient as our masters but we couldn't communicate with our own people. It took a child to make us feel what she was saying and even a mongrel like me got what she said, though I was unable to understand her words. I could imagine those outside our magic glass absorbing her meaning like potions.

The starting pistol fired the first shot and set off the fusillade; soon every gun in the house was firing. In the light exuded by the exploding shells I saw Trevor's face bewildered, not understanding how they could waste bullets meant to protect the people. I felt I could forgive him if he'd fucked Sharon, which I now doubted. Men had lighters in their left hands, guns in their right and I thought of fireworks displays in capital cities around the world on New Year's Eve, which I watched on the BBC on my 32 inch Samsung HD. Some held smartphones in one hand while they took pictures of their bright faces all the while fusillades of hot bullets fired in the background. Occasionally a bullet smashed into the metal poles holding the tarps and I listened for screams when they crashed on bare heads.

I was so drawn into the symphony of light I didn't hear when Rhino Man and the dancehall queen finished and the warm up musicians resumed their choruses on baby mothers and battymen and the need to kill all white men, so afrikkans could be free. The rum punch, air-conditioning, and sitting like a zombie did their work on my bladder and I wanted to exercise my legs before I got cramps. I knew Eddy had so much control I'd never seen him excuse himself to piss and I nodded to him as I walked toward the luxury, VIP wash rooms. As I neared the gents I heard the queen scream *'Fuck me! Fuck me harder! Harder!!!—'* and wondered why she was practising for her next session in the men's loo. Then, as I entered, I saw on the marble floors her top, hot pants, red thongs and the Rhino's enormous white jeans. He was squatting on the sink – the Chinese must make the most durable enamel in the world – cradling the queen who sat on him, his huge hands clasped around her buttocks, pressing her harder and harder into him as she thrust and screamed 'harder, Rhino, Harder. Fuck me, Man!!!!!!!' Looking at this little girl from the most notorious ghetto in the city I thought there was more passion in an atom of her than in a universe of Rihannas, Beyoncés and Lady Gagas. I couldn't wait, listening to the music and gunfire, no one else had the will to piss and I crept into the ladies to do my business. By the time I got back the 'heroes' had run out of bullets so things were quiet. Eddy's people must have radioed the soldiers to tell them people were just having fun, so there was no need to come with tanks, machine guns and grenades to massacre them.

'I have work to do early tomorrow, Eddy.' I stood up, he too, all his people except Moses, their grunts saluting power with more decibels than dancehall music and Chinese speakers of mass destruction. 'Yes, Prof., it's late, we should all go home now. Hope you enjoyed the show.' In the car I texted Sharon to say I was on my way. I was so tense I hoped she'd be awake enough to have rum punch with me, so I'd tell her what it felt like 'mingling with the people' before we fucked.

CHAPTER SIXTEEN

'Let's go to the Christmas fair in the morning.' Eddy had taken me to see Chinese construction projects on the North Coast. I felt something in my stomach as the engineers explained how they could organise the work to maximum effect and I was glad to be back home.

'I thought that was for little kids,' Sharon said.

'Yes, I remember when I was little my grandma or her maid took me there. I was scared of the horses on the merry-go-round – they looked so big. But once I got on I cried when they took me off.'

'Then I'll have to adopt you – take you as my naughty little boy!'

'Don't worry, I plan to naughty you extra tonight.' She slapped my hand away when I tried to grab her tits. Eddy got an invite from Putin to celebrate some Russian festival, and when I made an excuse he didn't seem to mind and I wondered if he really wanted me to go, or was taking Miss Vie's advice that I was a young man and needed to have fun. He certainly didn't believe my excuses anymore – that I had to write up notes, when

I could go and get a packet of hundred dollar bills for expenses. Then I'd seen the ad in *The Chronicle* about the new attractions at the Christmas fair. There was also a picture of Eddy meeting the King of Saudi Arabia and another of him shouting at people in his constituency, his face a mask of rage. Was he still mad at Winston Pinnock? I'd been here now over six weeks but it seemed like a lifetime.

Sharon had gotten a tree from the Chinese plantation and I saw the book she got for me as a present. I couldn't control my curiosity, when she wasn't looking I felt it, smelt it, tried to see through the Christmas wrapping paper. I sometimes thought I had x-ray vision when I was around a gambling table. When she caught me she shouted 'I told you you're a brat. Why can't you control yourself?' When we got into bed I decided to wear her out then when she slept I would untie the string, lift the sticky tape, check the title and redo the packaging. But she wasn't asleep, she grabbed me, wrestled me to the floor and I was so embarrassed I tried to get on top of her again. But she squeezed me in that place where it hurts most. 'I told you you're such a fucking child. How can I trust you?' I tried my luck again but she pushed me off. 'No more sex for you, Lover Man; I won't even talk to you again – ever.' But in the morning when she was showering I sneaked in, felt her up, and she didn't stop me when I made my move. She dressed in a white blouse, red linen slacks and black loafers, I told her how much she looked like Santa Claus, tried to open her zip, asked for my present now. 'No more sex – none of that till Christmas. You know that's when Santa hands out presents!'

On the way we passed the hotel and saw the first twelve storeys were up. The workers didn't like the 24/7 shifts, which interfered with times for their families, GBH, girlfriends, drinking, killing or dominoes. So they organised a strike for the day builders planned to complete the tenth floor. According to the *Independent* the construction company called a meeting with officials of the union where they showed the model and blueprints for the 'Palace of the Workers' they would start building as soon as the strike ended. They also asked the union to select twelve relatives, to be given scholarships to American universities, reasoning that American racism would make them even more anti-American and pro-Chinese. I couldn't remember the way to the fair, I couldn't recognize anything when we got inside and saw Sharon smiling at me as I stared with my mouth open, almost downing a big green fly. Back then the fair was in a dusty field with faded, chipped up horses and stalls where you could win made-in-Hong Kong plastic rabbits throwing balls you bought for a few local dollars. Now there were smart shops in a mini-mall, merry-go-rounds with glittering lights, polished, gilded horses and steel-and-glass stalls where you could win prizes firing replica Chinese AK47s. There were Chinese, French and Italian restaurants, plus several outlets for our local dishes and fountains of crimson rum punch. 'I'll buy you tokens and you shoot and win me that nice leather case. I need a man-bag to hold your love letters! '

'I don't shoot anything; we have too many guns here.' Sharon said dryly.

'Ok, I'll show you how good I am – a cross between John Dillinger and Billy the Kid!' When my ten shots missed the target by a kilometre, I was sure the bastards were cheats, grumbled and showed my displeasure, which increased when Sharon laughed at me. 'I told you you're a baby – you can't shoot, and you don't like to lose!' I jumped, turning sharply when we heard the ring, indicating the target was hit, and saw a ten year old boy with long black hair, thick glasses, pimples and snot running from his nose, which he wiped with the back of his hand while holding the prize bag I'd wanted to win. Sharon grabbed me – I don't know if she thought I'd jump him and grab the bag. He smelt of turpentine, blew fountains of snot from his nose, and wiped it again with his other hand. We followed the smoke from jerk pork, and bought a half pound, although we'd eaten a nice breakfast of fried dumplings, callaloo and salt fish she'd made. As we chewed the pork, sipped the punch, and passed the tent with the 'gypsy' fortune teller we saw the Stephen Walter family coming out.

'You here all this time and don't contact you friend, boy? I going lick you ---- ----!' I saw his wife turn red, Sharon look embarrassed, his daughter pretend she didn't know him and his sons laughed to hear their father use words their mother beat them for when they shouted them at each other.

'Haven't been here that long, Stephen. I meant to call but didn't know if you changed your number.'

'I get the same number, star, and you a celeb now. I see you pic with Eddy and his people!'

'Some people have to work for a living, Stephen.' His wife was nasty and it didn't help he couldn't keep his eyes off Sharon's tits. 'My wife, Maria, Prof. Elizabeth my daughter, my sons John and Stephen.'

'Nice to meet you, Ma'am, nice to meet you Elizabeth, John and Stephen.'

'You write that book about that poor boy; Stephen tell me when you out here last time,' Maria spoke. I didn't like the way she said 'poor' – it could mean because Joseph was disabled, or something bad happened to him. I hadn't asked Sharon. I didn't want her to lie like everybody else, and my first commandment was you don't nag the woman you're fucking.

'I'm Sharon, Ma'am, his girlfriend.' If she thought 'girlfriend' would soothe Maria, she was mistaken. I didn't mind when men ogled Sharon, I understood male weakness, even when confronting women not one tenth as beautiful. But I wasn't a wife or girlfriend and I knew Maria and Stephen had history. When I was out last time I checked them on Google and the archives and this time I checked again for the latest gossip. Stephen was a sportsman, gambler and all the women you saw him with were, or could have been, beauty queens.

Maria was his cousin, she had money in spades and was called Miss Tight, because she wouldn't give out a penny and some said she hadn't opened her legs till she was married. Her crack about men 'working for their money' was aimed at Stephen who married her when his money ran out and he thought he could have hers without keeping his cock in his pants because she was plain. But she was a good shot and the scandal sheets wrote she threatened rivals with guns, knives, acid and hired killers. She looked better than she did in her photos in the archives and in the bright sunlight I saw the fine red lines behind her ears, under her eyes and throat, and knew it was true what I read, that she spent a bunch on the same cutters & stitchers Michael Jackson used in LA. Her teeth back then were also like early Tom Cruise and she must have used his tooth fairy too to get hers as even and white. Stephen said Elizabeth Cairncross was his first love when he took me out last time and it took coconut-sized balls to name his daughter after her. 'Mummy, we want to go on the merry-go-round,' John and Stephen pleaded, almost whining. 'Go with them, Elizabeth, here's money for the rides.' Elizabeth looked with contempt at the money, just enough for getting on the rides. She must have been about fifteen, the age at which girls hate their parents and younger siblings, want to get fucked by boys a bit older and thought they wouldn't give a shit if their parents were gassed. It was obvious she thought she was too old for merry-go-rounds and didn't apply make-up badly to waste squeezing her thighs on wooden horses. 'You know I don't like fairs, mother. I'm not a kid anymore.'

'Since when? Go with your brothers!' Her voice said she wouldn't take 'no' for an answer and her daughter's face said she was ready for whatever shit her mother was prepared to throw.

'Go with them, Lizzie.' Her father spoke. 'I have tickets to that Harry Potter movie coming to the Palace Superplex next week. You can take two friends.'

Elizabeth's face lit up as she thought of the cinema, where boys could come and offer to buy them sundaes then fuck them in the back of their Hondas. Her mother wasn't happy, she'd been looking forward to the confrontation but contented herself that Stephen hadn't spent *her* money – his Chinese classmate who had just bought the Palace and the rest of the chain gave him the tickets.

'Let's go,' Elizabeth shouted at her brothers who she'd always thought too slow, too fucking stupid, like all men. She had problems deciding whether they were more cretin than her bitch of a mother. But for now she was a kid again, thinking of merry-go-rounds and ice cream instead of boys.

'Go with the other kids, I know you want to!' Sharon quipped, and I saw Maria smile, as if she forgot her husband would try to get some of my girl when I went back. She even gave Elizabeth money for my ticket and I wondered if a wizard had put something in the sports drink she was sipping from a bright green bottle. The horses were big, I felt my own trembling between my thighs, then looked at John and Stephen, hoping they wouldn't break as many hearts as their old man, or squander their mother's money on gaming tables. Would Elizabeth, who looked so happy and carefree now, suffer the horrors of her mother, Elizabeth, the dancehall queen, or my little girl of glass? Maria and Sharon were smiling happily as they watched the children ride round and round, in the sweet, endless cycle of youth. They were both taking pictures with their phones. It was so nice to feel like Sharon's kid I felt like weeping. Having a mother, whatever the pretence, produced a warm feeling, deep inside the guts, like joy.

CHAPTER SEVENTEEN

Eddy came back from Russia in a good mood at what he had accomplished, saying how much more personable officials were there than the fucking Chinese, who couldn't get their minds off work. He mentioned how everywhere they went beautiful girls surrounded Putin. He was around for about two weeks before he went off to Saudi Arabia and Dubai. He didn't invite me and I couldn't tell whether he didn't want me to go with him, or was tired of my excuses. But when he went to Bermuda he invited me and this time I said yes. I would be away for just two nights and the man who headed the Chinese subsidiary and who was building an enormous resort and shopping mall there was Chin, a classmate of mine at St Dunstan's. He was as small as me, brilliant, and a true friend. The bigger boys at school had stole our pocket money, our food, our things, and then threw us around, from one to another like fucking balls.

When Eddy and Chin finished negotiations with the Bermuda government, Eddy went off to an emergency meeting with the American Secretary of State while Chin took me to the house of Mr Wang, a friend from Shanghai who I learned was behind much of the big investments in the Caribbean. Unlike Eddy's pads with the brilliant, mass produced paintings by unknown artists, the walls of this one were covered with Picassos, Miros, Mondrians, a Kandinsky and, in a corner overshadowed by a glistening Klimt, a small Delacroix. I was afraid of breathing, everywhere you looked was Chinese porcelain so fine it seemed they'd explode if you even so much as glanced at them. I knew his made-in-Italy furniture was really made in Italy, a man like him wouldn't want any hint of falsehood in his home. But the most precious work of art was the man himself, who looked like a teenager but was older than Chin and me.

Despite his wealth, he wore slacks, a shirt and sandals you could pick up in Top Shop and his glasses were probably bought off the shelf in Boots. The house was part of a complex which included his offices, a zoo, and a private cinema where he viewed the old movies I used to watch with Indie, films by Bergman, Fellini, Antonioni, De Sica, Rosellini, Renoir, Truffaut, Kurosawa. Chin said he owned four of the biggest casinos on Macau, generating more revenue than the whole of Las Vegas. He was one of the richest men in the world but didn't appear on any list or give interviews and chose to live in Bermuda, because no one knew him there. He mentioned he had some property on a small island off the coast of our country and gave me a signed calling card. Later Chin told me he was from the family who had supplied economic advisers to Chinese rulers from the time of the first Emperor Chin. When scientists discovered gunpowder, one of Mr Wang's ancestors advised the emperor to encourage the manufacture of fireworks. When Admiral Zheng navigated the East African coast in ships bigger and more sophisticated than those Columbus used years later, another advised his emperor to dismantle the ships. Their thinking was that guns and ships meant conquest, and they would cease to be Chinese if they conquered other peoples. Mr Wang now shunned the pomp of the court of the Forbidden City, preferring the obscurity to allow him to indulge his obsession with old Bergman movies and the lyrics of Linda Ronstadt. When he saw me off, Chin gave me a thick white envelope and I wondered what currency was in it. I had no chance to check till I was in the airport and rushed into a loo – ten thousand US. It was nice when rich classmates knew you were poor as shit. At duty free I picked up more Ferragamo Incanto perfume, plus a Waterman fountain pen and silk scarf from Shanghai for Sharon.

~

I always thought beautiful women cooked food like shit but Sharon's was so good it tasted like the meal we had eaten cooked by the single mother with the restaurant in her living room. I'd soon look like a pig if I stayed too long with her. Since Eddy said he was going to the Caymans then the British Virgin Islands which I wasn't interested in seeing, I told Sharon we could go to the island off the South East coast she'd been pestering me about – she had told me her classmate managed a big hotel there. The island once belonged to a Hollywood superstar, killed in a duel with the husband of a woman he fucked. A drug dealer who financed the government before Eddy's, bought it and started building a resort with money from Pablo Escobar. But the Americans arrested one of Pablo's friends, he halted money to some right wing militia sponsored by them in Nicaragua and the Americans killed him. Last time I was there there were only uncompleted buildings covered with parasitic vines and populated by lizards, rats, mongoose, scorpions, squatters and wild dogs.

Sharon cooked us up escoveitched chicken, ackee and salt fish, rice-and-peas and fried dumplings, and we rented a small Audi from Avis, run by a high-school classmate who gave us a nice discount. Eddy wanted Delroy to take me on such trips but Sharon didn't like using a government car for private outings and I didn't want him to know how much we were fucking. Sharon drove, she knew the way, I was never confident of my driving skills. The hills we drove over were unpopulated and the vegetation seemed to have been there from the beginning of time. I had never seen leaves as green since the time I was sent on an assignment to Congo and Rwanda by a glossy German magazine. Before we got too high I saw what looked like a miracle from the past. I asked Sharon to take a right turn down a narrow lane where it seemed as though we were descending into paradise. I felt cold inside, despite the beauty.

'This used to be the most expensive resort in Woodwater', she said. Below there was a plateau hanging over the sea, and a bright cobalt and white stream thundered down the ash-coloured cliffs. There was a perfectly round waterhole – it looked man-made – with water bluer than anything I'd ever seen.

'An extinct volcano, love, most of this island was pushed up from under the sea. Get into this one and the currents take you down, down, till they fish your body out near Jamaica.' I don't know why I was shivering. There was a sign with huge red letters: SWIMMING PROHIBITED but it wasn't the sign I was looking at. There were glass-fronted round huts which seemed to be made of polished mud, with thick straw on top, I thought to myself, this was the kind of place Europeans would mortgage their houses to stay at.

'We'll come here sometime – it's one of the most beautiful places I've seen.'

An American woman came out of reception, her shabby clothes seemed tailored for her body; she wore a white t-shirt with a red logo – I Love Tampa and what looked like the tat of a heart was on one of her three chins that were difficult to differentiate from her neck.

'Hello, Miss. We'd like to stay here sometime. What're bookings like this time of year?' Either she had a stomach ache, hadn't slept well, it was her time of month because she didn't crack a smile and merely barked back to us. 'No booking needed, you just turn up. Place used to be full till those gooks built their shit on that fucking island.' She was obviously sensitive, she looked at us to make sure there wasn't enough 'gook' in us to cause offence.

'Thanks for the tip ma'am. Maybe we'll call on the way back from the 'shit the gooks built.'

'Fat chance – I'll be back in Tampa by then.' So she'd been sacked too, to add to her pain.

We drove on and as we approached the summit the trees linked across the road creating an intense green tunnel through which even the bright sun struggled to shine. Cavernous and dark, as we drove through Sharon had to keep the lights on. Then we were in daylight, looking down the mountain across the sea to the island I could not now recognize. When I finished the book on Joseph there was a review in *The New York Review of Books* and Chin had written to me. At the time he controlled imports from China on the Eastern US seaboard and owned the biggest insurance company in Canada, with branches in the US and Caribbean. He sent me a first-class ticket to Hong Kong and a draft for twenty-five thousand dollars.' In Hong Kong I had come across a gambling joint, had the unusual feel of money in my pocket, and the urge to put some on the 21 table. I had always been lucky, I judged the cards right and felt so pressured I was seeing the results in my head. I had changed ten-thousand into cash, was so nervous I lost five thousand then pulled myself together, won it back then kept winning till I had twenty thousand more. I remembered feeling sick, hadn't understood why I had felt such an irresistible urge and never gambled again. I was remembering a time I'd spent in Lake Tahoe when my Japanese girl went manic, wanting to gamble all her money on the roulette tables. She had told me she was proud of her Samurai ancestry till she found out her great-grandfather was a war criminal, who had stuck a dagger in his own guts when the emperor signed the unconditional surrender. After Indie I had had a penchant for unusual babes. I was thinking of Hong Kong again as we descende. There were wind turbines all round, they must have produced enough electricity to light up a whole city, the skyscrapers were as dense as in Hong Kong but laid out, designed and coloured better. I was thrilled by the architecture in *CSI-Miami* but thought the producers should move the filming here. If Escobar and our drug dealer were looking up from hell, they would have loved this place. It looked so much better than the suburb of Bogota they had tried to replicate here.

'We call it China Town, Sharon said, looking at the magic cityscape. 'They have a ninety-nine year lease.'

'Eddy didn't mention this. And he likes to take credit, even for things he had nothing to do with.'

'He doesn't want people to know this is now Chinese

property. We almost need visas to come here. My classmate got us passes. When Winston published details about the finances involved, they tried to blow up his car and torched his newspaper offices.' There were big, ultra-modern catamarans running every half hour and air-conditioned buses and cars filled with women speaking English, French, Spanish, Greek, Russian and I supposed any number of Eastern European languages. The marina here had boats I'd never seen anywhere before and made Miami or Cannes seafront look like fishing villages outside Mumbai. The Chinese men with small digital cameras wore linen suits or tee-shirts and Bermuda shorts. As we drove off onto the dock I looked at the unfinished four-lane bridge. 'They started three months ago, with plans to finish for Christmas,' Sharon said. 'But they brought too many of their own workers and ours went on strike.'

In the distance I could see the fantastic white sand beaches bordering the deep blue sea, where figures in bikinis and shorts were dotted like fleas. The hotel was small, with about twenty floors, but inside was all glass, steel, marble and hard wood panelling; the design would probably not be seen anywhere in Europe or America for the next century. Sharon was expecting her classmate, Marcie to meet us but she texted that at the last minute her boss had sent her to Miami to accompany the mistress of a visiting, high ranking Chinese official who felt uneasy for her. The mistress didn't speak good English and was bringing him two-million dollars to gamble in Mr Wang's casino. Marcy got us a freebie and her text said we should sign for all we ate and drank. We didn't yet feel ready for hotel fare, so we started on the food we brought and Sharon's perfect rum punch. The room was a junior suite but bigger than most presidential suites in a UK hotel. We saw the prices – we could hardly get a B&B in Bayswater for that. Hotel rooms here were subsidized by casinos making fortunes from Chinese highflyers. The floor was black marble, the walls white, the chairs the same leather we saw everywhere, the tables and bar, blue glass and steel. The TV was a 50 inch B&O and Sharon's friend had left us DVDs with the best blues and reggae hits, *Blade Runner* and *Three Days of the Condor*. The paintings were the same as those in all the hotels we had visited and we wondered if there was a Chinese factory where they were made.

'You must be tired after driving round all those curves. Let's drink more punch then have a rest.'

'You're a conman. I know what you mean by "rest". And you want to finish my punch.'

'Yes – then I'll finish you and go look for sexy women!' She tried to hit me, I grabbed her round the waist, we wrestled, then lay on the bed which was almost as big as the one in my guest house, with black, polished frame and white bedcover. 'I'll kill you when you fall asleep!' she said.

I fell asleep almost at once and started having the dream I had when I got to some new place, of a large mirror in which I couldn't see myself, a barren scene I couldn't recognize. Maybe it was dreams like this, which inspired creators of vampire, and zombie stories to think their creations were incapable of seeing their images in the glass. In the dream I tried to scream but the sound was trapped and I heard it like an echo. When I woke I was sweating though the air-conditioning was on and I heard Sharon taking a shower. I joined her, and we started spraying each other with cold water.

'You told me how you enjoyed *Three Days of the Condor*.

Let's watch it then go roaming. Maybe I'll find a nice man!' I'd watched the film many times, about a section of the CIA hiring a hit-man to wipe out another threatening to blow their operations in the Middle East. I now realised one reason I liked *Condor* was that Max von Sydow played the extremely cultured hit man, whose only concern was his own precision, not ideology or patriotism. I remembered Indie and I had watched him in all those Bergman movies the film club had put on, and thought of Mr Wang in his studio, watching the actor play chess with Death in *The Seventh Seal*.

We were relaxing in the bed, I recalled my time as a child 'I thought I could use my brains to get out of the ghetto but saw what happened to Trevor. He was doing well in school but the bigger boys picked on him: when they tried to get him to rape a little girl with Down's syndrome he refused and they beat him. When he couldn't take it anymore he stabbed one and they expelled him. Moses took him in. Then I thought of track – I ran the hundred and two hundred in times of Olympic standard but quit when I found the coach didn't expect me just to sleep with him but cook and wash his dirty underpants.' Sharon held my hand.

We drank more punch then went out. We thought our hotel was tops but each new one we entered looked more special. All the bars offered a free rum punch, some were good, some excellent, and after a while we couldn't tell the difference. It was late night when we got to the biggest, most gaudy casino and discovered the rum punches were free all night. Gamblers pulling levers for slot machines, glued to roulette wheels or Blackjack tables looked like creatures founded in the mind of Stephen King. This casino belonged to Mr Wang. Chin liked me, we were pals; whatever he said to the man had a good effect and he invited me to go with him to Macau anytime. I had his card, on the back of it he wrote 'my close personal friend' and I'm sure if I showed it to the manager he'd offer us the Presidential Suite, caviar, *fois gras* and a bag of thousand-dollar chips. But hanging around Sharon I'd become self-conscious about taking freebies and, besides, I didn't know the guy that well, and his wealth and lineage unnerved me. I was watching a Blackjack table when I noticed Sharon giving me nasty looks.

'What's the dirty looks for?'

'What dirty looks?' she asked, and I could hear the anger in her voice. Then I saw the bitch dealing the cards. even in the dim light I could see she was no beauty, her hair piled up on her head like a haystack, cheekbones like bunions, tits overflowing her bra like pumpkins. For Jesus Christ's sake! I was getting hot that Sharon could think I was looking at that but we were here to chill and I decided to let things slide. 'I'll tell you a secret about what I'm looking at ... but promise not to laugh.' 'I'm listening.' She still seemed angry – maybe she thought I was going to tell her I had a fetish for women who looked like Kirstie Ally.

'Ever since I started to gamble I thought I could read cards. The few times I played,I never lost and thought I had a gift.' I couldn't tell her it was one thing that had attracted me to Kiki, my Japanese lover. 'That's how gamblers get hooked. They think they have the juice to wipe out the bad side. You know there's no such thing as gambling? Owners fix the odds: you can't win in the long run. Let's try this one, I'll show you.' I was absolutely sure I'd win.

'I don't want you to ...'

'Don't worry, I'll just play a few hands, you'll see.' I lost the first two rounds.

'Let's go,' she said, 'I've seen— you lost money, like I thought you would.'

But by the third hand, after I'd watched the cards dealt, I was on a roll. I won the third hand, I started upping the stakes and the dealer stared at me like a cat said 'You're going to clean me out – then I'll have to go back to Sicily!' I was the one feeling hot now, that a bitch like her could think she had a chance while Sharon was there. Her make-up was like a rhino's hide and growing and Maria Walters would find it easier to smile with her surgically altered face and botox in her forehead. When I won seven hundred and fifty dollars I collected my money, put my arm around Sharon's waist and said bye to the frump. I'd made almost exactly the amount I had spent on Sharon's presents.

'Hey, big boy, you won all my money and now you're running away!'

'Maybe we'll see in Sicily.'

'It's much nicer here!'

'Yes, isn't it?' I kissed Sharon long on the mouth to see if the bitch would stop but she couldn't take a hint. 'See you soon, big boy!'

'Yeah,' I said. '*Very* soon ...' As if I fucking cared.

'You didn't have to be so nasty; she obviously thought you'd spend your winnings on her!'

No matter how sarcastic she was being, it always surprised me a woman who would kill another out of jealousy, could start feeling sorry for her five minutes later when she lost out.

We fell asleep watching *Blade Runner* and drank so much rum punch it was almost lunchtime when we woke. Instead of feeling hung over we were horny and worked up a huge appetite from the exercise in bed. We ordered room-service after we showered and agreed to continue with our unplanned forays into paradise, or Blue Island to give its official name. Chin's friend said he had a flat on an island off the coast; I didn't know anything about this place, and thought maybe the Chinese Construction Company had built an apartment building on an uninhabited island you could only approach with a chopper or boat. But after we'd passed through some more hotels, seen more spectacular women and scoffed more free rum punches, we saw the fifty storey bloc where the apartment was located. The forty storey hotel they were building in town wouldn't be the tallest in the Caribbean after all – unless our Chinese friends considered this place part of their country.

'The Chinese believe 'double days' are lucky. A man won ten million dollars in that big casino on October 10, 'double ten.' They said he gave the Venezuelan woman he was with one million.'

'I'll wear a wig, stuff socks down my chest and see if I can find a lucky Chinese man on December 12!' Quipped Sharon.

This place wasn't seventy stories but out-trumped Trump Towers with its Italian marble floors, stained glass windows, gold-plated statues and deep blue fountains. There was a giant illuminated portrait of Eddy receiving an honorary Doctorate of Law from Chancellor Angela Merkel, guest of honour at the graduation ceremony of Westminster University. But the portrait was not what caught our eyes. Sharon and I were staring up at the biggest Christmas tree we'd ever seen, decorated with the most exquisite luxuries. I recall the tree we'd seen advertised in Dubai with decorations worth thirty-million dollars. This one had a sign warning punters not to touch, the shit on it was worth *fifty million*. Twenty-five of the fifty floors were occupied by the offices of the big Chinese oil, construction and telecoms companies, plus, Google, Apple and Volvo held offices there too. I saw my publishers had an office on the tenth floor but we were chilling out and I had no desire to visit. The top twenty-five were flats, we saw the prices, between five- and one-hundred million dollars. There was just one left and we saw the offer price-tag of fifty million. Mr Wang's was a penthouse and these went for one hundred million. I touched his card in my pocket to see if I could sense what a hundred-million dollars, for a place you hardly used felt like. He'd told me if I was ever here, to show the housekeeper his card and she'd let me stay in the visitor's suite. A girl in a shiny red bikini came round with a tray of rum punches and daiquiris and with a smile to beat the sunrise she offered us her treasures.

'Isn't it too early for more booze, darling, after the damage we did last night?' Sharon grabbed two daiquiris, smiled at the girl who smiled back, as she imagined what the drinks would make us do. 'Thank you, Miss... We're on holiday, we can drink all we want.'

The daiquiris were good and strong; we polished them off quickly and moved on. We found bars full of Chinese men and foreign women on our quest to find better daiquiris and came to one where the manager was another classmate. He laughed at us when we told him we were in search of the perfect cocktail and nodded his head in the direction of the bar as if to say help yourselves. We needed no more encouragement. He had the white rum, lime, nutmeg and Angostura bitters, Sharon and I made up a batch, and he told his chef to steam one of the huge snappers they just brought live from the sea. We were almost completely wasted by the time we got back home, but we still tried to watch *Blade Runner* again. Ridley Scott's brilliant creations were no match for the quantity of rum we drank and we both sank into sleep within moments of starting it up. In the night what sounded like the Third World War started. We screamed in our sleep as the bombs began to explode. We woke entwined with one another, whimpering, our bodies rigid with fear and sweat. Then Sharon's arms relaxed as she kissed me and said: 'Chinese fireworks! – I don't know what festival they're celebrating.'

We put on the hotel tee-shirts her friend had left for us, she found my red Derek Rose boxers and we went out on the balcony bringing the daiquiris we'd brought back in a cooler. We drank more liquor, raising our glasses to each other's mouths and drinking deeply while the sound and fury of the fireworks exploded overhead. As rainbows of light separated and the sounds echoed inside our heads, the atoms of rum spread throughout our bodies and time slipped the memory so that we didn't know when we went back in and slept.

The fireworks still resonated in my head and I dreamt I was in Ciudad Juarez where the killers of two cartels were trading fusillades of shots, punctuated with brilliant explosions from grenades, and spurts of blood from severed heads catching the light.

My first beauty queen love was not admitted to the academy for her looks, she was awarded a full scholarship to Stanford where she graduated her MBA with distinction before landing a job working for Google. She had a meeting with the CEO of one of the biggest banks in America when she met Diego Suarez, there to deposit a container load of hundred-dollar bills. Diego was trained in the School of the Americas and acquired such a reputation killing leftists and indigenous people he was given the nickname 'El Diablo.' To perfect his killing without going mad the local hallucinogen he took made him see visions of the saints he imagined as a former altar boy. One day after a particularly brutal killing he saw the Virgin Mary who instructed him to become a Jesuit. At the seminary he excelled with his passionate devotion but could not rid his head of bodies when he meditated. He left the order, set up a squadron of former comrades to become enforcers for the cartel based in Ciudad Juarez and took over the organization with exemplary acts of violence. When he saw Maria she was the image of the Virgin Mary he had in his head and he immediately made her his business manager, with recommendations from the Nobel Laureate Professor at Stanford who considered her his most gifted student. Diego was now called 'El Tigre' and his signature was not the beheading of enemies, now commonplace among all cartels – he shot his victims in the back of the head three times – '*In nomine Patris, et Filii, et Spiritus Sancti,*' one for the Father, one for the Son, and one for the Holy Ghost.

I drove us back over the hills and it was a miracle. The car seemed to know the road and I followed like an automaton, my hands barely turning on the wheel as if I didn't need to be there. Sharon slept all the way, her head like a feather on my shoulder. I drove past the turning for the blue hole and mud houses above the sea. When we got to the house I woke Sharon, at first it seemed she didn't know where she was. As she opened the door she almost stepped on a small brown envelope on the floor. 'For you,' she said and when I opened it I saw a plain mobile phone and a type-written note: 'Will call you on this, Winston.' it read. I handed the note to Sharon; she looked at it then walked away. It was as if we had been breathing the sweet fragrance of heaven and suddenly our nostrils suddenly now took in the scent of the open sewer.

CHAPTER EIGHTEEN

The taxi to the club arrived at the same time as Stephen who seemed already drunk and almost hit an enormous red BMW SUV with the plate 'LOVER MAN 1'. From what I'd read about the owner and star of dancehall, his car was custom-made to hold his bulk and it was the last car you'd want to hit. Its owner thought his musical genius and closeness to the Minister of Security gave him license to maim, rape and kill. Stephen compounded his near fatal error by abusing the parking lot attendant who gently remonstrated with him, knowing him as a player. He got that job because he had connections to the Security Minister and was expected to share knowledge of who was fucking whom, who took whose wife or teenage daughter of a reverend to the club. I called the man over and slipped him two-hundred bills so Stephen's car wouldn't be 'stolen' or have an 'accident'.

'Do I call you, or take a cab when we finish? Maybe you want to sleep, Bunny?'

'Call me, sir. I do nights most days. No problem.' I didn't like the phrase, in Woodwater it meant you were likely be fucked over but Bunny was a good guy and we used him for short journeys when we didn't want Delroy on our case. Stephen was still in aggressive mode, even with me when he saw I came alone, he had insisted I bring Sharon. Something was bugging him but when he saw I was ignoring him he chilled. When he took me to the club last time it was a genteel, middle-class joint where they played 70s and 80s soul and blues music, but the exterior had looked tatty and people inside were usually dressed in synthetics. It was here I saw really pretty girls, dressed in almost nothing, and had wondered why Stephen ignored them. It was then he told me about Elizabeth, his first love, and how she broke his heart when she left him for her grotesquely huge, low-life, criminal lover Rhino Man.

Now the place was sparkling, people wore linen or cotton, the girls looked more expensive, there was an illuminated fountain room chilled by air-conditioning. But they still played the same old songs. Stephen picked out the spot we had before, far enough away from the music so you could hear yourself breathe and avoid men who were there with other men's wives and thought it a badge of honour to fuck them on the floor. As he went to get the rum, Pepsi, lime and ice I looked at the far corner where Lover Man presided over a table with other musicians and brightly dressed women, of various ages: our musicians believed in a balanced diet. I noticed the tables around their spot were empty. I thought it was to protect ears from the roar of their voices but when they rose to piss or 'powder their noses', I saw other reasons. Lover Man was as tall as the Rhino but twice as broad making the 9mm Glock he kept outside his short-sleeve silk shirt look like a water pistol. Neckless, his head seemed pounded with a sledgehammer and fused with his ass.

This wasn't really he and his cronies type of place but sometimes they found it amusing to put the fear of bullets into middle-class pussies here. When one of their table passed by, people scrambled to get out of his way so he wouldn't 'accidentally' bump into them or make eye contact. Men with pretty women had to be especially careful to avoid attracting attention. Fear swirled round like sewerage and I could smell it.

I recognised Lion Man's bandana but didn't realise it was him until a spotlight swung across his ebony black face now replete with splotches and stripes of white, green and grey. He had been the warm-up act for Janet Jackson, her entourage were impressed by his roaring vocals and seedy lyrics. One of Janet's people explained how her late brother entered the American mainstream when he 'became white' and told Lion Man he could rake it in if he bleached his skin too. There had been an article in the *Independent* about a father who reported the singer to police when the singer abused his ten-year-old son. The child later died from septicemia when his torn rectum became infected. On his way from the police station the father was abducted and taken to a house owned by Lion Man that was surrounded by a ten foot white wall and black metal gate. There the boy's father was tortured for days and finally killed and mutilated. To hide his crime the musician set fire to the house, bulldozed the ruins, and claimed the huge insurance payment, whose premium he upped when he bought it.

When people from the dead man's community demonstrated outside Elizabeth's studio where Lion Man was making a demo tape, a renegade CSP arrested him for this and fifteen other murders. But he was released, he had been in the same reform school with the Security Minister and his half-brother. Later, in a piece in the *Chronicle* online Lion Man explained how many extra millions he had made from changing his skin to look like a corpse.

Stephen returned, his glass filled with rum, a hint of Pepsi, slice of lime and two ice cubes. I didn't know what was bugging him and thought he might cough up once the rum took effect and opened up his brain. 'I know you working on this book about Eddy, Star, but you know he no longer fighting for the people, the only reason we old boy bring him back was Reds was fucking up the place.' I was mightily impressed this descendant of the biggest slave owning family in the Caribbean and now owner of banks and factories (at least through Maria) was now so concerned about liberating the masses from the counter-revolutionary Eddy, descendant of African slaves with his borrowed Lebanese name. In my glass I'd put about a third of the rum he placed in his, diluted it with Pepsi and ice but still felt like a fucking rocket primed for take-off.

'We put in fortunes to finance saboteurs, worked with the Yanks we didn't like, bought weapons to counter the AK47s the government got from Castro, till they couldn't hold on any longer. When he took over, a Cardinal came down from Boston to celebrate High Mass. The Cathedral couldn't hold all the old boys, we had to put up marquees in the school grounds to take the overflow. People had a lot to celebrate, the Americans brought a container ship of food, clothes, electrical goods while the C5A that carried Eddy and his five Lincolns had fifty-million dollars on board. Elizabeth, me, business people, dancehall musicians and a lot of other old boys were in his entourage and behind him politically.'

The two musicians were returning, I could tell because

talk went quiet and I heard the panicked scraping of chairs as patrons made sure they didn't accidentally attract attention and set off rounds of automatic gunfire..

'Now fucking Eddy has all that Chinese money and is getting even more he treat us who bring him here like shit. Now we have to make appointments to see the bugger!' I silently checked Stephen. He must have forgotten he'd told me classmates in Eddy's entourage made sure Maria's near bankrupt companies had enough finance to stay afloat, one reason she didn't kick him out and his companies got contracts so he wasn't totally dependent on her. He didn't mention the private gambling club owned by another classmate where he put money he made from other Chinese.

'You know Eddy Senior wasn't his father, don't you?'

'He didn't look like it but it's not the kind of stuff you discuss with a man you want to write about, Stephen. Besides people have the right to adopt, no matter the colour of the child.'

'He wasn't adopted, star. They say his mother get pregnant for Moses' identical twin when she a schoolgirl. So he's the nephew of the biggest Don among our local criminals. When his brother Aaron was killed Moses make a arrangement for Miss Vie to marry Eddy Senior, his tight friend.'

I stopped listening when a couple came on the floor and there was again a silence to the talk, even at the table of our musical celebs. I knew the woman, Cecilia, she was Eddy's special advisor on social issues and helped me prep when I interviewed him. Sharon said she came from a very pious family – her elder brother was a monsignor and she aimed to enter the convent till a lecherous professor sweet-talked her into opening her legs. She cherished and obeyed him, worshipped him like a God, never opened her legs for any other man till she caught him in their bed with a fifteen-year-old he said was his half-sister his father had with an outside woman. There were rumours she was getting it from Eddy, though the only women I'd seen close to Eddy were Elizabeth and Maria. More credible rumours said she was fucking the head of Eddy's Commando. She was pretty but looked plain. She wore big tortoise shell glasses and bought her clothes from M & S. Her husband did not, he looked like a show window, smiled when he twirled his wife on the floor, to generous applause. I read articles he wrote for *National Review* and the *Spectator,* which made Rick Santorum sound like Kim Jong-Un. He wore a powder blue *Zegna* suit, Armani tie with red and blue stripes and tasselled Gucci black loafers with gold 'G's. His opinion pieces in *The Chronicle* blasted the Chinese for using unfair practices to damage big American firms, for which his Google Profile said he was consultant.

I also knew the couple who came on the floor next. Sharon told me about the girl, Darlene, who wore a gown cut to the waist to expose parts of her breasts when she appeared at the Independence Ball with the captain of the national football team. There was also a story about a student boyfriend who beat her senseless when he found a Harvard class ring in her purse. She was pretty like Eddy's slut. Her date tonight was the same footballer, his one hand over both cheeks of her ass – his nickname was 'The Hulk'.

Stephen could not stop his spiel about Eddy – he was obsessive – with booze, women, sports, gambling and now Eddy's sins. Our strong rum has the reputation for stimulating obsession but now he changed subjects and revealed what had been bugging him all evening. 'Maria throw me out the house, star. I can't see my children or get clothes. She catch me with a old girl friend I swear I leave long ago and she tell me this my last chance. So I give the girl a money, keep paying the rent on her condo and instalment on her car, tell her to take a break till things cool down. But then I meet this wonderful girl who come to work at one of our company, fall in love like a schoolboy and buy her a condo and Honda SUV. Of course the old girl, the one I put on leave, find out, curse me and write Maria, with photo of me and her doing it. So I go home early one morning, find the lock on the house change, a overnight bag with a toothbrush, shirt and trouser and note from Maria saying she hope I enjoy my new slut.'

Educated people like us try to speak BBC English but rum and stress peeled off the veneer of a cut-glass accent and left Stephen sounding like Rhino Man. I didn't need the few courses I'd taken in philosophy to appreciate the logic of what he faced. Stephen's paradox was prosaic, he couldn't have the women he truly wanted, because he didn't have money. He wed Maria who had money but who he didn't want, so he could afford the women he did want – but he couldn't have those women if Maria cut off his money and maybe his balls. That was the position he was in now. But another of my principles was never to offer advice to people in relationships and even when I knew I was 100 per cent right I kept my fucking mouth shut.

It was getting late, even the weaker drink I'd had made me feel like a boxer after fifteen rounds with *both* Klitschko brothers and I could only imagine what Stephen was feeling now, with all the blows from the booze and his bitch of a wife. So I called Bunny. He must have been cruising nearby – he was there in ten minutes. Stephen was drunk but not stupid or insane.

Even if our roads were not designed by criminals and used by psychopaths he knew he had gone way beyond what was safe to drive. He agreed when I said Bunny would take him home and he could collect his car later. I gave another two-hundred to the man he'd annoyed before and called one of the small boys who hung around, wearing torn khaki shorts and an old 'Legalize Ganja' tee-shirt. He was about the same age as my little glass girl and I imagined her now lying in the same bed with her parents and five or six siblings. I gave the boy ten US dollars to stay with Stephen's car and promised Bunny would give him another ten if he were there when Stephen came back for it.

Stephen's girl lived in one of the new developments not far from Sharon's – maybe a classmate had given him the condo. Bunny knew the way, it didn't take long to get there but Stephen was in such deep sleep he was blissfully unaware we were at his home already. I rang the doorbell for what seemed a long time, and when she came out saw she was about Sharon's age, looked like a nice girl but haggard, red eyed and wild haired from waking so early in the morning. She wore a blue ribbed robe over her nighty and reached into the car to get Stephen. But he was an ex-athlete, his muscles were out of tune and he was heavy as fuck, she would have busted her gut attempting to lift him out of the car.

'We'll take him in, Miss, just show us where to put him.'

'I'm Jenny,' she said. 'I know you. I was in the same class with Sharon; she showed us your pictures when we went for debates at St Dunstan's.' She pointed to a new leather couch, we put Stephen down on it, she covered him with a red blanket. The leather wasn't as good as that in my place, so maybe the Chinese didn't bother with the 'Made in Italy' tags. She wore Carolina

Herrera – I'd read in the paper it was the scent for sex, thus explaining why Eddy's slut bathed in it. Jenny used oceans of it too, hoping her man would come home sober enough to fuck her but now she had to lie in bed alone while he snored like a fucking saw-mill on her couch. She was too young, too nice to waste herself on a man like Stephen, who chased new pussy like a dog on heat. But as my principle dictated, I kept schtum. 'You call Bunny when you're ready to collect his car, Jenny. He'll take you there.'

'Here my number, Miss Jenny. Call when you ready.'

'Thank you so much for taking such care of him; he said he knew you when you were at the school, though he was ahead of you. I read your book on Joseph; Stephen said you spent time together when you came out to do research. He said you're doing one on Eddy now – good luck.'

'Thanks, Jenny. Let him sleep, give him a big breakfast and some strong rum punch when he wakes.' 'I'll see you again sometime, I have Sharon's numbers and we see each other at meetings all the time.' She replied. If Stephen was younger and not such a shit she would be wonderful for him, as Sharon was for me. If she was thinking with her brain and not her cunt she would find a man her age, be moderately happy and get grey hairs much later. But I didn't give advice. 'Take me home, Bunny, I need some sleep and you do too.' Now he knew I was fucking Sharon he was almost like a good friend. Dawn was breaking; I looked in the side mirror and saw my face was pasty, as if I'd spent the night in lard. I didn't look for long though, afraid that maybe those people were right about zombies, and my image would disappear in fog like the living dead.

CHAPTER NINETEEN

I was writing up my notes on Stephen, on my new laptop; it made my old one look like a bar of hard soap. Sharon was in black knickers and a tee-shirt from the hotel, practicing her German by reciting Rilke's *Duino Elegies*. Rilke's language and rhythms were complex but she was doing a fantastic job, her accent much better than mine and when I stole a glance I saw she was looking proud of herself. Then I heard the cell phone ring. I picked up my new fancy phone but let the call go over to voicemail. The message was from Winston's throw-away cell phone. '*Taxi. Leroy. 2day 5PM.*' I showed it to Sharon and read the couplet she was working on over her shoulder as she read the note. 'Every brute inversion of the world knows the disinherited/ to whom the past no longer belongs, nor yet the future.'

Her face was set like plaster, she said nothing as she put the book down and walked to the kitchen. Rilke was complex but he made sense, at the rate Eddy was destroying the past not even the industry and efficiency of the Chinese could ensure the future he envisioned. Moses, Cairncross and Eddy belonged to this past but Eddy maybe had a reason for denying it. Tragedy had that effect on people. We all had a past determining what we did, even if we didn't know it. When Sharon didn't come out, I followed and found her looking out the window at the crews building the fancy houses above my place. The first rows were complete while bulldozers cut roads above and gardeners planted beds of red, blue and yellow flowers below. I was trying to remember what that flower seller said in *Streetcar*. Despite the brilliance, there was something of Williams' decay about this relentless construction of modernity.

'What're you upset about? You know I have to see Winston. I can't do a book on Eddy without him.'

'I know Winston, we grew up on the same estate. He can take care of himself. I'm not upset.'

'You are— okay, I'll cook lunch, I'm good at pasta and sauce. You bought that Parmesan and I took a good Chianti from Miss Robotham. After we eat we can walk, then come back and rest.'

'I already planned what we're having and I know when you say rest it's the last thing I'll get!' Women are so much smarter. While telling her not to worry, I was making elaborate plans for the last supper and the goodbye sex. 'Since we came to your place for lunch Elena wants those mahogany floorboards. If she tells her cousin he'll get it done. It's not worth it. I talked to her but if she says anything to you, say how much you love our tiles.'

'I *do* love your tiles – I've never seen blue like this. I like mahogany but I wouldn't change this for wood. She seems to like getting new things.'

'She's had a tough life. She wants something different for the future. '

'So did you, you grew up in the same place.'

'Hers was much worse. I don't like to live here but I have to be near her so she doesn't flip.'

'Okay, I'll discourage her, tell her how I hate wood.' I was wondering what had happened to Elena.

When the taxi came Sharon and I embraced and as I kissed her, I felt her body shiver while she tried to compose her face so I wouldn't see how upset she was. 'Don't worry, babe, this shouldn't take long, then I'll be back and we'll celebrate with rum punch.' I squeezed her: 'And maybe a little of that rest you enjoy so much!' 'Go away and leave me!' she said, pushing me off her but I saw her smile. I knew the score, she was tight friends with Winston but he wasn't fucking her, because when you fuck someone you feel special responsibility, you grieve when there's a possibility they'll be blown to shit.

The taxi was an ancient Lada, a remnant from the time when we were led by comrades and got our wheels from Russia. The driver had dirty old clothes in a brown paper bag for me. I put them on in the cab. I guess it wouldn't do for the pigs to see a man in a Boss polo shirt and linen trousers in a beat up taxi, driving in areas where only gunmen, street girls, addicts or unemployed crooks would feel at home. I even changed my Ray Bans for plain ones that made me look like an old maid Jehovah's Witness. As soon as we got out of the hills and started through the rougher quarters we passed Jeeps full of heavily armed soldiers and paramilitary police and the ambulance sirens were like a summons to the deepest pits of hell. Occasionally we passed a Land Rover with Eddy's Commando, criminals who according to Sharon were recruited from death row and supermax prisons by North Koreans who taught them to kill without question. When he came to power Eddy dissolved all security units from the old crew but them. We went through opposition areas and were waved through roadblocks where skinny Rastamen in brown rags and red, black and gold tams sat on wood boxes smoking herb or chewing nuts. We went through the area where Bunny first took me to see Trevor. I saw the twelve-year-old soldier again and he had been in the wars. His left arm was in a sling, his right leg in a cast and he was bent even further into the ground by his cannon. Half his face looked like stale hamburger meat, as if he'd spent a million years in Africa being buffeted in the rapids of the River Nile, and then dried out on the boiling sands of the Sahara. But he had survived and looking disturbingly like a John Galliano runway model, would go on killing.

We drove on, arriving at an area where the houses were so derelict they seemed uninhabited and abandoned. Occasionally scrawny men and women emerged from the ruins, looking like rejects from the insane asylum downtown. They stared blank-eyed as we passed, with such a Prof.ound disinterest it made me wonder what had compelled them to come out at all. Ahead the asphalt was gone from the roads and it was so dark you couldn't see the potholes. Even the security forces avoided this bit of hell where, if you didn't break your axle, ten-year-old gunmen, high on drugs, could ambush you. Heavy rain had fallen and the potholes along this solitary, wretched road were like bomb craters along a wasteland of war, famine and death.

'We're here, sir.' 'Here' was a low, grey building, like an old post office, that might have been a victim of the last hurricane but had not been repaired – maybe its people couldn't prove their loyalty to the People's Mandate Party. Standing in front was a small boy, whose rags and the caked dirt on his face would make him unsuitable for even the most desperate Dickens' novel. As I got out of the car he started toward me but the driver called out, 'Wait, sir.' He was holding out dirty old shoes which looked at least two sizes too large. But I guess a cop would have noticed my Russell and Bromley loafers and I would be forced to spend time in Eddy's fortress downtown near the sea, answering questions while my eyebrows were being plucked. The boy's acrid smell added a new wave to my sickness. Maybe he couldn't wash his clothes because they were the only ones he had or he was too busy staying alive.

I followed the boy ducking in and out of ruins, through broken doorways, some of which I could hardly squeeze through, up and down rotted stairways, with my heart in my mouth. Then we arrived at an unbroken door. It was closed, although by rights there was so little wall surrounding it the door was a wry practical joke. The boy knocked loudly and particles of plaster and dust fell to the ground. Fear and humour were at war in me. The door opened to reveal a large, dark room. There were cracks in all of the walls, and in a few of them a dim vision of the world beyond peaked through. A long time ago someone had painted on what must have been solid walls, but now the paint had worn out. There was no electricity, so only a dull kerosene lamp gave a flickering dim light to the room and showed, finally where Winston Pinnock sat, in a fetid easy-chair. The room smelled like a sewer being heated by hellfire.

'He's here, Mr Winston.' The boy's voice was more refined than his looks.

'Welcome, comrade', Winston thrust a skinny arm toward me. 'Good to see you! Wait outside, Leroy. Call if you see anything.'

He could have been a young Bob Marley. He didn't look

anything like his pictures on Google and the clothes he wore could have come from the same rubbish bin as the ones I now wore. Winston was a complex bag of contradictions. He had won the Rhodes scholarship after finishing at St Dunstan's. Without having Eddy's pedigree, his Oxford education gave him the opportunity to mix with the people who would in the end run our country and occupy the highest levels of government in the UK. Many of our nationalist heroes had gone to Oxford or Cambridge. From what I'd read he was also a better writer than me and could have made it as a novelist. Oxford graduates didn't do that kind of political journalism in Woodwater, especially not the kind displayed on the sign behind him which read 'BOMB ME!' above pictures of some of the islands grand ,new glass and steel constructions.

'I see Sharon's feeding you well – you're looking fitter than you did in your picture, on the sleeve of your book on Joseph.' His words were staccato, exploding like shells in the otherwise silent room. He looked at me as a scientist would while examining a specimen, his eyes intensely boring into my soul. 'I see they didn't tell you what happened to him … to Joseph.' He looked resigned to having to be the one to tell me, and it weighed heavy on his face, momentarily turning the almost sweet boyishness harsh.

'I tried to find out the truth, but everybody gave me a different answer.'

'You can't blame Sharon, I'm sure she was afraid she'd fuck up your time with Eddy.'

'I didn't ask her, I was too afraid she'd lie too.'

'You're doing a book on Eddy, so you have got to know what his people did to the man your words made famous.'

At last, this was the moment I had been waiting for and even as I knew I probably wasn't going to be hearing anything good, I allowed myself to hope for more, to hope that my country was better than I already knew it to be. Winston shifted in his seat, suddenly looking very small and vulnerable and began to speak in a rough, sad voice.

'We were so proud when the book came out. Everyone from St Dunstan's, the whole island in fact. Here was one of us, a disabled person in physique, but enabled in life and through your words into the type of hero we used to read about in Homer, Virgil or Shakespeare. You know what our leaders think about disabled people here – treat them like mad men, even worse than criminals. It was a triumph like no other. Joseph came to represent the best of all of us and his story gave him the world stage. You can imagine the way we feel here when we see him winning all over the world, accepting his trophies and awards, hand in hand with royalty and top celebrities. Everybody whether able-bodied or not, walked taller because of him and because of his success. The book coming out and doing so well, just add another level of class and enjoyment.

By the time he returned to Woodwater, Joseph was a celebrity himself. Bigger than anyone here and naturally that was going to be a problem for those in so-called power. Eddy's people wanted him on board badly. They controlled the people by drawing in the popular dancehall musicians and others but to have Joseph running with them that would be the icing on the cake. But you know Joseph – he was stubborn – not for sale. Besides he was enjoying his own success, and was looking at how to capitalise on that for himself and the betterment of others. Maybe he even imagined running in opposition to Eddy's party, we'll never really know. Joseph did not give them what they wanted and sadly for him it became public, and the papers reported it in a way that definitely made Joseph the hero and Eddy looked really ridiculous in the eyes of the people. For us as opposition it was the crack in the armoured glass we were looking for, the way for us to try to destabilize his government and finally get some real leadership for our people.

'The intimidation began slowly at first. Stopping Joseph's car whenever he was driving around town. Searching it for hours while he had no choice but to sit and wait. One time a fan, seeing Joseph's car on the side of the road and all the police buzzing around, assumed Joseph had broken down. The fan, an older man, offered Joseph a lift to wherever he was headed before the breakdown. Joseph, grinning and waving took off with his new friend, leaving the police to kick rocks, unsure as they now were as to what to do next.

When Eddy heard about this he became infuriated, sending a small army of heavily armed police and their dogs to Joseph's house where their campaign of harassment and intimidation continued for weeks. Joseph left to go on business and while he was out of the country, over one-hundred armed police and at least ten dogs surveyed his property. Apparently some of the wiliest thieves on this planet were able to enter his property and steal every last thing inside. When Joseph returned home, he was detained for hours at the airport and his passport seized. It wasn't until he was standing in front of his house, the doors hanging off their hinges, every window smashed, broken glass littered like brittle, silver grass, and what little possession he had left, strewn around broken and water-logged – it was only then that Joseph began to fear for his own life. Eddy and his band of killers were on a rampage to get him and would stop at nothing.

Joseph knew the only person who could help him at this point and went directly to see Miss Vie.'

I felt queasy. I knew what was coming next and only got momentary pleasure from hearing Winston relate how Miss Vie took Eddy to task, berating him as if he was a wet-behind-the-ears child instead of the leader of one of the world's growing economies. Miss Vie threatened Eddy with all kinds of unnatural consequences if he and his cronies did not leave Joseph in peace. According to Winston, Eddy was upset and bitterly resentful. He felt impotent at his mother's interference and equally at his apparent inability to just ignore her. But there was already too much at stake for Eddy. He loved his mother but he loved loyalty more. His ego would not let him rest. In his mind being beaten by what he termed a cripple and an old woman was something he could never accept. It was his orders, directly sent, which resulted in what Joseph then endured.

Some of Eddy's goons lay in wait for Joseph who had began to rebuild his life and had secured a new house high in the hills surrounded by a thick brick wall. Flagging down the car he was driving they captured Joseph, and began immediately laying into him with batons and fists until they beat him unconscious and in one last callous and cowardly move they cut his Achilles' tendons so he couldn't walk again, never mind run. Joseph's struggle to learn how to run after being stricken with polio had become part of the heroic folklore of the island. It was regarded as the ultimate grace of God, and for those so poor and destitute he was a figure of great worship. But he was also a man and one who had overcome the worst odds. Whatever strength had taken him there and had sustained him since his first success had depleted in light of his mistreatment by Eddy and his henchmen. Waking up in the hospital and finding himself being forced once again to rely on assistance, and on a wheelchair to navigate the world – Joseph broke down. It was too much for him to bear. His body was discovered later that day hanging from the mango tree they would later cut down to make way for the new school. They claimed it was suicide, that Joseph had hung himself and no-one questioned how the disabled man would have been able to climb the tree in the first place. Miss Vie, when she heard about it ran to her son full of questions. Eddy wept, he swore to his mother he didn't know anything about what had happened to Joseph, said how sorry he was, promised to compensate Joseph's parents.

Winston slumped back in his seat, his eyes brimming with yet-to-flow tears.

Later Eddy's government paraded a small boy, who was the son of a minor figure in the party, and was arrested and confessed to the Joseph's murder. He was sentenced to twelve years. But Winston had heard he was promised a house, money and a job when he came out, after serving maybe three years. 'What about Joseph's people?' I asked.

'Eddy promised Joseph's parents a house, money and burial in the Garden of Remembrance. But they refused, moved out of the estate and our people guard them so they don't have any 'accident'. This is where you came in'. I shuddered to think how I might have been caught up in assisting the low-life. 'Apparently the opposition got hold of a mobile phone video of Eddy's thugs cutting Joseph's achilles tendon. They also discovered that Eddy planned to use you to write a white-washed version of his life and they knew you had already achieved such success with Joseph's story that they planned to get you on their side. You writing an exposé instead of a glorification would have been a major coup for the party. Have you wondered about Eddy's sudden interest in you? He probably showered you with gifts and money.' Shame crept over me as I remembered the luxurious car journeys and exquisite places I had been on Eddy's dime. Even now my pocket bulged with one of the cash-laden envelopes he had given me.

'Eddy had to get hold of you, buy your loyalty so he could counter them. He also spoke to Bloom who said you were the best man for it. You know he recommended you to the Publisher for the Joseph book?'

I felt my insides fall, the distant sirens and the wind piercing into me like swords, and all I thought I'd accomplished in life was erased. I tried to make excuses for Eddy, perhaps he didn't know, as he said, maybe his tears were genuine. But I knew men as powerful and paranoid as he was created an atmosphere where none of their people would act without permission. While I was researching that book I'd become as close to Joseph as it was possible for one person to be to another. I always thought I'd wasted what talent I had, that I hadn't made use of my intelligence but Joseph made me feel worthwhile, that I'd immortalised courage, hard work, and determination, despite all the horrors. My work with him had made me alive, caused me to feel human, saved me from oblivion. And now he was dead.

'Stephen Walters – you know that old boy: good at sports, from one of those wealthy old families?' I asked.

'I know Stephen well, a weird specimen. You know he was a good writer, had real talent, could be one of Woodwater's most successful. But he had too much; you have to be in need to want to write.'

'Stephen told me things about Eddy I didn't know, how

unapproachable he'd become, how he's ignoring the very people who brought him to power. He said Eddy Haddad Senior, was not Eddy's father, that Miss Vie had an affair with Moses' late twin brother, Aaron, when she was a school girl, that Moses arranged the marriage with Haddad, his friend and business partner.'

'He said that? That's what people think but it's not true. Anybody with eyes in his head can see Eddy wasn't Haddad's son. He *is* the son of Aaron but Miss Vie didn't have an affair, he raped her. Aaron was notorious for raping women and killing men. Miss Vie's parents were Moses' good friends; they grew up together, were educated and got good jobs as teachers. Aaron was after the mother and elder sister but Moses warned him off and Aaron left them alone. He had this sick mind and he'd think the women he was chasing after were in love with him.

Moses had no idea his brother could harm a very bright, very beautiful little girl who was like his own daughter. But when she was fifteen and about to take her national exam to go to university Aaron convinced himself she was in love and, after almost beating her to death, raped her. His brother and her parents knew he was guilty. He tore her clothes and removed her underwear, keeping them as a trophy. That was one of his signature actions. Moses wanted to have him killed. He was one of the biggest gangsters on the island – Don of the ghetto where Eddy would get the strongest support in his political career. But they were identical, even close friends couldn't tell them apart. So Moses had him locked up in an asylum where he paid for the best psychiatric care. Years later, when they thought he was cured, Moses said they should let him out but warned him to stay in the country, never to approach Miss Vie, her husband, or Eddy. But he did, telling Eddy Miss Vie loved him and that

Moses was jealous, so he arranged for her to marry a 'Syrian'. That's why Eddy now hates Moses. He spent time in private institutions, trying to get cured of the illness his father had. That's why he was far behind you in school though he was older. Later Aaron started killing again, people he thought close to Moses. Psychiatrists said he was jealous, thought his brother was abandoning him. Finally Moses snapped when Aaron butchered a couple he, Moses, was really close to. Moses ordered his people to get rid of his brother but told them he didn't want to know when, how, or where. They obliged, chopped Aaron into little pieces, dissolved the pieces in acid and burnt anything left over. Eddy has the same issues about being abandoned and demands total loyalty. Boys teased Eddy about his White father and to compensate Eddy glorified the late Aaron and hated Moses, even though his uncle built up Eddy Senior's business and made Eddy what he is now. Eddy's a sick man though his power covers this up. He would kill anyone who knew his secret, which is why Stephen couldn't tell you, out of fear you might let things out, even by accident.'

The room was humid, stifling, there were no windows and the door was pulled tight. The clothes itched. Maybe there were bedbugs, though this could be paranoia but I was scratching like a dog with mange. The sirens were distant but the sound throbbed inside my head. I was thinking of Sharon and the happiness we felt in our little place on the hill, with its blue tiles, among the gardens full of rainbow flowers. Winston was strong, he didn't go to pieces the way I did. There was brightness in his eyes, a force in his voice that spoke of everlasting life. I tried to remember the words of that Dylan Thomas poem: '*Do not go gently into that good night./Rage, rage against the dying of the light.'* The lamp flickered in the gloom, as if the oil was running out but Winston's face was bathed in the first light, as from the beginning of the world.

'I went to Oxford thinking you would be there, to be a mentor to this lonely boy, brought there by the fortune of a man much worse than the slave masters who raped our ancestors and keep raping our mothers today. But you were gone and I had to find new ways overcoming my loneliness.'

'I went there hoping to be a role model to our people dispossessed for centuries by graduates of that same noble institution. I knew of the scholarship you won, endowed by a racist murderer. But when I got there I saw so few of us, all more English than the English. I spent three years in one of those schools in America, wasn't prepared for more time in another maximum security prison of the mind.'

I felt the pain in my body of wanting to tell Winston the truth. Instead I told him what I'd repeated so often I began to believe it. I was Berg's star pupil. He thought I'd one day be Professor of Modern German Literature in a great American, British or German university. As a graduate student I was publishing papers in journals some of my teachers hadn't heard of. When I told Berg I wanted to go to Oxford and already had a fellowship, he wrote to one of his protégés, now Head of German, telling him that I was 'the man'. When I got the acceptance I was overjoyed. I thought Oxford would open up something that had been blocking me from achieving what I dreamt. But once there I experienced the horrors too, as if ghosts hid in those ancient crevices, crawling out to haunt me when I was lost in fogs of daydreams. When I was feeling haunted like that I went up to the rooms of Berg's student on the top floor for a sherry. On the way I passed the offices of an eccentric German professor who changed his name from Joseph Battenberg to Barton to conceal the fact his father was a disciple of Heydrich and expert in vivisection. Barton had a mirror on his door so students would make sure they were properly dressed when they came to see him. He had attacked one who wore trousers so low his boxers were exposed and it made the papers – the student was the stepson of some famous, washed up rock star. As an expert in drugs manufacture Barton was hypersensitive to suggestions his animal testing was related to his Nazi ancestry and history of eugenics. So when on his mirror he found the sign in red lipstick saying 'Save the animals. Die Nazi Pig!' he smashed it with the steel knob of his big umbrella. When I was on the stairs and saw the broken mirror on Barton's door I thought it was blood, thought I saw the head of a woman reflected, whose face had been smashed in the glass. I screamed, cracking my fist as I fell and convulsed on the hall floor, and was out for I don't know how long. I'd found teaching German literature at Oxford easy, I was an expert on Franz Kafka and Heinrich Böll. Berg told his protégé I was special. But now when I tried to teach I kept blacking out, seeing the face of that woman.

Winston was still chipper, as if we were on that beach on Blue Island, bathed in the Chinese sun. 'We heard rumours about why you left; the one most widely repeated was that it was woman trouble – you know our reputation. They said you spoilt the daughter of the head of some really important family, he had a word with you to get out if you valued your life!'

'Nothing so interesting as that, Winston. Just the banal thing that I looked at the place and couldn't see myself reflected. Like Alice's looking glass but I couldn't see my image, only ghosts of things past.'

'Glad you cleared that up, comrade,' Winston said. 'Now I must get you back to Sharon before she launches a killer drone attack! I called her after you left and she cursed me out! Leroy...'

The little boy came in, like a shadow in the dim light and I embraced Winston then followed the little shape back out into the pitch black night. 'Take care, comrade, we'll meet again soon,' I heard Winston say.

All along the route back the construction sites were lit up like bright forests of Christmas trees; in poorer areas lights on police cars and ambulances shone like stars in a nearby galaxy while sirens wailed like drunken angels, swinging the shorn heads of men and women between heaven and hell.

CHAPTER TWENTY

Eddy said he wasn't sure what he was doing this weekend – for a man as organised, who stuck to decisions he made months in advance, this would have been a shock had I been in a better mood after seeing Winston. But I was secretly glad. I wanted time to compose myself so I wouldn't show the contempt and terror I felt. I didn't want to burden Sharon, to tell her what I'd heard and get her fearing what Eddy would do to me if he found out. But she was intelligent, very sensitive and would know I was hiding something. Besides, when you feel very close to someone, love them and fuck them well, it's hard to hide what you're feeling. So I told her, felt her body stiffen but then relax and feel even closer as she sensed how much I trusted her. We were glad we'd have more time by ourselves as I tried to come to terms with the enormity of the task I'd taken on, to write about a man for whom life was entirely disposable. I'd always had the Romantic idea that the powerful were not bound by moral precepts, as Nietzsche said of the Ubermensch, the man who operated beyond good and evil. Stalin had said 'kill one man and it's murder, kill a million and it's a statistic.'

Occasionally we saw Eddy on national TV, exhorting his audience to obey the rules of their Church and God, to love their fellow men and women, be moral, upright and faithful. He urged students to sacrifice. On the BBC World Service we listened to him as he convinced reporters that the people they accused his followers of killing were massacred by their own side to embarrass him! The bastard should be in Hollywood; he made the shits prancing around look like fucking cardboard zombies.

We wanted to watch *Blade Runner* to the end having failed to do so on so many occasions, drinking too many rum punches and falling asleep. Or Elena taking us to unheard of places for fantastic food when her 'cousin' was busy with Eddy, his butch wife, or official duties. Having one of Sharon's classmates pop up, having to take them places – a jam session by a new band, or one of Miss Robotham's fantastic suppers, with a cellar of fine French and South African wine. But now we nailed it.

Sharon made a fantastic meal of very peppery ox-tail, cowpeas and rice, potato pudding, and we planned to have the rum punch *after* the film so we wouldn't fall asleep. She was eager, after what she'd seen of the fantastic direction of Ridley Scott when the film began. Then the half-naked girl from Eddy's office called, saying the PM wanted me to come to Blue Island where we could continue our interviews. Delroy called to say he'd be there in an hour. I tried to hide my fury but Sharon felt it and tried to calm me down, telling me to be patient, we'd have time later to watch the film, and she'd keep the food for me. To make me see reason she also gave me a lot of tongue, stroking me where I wanted as a promise of more.

Delroy arrived in no time and I joined him in silence in the car. I was scared at first at how fast he took the hairpin bends on the road. This was a new feeling, so different from the deep sense of relaxation and privilege I had become accustomed to feeling being chauffeured everywhere. We switched back and forth along the dark winding road, in the pitch black night, across the mountain where the canopy of leaves blocked out even slivers of moonlight. Since Eddy wanted us to be inconspicuous we drove a new Audi, the boot of which I discovered was full of coolers stuffed with bottles of rum punch. Then we saw Blue Island. The bridge was lit up, the Chinese liked working 24/7 and it was nearly complete. A catamaran waited for us at the dock and we were across in no time. The hotel was similar to the one where Sharon and I stayed before but my junior suite was bigger, the fittings more luxurious, the glass and stainless steel shinier, silk sheets instead of cotton but the same size B&O and paintings from the collective of hallucinatory colours and shapes.

Eddy's suite occupied the whole top floor, the room for the party was like an auditorium, the Christmas tree with brilliant decorations and expensive presents, the bar with every brand of liquor imaginable. But the Ministers present and their hangers-on were drinking rum punch. They knew I was Eddy's image man and sprung up like jack-in-the-boxes, greeting me as if they really cared. The Donovan clone who had taken me up to the suite went behind a black door at the far end the hall and came out trailing Eddy, who spurted charm out like whipped cream. He gripped me around the shoulders as he did on Eaton Square, said how happy he was to see me, apologised for dragging me away from Sharon! He promised we'd get down to business as soon as he sorted out a few problems. But at Eaton Square I didn't know him, thought he reminded me of the diffident yet effective, Forest Whitaker. Now I took Sharon's advice and put on a convincing act. I saw the Foreign Minister stumble up the stairs from our floor, his shades in place but failing to wipe all the coke from his nose. His voice quavered as usual when he greeted me and he shook when Eddy struck him on the back. 'Went to powder your nose?' he asked in mock jocularity, not hiding his contempt.

The Brazilian Ambassador arrived with four very pretty girls who wouldn't have shown more skin if they were at Carnival. They gave me, Eddy and all the other men cursory looks but decided it was too early to put their chips on any number. The man knew me, we'd met at one of Eddy's houses, greeting me warmly after embracing the PM and trying out some of our colourful 'bad words.' He was a very fat man, his psychedelic shirt could have made a tent for his bevy of beauties; he was bald but tonight wore a brown rug. 'Excuse us, Prof., the ambassador has a little business we have to discuss. Soon come,' Eddy said. The youngest girl, in what looked like a strip of kite paper, gave me a look suggesting she might come back if she didn't find anything better in the room they were going into.

Colin Shepherd didn't want to sit with his colleagues but the Agriculture Minister grabbed his arm and pulled him in as he rubbed his nose. The others guffawed as they looked toward the door, their eyes staring brightly like inebriated ferrets. When I followed the trajectory of their gaze, my jaw dropped and I was happy there were no flies to zoom in. None of the girls entering that room could have been more than sixteen and I doubted the youngest was in her teens. They looked like typical girls from the Academy and since we were almost all St Dunstan old boys, this was almost certain. Their ancestors had owned slaves, and their descendants now owned companies, or worked as lawyers and doctors. The young girls had obviously been taken on a tour of the huge mall with an official credit card that had no limit and streamed through in their Prada, Louis Vuitton, Gucci and Christian Louboutin finery. The eldest girl gave me the look – she obviously assumed all of us were child molesters. She wouldn't need a bra for another year but had stuffed this one with tissue, pushed it up and twirled what she considered an ass in the pimp roll she probably saw on television. When we were in school, girls like these would prefer being in a maximum security prison in America than with the Mother Superior and her nuns, who were more efficient than Himmler's guards. Their belief in the Blessed Mother and their fathers' money were the best burglar alarms for their crotches. Not even the Governor General, Prime Minister, Archbishop, or the biggest businessman could get one out and only geniuses with Houdini-like talents like Elizabeth could breech the security. Now a baker's dozen could get out to practice in designer bras four sizes too large and get brand new hundred dollar bills to buy the next Prada frock or Hermes belt.

I saw the barman open his mouth to ask something when three of them went to order drinks but whatever they answered was so sharp his mouth shut fast like a trap. The eldest one licked her lips as she took a swallow of the punch and said something to the others when she saw me watching them. She took another swallow then arranged the tissues in her bra as if to make herself look older. Rum punch is a drink for adults, you need to sip it as it's usually so strong you can find yourself on your ass if you swallow. This one kept swallowing then, with encouragement from her mates, placed a cigarette between her lips and pimp rolled over to me. She looked like Leona Lewis but horseback riding, swimming, hockey and casual sex had toned her body and her face had the arrogance of four-hundred years of money, privilege and idleness. Her brain was stainless steel and could calculate to the nearest $100 how much a man could pay for fucking her front, back or sideways.

'Got a light for my cigarette?' she asked.

'I don't smoke and neither should you.' I saw the shock in her face as she turned away and swung her ass back to her astonished comrades. She said something to them and the look of pity they gave me said 'The fucker's a perv, he doesn't like little girls!'

Eddy came out again when the Donovan clone went in, and before he got to the door and heard the chime, the Cuban head of intelligence had bounded into the room with three girls who could have run for Miss Cuba World, if Fidel allowed such bourgeois selling of the flesh. As Eddy and the man embraced, the girls gave all the men very quick but Professional appraisals, all without commitment. The spy man was considerate; a consummate diplomat who thought modern Cuba needed no more beards or Marxist slogans, that he could serve his country with magnificent physique and fists of steel, as he did winning Olympic gold as super heavyweight twice.

'Come, Ernesto, I have friends I want you to meet. I soon come, Prof.'

'Yes, Amigo, we have good business to discuss.' He stuffed a packet of ten-inch cigars into Eddy's shirt pocket then herded his three beauties towards Eddy's big black door. None gave me a last look as they probably figured I was too low on the food chain, had no big muscles, fat wallet, or proletarian ideology. The little girls gave them dirty looks as if they resented the fact adult women were being admitted to Paradise. I was surprised they weren't looking wilted with all the punch they swallowed and now the look on the face of the one I jilted said if she caught me alone in an ally she would beat me to death with her Barbie doll.

I noticed now that one looked like Stephen's daughter but didn't think even Maria's stinginess and mean temper would drive her child to look for designer gear selling pussy. Unlike my Lalique girl, these ones were hard as basalt, (they only resembled her in age) with brains functioning like cash machines. My one made a mistake with me; she believed any one close to Eddy oozed Chinese money like sweat. Her father must have told her she shouldn't judge a man's worth by the gold Rolex he wore, like those fucking cabinet ministers, whores, drug dealers and Yankee businessmen. A real man wore a truly expensive watch, looking like Chinese made shit that cost less than a Big Mac. Maybe they mistook me for Money, my watch *was* Chinese made shit, which I picked up in a back street of Hong Kong for less than the price of a hamburger. When Eddy came out again I thought there was another luminary at the door but then he came over and I wondered what was going on behind his big black door, what type of nuclear reaction took place when such hot women and power drunk men came into contact?

'I'm sorry I haven't had time to discuss work with you, Prof. You've been back now after a long absence, seen the changes we made but you're not a stakeholder, you have nothing to keep you here.' He phoned and a pretty black haired girl appeared with a pink file, a red cross with SECRET marked on it. I thought I would have checked her out if I didn't have Sharon and noticed she was the same girl from the house by the sea, when I was overwhelmed by the smell of the ocean of her Carolina Herrera perfume. Her hair was black now and I realised she was wearing a wig. She had on knickers and a bra this time – you could see through the dress she wore when she bent over to hand Eddy the file. She was still giving me the eye, even bolder now, and I wondered if she thought I ignored her last time because she tried too hard, showing me she had nothing on under her skirt. Did she think wearing knickers and bra would persuade me to fuck her?

'Look at this, Prof.,' Eddy said, as he gestured for her to go away and she went over to the DVD player where she started playing Barry Manilow, Tom Jones and the Beddingfield's. That was shit I really hated and I looked at her with even more distaste. But she was busy exchanging dirty looks with the cigarette girl who hadn't given up on me yet and didn't want her moving in. Eddy saw the look in my eyes as I surveyed the contents of the file with an intensity approaching lust. 'Beautiful, isn't it, Prof.?' I'd never seen a house like it – like Sharon's beauty, a whole that couldn't be broken into parts. But this one was divided into quarters, each with an integrity in its own right, fitting into the beauty of the whole like a key into a lock. My garret on the Green would not serve as a servant's quarter for the servant of the servants here.

'You have no place here, Prof.; a man like you needs somewhere to call home. Donovan told me about your place in Shepherd's Bush. Even in a country barbarous like that where they have no respect for talent, they should provide a man like you with something better.'

I couldn't afford it if I lived a thousand years. Winston told me even small houses in the new developments started at a million American dollars.

'I'd like you to have this, Prof.'

'You know I'm an ex-academic, Eddy. I wrote just that one book on Joseph, I can't afford such expensive real estate.' As I alluded to Joseph I looked for even a flicker of guilt, a recognition he was sorry for what his people had done. But there was nothing. Instead there was a flash of anger, as if he resented me implying he was trying to sell me something. Like a fucking peddler. 'Who said anything about buying, Prof.? I have so many houses I won't notice if you take this one.'

'That's great, Eddy, I never dreamed of owning a house. But the offer's so sudden I need time.'

'No hurry, Prof., take all the time you need. I have some people waiting.' When he passed he said something to the girl and the new intensity with which she looked at me confirmed she was still on. She came over, passing through a spotlight so I could see there were sequins studding her underwear. She would light up like fireworks if I decided to slide in.

If a man like Eddy had offered me a house like this a year ago, I would have jumped so fast it would be mine before he finished speaking. I'd regard it as a gift of nature. But now I had Sharon and she wasn't one to accept freebies with open arms, well aware of the catastrophe when the Trojans thought they had a gift horse from their Greek enemies. But there was another reason I had to think twice about accepting. In Eaton Square Elizabeth had spoken of the boarded up house she explored when she walked from the folly her ancestors built. On the map showing where the house was I saw the castle nearby and figured the house, mention of which had made me black out, was not far. I heard Bob Marley singing 'No, woman, no cry,' looked up and saw the half-naked bitch still staring at me. I don't know if someone warned her Barry Manilow and Tom

Jones made me sick. She was still watching to make sure the girl with the Prada shoes didn't make a move when the Foreign Minister signalled and she went over. He was whispering in her ear and from the time it took he must have been giving her very complicated, very precise instructions. He struggled getting up and tottering down the stairs as she walked over to the children and picked out the smallest two, including the one who resembled Elizabeth Walters. The girls were a pack, the bigger ones were leaders, they drank a lot of punch and looked as if they would attack the chosen ones at little provocation. The two looked chuffed, and exaggerated their pimp rolls walking down the stairs. I wanted to go to my suite to call Sharon, brief her on what Eddy said, but if I went now, the one who tried to pull me might misunderstand and follow me. Or Eddy's girl might try her luck, thinking I was so drunk I couldn't hold her off. So I stayed and listened to more Bob Marley, Jimmy Cliff and some popular songs of the eighties and nineties. I kept ignoring the chimes when the door opened and noticed the room was filling up with more women, ministers and ambassadors.

Although this island was practically owned by the Chinese I saw none of them here and figured they preferred to do their own shit, not crashing Eddy's parade. Then a tall, distinguished white man in a Saville Row suit strolled in and the ministers and their hangers on rose to greet him. His hair was very black on top, blue rinsed at the temples and he looked like a Tory MP. I knew him: he was a cousin of Elizabeth's father, was born in England, went to Eton and had ambition of becoming a Tory Prime Minister. But the UK had become too democratic for his tastes and he had come back to Woodwater where he now had polished twin black mistresses – fifteen-year-olds – whose mother he gave a house in a former upper-class suburb uptown. His family still owned two plantations he used as a symbol of his commitment to the old ways – that times had changed but not for the best people. When the Chinese bought up most of the old sugar estates, however, and he heard the price, he came to see if his old friend Eddy could put in a word with them. His twins were demanding that they be transferred to the Academy from government schools then sent abroad for their further education.

I wanted to piss now and didn't want to queue up for Eddy's toilets. So I went downstairs, planning to call Sharon, though I knew she would be fast asleep. Then I saw the girls giggling as they came out of the suite next to mine, wiping powder from their noses with one hand while counting rolls of new hundred dollar bills with the other. They were so high they couldn't blink – they stared at me, laughing, as if they planned to follow me in and double their money. But I rushed in, slammed the door and heard them shout obscenities as they skipped up the stairs.

When I got Sharon on the phone, she was too groggy to talk and I told her I'd call her first thing in the morning. As I was going back up the stairs I heard the door next to mine open and Colin Shepherd crept out, mumbling something I couldn't understand. I don't know if he'd feel better if he thought I didn't see the girls leaving but at that time of the morning I really didn't give a shit. Back upstairs Eddy's girl now played the Manhattans', *You Are My Shining Star.*

I heard a buzz as the crowd parted and I saw Donovan lead in two men whose costumes were so similar they could be lodge brothers. One drank from a bottle of our twenty-five-year old rum and handed it to his comrade. All the ministers and their hangers-on leapt up and I saw Elizabeth's father's cousin try to out-smile the others and seemed to salute the newcomers with his hair. The Chinese and American ambassadors had their arms around each other and waved to the revellers like rock stars. Even the little girls stood up and would have applauded if the adults had given them a lead. As I watched the Americans swallow the rum, I recalled that I could no longer call it ours as the Chinese had bought the distillery too, for what *The Chronicle* called a 'record price'. Then Eddy, the Brazilian, Cuban, and reps' of every nation of the earth surged from the magic room to salute the brothers in arms. I heard a man in a striped blue and white shirt with a gold Rolex and South African accent whisper, 'They found the biggest supply of gold in the world and are offering the Yanks some if they stop supplying arms to Taiwan.' Eddy's face was beatific, as if he'd found the password to heaven. He had succeeded in all there was in the realm of politics, in which he'd chosen to flaunt his talents.

As I watched the black door close behind them I figured there was no point waiting any longer for Eddy. So I nodded to Indie's double, who smiled above her glass of rum on the rocks as I stood up and left. I didn't look at the DJ, now playing *Young Hearts, Run Free*, by Candi Staton, nor at the little girls, now desperate they'd run out of child molesters to tuck them in tonight. I was thinking of that boarded-up house on the hill where Elizabeth had ventured. I hoped to get up early enough to call Sharon before she started to worry. But just as I nodded off I got a call from Eddy hoping I wasn't yet asleep. When I went up he was excited, yelling, 'We're going to Cuba in the morning, Prof.! Me, the Chinese and American ambassadors – it's going to be a treat seeing the old rogue Fidel!' So the old commie basher had a crush on Fidel too, just as Nixon wet himself when he met Chairman Mao. I'm glad he didn't mention me going with them. I'd thought I'd become mercenary but the amount of money I was missing by not going on these trips was mounting. When travelled, some girl from the Foreign Ministry would give me an official white envelope stuffed with hundred dollar bills so new you'd think the ink would run. I also got a gold Amex card with a $5000 limit. But now I preferred my sleep and my girl to the Yankee dollar. One thing made me regret not going; the American ambassador was son of the CIA Director who had planned 654 attempts on Fidel's life. Would the *Commandante* joke with the son about the sins of his father?

193

CHAPTER TWENTY-ONE

Eddy must have felt like a burst balloon when the Deputy Director of Central Intelligence called to tell him his mother had died in a Florida hospital, where she'd been flown, unconscious after an attack of dengue fever. It was just over a week since his triumphant return from Havana. Delroy was weeping when he called to say Eddy had already left for Florida, that he would pick me up for the airport when he knew the time of arrival of Miss Vie's body. I couldn't say anything. I tried to speak but the sound didn't come out, it turned inside and reverberated like an echo.

I was afraid to tell Sharon, who was asleep when Delroy called and waited for her to be fully awake. But when she saw my eyes she knew instinctively something bad had happened and she started screaming before I formed a single word. Sharon took it hard, went into shock. When I finished she stopped screaming, seemed to stop breathing and for a moment I thought she was dead. She lay motionless in my arms and as I screamed her name I tapped her face firmly and she started whimpering. Her eyes were open but moist and unfocused. I had to call her doctor who reassured me Sharon was okay. She was in shock but would recover after rest and medication. I called to ask Elena to stay with her when I went out. She too was crying and she told me her 'cousin' had gone with Eddy to receive the body of his aunt. Eddy didn't waste time in Miami, a 747 with the coffin was waiting on the tarmac when he arrived in a Falcon jet and he ordered it to take off immediately.

Delroy drove me right up to where it was parked, joining the crowd who had gathered. All wept, some quietly, others howling like moon-struck dogs. When the jumbo jet came to rest, the stewardesses promptly opened the doors but no one emerged until I saw at the top of the steps a man about my height but with muscles to spare, older than me but with the panache of the forever young, in a three thousand dollar J. Press tweed suit, blue striped tie, Bass Wejun loafers and Brett Farnham style Ray Bans. He didn't spend five seconds before descending but I'm sure his eyes took in everything, memorised all the faces, and would have alerted those inside on his sleeve mike if he saw anything out of place. He loped as if he arrived for vacation and absorbed the island's mantra of 'Woodwater, No Hurry.' He stopped next to me and I thought nothing of it as I was near the head of the queue. When he spoke I could hear each word distinctly but was convinced people on either side of us could hear nothing.

'I'm a friend of John D. and Brett. They spoke highly of you, and I enjoyed your book. I'm Clayton Whitney.' He emitted words like radioactive metal. We shook hands. John D. was a big man then, I hear he's even bigger now.

'What's the holdup? Our PM's not a patient man and I'm sure he wants to get his mother home.'

'Some man called Moses – they're exchanging words'.

Moses was shocked when he saw the coffin Eddy ordered. He said Miss Vie was a simple woman, champion of the poor, and her son was making her look like an expensive whore. The PM used some obscenity, said she was *his* mother, he had the right to pick what coffin he wanted, repeated the obscenity and Moses had slapped him.

'Oh, by the way, Brett's here. He flew down before they broke the news so he could console his friend.'

'He has my number, why didn't he call?' He gave me a quizzical look. But before he could say anything else I saw the coffin begin its descent from the belly of the 747. Moses was right, it was bronze, ornately decorated and so heavy it had to be pushed on wheels so as not to crush the spines of pallbearers. Eddy didn't look like Forest Whitaker anymore, there was no acting in his ashen countenance, his wide-staring eyes, or the tense muscles of his face he screwed up to keep in the tears. The death of his mother had penetrated the impenetrable defences of Mr Total Control and the toned muscles collapsed into mush. His cousin looked more solid, his shades off, not pinching his nose and I could see no trace of white powder. He stood close enough to steady Eddy if he stumbled. But he kept his hands to himself, so his cousin could continue to think he was Superman, even if he looked more like a corpse than his dead mother. Moses stood behind; he too looked forlorn but was the only one with enough composure to greet me and the other mourners waiting on the tarmac.

The government didn't have to declare a period of mourning; there didn't seem to be a government – Eddy Haddad had disappeared into his grief. When I went to give him my condolences he barely seemed to recognise me but thanked me for honouring his mother, embracing me, as he seemed to now embrace the entire population sharing his grief. When we went to pay our respects in Miss Vie's old house Eddy looked more alive, as if being in the house where he grew up gave him a new lease of life. Apparently when she put up the house for sale, she didn't know her son had set up a front company to buy it, having bought the adjoining houses. The Chinese had already started building the ten-foot wall that would surround the whole compound and I was sure they'd complete the work as soon as she was in the ground.

Sharon told me about the collection of glass figurines Miss Vie had started when her dream of becoming a doctor to cure the ills of the poor had been cut short by the man who forced the seed that would become Eddy Haddad into her unwilling womb. I don't know where she got so many but they were displayed on three large tables in the hall where her body lay in the plain wood coffin for a week. Moses' will had prevailed and the local carpenter who made Miss Vie's furniture had constructed a simple planked wood coffin. Miss Vie had called her glass menagerie her 'precious little ones' in memory of what she held inside her, the weak and lame she would nurture and now she looked like one of her collection in the glassy sheen the dead assumed when the skin was drained of blood.

I forgot about my book and spent most of my time with Sharon, cooking, cleaning, washing clothes and even giving her a shower. When I had to go somewhere Elena was there and we acted like loving parents, taking care of our little girl. We insisted the doctor keep checking on her, and although he said she was fine, he continued giving her mild sedatives and antidepressants. She hardly said a word, we practically had to force her to eat and wash and she remained in an old M&S nightie Miss Vie had given her, which we had changed her into when she'd collapsed. I told her everything I could about what I found when I went out, of the people who camped outside Miss Vie's little house even while her body lay in state in her late husband's mansion. The heads of state and government who sent Eddy and the Governor General condolences, the people who came from all over the Caribbean and Africa to grieve for a woman who had given up all for them and overwhelmed them with the bounty of her goodness.

But I didn't tell Sharon how broken, wasted and alone Miss Vie's son looked, or how her embalmed body looked cold and glassy, like the menagerie in her collection of glass. I couldn't tell her how I felt my heart stop and my breathing disappear as I gazed at Miss Vie and realized this was the last time I would see her, that wherever she was now and wherever she would go, she would go alone. I was glad I no longer believed in heaven or hell, so I had no fear she would see her violator, Eddy's father, ever again. As I looked at Sharon prostrate in her bed, I was glad I had her, glad she survived the death of a woman who could have had it all but said no. Gently I lay beside her, put my arms around her and tried to get the image of Miss Vie out of our heads.

So many came for the funeral that the Governor General cancelled all leave for the security forces and declared a state of alert. All the airports and seaports were full as people poured in from all over the world, Kings, Queens, Emirs, Chiefs, Presidents, Prime Ministers and all the little people to whom she had dedicated her life. There was no protocol, no one seemed available for organising the funeral but there was order, dignity and security, as each mourner felt and did nothing beyond the cordon created by the immensity of grief for us. I felt a strange calm, there was peace in the air as I watched the people in rags take her simple coffin from the official pallbearers and carry it to her little grave in the Garden of Remembrance. I saw Moses and the Ministers bow, weeping with their heads in their hands, people prostrating themselves in the red clay around the grave, old women stripping their clothes off and attempting to set themselves on fire. Eddy's Commando had to surround the grave to prevent people jumping in. Eddy himself looked more composed, there were no tears but his serenity was the peace of the dead and although he tried to put a smile on his face, as if he had reconciled himself to his mother's death, there was more vitality in her corpse than in him. He looked like a dormant volcano, ready to explode any time. As her body was lowered into the ground a wail as at the end of the world went up and I could hear but faint echoes of the priests: *there is a time for living and a time to die; the Lord giveth and the Lord taketh away; ashes to ashes, dust to dust; agnus Dei qui tollis peccata mundi, dona eis requiem sempiternam...*

After the burial people sat or lay on the bare earth to await the second coming of Miss Vie. I hadn't the energy to look for Delroy or sense to call him and started drifting in the general direction of the house, walking the three miles, unable to ring the bell, waiting till the gateman saw me and rushed to open the gate. Delroy sat outside in the car, weeping into his hands and when the guard called him he sprang out, fell to his knees, pressed his arms round my legs and drenched my trousers with tears.

I had been taking care of Sharon full-time and when Elena and I decided she needed a change of scenery, I called Bunny and told him to take us to the resort by the blue hole with the round mud huts and expansive glass windows. I told him before he left he should go to a local market and buy provisions for me and my guests. The new manager knew us and I told him we would take care of our cooking. But occasionally he came by with some special dish and we would sit on stone chairs in the garden, trying to make conversation while we looked out over the sea. After a while Sharon started joining us, she said how much she enjoyed my cooking, how she loved the polished mahogany floor boards, giant glass windows which made electric bulbs superfluous, the big, solid Jacuzzi, the incredibly intense colours of the flowers in the ornamental beds. When she insisted she do the cooking and I started enjoying her rum punch, I decided she'd recovered enough, called Bunny and he took us back through bad country roads, allowing us to buy fresh pineapples, oranges and jackfruit. Elena was so glad to see us she embraced us. Then they wept in each other's arms for Miss Vie.

CHAPTER TWENTY-TWO

T*he Chronicle* and other right-wing media, including the Cairncross press, began a campaign built around demands by the American government that Moses, Rhino Man and other dancehall musicians connected to the Bathtub posse be extradited. They listed their crimes: multiple murders on the island, in the USA, Canada and the UK, the massive drug dealing, gun running, kidnaps and smuggling of cars stolen overseas. Raping of children was one of their specialities. The media revealed torture chambers on ghetto gangster-controlled estates, mass graves into which enemy corpses disappeared. It avoided mentioning that during Eddy Haddad's leadership the PM's own constituency was the most notorious.

The *Independent* and other left-wing media pointed out that the Americans would never have made these demands without the agreement of Eddy Haddad, since they wanted to retain access to the oil and other mineral industries on Woodwater. Winston Pinnock argued that the Americans would never have made the request unless Haddad asked for it. Eddy was so unhinged after his mother died that he decided to settle scores with all those he considered responsible for her death, which could include anyone his twisted mind thought should be punished. He was a certified lunatic. Winston mentioned American Special Forces operatives who had come into the island and ships with heavy equipment unloaded at ports controlled by the unions connected to Eddy's party. There were pictures with crates marked 'Tractors' and 'Car parts', cracked open to show components of computer guided self-propelled artillery pieces, mounted multi-barrelled mortars and cluster bombs with bomblets that looked like toys, and were designed to maim children. He warned comrades to be careful with phones, citing the case of someone he arranged to interview who escaped being killed only because the security forces blew up the wrong Toyota Camry, having transposed two numbers on the plates. Eddy kept referring to 'the nights of the long knives' when he would wreak God's vengeance on all his enemies who had killed his beloved mother. I guessed the genes he'd inherited from Aaron were coming into bloom.

His chief spin doctor, quoting his Harvard Prof., said that Moses, though uneducated, was the new Machiavelli. 'The power to hurt is more effective when held in reserve' ... 'spectacular acts of violence, judiciously utilised, is pain, shock, and the promise of more.' As examples he listed Moses' use of beheadings, castrations and gang rapes. I was tempted to find the phone numbers for Brett and Clayton but saw no purpose. any intervention of mine would be futile and people like that knew how to stay hidden. Eddy never appeared on national TV – he was still in mourning. But occasionally we saw him on BBC World Service, Deutschewelle, CCTV or France 24. He seemed like a zombie and his eyes looked like water balloons heaving and ready to explode.

CHAPTER TWENTY-THREE

Sharon tried hard to show she'd gotten over Miss Vie's death, perhaps in appreciation of how I took care of her while she was down. After the period of mourning she agreed to come with me to a very old restaurant on the hill where they served food using recipes from the days of slavery. Not long after we met I pestered her about finding an old eating place on a hill. It had been there forever. When she found it and called to book, no tables were available till after Christmas and she had to tell them I was visiting from London, had been to Oxford and was the biographer of the PM. They seemed to be impressed, said while they couldn't promise anything – all the tables were booked – we should come up. So we went, sat for ten minutes, drank strong rum punch made with sugar syrup, ginger and nutmeg and were ushered into paradise by a deputy manageress Sharon had been to school with.

Sharon looked stunning in her blue dress, as if she was poured into it and it was slit up to near her hips. I'd watched her putting on the blue set of undies I bought her after her shower so when I looked at her now I was seeing her naked. 'Your dress is giving me problems – you look so good I don't want to take it off but it's making me so horny I want to rip it off right now!'

'This is a high-class place, so no ripping off! You know I usually wear slacks – it's safer with the kind of men here – including you! I bought it in a shop owned by Jenny's cousin – you remember Stephen Walters' girl? I kept resisting till you said we should go here.'

'It matches your watch, necklace, earrings, bra and knickers.'

'That watch I saw, loved, knew I couldn't afford but it was calling out to me, as mermaids are supposed to lure horny, stupid men like you to drown yourselves!'

'You're too colour-co-ordinated – I'm going to have to remove your knickers!' My hand was almost there, she removed it but left it resting above her knee, leaned over and kissed me, putting rum punch in my mouth. It was homemade, like the one she mixed from her father's recipe. They had been playing Bob Marley since we came but as I felt the punch go down they started Christmas Carols, the first by Dame Joan Sutherland, and I remembered hearing it on the Green while on the way to Eddy's pad in London. it came from an internet café owned by the king of pirates in Somalia, who financed al Shabaab, or any force in charge in Mogadishu. Then they put on carols by the choir of King's College, Cambridge. I brought their CD last year and we'd listened to it a lot in bed – we liked *The Little Drummer Boy*. It added to the general festive atmosphere and reminded me why I got interested in the restaurant in the first place, when I saw it featured in a guide prepared by the Tourist Board.

It was the oldest restaurant in the country, part of a former Great House left by a plantation owner to a slave woman he married. The plantation had not been doing well – the woman refused to use slave labour and freed those she inherited. Her eldest son set up an eatery and told the cook to use all his mother's recipes. The place did well for a long time but started going down when the Chinese and Americans set up modern, cheaper restaurants with more accessibility nearby. But lately business had picked up when a son the family sent to Cambridge to study Law decided to become a restauranteur. In a piece he wrote for the magazine he said when he got to Cambridge he was terrified his classmates would be vicious racists who'd mock him for being a descendant of slaves and call him 'golliwog'. He decided offense was the best defence and went on the attack, belittling them for their skin like lepers, their incapacity to bear pain, their failure with women due to their small pricks. Soon they were begging to be his friends, hoping to win his acceptance and when he became the first black to enter the choir they treated him almost as a God. He discovered he had a brilliant voice and his fellows and choirmaster treated him even more divinely. I tried to see if I could detect his voice but couldn't.

It took them some time to bring the first course – thick, very spicy pea soup and by the time they did the rum punch was having its effect and Sharon stopped bothering how far I pushed my hand. I was happy we had come with Bunny and told him there was no point going back down the hill then up again. Sharon's friend gave him a place to rest and sent him superb food. From where we were we could see the whole town spread out below like an illuminated garden. If we looked on the other side there was a gap between peaks and we saw the spectacular skyscrapers of Blue Island where the Chinese tried to create their Shangri La. From up here it looked like a jewel, a carousel of rainbow lights and I tried to see the fifty-storey tower where Mr Wang had his hundred-million-dollar penthouse. I learnt that the hotel where we stayed and the one with Eddy's penthouse belonged to a consortium registered in the British Virgin Islands and Eddy, Mr Wang, and Chin had shares. 'You didn't tell me much about your weekend with Eddy in that hotel,' Sharon said.

'Totally boring, nothing to tell. I don't know why he called me, he was having a big party, I thought to celebrate his conquest of the universe – the American and Chinese ambassadors were there, going to Cuba to discuss oil with Fidel and Raoul. Then his mother died.'

'My spy told me all – the little sluts from the Academy eying you, the Latin American hotties, a beautiful woman who looked Indian – most likely Brahmin – who kept checking you out.'

'She probably was – she looked like a classmate from university who married a telecoms billionaire. I almost screamed when I saw her. Who was your spy?'

'That girl who apparently doesn't like wearing clothes. Eddy sent us to check out some house on the hill once. We took nice photos. Her name's Rosemary but we call her 'The Man-eater.'

'That bitch? Did she tell you how hard she tried with me?'

'No need. She knows we're together, but she'd love to fuck you then tell me about it. She's like that – she even told me about the girls she picked for the FM. I had to beg her not to tell Elena.'

'In other words, a sicko. I saw her at another of Eddy's places but didn't recognise her, she changed her hair.'

'Elena's friend in Security said she freelances for them sometime – honey traps.'

A man I supposed was the owner stood talking to the manager and looking over at us and eventually he strolled over.

He looked toned and healthy and I supposed he played polo or golf, or some such activity people of his class used to show they were not like the rest of us.

'Hello. Hear you went to Oxford, I went to the other place,' he said

'Grad' student. I was doing a DPhil, took tutorials and a few lectures but got bored and didn't finish.'

'Same here, I was undergrad'; went to do law but discovered I was more interested in cooking! Broke my parents' hearts to hear their son became a cook.'

'Brought a CD of your choir doing carols – but you were there long before. Sharon and I love it.' He didn't ogle Sharon or sneak a peek at her tits, more of which she displayed in this frock.

'Didn't think I'd like the place but being in that choir made me find peace. It's a bit busy these nights; we'll speak later. Sally...' He called Sharon's friend. 'Put them upstairs, they can enjoy the view, maybe see a few ministers with their teenage girl friends!'

I'd seen the alcoves upstairs for special guests – a merchant with another man's wife, a minister with an undergraduate mistress, a male celebrity from overseas with a boyfriend. I was surprised how much more we could see from up here, just a few metres higher. But I suppose that was the architecture of slave times, where you could see heaven from your house on the hill.

'I'm glad we came. I was beginning to worry I'd never get out of bed.' Sharon said happily.

'And now I'm feeling the punch inside, I want to get you back in bed!' My hand was sneaking up further, it was almost there, she held it, and I saw her looking down. 'Donnie and Lizzy!' she shouted. They were looking up, Sally pointed, and Elizabeth leapt up the stairs. I didn't recognize her at first; she looked more like when she was sixteen, the beautiful Ice Queen in *The New York Times* but now she was a more mature woman. Last time I saw her she was on a stretcher, like a homeless person they picked from the gutters, her hair like burnt weeds. She and Sharon grabbed each other as if they wanted to wrestle each other to the ground.

'Sher, you look so good; if I was a man you wouldn't stand a chance with me tonight!'

'Donnie, is why you don't control you woman?'

'You know Elizabeth, Sharon. You can't control her – and she's my manager!' Donnie and Sharon embraced while Elizabeth held onto me and squeezed.

'You know I meet the Prof. at Eddy's place in London, Sher. I laugh when Eddy call him 'Lover Man'! Ten of him would fit in Lover Man and still have space for a truck load of yam and stew!'

'I telling you, Prof., if I was a man I fighting you over this sweet gal tonight!' Raucous laughter shook the room.

'This is Donnie, we grow up together.' Sharon introduced us, smiling wider than I had seen her do in some time.

'Hello, Prof., enjoyed your book on Joseph. Hope the one on Eddy will be as good.'

If the Creator had looked at Lover Man and decided he needed an absolute opposite he would have made Donnie. The dancehall stars were huge but it was not their size that overwhelmed, you knew their fists, feet, forehead and guns could take you out. Their beards were like flags though not red, warning you of pain and shock. As I looked at Elizabeth I could imagine how much damage men like that had done to her body and knew the imprints left on her mind would never be erased.

Donnie was not a dwarf but you wouldn't notice him in a crowd and the new beauty in Elizabeth showed what his goodness brought out. He had a beard but like Che Guevara or Bob Marley, enhancers of gentleness. I could imagine Renaissance painters fighting over him, to find the perfect angle. Sally came up with a waiter bearing extra table settings and a new pitcher of rum punch. 'Tony said all this on the house!' she said, 'so I hope you have a driver!'

'I hoped this one would spend all his cash on me! What does a girl have to do to feel wanted?'

'You know how much I want you,' I said, pushing my hand further up. Sharon shot me a stern look, but her eyes were full of desire. I smiled, reassuring her I would behave.

'You haven't seen the contract Donnie just sign, for five record!'

'Almost enough to buy one of Eddy house, Sher!' Donnie said.

Winston wrote on politics and I'd forgotten the book he published with Jonathan Cape had won the Commonwealth Prize for first book. His piece on Donnie's music was a gem, he took it apart like he took apart Eddy's power base, only there the parts were all good; he predicted Donnie would be the first superstar from the Caribbean since Marley and would remain grounded, a genuine hero. The people downstairs were shouting Donnie's name, demanding he give them 'some tunes.' He ignored them but I knew a man like him was too thoughtful to avoid answering their call sometime tonight. He had to satisfy Elizabeth first and us, their friends, before getting to his fans. Elizabeth was so touched being with a man who didn't have to hurt her to feel pleasure. Suddenly she jumped up, pulled up her red silk smock with Chinese dragons and willow stems, grabbed Sharon's hand and pressed it against her stomach. 'Feel her kick, Sher! She's a girl but could be a footballer! Let the Prof. fuck you tonight to make you pregnant, Sher. Fuck her, Prof., give her a boy so he can marry our daughter!'

'Lizzie! You're such a naughty girl! Donnie, I told you to control you woman!' They play wrestled and I could see how happy they were. Donnie didn't want to get involved; he was under pressure from the shouts below to sing his latest hit, *Black Christmas,* for which bookies stopped taking bets on it to be number one on Christmas Day. The chef sent up their soup. Elizabeth wolfed hers down. But when they brought up the spiced chicken with green and red peppers, tomatoes, pimientos, shallots, and rice and peas she got that down fast too and Sharon gave me a look which said leave her alone, she was eating for two, eating her past drug addiction, past the pain she had endured from fists, elbows, foreheads and belt buckles, dealt by men who swore they loved her. Donnie took a long draught of rum punch, drank tap water we ordered without ice, stood up, kissed Elizabeth long on the mouth and squeezed Sharon's shoulder before going down to the deafening applause of his fans.

His first song was not the hit they demanded but a gentle serenade about a bird with a broken wing, its beak sunk in its breast feathers as it hung from the telephone wire, drenched with cold rain. Then the rain stopped, the sun emerged, its feathers dried, its wing was healed and it soared into the sky like a newborn star. Elizabeth was weeping, silently at first but then she started to mourn and Sharon took her in her arms and hushed her like she would her unborn child. 'Don't cry, Lizzie, don't cry. Donnie's here for you now, we're here for you.'

I'd always hated the dancehall musicians who used their voices and words like weapons, worshipped killing and violence, boasted of the young girls they 'tore up', the 'battymen' they beat to death, men they 'minced'. But here was a voice that was like honey, clear, sweet, smooth, entered your soul like a pleasant wind that cooled and comforted you. You could understand *words*. They burst inside you like bubbles from a drink you liked, turned round inside your head like the brightly painted horses on a carousel. Poor people reacted to lyrics by Rhino and Lover Man because they echoed the staccato of machine-gun bullets, the shouts of judges, soldiers and policemen, the screams of men being tortured, women raped, children battered and violated, the rumble and ache of hunger in their stomachs. When their words exploded from the giant sound-systems people heard the sirens warning them of pain, shock, horror, and the promise of much, much more. For the people terror was what they knew. Its echoes from musicians who boosted their thoughts of violence with drugs, while flashing the gold and silk of the music industry, gave them more of the same, leading them further into darkness, to which it seemed there was no end. But Donnie's voice spoke of hope, burst with light, told victims like Elizabeth they could be reborn.

When he finished his first song Elizabeth leapt to her feet, we followed her and soon the whole place was full of people standing, shouting, to Donnie that he had brought them back from hell. Then while the applause was at its highest his voice inserted itself and the shouts and screams flowed into silence as the lyrics of *Black Christmas* seeped into them. Donnie's words didn't echo Bing Crosby's. He did not sing of snow, the cold white flakes which reminded these men and women of waste, loss, desperation – purity and joy that was empty, cruel, sterile – which repeated its deceitful cries of happiness while men and women continued the cruelty and mercilessness of the year passing, which would come again, over and over, while the Saviour gave nothing and the souls of the tortured remained unhealed. For Donnie *Black Christmas* was the time when multitudes disinherited, despoiled, transported, alienated, tortured, impoverished and humiliated, found joy, love, hope, a promise for a tomorrow that was better than yesterday. People who had nothing could see their children living secure in the knowledge that the horror would end. People here were black, white, yellow, brown and mixtures of every colour between, but the song affected them as it had done among the descendants of slaves downtown when he sang in Miss Vie's old church, redemption was not just for the victims. These were rich people, the poor could hardly afford the fares to get up here to sweep the floors or wash the dishes but the song linked them to the poor, into a humanity that was possible if men and women had the courage to let it be.

Sharon and Elizabeth were in each other's arms like lost lovers, weeping like abandoned children, and for a while I felt empty and superfluous. The owner and Sally formed a circle with the other waiters, waitresses, and barmen, holding hands and weeping. I recognised the feeling. I'd felt like that when I saw Miss Vie's shining face, an image that would remain in my mind for as long as I lived. When Donnie finished some screamed 'Encore!' but the majority were satisfied, and as Donnie left the stage they sank back in their chairs to enjoy the rum punch and memories, while the singer returned to his woman. After the hurricane there was need for calm. Elizabeth dried her tears before she rose to embrace him, they held together for a long time, then Elizabeth pulled Sharon in and Donnie held me.

'Well done, Donnie. This will be the most deserved number one ever!' We clinked glasses – 'To the future,' we said. 'To Donnie,' the three of us said, as Elizabeth and Sharon kissed him and I shook his surprisingly firm hand. Unlike most of our current musicians Donnie didn't stir up heat, rage, the desire to set fire or violate. Instead there was peace. We sipped our drinks, allowed all that had entered us to digest slowly, become part of us, as we spoke of all that had been and would become tomorrow. Bunny rested in Sally's room but slept lightly and when I tapped the window he was immediately alert. Sharon brought him a cup of our refreshing coffee with milk, sugar and cinnamon, and he drank it slowly. I said 'our' coffee, forgetting the Chinese had bought that too. Donnie hadn't drunk much, but he was steady when we stood to leave, head and tongue sharp and clear. But the owner wouldn't take chances with such a national treasure negotiating lunatics and murderous bends downhill. 'I'm spending the night up here, Donnie. My driver will take you.'

'No need, star, I can drive.'

'You not driving tonight, Donnie – you know most of our drivers should be in the nuthouse!' Tony's voice was firm, brooking no refusal.

'Bye, Tony, bye Sally, and thanks,' we all said. 'We'll see you again.'

I looked at the crown jewels of skyscrapers on Blue Island, bright and shining like the sun rising in the morning, imagined a Chinese man winning ten-million dollars in Mr Wang's casino, handing a million to his companion from Brazil, Slovenia, Cuba, or anywhere else they conquered with their money. In the back seat Sharon and I folded into each other's arms, feeling no need for sex and slept before the car started and dreamt of Christmas day when we arrived. Bunny waited a while before waking us in the backseat.

CHAPTER TWENTY-FOUR

Christmas Day. I never believed in Christmas, always planned to spend the day alone, never acknowledged its existence with trees, presents, cards, or celebratory meals. I was in high school when I learnt the birth of Christ could not have taken place on twenty-fifth December, that Christians co-opted a pagan holiday to make their religion more acceptable to the unbelieving multitudes. But really my doubts began earlier, when my grandmother who saw nothing to celebrate on birthdays, implied that Christmas was just another day. She was supposed to be a good Catholic, a pillar of the church but refused to go to mass, gave no presents or cards and refused invitations to dinner or carol singing. She seemed to have had an argument with God and I never thought I had the right to question differences between two such omnipotent beings. But now I had Sharon and having her made me feel justified in celebrating. I felt like a new man, with no need to remain lonely and alone, now capable of joy and hopeful the horrors would end. I'd read something of Guevara where he wrote of new, socialist man, born of a society in which exploitative relations no longer existed. But my liberation had nothing to do with material relations or the politics it reflected, of power arranged in a pyramid where men oppressed and exploited men and women below them. Mine was the very un-Marxist, immaterial liberation of the spirit in which I could breathe.Donnie's *Black Christmas* had also given content to the debased idea of Redeemer, gave meaning to the idea of Saviour who could rescue the suppressed victim from the depths, as Miss Vie had rescued herself, then those who lost everything.

As he sang, his words made me feel wholesome as I now knew what it was to be free. All the works I'd read in philosophy, Marxism and Existentialism, in literature and science, I understood only in theory, as the Idea of Freedom. And now I felt it as something I could grasp. I saw what Elizabeth had become, saw in her restored mind and body the power of Donnie's healing words. And she was white, child of the most powerful slave owning family in Woodwater, heiress to its colossal fortunes.

Through abilities and opportunities she inherited from the oppressors she made another fortune, became manager and plaything of musicians who now dominated the social, political and cultural scenes and brutalised those they should have saved. But she too was a victim, because she bore the image of her ancestors. Like the mark of the beast, the musicians she promoted wanted to beat it out of her, in their perverted mission to seek redemption. They were now brutal oppressors themselves, just like the slave masters who exploited their ancestors, raped their grandmothers and wanted to take revenge, to crush the features they thought reminded them of their shame. They had money, power and this woman had brought it to them. But she was still

Cairncross and therefore deserved the tortures and humiliations. Like slave masters they tortured, plundered, raped, dominated, but still bore the mark of the slave and thought they could cut it out with blows to her head and body. But Donnie's healing words dissolved the master-slave relation and his love made her divided body and soul one again. And now we who had seen them, could enjoy Christmas.

On Christmas Eve Donnie invited us to a club where they played music by old musicians like the Mighty Sparrow, Don Drummond, Bob Marley, and now Donnie himself, the new, divine star of the musical firmament. We enjoyed the old music, felt the bond their lyrics and rhythms established with the people. But while we feasted on these great heroes, we were hungry for the new star, the simple man who did not need hysterics and braggadocio to impress. As he sang each tune seemed to open up new windows on reality, so we were swept into virgin arenas of the spirit. I looked at Elizabeth, a beautiful woman again, a mother expecting his child. She couldn't stop weeping and Sharon wept with her, celebrating redemption from the horrors. Bunny wanted to take us but we gave him money and told him to celebrate Christmas with his family. We told Donnie and Elizabeth we wouldn't stay late, that we had to drive home and wanted to be alone when the day arrived. They thought it a good idea and Donnie was cheered by the crowd when he announced that all lovers should be alone when the Saviour was born again. He sang his new song, with added feeling and intensity, they cheered again and again, wept copiously. Then we were gone.

Back home we drank more rum punch till midnight, kissed in celebration then gave each other our presents. Elena's 'cousin' – the FM said he had to be with his family at Christmas and when he saw how broken she looked, bought her mother a mansion in the hills where the Chinese just finished yet another development, which could be afforded only by drug dealers, politicians and contractors. She wanted us to spend the day with them but Sharon told her it was a special day for us. She knew how much I wanted to see the new book in the packet, how she had had to hit me and curse me for trying to peek. She knew how much I liked Scandinavian crime fiction, knew I'd read all the Stieg Larssons, Joe Nesboes, and most of Henning Mankell. She'd heard me extoll Wallander, the hero of Mankell's books, heard me say how cool he was, how believable the Swede, how tragic the actress who played his daughter, and when I heard she committed suicide I found it difficult to distinguish the actress from the character. So I was sure she had ordered the latest Mankell, recently reviewed in *The New York Times* online. I loved the review so much, looked so expectantly to reading the book that I couldn't shut-up talking about it. So when she handed me the packet and didn't shout 'Now you can shut your big fucking mouth, asshole!' I admired her control even more. My hands fumbled while I loosened the ribbon and I was seeing the cover even before I tore off the paper. Then I let out a strangled cry as if I opened a door and saw an old friend I thought had died. 'How'd you get this?' I had problems getting words out, there was too much air going into my lungs.

'You remember when the German embassy celebrated Goethe's birthday, and you said you wouldn't come – you wouldn't wear black tie? I met a First Secretary who I told about your obsession. He knew you; he said Böll would have liked your book because it was all about compassion. So when I told him what I wanted he said he knew an old companion of the writer who had two signed copies of *Billiard um halb zehn*. He said the man was a good friend of his father, a Professor at Heidelberg, so he was sure he could get me one.'

I was paranoid, jealous of any man she mentioned and should have got all rattled about some handsome German who had such contact with one of my heroes. But I was so thrilled holding the book, seeing the signature I'd regarded as scripture that I couldn't have budged if a grenade went off. The cover still looked new, though a little faded and I couldn't smell the new book odour. I remembered seeing a copy once, among a collection of signed works presented to our Rare Book Library by an uncle of John D. and Brett Farnham, the Ambassador to Germany. It had always been my dream to have a copy like this, confirming my belief that dreams never came true for those without power. I recalled the first time I read the book in German, the euphoria when I heard 'full of compassion the eternal heart' and thought all the horror had ended. I kissed her and almost couldn't stop until I broke off to hand over her own presents. I was embarrassed after getting the sacred work. What would she think of me getting her knickers, bras, slacks and blouses? But when she opened the package I saw her eyes brighten, her face light up when the colours confronted her. I saw her strip off and try the red set.

'Before we sleep we'll make love after I change into each colour! Merry Christmas!'

We were so exhausted when we fell asleep I was afraid we wouldn't wake up on the day. But I had a plan and woke early. She slept so soundly I had to check she was breathing. The peace I saw in her face was more Prof.ound than that I saw on Miss Vie's when she achieved relief from the hell Aaron had inflicted on her. When Sharon collapsed after hearing of her death, it was almost impossible to get her to eat. Elena said to try macaroons. I went out and bought some from *Emanuelle*, the new patisserie down the hill. She took a bite when I forced it into her mouth and from then on her recovery began. I searched 'macaroon' on Google, found a recipe and decided to surprise her. Although I didn't have moulds they came out fine, I tasted one and couldn't believe how well I'd done. I found a place in a cupboard where Elena had kept old dishes inherited from an aunt who returned after migrating to England. I hid the macaroons, so when Sharon finally woke and we showered together and had our Christmas dinner, I took them out for dessert. She couldn't believe I'd made them and when she tasted one she started to cry. I'd gotten carried away, put in a little white rum, Angostura bitters, cinnamon and nutmeg. But they kept their macaroon taste, now enhanced.

We drank more rum punch, decided to watch *Blade Runner*, and we finally saw it to the end. She was impressed by the character played by Rutger Hauer, the efforts he made to find his maker, his desire to extend his truncated existence of four years and the compassion he showed in sparing the life of the puny adversary sent to assassinate him. She was crying again and I was so moved by her tears I almost cried too. With her I now felt so fulfilled I didn't want this day to end and began to feel what a true believer must when Christmas comes. When the courier arrived with a throwaway phone from Winston, we both felt like a deflating balloon. Sharon cried for the third time and now there was no joy. A woman called about fifteen minutes later, said that a motorcycle rider would collect me at seven. I tried but couldn't get Sharon to stop crying and when I held her body she was shaking like a leaf in a hurricane. 'Don't cry, darling, it's Christmas Day, he won't keep me long.' But she couldn't stop and I had a vision of her drowning in her tears.

CHAPTER TWENTY-FIVE

The motorcyclist had old clothes and shoes for me again, and these stank even more than before, because my mind and body were now accustomed to the higher plane of joy I felt with Sharon. I recognised the boy, I'd seen him at the entrance to the estate when I went to see Trevor, the Colt 9mm under his green sports shirt stuck out like a promontory. I didn't want to go, it felt like cutting my arm off to escape from a trap but knew I had to – Winston wouldn't have interrupted our Christmas if it wasn't something important. When we rode up to the taxi, parked behind an old Chinese restaurant, Winston was driving, though I didn't recognise him. He'd shaved, his locks were cut off, clothes frayed and dirty like mine. He wore an old Michael Jordan baseball cap and drove like a taxi driver, his accent rough as some of the roads we passed on. 'Welcome, comrade. Sorry to take you away on such a day. It won't be safe to be near Sharon after this! Eddy and the Chinese plan to displace a lot of people from ghettoes near the sea, put them in dormitories to work in factories reassembling goods for the American market. In the old days this was the commercial centre, between the countryside where sugar and rum were produced, town where craftsmen and traders made the economy run. The rich lived on plantations but had places in town where they came for sports, the theatre, or to travel to the mother country. When we got our 'independence' we forgot about the economy and let this whole sector develop as a no-man's-land between the countryside, sea, and upper class suburbs, the so-called 'uptown'. Eddy and his Chinese friends think they know how to run an economy. They want to invest revenues from oil and other minerals in industry, some to supply the local market, some for exports to America and other Caribbean countries.' Winston hadn't said why he'd dragged me out, where he was taking me and I didn't ask, he was a smart guy and I could afford to be patient. The big hotel was almost finished, workmen were cleaning the multitude of shiny windows, each giant pane reflecting the fluctuating rigidity and fragility so unique to glass. Eventually, Winston began to talk.

'Moses wants to see you urgently, he has news about Eddy's plans since his mother died. You know the Americans did secret surveys, they knew the island was choc-a-bloc with oil and other treasure. They didn't tell the previous government, they didn't even tell Eddy, they thought they could get him to sign agreements like they used to with Batista, Mobutu, and other Arabs and stooges. They thought he was their boy and he bowed and scraped to convince them he was an Uncle Tom. But he knew their plans, being friends with Brett Farnham whose family ran the CIA and other branches of the American government. Eddy got the Chinese to do their own surveys, they found the treasures and were willing to pay the full whack to exploit them. The Americans were angry; they tried a coup but Chinese intelligence told Eddy and the officers were shot. You see what the Chinese are doing – they know Eddy won't double-cross them with the Americans. They can't do what the Chinese are doing. But Eddy resented the power people like Moses and the others who made him PM have. When his mother died he decided to settle scores; he couldn't ask the Chinese, that's not their style. So he turned to the Americans, saying he would let them have some of what the Chinese had. You know the American gung-ho attitude, the idea if force doesn't work you're not using enough. In Vietnam, Air Force General Curtis Lemay said. 'It was necessary to destroy the town in order to save it' after taking Hue, which the NLF captured without destroying a single building. From the time of Sun Wu Tzu Chinese generals knew the virtue of conquering without a fight, using deception and tricks. Mao said, 'When the enemy advances we retreat.' Eddy worked out a plan with the Americans to destroy the Estate Moses built and kill the man himself. The idea of asking for his extradition was a smoke screen. He wants to see you, spies in Eddy's camp said your name was on the kill list. He couldn't understand it – Eddy seemed to like you, he wanted you to write that book to immortalize his image, as you did for Joseph. I didn't believe it either – the spy must have concocted a list to increase his credibility with Moses.

I was in shock and disbelief. Eddy was smart. He had nothing to gain from killing me. My book on Joseph must have really got into his head, he believed in the magic of the written word. He thought he could live on through them if I put them on paper. To keep me on track he'd given me Sharon, with whom I was now hopelessly in love, given me money, and offered me a house that was like a fairy tale castle. He knew nothing of what Winston and Stephen told me, and drafts of my chapters, which

I e-mailed to myself in London were in code. So I had nothing to fear but would go see what Moses had to say. When we went through the opposition stronghold I saw the injured boy had survived; he sat on a rock like a thinker, his cannon pointed at the sky like a rocket, part of his shirt covering the wounded side of his face. His mouth was open and flies were buzzing around him. The vulture had not survived, as Winston slowed for a pothole, I saw feathers and what appeared like a beak.

Winston had been cheery since we met. He seemed full of vitality as he recounted the plans for mayhem Eddy and his American friends planned. I knew some of it was true – I knew Farnham and Whitney weren't here for the suntan, cheap rum or fucks. But Winston had gone quiet, that still silence you hear when a long, loud sentimental record you love comes to an end, and as I looked over it seemed he had retreated deep into himself, perhaps dreaming of a woman he loved deeply but now, like me, had to abandon on Christmas Day.

'We're taking the new road the Chinese just finished, comrade,' Winston said as we started seeing new blocks. Then out of the sky there was an explosion of light, colours and sound, and for a moment I thought Eddy had begun his war, forgetting Winston had said it was planned for New Year's Day. His face lit up, with fantastic special-effects and colours. I recalled the fireworks on Blue Island, how Sharon and I had gone from nightmare to joy as we realised how eastern magicians had transformed the tedium of night into nebulas of spectral beauty. I read where the inventors of gunpowder and fireworks had become victims of their own success when giant factories exploded resulting in hundreds of deaths. When they thought of shutting down the industry, Eddy came to the rescue, offering them the lease of another uninhabited island occupied by noisy birds for the past twenty-million years. It was called Guano Island, the British harvested bird shit from it for hundreds of years. Then they used it as a firing range, killing most of the remaining birds. The Chinese relocated their factories, introduced amazing technologies and now were producing the most spectacular fireworks in the world.

On Blue Island we were transported by the lights and colours; the bright explosions in the background. We felt we were out there, deep in space and time, at that instant when all that would be had emerged from a single infinitesimal point. The Chinese had transcended their own creations, now revealing colours and shades of light unseen since the beginning of time. I saw a point of intense light explode and expand till it was like a galaxy, filling all the space that was, then each star expanding again and again, filling space over and over, until nothing else could be. Then the stars were transformed into flowers, and I thought of Kew Gardens expanding till its blooms filled the universe.

Since I came to Woodwater I'd seen the most fantastic gardens, flowers with colours of such intensity I thought they could not have been of this world. There were stories of a woman, the late landscape architect, who tried to cover the island with colours of flame more radiant than the sun. I remembered the flower seller in Tennessee Williams' *Streetcar* but still couldn't recall her words. Now I beheld her, stark and unclothed, with bunches of wilted flowers saluting the bleak, grey sky. I saw every flower that had been and would ever be, each evolving into the other as the magic of explosions recreated infinity. I began to hear a sound more steady than the exploding fireworks but ignored it, The flowers were coming together, forming a tree of colossal proportions, and suddenly I realised this was the Christmas Tree I imagined and longed for as a child, when my grandmother said there would be no tree or presents as there was nothing to celebrate. And it was then I remembered what the flower seller said, heard the whine in the edge of her voice as she wailed '*Flores, flores, flores para los muertos flowers, flowers, flowers for the dead.*' Williams, whose work was suffused with decay, corruption and death, was homosexual in an American South where, like our country, being gay was far worse than being a murderer.

Winston too was caught up in the magic of light and flowers, as he handed me his phone; 'Call Sharon on this, comrade. Tell her we're almost there, we'll be home soon.'

'There's no signal,' I said.

'These people have the best network, comrade, never a problem with reception.' I showed him the blank space where the signal should have been, showed him my phone. Then I heard the steady sounds that were helicopters and thought of *Ride of the Valkyries* accompanying swooping choppers in *Apocalypse Now.* We were nearing the estate, I could see the tops of the towers surrounded by fireworks.

'The son of a bitch,' Winston shouted. 'Eddy brought the war forward; he's fucked up our phones!' By the time we got to the estate we saw Trevor and the boy who came on the motorcycle with AK47s in their hands, frantically signalling us to turn around. Tires squealed and I smelled rubber as Winston swung round and we swept back down the street we'd come along before we turned off on a side road I'd not seen. Trees joined across the road, we couldn't see the sky. Then as we sped along a curve in the road I saw the black Commando Land Rover parked in the shadow of a big mango tree. Winston tried to swerve out of the paths of the flaming bullets. Time stood still in an instant. I could see all there was from the time I was born, the childhood joys and horrors, the pain in my muscles as I ran, the medals, prizes for exams, scholarships, beauties I lusted after, the frustration and pain. I saw all that had been since the world began, saw Indie – we were together for thousands of years, went through the endless cycle of rebirth till the emptiness we could never refill exhausted us. With Indie I learned why I could not keep time, why it speeded up, slowed down, came to a stop. She thought of cycles of a thousand years, repeating until time ended. And now it was over, I saw a line of women I thrust into endlessly, dumping what could no longer be. My little girl of glass and all her companions traversed the horrors, drowning in bottomless torrents of tears, suffering beyond pain. And then I was in Sharon's redeeming arms, feeling her love and compassion, knowing what it was to be. Here was a woman that was pure, wholesome and true. And it was then I knew we would be together forever and ever and ever. 'I love you, Sharon, I love you so much. I will never love another woman the way I love you.' I waited for her answer, and thought it would echo and echo and echo.

CHAPTER TWENTY-SIX

The first time Moses looked into the mirror he thought he was seeing his brother Aaron. He looked behind the glass in confusion when he didn't see his twin. This confusion, of seeing double, would remain with him all his life. When he was alone, he felt his brother within him. When they were together, he felt they were one. Good and evil raged within them both and he couldn't tell his own acts apart from his brother's. Whatever Aaron did, he felt responsible and was torn apart, mutilated when Aaron started raping and killing, first their baby sister, then countless other women they loved. He hated Aaron for his acts of terror but in hating his brother he found he hated himself. He wanted to punish, annihilate him to remove the stain. But it made no sense to negate what he was. It took more horror than any man could bear before he found the courage to cancel what he knew himself to be and even after he knew Aaron was gone, that there was nothing left to grieve, he still had this nightmare of seeing two as one, the consciousness of experiencing the same and opposite inside himself, of being torn apart in his vision of the one. And now this schizophrenia had been enhanced by his nephew Aaron's son, the one he loved and thought of as his own. Despite all his efforts Aaron had got to his child, convinced him that Moses, the man Eddy could not distinguish from his own father, was the enemy, who threatened his ability to be. From when he was a boy, in and out of mental hospitals, Eddy had loved Moses as a father and hated him as a betrayer. As a man Moses sacrificed all to protect Aaron from the consequences of his own actions. To acquire the power he had, he gave up family, education, decency, human feelings, pleasure and when he failed with the father, he tried with the son. Now this son was gearing up to destroy him, the killer of his father, a project of revenge which consumed Eddy from childhood, seeing nothing beyond the darkness of the padded cells he was confined to, when the demons rose beyond his control.

Even without the oil and other minerals Eddy now controlled, Moses had money and power. As a powerbroker and kingmaker he had access to every luxury Woodwater had to offer, and much more powerful countries besides. Moses could afford and had been offered houses, money, jewels, women but preferred to live in the same community where his poor parents had relocated from their country village when he and his twin were boys. He had demolished the slum and built this estate to provide a base for his nephew's political career. The flat he lived in was no different from those of other residents, his friend – a great architect – had also designed the furniture. Now he sat on the couch made from mahogany and leather tanned from local cattle, stuffed with silk cotton from trees their slave ancestors believed harboured spirits dominating their lives. His friend had designed the buildings too, with huge glass doors and windows to let in light and drive out the demons. And everything reminded him of his brother, Aaron had killed his friend and his wife out of jealousy and fear.

He'd known of Eddy's animosity since he was a child but the goodness of Miss Violet made him suppress his hatred. When Miss Vie died Moses saw the hatred boil to the surface, knew the day of reckoning was coming. Moses recognised what to expect when he confronted Eddy over the shameful coffin he chose for his mother, saw the same inky incomprehension as in the eyes of his late brother. His nephew had spent a fortune to honour Miss Violet who had given up all to become what she was, a lone beacon of compassion in a land with nothing but contempt for the poor and weak. Just as he had shielded his brother from the consequences of his acts, Moses had ignored or compensated for his nephew's misdeeds. Eddy had made his first fortune selling weed, ganja was a natural herb the Rasta regarded as sacred and others used as medicine. Farmers grew it in the same way they cultivated yams, bananas or breadfruit. But heroin and cocaine, products of the white man's industries, killed the flesh and spirit, then corrupted what was good through its excess of profits.

When Eddy got involved in the trade on an industrial scale and killed without compunction to retain his place, Moses had the power to stop him but left him alone in honour of Aaron, his father. And he tolerated much more when Eddy neglected the poor to whom his mother devoted her life. But Moses had to act, when his nephew threatened his whole community and the uncle he associated with people – people he considered disloyal. Moses ignored the rumours of what people said he was contemplating, the intelligence of plans for destruction, of weapons imported and American Special Forces coming in to operate their machines of annihilation. His spies in Eddy's camp told of the plans scheduled for New Year's Day, the units to be committed, their deployments and weapons. There were lists of those to die and he was at the top. So Moses had designed a counter-offensive with the aid of his soldiers, a plan to attack Eddy's people before they could launch. Although he'd ignored rumours of his nephew's intentions he stock-piled weapons just in case, and his soldiers practiced operating them. He believed while it was wise to expect the best, it was wiser to prepare for the worst. Since the union he controlled represented all taxi drivers in the capital, no one would suspect when they started delivering soldiers on the night of New Year's Eve. And although he hated taking him away from Sharon on Christmas Day, he'd sent for the son of his friend.

When he heard Eddy brought his attack forward by a week, and was now launching on Christmas Day, he knew it was too late to put the counteroffensive into play and decided he had no choice but to rely on Donnie, the one man capable of taking out Eddy himself, to defeat the snake by cutting off its head. Moses' anger that Gimpie, the man who informed him of the attack on New Year's Day – Eddy's deceiver – was allayed when the Gimp risked his life to come and warn Moses of the change. His problem was now to contact Winston and warn him not to bring the writer who had done that wonderful book on the late Joseph. But when he tried to call he discovered the networks were blocked. Moses was angry at first and cursed the nephew so treacherous he would interfere with people's ability to feel joy on Christmas Day. But Moses smiled, acknowledging he would have done the same if he planned to destroy his enemies!

CHAPTER TWENTY-SEVEN

Elizabeth couldn't take her eyes from the sleeping body of her lover where she lay on his arm, her hand caressing his face, as if she were an artist trying to find a way to improve on perfection. She concentrated on that face of incandescent beauty, as if to compensate for scars maiming his body like craters on the moon, white zebra stripes where the flesh was stripped, marks of belt buckles. Just below his trembling heart two bullet holes, neat as coins, looked out like birthmarks. She knew his pain, she too had experienced the horror. The morning was warm and since they didn't like air-conditioning they hadn't used sheets to cover. Birds kept up a steady chorus of chirping, as if to celebrate the joy of Christmas Day and communicate with lovers the promise of rebirth. She felt the child inside her move, had to suppress the sob threatening when she studied the fine features of the man who cherished her enough to commit this loving part of himself to her. This was paradise, a day so unlike any she'd experienced – a day she didn't need drugs to blot out reality, fists, foreheads and belt buckles to keep reminding her that life was pain.

With her money and the contract Donnie signed, they could afford the most expensive houses in the capital. Her father had so many he had no idea where some were. But this apartment on the estate was where they found peace and joy. Donnie was brought-up here, and when he asked for it Moses gave him. His breath was so smooth she could hardly see his chest move below the bullet holes, and her longing for his love was in the words of his track on the CD now playing.

The night before, they were together with Sher and her friend, Prof. He looked so neat, composed and controlled, she thought he was one of those very normal people whose behaviour you could predict and be bored to death. But when she looked into his eyes she saw what she experienced when she looked in the mirror. When she mentioned his parents old house he appeared to shrink, though he showed no sign he recognised the place, or had any memory of what happened there. She identified with him but his situation was worse. She knew every measure of what she suffered and, until Donnie, could not get them out of her head. She saw compassion when she looked into his eyes. She remembered the massive houses where she lived as a child; her quarters could have been in another country, even another planet. She remembered her mother, a spectral presence even when she was small. She was locked away in a mental institution in England for years before she died, though Elizabeth's cruel friends said she was imprisoned in the dungeons of the castle, together with her zombie grandmother. The same 'friends' said John Cairncross was not her father, that her mother had Elizabeth with her own brother. Cairncross didn't act like a father, he was hardly around, and there were so many servants acting as parents she could hardly remember their names.

When he was around she saw him in the distance, hunting on horseback with drunken friends or in big rooms with drunken companions, doing things to servant women or children. She remembered the little boy kicked by his horse; her father didn't stop to tend him but continued the hunt and the boy died. She wandered the land like a hermit, seeing strange people working the farms or strange animals waiting for the hunters. She remembered the bird with the broken wing clinging to the telephone wire, how frightened it was when it fell and she took it in to make it whole again; it did not lose its fear when it healed and she set it free to fly again.

When she was seven she saw a gardener doing things to a servant girl from the kitchen and when they saw her, they called her the crazy one and told her what to do. She felt the pain when the man entered her and after that she could never enjoy what men did to her – until Donnie. When she was ten a driver took her to the Academy in one of her father's Rolls Royce's and the other girls never stopped mocking her for being 'crazy' and a Cairncross. She felt so lonely she sneaked out to the ghettoes to find men who would give her relief, to make up for the pain and frustration she felt with the gardener who mocked her for being her father's child. When the nuns wanted to expel her for leaving the school at night, Miss Vie said 'No!', that she would take care of the child. And Eddy's mother became the first person to make her feel love, show she was wanted, make her stop mutilating herself. From that time Miss Vie was there for her when she overdosed, when her musicians beat her unconscious and she felt she was about to die. When others criticised her and said she should stop wasting time and let the little slut die, Miss Vie said, 'It's not for us to judge.' When Miss Vie died she tried once more to end it but was too weak to kill herself. Donnie rescued her and now they lay in peace on Christmas Day, as if they were in heaven with Miss Vie.

'You're so far away, darling, thought you were on another planet,' Donnie whispered.

'You was sound asleep, I don't want to wake you. Our little girl movin' as if she know is Christmas!'

'I'm sure she does; she going to be spirited as her mother!' He rubbed her stomach and felt the tiny feet and hands move.

'God forbid she going be like her mother.' She sounded like she would cry but he hushed her, covering her mouth in a kiss that was soft and comforting. 'That was a good night we have, Donnie.'

'Yes, darling. Sharon and her man get along so well; they really good people, so good for each other. Like you said, hope they get a boy so he can marry our princess!'

'Yes. He so quiet you think he have nothing to say but Sharon say you can't shut him up when he start teasing or playing trick on her. And he write that book on Joseph which no-one who read it can forget. Joseph now in everybody head, no matter how hard Eddy try to make them forget. Eddy change, he use to do some bad thing when we small but Miss Vie control him. Now she not here, I don't know. I looking on you while you sleep and thinking of Miss Vie, Donnie. I almost cry when I remember seeing her in that coffin. I don't believe she dead, I think she just sleeping, you know how calm she look when she sleep. But the nurse said no, she gone, and I go so crazy they have to hold me down and give me drug. When I wake up I find myself in a bedroom in one of Eddy house.'

'Is Christmas, sweetheart. Miss Vie at peace, she don't want us to be unhappy. I going have a shower and dress in that new clothes you buy me. Then we go to Moses' for dinner. He say he going make nice food like Miss Vie use to make for you, Eddy and me. Me looking forward to cow peas soup!'

She was still so full of joy she cried while he showered, thinking of the night before. Sharon's man said the taxi driver needed to spend time with his family at Christmas so they came in an Avis rental and said they had to leave early before they drink too much. Donnie say it was a good idea and tell his fans they should all go home early if they didn't come with taxi. The drive home was magic, there was a full moon which made the streetlights look like candles. The BMW almost drove itself and she slept in Donnie's arms, dreaming of Miss Vie up there, cooking Christmas dinner for them.

~

She'd never seen Moses so happy, he was almost boisterous as he teased Donnie about his woman and daughter, his shiny suit as if he was a little boy showing off for Christmas! He did look so fine, in that special blue outfit the tailor make for him when they sign that contract. It looked like silk but it was satin and had a lot of pockets and flaps. People kept coming in from all over the estate, some eat and drink then leave, making way for others, and men their age tease Donnie, now he was a rich superstar, with Elizabeth, his woman, bearing his child!

Elizabeth was so happy she almost cried again but kept it down to enjoy the jerk pork he brought her with a piece of snapper seasoned with scotch bonnet peppers and vinegar and red peas cooked with long grain rice. They had a rum punch when they arrive but someone bring Moses some really good sorrel with white rum, cinnamon and ginger, and they drink that before they go home to sleep, promising to come back later.

While Donnie slept they listened to a CD with a collection of hits over the ages and she got impatient listening to Harry Belafonte, Lord Kitchener, the Mighty Sparrow, Ossie Davis, Don Drummond, Burning Spear, Bob Marley and Peter Tosh before Donnie come on. She started crying silently when she heard him sing about the bird with the broken wing clinging to the cold telephone wire then couldn't control herself when she heard the lyrics of his *Black Christmas*. She couldn't stop when Donnie's little brother banged on the door, shouting Moses wanted to see him, that it was very urgent. The little boy was another of the orphans Miss Vie brought for Moses to bring up. 'Don't cry, darling,' Donnie said, wiping her tears then kissing her cheek. 'Don't cry, baby, I soon come.'

She cried and cried; she knew she could not stop crying till he returned. She was crying when the explosions started and she thought the world had come to an end. She felt her body expand to fill the void; she was cold, her body shivered like it did when she was coming down from a heroin fix or recovering from a beating so bad she thought she had died. Then, from the steady flashes and expansion of light she knew the Chinese were setting off fireworks to celebrate a Christmas they didn't believe in. But she couldn't stop crying and when the explosions were louder and she felt vibrations in the floors and walls and saw the masonry falling, she knew why she cried.

CHAPTER TWENTY-EIGHT

Donnie's mother was the most beautiful child in the school, so beautiful the nuns spoiled her, believing she was the image of the Holy Mother of God. She also came first in her exams, was so good in sprints they expected her to make the Olympic team. And her parents also spoiled her – they thought she was a gift from God. But she met a boy who was equally beautiful, he too was spoiled, worshipped by all, and she thought of him as the God of her heart. When she stopped seeing her monthly blood and felt the child moving inside she knew what horror was and wanted to get rid of it but she loved life and loved her beautiful boy and thought it sinful to contemplate ending what was so without peer. When she told her parents they too felt as if they were sunk to the depths: they had hopes of their daughter becoming a lawyer, doctor or Olympic champion. But he was a pastor, his wife a good woman who loved him as much as their daughter and they tried to find hope in their despair. The pastor had grown up with Moses, whom he regarded as an older brother, until his friend became the most powerful criminal in the country, the don of the most notorious ghetto, mass killer of repute. The pastor made his name by his strident condemnation of gangsterism. Now so far down was he that he called on the don, who advised him life was too precious to be wasted, that as the parents of his unborn grandchild were children themselves, he should find a good man to marry his daughter, promising to help in any way to provide means to build a foundation for the couple. The pastor was too holy to accept Moses' capital but wise enough to take his advice, thinking he knew just the man. He was a naive and forgiving man and thought a young deacon in his church would be ideal, especially as he would cash in his savings to buy them a nice little house. The young man was handsome, he thought his female parishioners were gifts from God but his would-be stepfather thought responsibility for his wife and child would ground him, that the security of owning a house would cure him of his need for constant conquests. He thought Moses had done enough, that he might risk the wrath of God to involve a don any further in his family's affairs. So when Moses advised him it was necessary for the deacon to be sent to him to ensure he would not take advantage of his wife and the generosity of his stepfather, he thanked Moses, said he had it all under control, that he would leave all to God, in whom he had absolute Faith. But the young deacon thought the God who made him had done him wrong. He had an obligation to continue giving him gifts. He regarded his new wife, her son, the house, and the good name of the family as part of these gifts, saw no reason to relinquish the others. He was adopted, through research he found out his real mother too was a beautiful schoolgirl who gave birth to him and was disinherited by her rich father who took her child away. His mother was now a notorious harlot, a drunk who flipped between life on the streets and stays in the insane asylum. So he regarded all women as prostitutes, thought he could redeem them by fucking and beating, and believed his whore of a young wife was no different. When he looked at his stepson, he saw not a beautiful child but the man who defiled her. He saw his wife as a harlot who had betrayed him and now regarded himself as a whore also – her father had paid him with a house.

Donnie's mother was remarkably mature for a teenager. Having a child made her into a woman and she did everything to make a home for her husband and child, no matter how much he drank, stayed out late, or slept with every woman in his congregation. When he came home and saw her and her child he thought of his mother and visited his wrath upon them to cleanse himself. When he woke up sober he often felt guilt and tried to show his family he cherished them but when he went out and got drunk again, fucked women whose faces he could not remember, he came home to beat the mother and her bastard child with even more ferocity, using his fists, feet, belt buckle, whips, sticks and iron pipes. His wife started using make up, wearing special clothes to hide her bruises and explained that the injuries to her son were because boys could not keep still and had accidents. And since her father was a man of faith, thought he had no right to interfere in what God had put together, he left them to their devices. His wife was a good woman, she believed God put the yoke of leadership on men and left matters in the hands of her husband. But in the nights while the Pastor slept she wept for them, wishing that God would perform a miracle to save them, or take her up to Him so she could have peace.

Despite her finest efforts Donnie's mother could not get her son to grow and by the time he was five he looked like a three-year-old. His speech was that of a two year old and when he was seven she found it difficult getting him into school; the teachers said he was retarded. It took her father's influence, aided by Moses, to get him into an elementary school, and she warned him never to take his clothes off, so his teachers and other children wouldn't see his scars. She looked ten years older than her sister who followed her by a year but her father warned concerned relatives that marriage was the concern of a family and their God, and that no one had the right to interfere. But as he didn't want his daughter and grandson to starve, he gave money, food and clothes to her when he went to visit while her husband was not home. From the day she was married his mother hid Donnie in closets, drawers, under beds and chairs when her husband came home drunk, sometimes with his flies open after fucking his women and pissing on himself. In his hiding place Donnie heard the smack of his stepfather's weapons on his mother, heard the hysteria and hate in his voice as he cursed her for whoring, those sounds magnified to infinity as they exploded in his head. Occasionally the deacon was sober enough to remember him, seek him out and visit punishment on his head and body as his mother tried to restrain her husband, pleading that he spare her innocent child. And next time, crouching in some dark recess, feeling the wet sneak down his legs, he heard the poundings on his mother and felt ten times her pain. Each time he was hit he thought the pain could not get worse, till the next time, and soon his body was one massive sore and his mother had to beg for antibiotics from an aunt who was a nurse to stop him dying of infection.

When he was eight and saw how bigger boys punished others with their fists, knives and iron bars, Donnie began to have visions of his stepfather no longer around them and his mother and himself at peace. After some time he could not distinguish his visions from reality and smiled at his mother for the peace he thought she was now enjoying. But then he saw the terror on her face when she heard the bangs on the door, the screams of 'Whore!', and her frantic efforts to hide him. But he was becoming tired of feeling his mother's pain from the darkness of concealment, tried to resist her attempts to spare him, only to find she had superhuman strength to shove him where she thought he would be spared.

The school wanted to expel him; he was learning nothing, was absent most of the time, and wet himself when confronted by teachers or other boys. But his grandfather and Moses appealed to the principal, who let him stay until he disarmed a much bigger boy and almost decapitated him with his knife. By the time they expelled him he had grown and now had muscles. He was ten and cooking and washing for his mother who was confined to bed by the beatings and lack of food. She was also hallucinating, seeing her husband as the devil poking her with his blazing fork and Donnie's angelic father swooping to rescue her from his magic castle. Sometimes she asked her son who he was. Her husband was away longer than usual; perhaps he found a woman drunk enough, or desperate enough, to think she could keep him. When Donnie heard him banging the door and cursing his 'Whore!', he saw his mother on the couch, her eyes wide and empty, her mouth gaping, the spittle foaming from the corners like crests of waves. As her husband kept banging and screaming he was becoming hysterical and accusing her of hiding inside to fuck men and give him another bastard. Donnie didn't see when she rose and opened the door and as the man rushed in he passed her to find her man in the bedroom. Then he was back, fists raised and she crashed to the floor as he slapped her time and time again then punched her down. Her eyes were glass and she was hardly breathing. 'Is where him is, woman? Is where the man is who fuck you and give me this grey eye jacket?' He became angrier when she didn't reply and started kicking her in the ribs. When she didn't respond his face distorted more, he was choking, his mouth frothed and he looked for something special to hit her with. He saw the glint of the trophy she won in the 100m when she was fifteen and raised it to smash her head open when he was shocked into silence to hear her bastard, 'Leave my mother alone, you coward, drunken, whore monger. Put your hand on her again and I going cut you head off.'

The deacon couldn't remember ever hearing the boy speak, he had grown but still appeared stunted and the butcher knife he held was almost as broad as his chest. Then the deacon laughed; this was the funniest scene he had ever seen, the whore of a woman on the floor and the weed she produced to shame him about to join her, both heading for the deepest pit of hell. He raised the trophy to consign this boy to the perdition he deserved before the day he was born, in humiliation that could never end. He was still laughing, he felt himself euphoric when his arm stopped in mid-air, the laugh froze on his face, the alcohol in his system solidified. His arm was still raised, his fingers gripped the metal trophy but he felt the arm was no longer his, experienced the same disembodiment as when he found out about his mother and the men who fucked her. Then he tried to raise the other arm, to see if he could find its mate in the void where it floated but saw droplets of blood splash out like shooting stars. His other arm went numb too as the steel flashed and he saw his body detach as the blade thrust into his abdomen, chest and face, again and again and again. Now, for the first time in life, he felt peace, watching his body float in emptiness, silence, eternity, light and ice.

When Donnie's aunt came to look for her sister who had not answered her call, she whimpered as she knocked and received no reply. Tears ran down her cheeks as she cursed the useless drunkard for killing her sister. She screamed when she saw her lying on the floor, her fears confirmed, and in the dull light she thought the husband was in drunken sleep, next to the woman he had killed. But when she came close enough she was confused, wondering how the man could sleep when his body seemed so strange, arms twisted at impossible angles, head in shadow. Then she saw her nephew squatting on the floor, knife upheld like a crucifix between his crossed legs; her screams rushed back inside her, echoing like a distant drum. The boy was staring into the empty eyes of his tormentor's head, emptiness into emptiness. Inside the aunt's chest the whimpers echoed, as if forever.

Psychologists at the juvenile court told the judge the boy had an IQ of nearly two hundred but was so damaged by abuse it was impossible to cure him. So they recommended he be locked away in the asylum as his mother was, never to be released. The judge agreed and was about to sign the papers when his grandfather again appealed to Moses. The don was so struck by the beauty of the boy, the innocence in his features but also the horror in his eyes, he decided to save him. He felt he was seeing Aaron's eyes again, the depths of blackness from which light could not escape. He had an audience with the judge and the man agreed to release Donnie, Moses had the power to protect the public from his evil far better than any asylum, even if the walls were a mile thick, made of special steel. He was also becoming wary of the crazy people running the country, threatening to take his beautiful house uptown and give it to whores, musicians and madmen. So he was grateful when Moses gave him the title to a magnificent house in Palm Beach, with heart-shaped swimming pool and automatic gates, an endless supply of young girls and old rum. Moses was surprised by the gentleness of his newest adopted son, whose name the judge had agreed to change so people wouldn't know he had butchered his abusive stepfather. He was a beautiful child but anytime someone approached he whimpered like a sick puppy.

It took time for Moses to convince him that even with his power he would never hurt him and he learnt to smile and say 'thank you, sir' or 'ma'am' when anyone did him good. Soon he acquired the reputation of a polite, well-mannered young man and women began remarking how different he was from other boys. He taught himself to read, was soon enjoying books for adults, works of Fanon, Achebe, N'gugi, Greene, Marquez and Marechera. Moses hired tutors who said how brilliant he was, one of them entered him for the exam to St Dunstan's and he won a scholarship. Moses was proud when he read the school reports, the statements by the priests that he was the most intelligent, polite, kindest, boy they ever saw. Everyone said he was a shoo-in for university, and more pious priests swore he would enter the Jesuit order and become the first indigenous Bishop of Woodwater. But Donnie had suffered from the time he suckled at his mother's breasts, seen the person he loved more than any other battered and bruised into madness. He had seen the adults who had power refuse to fend off the blows, watched them pray to a God they said was all-knowing, all-powerful, merciful, full of compassion. But none of this had provided a shield or dulled the pain. He and his mother had gone to hell, been dragged out, beaten, battered and kicked down again and again and again, till suffering was like breathing air. God, His Angels, the church, his grandparents, all his adult relatives left them to drain the bitter cup, with no milk and honey to cut the gall. He could no longer visit his mother in the asylum, she looked at him with those empty eyes, not knowing his name or acknowledging his existence. What had put an end to hell and pain was steel and he remembered the relief when the blade struck and struck, smelt the fear in the convulsions of the man whose blows had tormented him and the woman he loved more than the world. In his mind he could appreciate the strength and generosity of Moses, the kindness, dedication and intelligence of the priests, the goodness of strangers who did good for others who were down trodden and weak.

When he read the books of great masters he was transported into their visions of heaven, paradise, nirvana, the universes where nobility, honour and compassion reigned. But nothing approached the joy he felt in killing, the relief in destroying the enemy, the redemption he experienced from mutilation and death. So when he was not in school, or burying his head in a book, he sneaked out and joined the gunmen sent by Moses to ensure his word was law. He rode pillion on their Jingchen motorcycles and they let him – he was favourite of the Don. Then, when he asked to participate, they let him and found he was a good technician – there was no tremor in his hand when he pulled the trigger. But he asked them to wait when they hastened to escape, and when they saw what he was doing everything they ate that day came up. With multitudes of dons in the ghettos, killing had become routine so gunmen regarded it as a job, like civil servants obeying the General Orders. Mothers were proud of their sons; they benefited when their boys died and the Don made them presents of a house or money. They felt honour when their child was sent off in a magnificent mahogany coffin and air-conditioned hearse.

When a killer was big enough to merit burial in the Garden of Remembrance, mothers felt like their sons' had been knighted by the Queen or welcomed into heaven by St Peter. But what Donnie did after he shot his first man changed all that. Beheading was worse than castration; it was visible, told the world the dead was no longer a man. A mother could no longer feel proud her son was in heaven, waving his 9mm Glock on the right hand of the father. They felt horror without end when his head was dumped at their front door or suspended from a nearby light post. Just as a woman could not grieve if she lost a son who was a battyman she could not weep for his corpse without a head. So Donnie became a legend among gunmen, because they feared oblivion. Moses was unhappy, he loved Donnie, hadn't wanted him to become like other criminals who regarded killing as a trade. But due to his love he wanted his son to do what gave him pleasure and he was good at it. Moses found opponents now respected him more, they feared this new dimension of terror Donnie had brought. But he still hoped Donnie would become a doctor, engineer, lawyer, or something his talents and intelligence merited. When he started to sing and Moses saw how wonderful his voice was, it gave him great joy and hope, this talent would detract him from murder. He had Elizabeth to thank, her love saved Donnie and made him a superstar, just as Miss Vie's love had saved Elizabeth from killing herself through drugs and fucking men. She looked so wonderful now, so full of joy, with Donnie's child inside her, that Moses wept when he was alone. Which was why he felt such sorrow now, when he had to call on Donnie to save them from the madman. 'You can say no, Donnie. You have a woman now, expecting you child; you is a big singer. Me have no right to ask you to give up all that.'

'You more than father to me, Pops. Without you I in that cell with my mum. I sure I dead by now.'

'I never want you in this business, Donnie, you know that. You the best student in school, priest expect you to be doctor, engineer, lawyer, even bishop. This is the last thing I expect from a boy like you. Eddy become politician and he don't have half you brain. Is only because he now like Aaron I have to ask you. If you say no I can't blame you, son.'

'I can't say no to you, Pops; is you make me what me is and what you need now, what we people need, me can do best. So don't worry; I going get Eddy, cut the head off the snake.' Moses held him and there was wet in his eyes.

'Goodbye, Pops. You know I soon come back.'

'Goodbye, son.'

The gun he always used was in the flat but he couldn't go there: Elizabeth would be crying and the thought of her and their daughter might unsettle him when the time came for total concentration. He had a spare in the armoury under the generator house and that's where he went now. The British set it up during World War II when they heard the Germans planned a base in the Caribbean to attack America. They forgot about it, but when Moses became Don he knew he needed one and had the Americans build a big Lister generator house on top to hide it. Donnie went down the steps and admired the weapons Moses imported from Florida to protect the estate, the mortars, RPGs, sniper rifles. He ignored the fantastic 9mm automatics with laser sights, the Glocks, Smith & Wessons, Scorpions and Colts, and opened the wood cupboard where he kept the old spare .38 Colt, along with the bullets, sport shirt and khaki trousers he wore on missions. Then he went to the shed where they kept the bikes, avoided the Hondas and other modern, high powered jobs, and mounted the Jingchen he always used, feeling he was united with an old friend.

CHAPTER TWENTY-NINE

The wind teased through his hair gently. He wore a tam of green, red, gold and black, and as the threads were broken by the wind he felt tiny raindrops on his scalp. It felt good to be on the road again, knowing at the end of it was salvation, the sacrifice of the beast. Eddy would be dead and the community would live again. He was so used to the Jingchen he felt it was part of him, like his arms and legs. Its simplicity was organic; it was his favourite horse. He hadn't forgotten where the roadblocks were, the secret outposts of Eddy's Commando, CCTV cameras the Chinese introduced as part of their construction programs. Although they had made such changes in the geography of the city, the back roads, gullies and unfenced backyards were still there, so if he thought he saw a suspicious vehicle he knew where to slide off. What he did was so much a part of him it was like writing a song, the order to put the words in, the tune to fit like the sports shirt he now wore.

One thing he liked about masters like Achebe and Greene was that he could predict what was to come by following the relentless logic of their actions. Eddy had so many houses it was difficult for one who did not know him to figure where he would use for command and control. But Donnie knew him, they grew up together, Moses and Miss Vie were like their parents, and he knew exactly where he'd be. He'd seen Eddy on top of the world when he boasted as a child about changes the Chinese were now making. The transformation of a small, provincial, decrepit and decaying capital of a poor Third World country into the modern city he was now passing through; where the massive forty storey hotel was near completion. He'd also seen Eddy stricken, unable to move, talk, almost unable to breathe, uncertain his heart and mind were moving, so his mother, Eddy Senior, and uncle Moses panicked, prayed to God to keep Eddy alive and wept, shaking and gently slapping him, till the psychiatrist came and said he had to be re-admitted. Donnie knew where he would be, where he felt comfortable when he was growing up, where his mother and Uncle Eddy gave him all the love a child could wish for and Aaron, before he was butchered and dismembered, poured all the hate which now impelled him to destroy all who had made him what he was. Though he would not do what he was now doing if she were alive, he would be in his mother's house where he thought her spirit would still protect him with her love. Her husband had died and she moved to more humble surroundings but she was there in the old house and that is where her son would seek relief from the horrors inside his head.

When Donnie went to pay respects to the bier of this sainted woman, he saw where the Chinese were transforming the house and those next to it into an almost Germanic blockhouse of impregnable power. He'd driven past later, seen its near impenetrable façade, recognised that Eddy had been humiliated when his mother sold it to live in a hovel like the ordinary people he mobilised to worship him like the king of kings, the Prince of Addis the deluded Rasta bent their knees to. He even knew where in the giant compound he'd be, where his mother had been moved by compassion to forgive the man who violated her and pledged to give all she possessed to the poor, recognising that the child who suffered from the violation was poorest of the poor. Eddy loved his mother with an intensity that was part of his illness but hated her for never wanting anything for herself, so all he acquired to be worthy of her were like empty buckets.

Donnie knew when the Chinese built a fortress they always dug a tunnel to let the commander escape if he was overwhelmed. They had learnt this through five thousand years of siege and their belief in *Feng Shui* dictated where it should exit. The cheap Chinese bike was like a magic steed, he lost all notion of time when he mounted it, and between departure and arrival he could see no difference. As he approached, the floodlights were powerful enough to intimidate would-be enemies. But the door to the escape exit was concealed, hidden from the coruscating light. On his way he passed the electricity sub-station where he asked a friend to kill the lights on the next time signal of the BBC World Service. He waited by the escape exit till the lights went out and before they were back he was inside. The sub-station was off for just twelve seconds, before the fifteen it took for the emergency generators to kick in. In the dark he already recognised Miss Vie's living room, could sense Eddy close by, and felt his love for his daughter, Elizabeth and Moses well up within him as he anticipated the end of this madman who threatened all he loved. The gun in his hand felt as if it had always been there, a feather, born with him when he felt the blow on his mother's head from the first man he killed. Then the light exploded like the sun, so sudden he could see nothing before he was on the thick carpet and the smell of Gillette deodorant and gun oil was drowning him. The hands holding him were so strong he felt his face push through to the wood floor beneath. They didn't need to say 'Don't Move' – their strength made that superfluous. He was down for an instant but such moments seem forever, and it was an eternity before he heard Eddy, 'Let him up and get out of here – all of you.'

There was warmth in his voice like when they were boys telling stories about triumphs they made on the sports field. Eddy had never been patient, when he gave orders he expected to be obeyed. That was part of his illness. 'What part of "let him up and get out of here" you didn't fucking understand?' Eddy had such inhuman control Donnie enjoyed the times he lost it. When they freed him he saw there were five, in jeans and polo shirts, two holding his arms, two his ankles, and one the back of his neck. They held M16s in their left hands, pointing down, and one placed Donnie's old .38 on a glass table near Eddy. 'That's what he came with,' the leader said dismissively, as he entered numbers into a keypad with glowing red circles. The door was thick, opened slowly and took forever to close. 'Welcome, Donnie, we expect you with Elizabeth to share a Christmas drink and food!'

'Leave Elizabeth out of it, Eddy.' He was holding on to Donnie, real tight, as he'd done when a boy. They'd loved each other as children, when Eddy wasn't in the mood – when he thought everyone except his mother wanted to destroy him. Eddy had come in with a tall man in skin-tight blue turtle-neck, faded jeans and aviator sunglasses. 'This is Donnie, Brett; we were like brothers when we were growing up. Donnie, meet

Brett Farnham, my classmate from Florida State.'

'Nice to meet you, Mr Brett. Any friend of Eddy's a friend of mine.'

'Good to meet you, sir. My wife and I heard you in Madison Square Gardens – she said you reminded her of her brother; he too had a beautiful voice. Media described you as the new Bob Marley.'

'Glad to hear that, Mr Brett. Glad you all liked my singing. My friend Eddy here likes my singing too.'

'I have some DVDs I'd like you to sign for us, sir. Maria will be so thrilled to hear I met you.' He tapped in the numbers and Eddy waited till the door shut before he spoke.

'Sit down, Donnie, sit down. *Mi casa, es su casa*, as we say down in Florida! Brett and Maria just married, they're here on honeymoon, but you understand Maria couldn't be here tonight.'

'We're so old fashioned, Eddy, we keep our women out of our wars.'

'This don't have to be a war between you and me, Donnie. Miss Vie treat you like a son, me father love you so. Moses more than a father to both of us. Any difference between you and me we can talk about, settle like we always use to.'

'Before I leave for here, Moses say the attack coming, I hear the helicopter moving in, Eddy.'

'Moses is a old man, star. I surprise you stay with him so long. Every time I expect you and Elizabeth to come round. When you going ask me to be godfather to you pickney?'

'You know what Moses do for me, Eddy, you know the man more than a father to me. How I going betray such a man?'

Eddy so rarely lost it that when he was angry he looked like a totally different person, as if he pulled on a new skin. 'You know Moses is *blood*, Donnie. Without him me and Miss Vie wouldn't be for this earth. But nobody talking about betray. We need change, we can't have a man who stand in the way of progress. Moses belong to the old days; him was necessary to fight the old slave owners like Elizabeth father and the Walters and our people who suck their ass. Look what our Chinese friend doing – they the future. This the twenty-first century, Donnie!'

'Moses fight the slave master, he fight the ones who suck up to them. But as a man he get along with them, he never kill a man it wasn't necessary to kill. The Chinese love him. Any of them come here they ask to see him. How many time they invite him to Beijing? Chinaman not hypocrite like Englishman or American. They not fool. They know what he do, all the good, all the evil.'

'You a young man, Donnie, you have a woman, you expecting issue. You know how much me and Miss Vie love Lizzie, more than her own father, any of her people. We don't want to bog down with the old people. It not too late, Donnie, you get time to come aboard. Just say the word and you leave here on that old Jingchen you love so much! No time at all you in the arms of Lizzie, feeling you daughter foot moving inside her belly!'

'No, Eddy. I can't betray Pops Moses, the day I raise me hand 'gainst him the day I stop being me.'

Eddy really lost it again, big time. 'I keep telling you, me and Moses is *blood*, Donnie. You have no obligation to a man who keeping you, me and the country down. Look at you now, we know all you plan, we bug you phone, that old furniture he keep, what him dead friend make, you bed, you Jingchen. We know more 'bout you than you know youself! We watchin' you since you leave, we see when you go to that sub-station. You friend already lock up. Soon as the light go off we just wait for you, we know where you coming in. Look at what you come here to kill me with!' He picked up the gun and the look on his face could not have been more aggrieved if it had been a used sanitary napkin. 'Moses buy all them brand new equipment from our Cuban friend in Tampa, we know that. Is why you don't use a proper gun, one with laser sight and exploding bullet they can't trace?'

'Is true what you say, Eddy. Me and Moses love the old ways. When we accept the new, we don't have to mash up everything we have before.'

'That really a pity, Donnie. You know how much me love you and Lizzie, more than if you me blood brother and sister. And you daughter going be me little niece, me beautiful goddaughter!'

He didn't hear Brett until he was in the room and he marvelled such a big man moved so like a cat, and now his glasses were off he noticed his polo shirt and jeans coordinated with his eyes.

'I have the DVDs, sir, Maria's going to be so pleased.'

'"To Maria and Brett", that okay, Mr Brett?' Donnie asked, his voice smooth as honey.

'Very fine, sir. I'll tell her you said hello.'

Donnie took the blue biro he wrote songs with from his shirt pocket and wrote: *'To Maria and Brett, best wishes. May you have a long life and a thousand children. And may your days be full of joy.'*

Brett looked at the writing on the DVD, his eyes widening till they were twin lakes of pale blue ice. 'Thank you so much, sir. It was nice meeting you. Goodbye, sir.'

'Goodbye, Mr Brett. Please tell Maria goodbye and peace

and love to both of you.'

Donnie looked at Eddy's eyes after Brett left and thought he saw a thin haze. 'Goodbye, Donnie.' When Eddy embraced him Donnie thought he would never let go; he could feel his heart pounding. He never expected a man as cool and hard to shake so like a leaf. 'Goodbye, Eddy.' Donnie thought he heard a sob as Eddy opened the door and the men who had held him down before came back in.

'Hope you're comfortable, sir? Everythin' alright?'

'Yes, brethren – I feel as comfortable as the world. Peace and love.'

'You're sure you're ok, sir?'

'Yes, I'm sure. Thank you so much for asking. Say goodbye to your families for me.' The door took forever to close and they didn't raise their rifles till they heard the final 'click'.

CHAPTER THIRTY

Elizabeth couldn't stop crying. She felt all substance drained from her and she was an emptiness into which the explosions echoed and the screams of all the children dying could not fill. She floated on an ocean of tears but refused to drown and join her beloved until the end. This was more than emptiness she felt now that Donnie had gone. There was darkness from when the explosions started and they took the electricity and she could not find the image of her Donnie. When she rose from the bed it was not with her own volition; she was a wraith and gravity no longer applied to the emptiness that she was.

Donnie had kept his gun in an alcove in the wall, hidden by loose bricks, behind the bookcase where he also kept his collection of African writers. But she couldn't take the gun or its bullets, she had not the strength and when she found them in her bag, together with the keys to his BMW, they had got there by themselves, had the power to move which she did not. Clothes moved and draped themselves over her body; she could not shower, brush her teeth, comb her hair and the door opened for her so the car would let her in and drive itself.

She passed the school where they evacuated people, the generator was on and she saw ghosts walking with injured children in their arms. Before each atom of her body would have trembled with compassion for the pain of the children as they had for the bird with the broken wing clinging to the cold wire. But she was already dead, her eyes empty, could not receive images of her desolation. She thought she saw Miss Vie and Donnie waiting for her, up there in the bright sunrise of heaven, to comfort her and her child.

The car drove itself but the places she passed had not been there the night before when they lived in joy in the words of Donnie's songs. The church was empty; it was like a drawing made by a child. So too were the barracks, ghostly silhouettes in the dark, tanks, APCs and artillery pieces parked like empty match boxes on the lawn. There were road-blocks manned by ghosts but they didn't stop her. They knew Donnie's car and when she came closer they saw his woman, pale and frazzled inside. Donnie was son of the Don, a musical superstar, a Man.

The Chinese were still working on their construction projects and they were on the last floor of their famous tall hotel, its windows mirrors of lost desire. But these did not exist, suspended in the emptiness where Donnie floated now among the stars where she would join him soon. Miss Vie's new house seemed alive for a moment but receded when the car drove past. She had no memory of the times she spent there, in the arms of the loving mother, being fed back to life, helping Miss Vie plant seeds of corn, peas, carrots, scotch bonnet peppers, tending the poor man's orchids and wild flowers she said were parts of God's creation. The Chinese had rebuilt the university but she couldn't see the classrooms, dorms in towers like those on the estate, students wandering frantically to the new stadium where sprinters flashed into orbits around the sun. Joseph had risen like a meteor into the sky and now he was gone. All was grey and lifeless in the emptiness without Donnie.

When she got to Miss Vie's old house she didn't recognise it, couldn't see the mango, palm, breadfruit, orange, soursop, pimiento or orange trees, smell the thyme, mint and fever grass, hear the crickets, cockerels or tree frogs the size of thumbnails. There were walls that ran forever, floodlights so powerful they could light ten football stadiums and enough soldiers and policemen to start a war. But none stopped her – she was Donnie's woman in his brand new white BMW. They saluted and waved her on and when she recognised she had passed the entrance and drove back they saluted and waved her on again. They were superstitious, she looked like a ghost; they wouldn't take chances. And she was Donnie's woman. Then she was back to the giant black gate she hadn't seen before and the guards didn't stop her when the gate slid open. Donnie was the PM's best friend, almost a brother, and Elizabeth was Donnie's woman, another childhood friend of the great man.

The gates to the PM's houses were so used to the car they would have opened even without the guards. She had no problem, the car kept driving till she came to a smaller gate where an American like a wrestler, in blue polo shirt and aviator sunglasses approached her with a huge gun in a shoulder holster. 'What can we do for you, Miss?' She saw her ghostly reflection in the curve of his lenses and images of others with M16s pointing down looking on from the guard house at the side. 'I come to see Eddy,' she said.

'I'm afraid the PM's not receiving visitors, Miss. Out of curiosity – how did you get past the guards?'

'I come to see Eddy,' she repeated and the man could hear the strain in her voice. He could also see the black Mercedes 500 driven by Eddy's Chief of Staff, the flashing lights, and hear the horn blaring like a siren, call signs of the most impatient and bad-tempered man he ever saw.

'Please move your car to the side so the man can get through, Miss,' hand moving up to his holster.

'But I come to see Eddy,' she insisted. Then she heard a car door slam, the scream of Eddy's man. 'What the fuck is wrong with you, rednecks? You know you not in Alabama now, you can't be holding up people!' The guard was pointing to the BMW, his mouth started to open when he heard '*Elizabeth*?' Frank Walters looked from her to the guard, his face a picture of incomprehension, 'Is why you trying to stop Elizabeth? You don't know who she is?'

'We have orders, sir. No visitors.'

'Fuck your orders, redneck! Tell your crackers at the barriers to let us through!' Elizabeth heard the man's voice, an empty echo as he told the radio a white BMW and a black Mercedes were coming through. The other barriers were opened, the one to the car park raised up and Frank showed her where to put the car. At the entrance to the house five men in polo shirts and jeans, aviator sunglasses and M16s stood in front of Elizabeth and tried to open her bag.

'Get the fuck off, you assholes. When I tell Eddy you fucked with Miss Elizabeth you'll see your asses fry!' Frank Walters had gotten an MBA from Georgetown and always exaggerated his accent when he spoke to Americans, whom he'd grown to hate in their country. He was supposed to be related to Stephen Walters. 'Come on, Miss Elizabeth.' He tapped in the numbers to the keypad on the black metal door and guided her in by the elbow. He hadn't calmed down when he walked her down a corridor and opened another big black door where Eddy sat on a Steelcase Straffor chair. She felt nauseated from the smell of bleach and damp on the thick red carpet, saw the wet spot where something had spilled.

'Your rednecks tried to stop Elizabeth, Eddy! Nobody taught these people manners!' He didn't seem to notice the two other Americans in aviator sunglasses, one of whom tried to search Elizabeth's bag as she clutched it tight to her body like a favourite pet. 'Leave her alone and get out,' Eddy said, in that voice like new honey, which Elizabeth knew spelt t-r-o-u-b-l-e.

'We have to check her bag, sir ...'

'I said get the fuck out – you don't understand *English*?'

'I tell the others outside they not still in Alabama, Eddy! *Fucking Rednecks*!!'

'You too, Frank, give us a minute.'

'See you soon, Miss Elizabeth. My love and merry Christmas to Donnie.'

'You didn't come with Donnie, Liz. Hope no problem? If you tell me before you come, me can arrange a little thing for you and my brother, a little drink and small food.'

'You didn't have to kill him, Eddy. You know him is all I have.'

'*Kill* Donnie? Is what you saying, Lizzy? Donnie not dead. When I see you and Frank I think Donnie just outside there, signing autograph. Is you make me brother a superstar. Soon, instead of Bob Marley they going be talking about Donnie Boy!'

'Whatever argument you have with Moses, you don't need

to kill Donnie, Eddy. We grow up together, Miss Vie and Moses more than mother and father to all of us.'

'I telling you Donnie not *dead*, Lizzie. Anytime now I expect him to come in, like him use to when we small and Miss Vie cook up some fry dumpling, callaloo and salt fish.' She could hear the strain in his voice, like when he used to hiccup before he shut down and they had to call the doctor.

'Donnie was all I have, Eddy. After Miss Vie I think I already dead but is Donnie make me want to live again. You know all them man fucking me, beating me up from we small, Eddy. I take all the drug to kill the pain but nothing help. I never think I ever going have children, all them man want to use me, fuck me, take me money and dash me way like use toilet paper after mashing up me face. See —' She lifted her black blouse and showed him her bump, where he thought he could see the baby's little feet kicking. 'See her, Eddy, is Donnie who give me hope, make me feel alive again.'

The sweat formed like marbles on Eddy's forehead, even though the air-conditioning made the room feel like a morgue and she was afraid he might melt down again as he used to as a child. The heat was in his voice as he picked up the gun from the table, holding it like road-kill. 'See what Moses send Donnie to kill me with, Lizzie.' The resentment had grown and there was rage and humiliation in his voice. 'We grow up together, we like brother and sister. How he can come here with *this* to kill me, Liz? *In Miss Vie old house!*'

'You rocket knock down the tower, Eddy; people dead, even old man and woman, pickney. Donnie just trying to save poor person. Remember what Miss Vie say about protecting poor person?'

'You, Donnie and me is modern people, we want progress, we want to see our life go forward, get a nice future for our children - like you daughter there, Lizzie. Moses is a big obstacle, he want to stop the clock, make us go back to the old ways, when nice boy like Donnie have to kill so many man. He know he have you, Liz, he know you have a daughter on the way, he shouldn't get involve in thing like this anymore. Him say him give up that life, that him making it as a singer now. Him can't do the business him do before when him is a husband and father, Liz. See what happen to him now?' Elizabeth took out the gun and it felt like a feather in her hand. Donnie always kept it loaded and checked it regularly to make sure it worked properly. Although he thought he'd given up the life he was a workman, it was his tool, and he kept it in order, even though he'd sworn to kill no more.

'No, Elizabeth, don't do it. You know Donnie wouldn't want you to, you have a daughter to take care of now - for both of you.' Elizabeth raised the gun, she was in New York again, was sixteen, the target bright and wide as the world. She could not miss. But instead of an Olympic medal her prize was now in heaven, where Donnie awaited them with loving arms. When the bullet exploded it would be like a rocket and she would ride its trail into paradise. Her daughter would be born in heaven and her beauty would arch across the sky, its brightest star, forever and ever.

'No, Elizabeth, no,' Eddy's voice whined shrilly, as when he was a helpless child, crying for his mother to rescue him. He thought he saw the flash of the bullet before he heard the sound.

CHAPTER THIRTY-ONE

I t feels strange to be back, in what looks like a new world. I was unable to write the last chapters as normal. For the past weeks I've been in hospital in a coma, having received fragments from explosive bullets in my head and suffering concussion from collision with the dashboard of Winston's old taxi. Apparently I also shattered my right arm. I was sure I was dead; I saw incidents of my life pass before my eyes as they say in the storybooks. In the coma I even thought I was living another life as I was seeing images with such vivid intensity, far brighter than I did in real life. I suppose this is where religious people got the idea of resurrection, of rising from the dead.

At first I was in a place without dimension, like an ocean or alien atmosphere where there was no time, movement or progression. I saw unspeakable cruelties and felt myself inside the mind of an insane African leader where I could not distinguish hallucination from the routine violence in the rule of the dictator. I was in an African village where the hero sacrificed another human being in accordance with the traditions of his people and hanged himself before his British conquerors could murder him, claiming *their* killing was civilization. I was confined to prison by a leader who refused to give reasons and almost went insane trying to find out until the man died and I was free again, but in a world I now did not recognize. I was a boy on the brink of a nervous breakdown, alienated from parents, relatives, society and all its institutions. Then I was killed when I fell in love with a woman too far outside my league and pursued her, with the weight of all the society I was not, stacked against me. I heard music from all the acts I worshipped – Sam Cook, BB King, Jimmy Hendricks, Bob Marley, Tina Turner, Bob Dylan, Stevie Wonder, Bruce Springsteen, Eva Cassidy, Emeli Sande.

When I began to regain consciousness I mistook images I saw of Sharon, doctors, nurses, hospital equipment and smells as part of what I experienced for all the time I knew. Roberta Flack was singing *The Very First Time I Saw your Face* and thought I smelt her perfume where she sat on my bed. Then, as her song finished, I knew my love for Sharon would last until the end of time. I was afraid when I saw the handsome young doctor make his moves on her but relapsed into unfeeling when I saw her smile with him but keep glancing at me with horror in her eyes. I was seeing all this but unable to move a finger, words I wanted to say kept bouncing inside my chest like echoes in an empty room, and although my eyes were moving I could not focus.

'We still can't tell when he'll regain consciousness, or even *if* he won't remain like a vegetable, Sharon. You have to start accepting he might be like this for the rest of his life, a perfect angel, at peace with himself but condemned to silence and unconsciousness.' The old doctor spoke and when I saw her face contort and the force of her will as she fought to stop the tears, I wanted to cry out, reach out to her, take her into my arms. I thought of my little *Lalique* girl who couldn't let her eyes overflow for fear of drowning.

'Sharon!' I kept screaming but my perfect, peaceful body and mind absorbed the echoes of the sound. It took me hours, days, weeks, infinity, gazing at her, having doctors pronounce me permanently comatose, nurses crying with her and telling her to hope and pray, before I began to think I might wake again. She kept looking into my eyes, saw nothing though I thought I was communicating encyclopaedias of feeling. It was a nurse her age, the friendliest of the lot, who kept teasing her about how lucky she was to have a man who slept all the time and could not cheat, who shouted 'he's blinking!'

'He's always blinking, Debbie. First time I saw him here he blinked. The way he was looking at me I thought he was conscious. But the doctors said they weren't sure he'd live.'

'No, Sharon, he's waking up – see!!'

I managed to focus on her, blinked and was able to raise the tip of my little finger. I saw Sharon's eyes open, was almost blinded by the light from them, and saw Debbie grab her as she lunged at me. 'You crazy person, you want to kill him? He may be waking up, but he still has all those drips and needles in him and the doctors don't know how to get the metal out his head.' Sharon was weeping, Debbie was shaking her gently, saying, 'Hush, baby, don't cry,' as she would to an infant. I was so moved by her concern I grunted, they both stared at me like they were seeing a ghost, I found the strength to lift my left hand about a millimetre and when Sharon held it I was able to squeeze.

'She wouldn't leave you alone for a second,' Debbie said. 'We worried she'd starve!'

'Everyone knows what nurses are like – all man stealers! I leave him for a minute and you snatch him!' Sharon grabbed her throat, they wrestled and laughed as they play fought, looking at me all the time. Apparently when Moses told Sharon, she flew to the hospital and hadn't left. The old doctor said it was forbidden for visitors to stay beyond visiting hours, even if they were wives, and ordered her to go. But his Deputy was a Nigerian who told him in Africa hospitals depended on relatives, especially wives and mothers to help with the rehabilitation of seriously ill patients. The Head was still reluctant but agreed to let his Deputy try, as he was the most effective doctor in the hospital. Apparently Sharon ate the hospital meals meant for me. Elena also brought food, as did Moses. She asked Elena to be bringing her changes of clothes as well as books she knew I liked. The nurses let her use their showers but insisted she go for a walk sometimes, so she would get exercise and sunlight. When she told me the books she read out I recognised the source of all the hallucinatory images I experienced. To fill the breaks between reading she bought me an i-Pad and downloaded all the music I liked. I'd heard stories of coma patients being affected by music and people talking to them but dismissed this as urban myths. Then I was able to recall scenes from works by Heinrich Böll, Chinua Achebe, Ngugi wa Thiong'o, Graham Greene and J.D. Salinger, and knew they were right. The Head was so impressed he came with his Director to praise Sharon, who Debbie teased when she cried.

'You're very lucky, young man. When your lady wanted to stay, I said "no", hospital rules don't allow it. It was our brother here who convinced me, telling me how it's done back home in Africa. Without this young lady you wouldn't be conscious now, if ever.' Words were milling inside, not coming out. Winston hadn't been as lucky, his injuries were so serious they had to airlift him to America, and he had no Sharon there to keep his mind alive. The Director was born in this country but emmigrated to England, was educated in Manchester, worked there, and came back when he heard the progress made in medicine and the country in general. He kept nodding as the Head spoke, and when he opened his mouth I heard his voice was hesitant but impressed.

'Tremendous, doctors; when I saw this young man I gave him a fifty-fifty chance of making it back. We need to study what they do over there in the Motherland, just like the Chinese doctors have to know their own traditional practices when they study Western medicine. Congratulations again, we must do a pilot, see how this works; start with private rooms like this one. Good luck, young man; congrats on finding a woman in our selfish country who behaves like an African!' Sharon hid her face in her hands as she wept. 'Hush, baby,' Debbie whispered, 'don't cry; your man is back. Don't cry.'

I felt like crying too but although the tears were there I didn't have the strength to make them flow. I made rapid progress and Sharon knew when I started sneaking feels that I was getting back to myself. She was gentle with me at first but when she saw how insistent I was her slaps and pinches started to hurt. 'I'll bring you the papers and memory sticks,' she said. 'If you have the strength to be naughty, you can do something productive.'

After I tired of reading I started watching the funerals of Eddy and Donnie she had recorded for me. Both were grand affairs with services at the Cathedral, the National Stadium then internment at the Garden of Remembrance. Eddy was buried in the elaborate lead coffin he picked for his mother while Donnie's was plain wood. I saw Moses wiping his eyes with a big white handkerchief until he noticed the camera-woman and sent a boy to block her view. I suppose he was weeping for Donnie, maybe even for Eddy, his brother's son.

Brazilians and most of the African and Caribbean countries sent their Presidents while the Chinese and Russians were represented by their Premiers; the French by their Foreign Minister, and the Americans and British by ambassadors. There was one Cardinal from the Vatican, one from Brazil, and another from Benin. The Vatican said that God had blessed the country by giving them two such outstanding leaders and had taken them prematurely to test the spirit of the nation, as He had with Job. The Nigerian President recounted the links binding the two countries together since the people made such tremendous achievements after being taken from his country as slaves.

The Foreign Minister gave the best speech, composed, his glasses just vaguely tinted. He said the foundations lain by his cousin Eddy guaranteed the country would continue to prosper and thanked the compassion of Miss Violet, his beloved aunt, for giving all the power to succeed. People wept and screamed at the sound of her name, as in the background I heard songs of the latest superhero, the great Donnie. Then I saw Elizabeth in close-up, dark glasses covering most of her face, the black veil and gown not enough to conceal the sedation or her desolation in the crowd of weeping women. Apparently Moses called the Chinese and American ambassadors, John Cairncross and the Foreign Minister and told them the official line to take. There were people in the country who didn't want to see the nation go forward, resented the progress being made, and jealous of the achievements of Eddy and his close childhood friend, Donnie. They had done their worst, taken out the two National Heroes and been killed while resisting arrest. The Foreign Minister was the most senior after his first cousin and would become PM till elections were held. I'd watched the funerals of Kennedy and Diana on tape and this one was ahead on points in drama and spectacle. I also saw some YouTube videos Debbie and her friends had taken. Not a single media outlet queried the official line.

My first visitors were Moses and Trevor. Muscular boys in huge shades, white tee-shirts, black slacks, Michael Jordan trainers and Colt .45s bopped in, greeted me and Sharon, then bopped out before Moses came in his faded grey sports shirt, brown trousers and scuffed black shoes. He looked bigger than I remembered; I could see the pain in his face for Donnie. Trevor was in the same crumpled old clothes as in the session for Cabal. 'Welcome, Uncle Moses,' Sharon curtsied as she greeted. 'You looking very fine, sir.'

'You looking more than fine now you have you man back! Is good to see you better, sir, you have the best doctor in this woman! When she see you in those bandage I think she going die crying!'

'Sit down, Uncle, you're a very bad old man; you always like to tease!'

'Nice to see you too, sir. I saw you on the T.V. May God grant you the courage to bear your loss.'

'Thank you, sir. Is always tough when you lose your close one. But God there to help the helpless.'

'You look so much better, sir. Doctor say you arm healing; they soon take off that splint,' Trevor said.

'Thank you, Trevor. It itching under the plaster but I have a slave here to scratch for me!' Sharon gave me a look that said 'Just wait till they leave!' I felt like a shit suspecting Trevor of fucking her.

'We have person watching that road, sir. When Winston drive up we see them fire, see him try get out the way. We take out the Commando inside then go call Pops. He drive you to the hospital.'

'Thank you, sir. I was sure I was dead, all I saw after the bullets looked like what you see at the end.'

'God spare you life, sir. Then I call this woman to continue God work! She never leave you side, not once! I don't want you to tire, sir. I going now but we have to talk when they let you out.'

'Yes, sir. I'm feeling much stronger now.' Hospitals here were expensive and I wondered if the money I had would be enough to settle the bills. But Sharon said Moses had paid; I wanted to thank him but thought I'd wait till we were alone. The boys kept popping in to see their Don was okay but when they saw how comfortable he looked they went off and Trevor had to phone them. They popped back in, said goodbye and Moses whispered something to Sharon, making her face turn purple. I wanted to say something, heard myself speak and saw her like a shadow in the sky when Debbie came in and I heard Sharon say, 'He looks so peaceful when he sleeps I feel like crying.'

CHAPTER THIRTY-TWO

I was dreaming again of battles, heard sirens, the crash of boots on concrete, I screamed but the screams were trapped in my head. My eyes opened and I saw Sharon but couldn't tell if she were real. I saw the fear in her eyes, her face contorted as she tried to stand between me and the door when it opened and men in black with Heckler & Koch machine guns and visors like steel surveyed the room. I heard commotion approach, official bodyguards with earpieces looked in, then the new PM, Elena and aides I couldn't count burst in. Elena and Sharon were crying as they squeezed each other, the PM looked uncertain in his tinted glasses. There was no powder on his nose as people pressed in behind him. I saw Frank Walters, Eddy's former Chief-of-Staff. My girl was there too, her hair now blonde and conservatively dressed by her standards, with a skirt that concealed her knickers unless she bent over. She looked at Elena and Sharon embracing, gave me the eye, reminding me she was still ready. Cameramen and women were pressing them into the room. Then I heard the head doctor scream: 'Dammit! This is a hospital, not a market. Get the hell out of here!' A lanky yellow colonel with a Glock 9mm in a black holster strapped to his hip pushed through.

'Get out,' he shouted. 'Only those with the PM can stay.' The Doctor hadn't noticed the new PM until now. 'Sorry, sir. The patient's recovering but still has a long way to go.'

'I'm sorry, Doctor – didn't realise they'd all try to come in – Colonel, get these people out of here.' Sharon and Elena still had their arms round each other and my girl took the opportunity to adjust her blouse so I could see she was wearing a scarlet lace bra. Her perfume still overwhelmed.

'We were just passing by, Prof., and decided to look in', Colin said. Elena must have told him, druggies don't have that decisiveness. 'Elena said you were so much better.' I'd heard on the radio that the Chinese and American foreign ministers were in town, and supposed he was on his way.

'We're just from the Chinese embassy,' Elena said. 'You know it's just down the road.' I could see my girl was becoming desperate and worried she might try to flip a tit out.

'We discussed with Elena, Prof.; we decided you and Sharon can have that little house where they stay.' I was about to say I'd discuss with Sharon but she beat me to it.

'That's kind of you, PM, Elena mentioned it. I told her we'd think about it, wait till he recovered.'

'That's okay, Sharon, it's the least we can do after all that happened.'

'Thank you, sir. We're very grateful for the offer.'

'We have to go, PM, the Americans just called,' Frank Walters said, giving my girl a look which said he was still around if she didn't succeed with me. She still stared, smoothing her skirt, assuring me she would come back if I got rid of that bitch, Sharon.

'I should come back soon and stay with you, Sher; we been so busy,' Elena said.

'Goodbye, Prof.,' they waved, and soon I was asleep again, thinking the sirens were part of my dreams, Miss Vie and Donnie waving to me from above, so near, so very near. When I woke with the smell of Carolina Herrera in my head I thought it was my half naked slut but saw Stephen Walters with Maria and her daughter Elizabeth. I wondered what had happened to poor Elena, did she come to her senses and kick him out? Did he run out of Maria's money and leave her? Or did Maria go round to her place with a pistol and bottle of hydrochloric acid? Their faces looked broken up as they stared at me sleeping but Elizabeth looked thrilled and noticed I was awake before her parents and Sharon did. 'Do you still have the bullets in your head?'

'*Elizabeth!*' her mother shouted.

'Don't worry, Maria, she's still young, and young people want to know it all. No, Elizabeth, I didn't get whole bullets, just fragments, they were explosive ones.' I could see the disappointment in her face. I knew where she was coming from: 50 Cent was supposed to have nine bullets in his brain and this hadn't impaired his intellectual subtlety, his voice was a dream, Fort Knox borrowed gold from him, and women lined up round the block, legs open, waiting for his big bamboo. Tupac Shakur and Biggie Smalls were pussies – they succumbed to lead like women.

Elizabeth had started growing tits since we saw her; either she was taking the pill or stuffed toilet tissue in her bra. I couldn't tell if the perfume was from her or her mother but suspected it was Maria, as Stephen must have warned Elena to wear his wife's scent so Maria wouldn't suspect him. I suppose I was a minor celebrity since I was in the papers with gunshot in my head. That's why Elizabeth was here on Saturday afternoon when she could be at the cinema with friends, hoping to hook up with that big footballer from the upper sixth. 'You go away to escape this, Prof., I don't know why you come back. I try to warn you but guys like you think this place like England or America.' Stephen sounded peeved as hell.

'They said you were lucky, Prof.; the people who killed Eddy and Donnie just missed you and Winston,' Maria said with a concern that belied her reputation for meanness and cold steel.

'You don't sing?' Elizabeth asked hopefully, thinking I may not be a completely lost cause, that I might share something with 50 Cent, Kanye West and Justin Bieber.

'No Elizabeth, I'm afraid I don't have the voice.' My tone was hopeful, to kill her disappointment.

'Sometimes he tries in the shower, Elizabeth. All the animals run for the hills!' Sharon said, smiling.

'Like your father, Liz. When I hear him sing I think he's snoring. Men's voices aren't made for singing.' Elizabeth disagreed with her mother about men – not old men like Stephen and me – but 50 Cent, Snoop Dog, Justin Timberlake and that sixth form athlete who was rumoured to make older women scream. The family was Catholic, they thought pleasure should be conjoined with pain and Elizabeth didn't regret knowing the first boy who fucked her would make her bleed and weep. I'd seen an underground movie called *Blue Velvet* with a line saying 'take my whip and bleed for me.' Young, well brought up Catholic girls like Elizabeth wanted men like 50 Cent who looked and sounded like hardened criminals, didn't believe in stroking, foreplay or lubrication. They fucked to hurt.

'He's looking exhausted, Stephen, his eyes keep closing like he wants to sleep. We'll come again, Sharon. When he's discharged you should bring him round.' I was dreaming of Elizabeth hooking up with 50 Cent and Tinie Tempah, ecstasy brimming in her eyes as she screamed with pain.

CHAPTER THIRTY-THREE

I heard Elizabeth before she entered – I recognised her voice and she was the only one I knew who screamed like that in public. Sharon knew too, she whispered 'Elizabeth' as she went out and by the time they were back in they were both bawling like madwomen, holding each other as if they were drowning. I saw the nurses rush out but when Debbie saw who it was she pushed them back, saying 'Elizabeth – nothing to worry about.'

'You're so lucky, Sher, you still got your man.' They bawled some more and I felt the pain in my head and arm as I saw what had become of her since Donnie. If she'd looked like a charlady in Eaton Square, she now looked like a madwoman who slept on the streets. Her uncombed thatch was again full of grey, there were lines on her face, including those from the tracks of her tears and I saw new needle marks on her arms. She seemed like a magician, able to shed or put back on thirty years, to go from infancy to old age without any intervening period of adulthood. She came with another of Moses' sons, Roddie, who played bass in Donnie's backing band and after he greeted us he sat in the corner, silent tears pouring down his cheeks like waterfalls. I know Sharon didn't like it when people said how lucky she was I was still alive, I saw her face tighten but she hadn't reacted when Elizabeth said it and her tears were for Donnie and Winston. Elizabeth looked as if she would drown and when she screamed 'Sharon!' I didn't think the world was deep enough to hold her grief. She pulled up her blouse and I saw she wasn't just back on the drugs but fists of her musicians were trying to punch out Donnie's child. I saw the hurt on Sharon's face when she saw the purple welts.

'See our child, Sher, every night I call for him to come and be with me and our daughter.' I saw the total incomprehension on her face, as if she couldn't understand why Donnie couldn't be with her, to comfort her, tell her how much he loved her, that he would be there for her and her daughter forever. The wails were coming from so deep I thought she could swallow the world and when Sharon joined her I felt I too would never surface again, ever. Inside my head I was hearing Donnie's voice, seeing the ineffable beauty Elizabeth had drawn on to come back from the depths of despair. And now he was gone and I couldn't put a stop to Elizabeth's tears. I remember after Indie, before Sharon, how impotent I would feel, how I didn't have the energy to walk out and see, thinking Google World was all I needed. Roddie too was affected by the women's grief but stronger than me, stood up, and said, 'Is time, Miss Elizabeth. We make that appointment with the Doctor in Bogle Square.'

I felt like shit I could do nothing to help give her hope, prayed the doctor could save the child from those killing blows, get her to give up drugs. 'Go, Lizzie, we'll see later. Hope the doctor can help,' Sharon said. 'Yes, Elizabeth,' I said. 'You have to be strong for you and Donnie. Your daughter needs you more now.' I wish I had enough strength to kill myself. When I said 'Donnie' it brought back the pain and she started a wail so intense the nurses came out again, tried to help Sharon calm her. 'Let's go, Miss Elizabeth,' Roddie said, 'is time.' He was younger than Donnie, worshipped his big brother, and Elizabeth felt the strength in his urging voice.

'See you soon, Sher; get well, Prof.' She sounded almost whole again and I hoped Donnie would be able to help, from whatever corner of our empty universe he now occupied. As Sharon escorted her out I rested my eyelids, finding myself in a state between sleep and waking. I saw Debbie with Sharon when they came in, but as in a dream. 'He looks so like a baby when he's asleep. You should take out your titties and feed him when he wakes up!'

'*Deborah!* You're such a naughty somebody – and he thinks you're a little angel!' She hit her and they play fought a while. 'You should see him when he's awake – I never have rest, he's like a devil.'

'He's waking – see you later.' I watched as she left, her uniform tight in all the right places.

'So you're awake – hope you didn't hear us.'

'No, I didn't. But come take out your titties so I can have a feed!'

'You idiot, your mind should be on your health, not sex… you're such a menace, I never understood why you were playing hard to get when we first met.'

'Hard to get? How many times did I call you?'

'You were replying to my calls. How many missed calls did you have on your phone?'

'I explained to you about Indira…'

'It wasn't that, you acted like I was pestering you.' I couldn't tell her I was angry Eddy sent her. 'I wanted you since I saw your picture at St Dunstan's when we went for debates or watch athletics. Then I read your book on Joseph and thought how different you were from the men I knew here. I wanted you. I tried everything to get your e-mail, number or postal address.'

She seemed still so upset I decided to risk it

'I thought Eddy sent you, I wasn't in a good mood after I read what Winston wrote. I also saw the YouTube video where his boys killed those people.'

'Eddy sent *me*? He wanted to send you a woman all right but not me. Elena heard and told me. That day Delroy phoned you were coming home early, he was to bring her in the evening.'

'Who's this woman?

'You think we didn't see you eying her when she came to the hospital?'

'I still don't know who you're talking about, you idiot.'

'That half naked girl, who looked like she'd jump you, even with us there. Rosemary.'

'Oh, that one?' So I was right about Eddy's choice after all. A fuck machine. 'I didn't even know her name till you told me, though Eddy brought her to me twice and she showed she was ready and able. Fucking Eddy – so that's the type of man he thought I was!'

'You're a man. With a girl like that you'd be inside her in twenty seconds, and she'd fuck you comatose. Eddy offered her ten thousand US if she got you from me.'

So she was inside my head, seeing what I felt, and for a moment I thought I was dreaming. I heard another woman weeping and when Sharon opened the door I saw Maria and Brett. Maria grabbed her and they clinched.

'You're so lucky the Prof. survived, Sharon. Just saw Elizabeth in the parking lot, she couldn't control herself over Donnie. He was such an angel!' Sharon couldn't control herself either.

'The Prof.'s awake,' Brett said. 'Hello, Prof. Hope you're getting better. Maria still held on to Sharon but cried even more when she saw me looking at them, with no hand to shake since it was in a cast. 'Welcome, Maria and Brett. And congrats – hear you got married.'

'Thank you, Prof.,' they both said. It seemed like a million years since we met in Eaton Square and I thought she was the girl Eddy had on the menu for me. It seemed I'd known Sharon forever and I felt like a different person.

'We met Prof. in Eddy's house in London, Sharon. We had such a wonderful time. Eddy said what a genius his schoolmate was.' Each time she said 'Eddy' I heard the catch in her voice and saw the crest in her flow of tears. I was sorry I couldn't shake her hand, try comfort her, but I was remembering how my hand disappeared in Brett's in Eaton Square and seen him at the control centre in Eddy's house, directing the assault in which I was almost killed.

'We heard Donnie play in Madison Square Gardens, Sharon and Prof. We thought his voice was so divine, I cried. He signed DVDs for us when he came to greet Eddy. Brett likes those rough boys like Rhino Man, Cabal and Lover Man!'

'I told you I liked him, darling. We enjoyed his DVDs. His death'll have the same impact as Bobby's.'

Looking at Sharon and Maria weeping and clinging to each other, I was amazed men like Brett and Eddy still had their

Medieval codes for warfare, where they didn't tell women of their killings. Even if we showed her the images Maria would never believe Brett had anything to do with the murder of her hero, Donnie, reminding her so much of her choirboy brother who became a Seal and got shafted by Fidel. I didn't want to ask him about Clayton. I'm sure he left the island right after the operation and mentioning his name might make Brett uptight, talking shop in front of his wife. It was Clayton who saved Elizabeth after she shot Eddy when his Special Ops killers' fingers tightened on the triggers. He recognised her as the daughter of John Cairncross, buddy of two former presidents to whom Clayton was related. She was a junkie, a whore, and spoke worse *patois* than the criminals she fucked. But as a daughter of Cairncross her death at American hands would embarrass his relatives. While I was here in the hospital Elena noticed my phone and laptop blinking on and off. She took them to her friend in Security who found they were riddled with spyware so Eddy could listen to or read all I said or wrote, and know where I was at all times. I don't know if Brett and his friends fixed it, or Eddy's Chinese pals who manufactured the gear. After all the Americans were fucking enemies for only four-hundred years while the Chinese were doing so for four-thousand.

'We have to go, Maria… Maria has a cousin here, who runs a renewable energy company, Prof., then we have a trip to that waterfall near the village where Rhino Man was born. Our honeymoon lasts another week so I'm sure we'll meet again. Bye, Sharon, hope the Prof. gets well soon.' His hand almost covered Maria's back as he ushered her out and I thought he must truly love her and she would help with the Hispanic vote if he ever tired of killing directly and decided to run for President.

'The two of them were so nice in London.' Sharon said.

I couldn't tell her of my fantasies about fucking Maria.

'He looks so nice in person; you wouldn't believe the things he does. His big brother was the same; he was a senior when I entered the school as a sophomore. A nicer guy you could never meet. Really tried to make me feel at home. Now you can't imagine the operations he runs in Iraq, Afghanistan, Iran, the Middle East. I'm glad I'm not schizophrenic like that, though some people can't decide whether I'm innocent like a babe, or a devil in disguise! In either case I still want your nipple in my mouth.'

'Keep your hands to yourself – I told you you're too weak for sex!'

The doctors said I was well enough to be discharged though I was welcome to stay if I wanted. They joked I would be well taken care of as I had a live-in nurse and Sharon tried to hide her blushes. Moses offered us a 'nice house' up in the hills, Elena and her 'cousin' said we could stay in the condo but I thought if we stayed in town we wouldn't have peace. Now the man was PM all the hustlers would want to be with Elena and Sharon, her best friend. Sharon agreed when I said we should go to the resort with the waterhole at the beach. When Elena told Moses, he instructed my schoolmate, the manager, to give us the VIP treatment. Sharon said she would do most of the cooking and went with Bunny to the local market to buy breadfruit, bammies, ackee, salt fish, rice, peas, oil, peppers, callaloo and fruit. Kenny said he had a good chef who could make us whatever we liked when Sharon got tired, and the guy was good though not as good as Sharon.

She wouldn't agree to have sex till the plaster was off my

arm and she had the doctors' assurance that 'vigorous activities' wouldn't impair my health. When they asked what 'vigorous activities' she had in mind she said tennis or ping pong. They said tennis, ping pong and cricket were fine but I should avoid football or polo. I asked her why she didn't mention sex, if she was afraid I'd die on top of her. She swore never to have sex with me again and regretted being foolish enough to have agreed before.

Coming to the resort was a brilliant idea. We had no visitors, the place was far and out of the way and people made the excuse I needed rest. It took me time to walk properly and at first Sharon had to hold on to me. My schoolmate sometimes joined us when we sat out in the sun or came to check on us when he saw lights on at night. He always brought us rum punch or daiquiris and if he went to town he brought us little treats like jerk pork, chicken, or special patties made by an old woman he knew, who ground the meat herself and used very hot scotch bonnet peppers and other spices from her garden. Since the accident the place seemed different and I spent time scrutinising, inside and out. I noticed how cool it was though the glass should have produced greenhouse heat. I guess the architect had designed it with climate in mind, so there was no need for air-conditioning, and ducts and vents kept air from the sea in constant circulation. The furniture was also carved from local wood and outside, the flowers were arranged in beds so no two were alike. All in all Moses' friends had created a masterpiece, though they were unable to compete with the Chinese on Blue Island.

Elena and her 'cousin' were our first visitors but instead of the noise and chaos of last time, they came like thieves in the night. There were three Range Rovers with Commandos but these were left in the parking lot; there was no press and no Rosemary. Frank Walters came in but just to greet us and went off, perhaps to check on a woman. Elena ran in, bent down to kiss me on the forehead where I lay on a couch in blue satin pyjamas Sharon bought me. Then she dragged her out, giggling like schoolgirls and ordered her 'cousin' now the PM to watch me, as if I were a mischievous brat. The the PM was more resolute now, looked more like an adult, joking with Sharon that her man was 'now in action'. There was no powder on his nose, he wasn't rubbing it, and his glasses were so clear you could see his pupils were not dilated. 'Hope you had a good trip, sir,' I said.

'Yes, Prof., you know it's not that high up the mountain before the turn off. And we told those crazy people there was no need to drive like lunatics... you're looking much better than last time.'

'Yes, sir, I needed the rest, and I have the best nurse and cook in the world!'

'Yes, they're two exceptional women. Don't know why they're so excited.'

'Men can't tell what excites women.'

Sharon and Elena were still whispering, giggling and holding onto each other when they came back in, laughing at me and the 'cousin' as if they had been comparing notes on how we fucked.

'Care to share what's making you giggle like schoolgirls?' Colin asked.

'None of your business; nothing to do with men!! I was pleading with Sharon to take that little house, Prof. Please talk to her – you're her boss after all!'

'They told you they didn't want it, Elena. Leave them in peace!'

I thought she would be upset at the rebuke but she looked at him, smiled to herself, as if surprised he was being assertive, like a man. Maybe he was getting his high from being PM, rather than sniffing Colombian powder or fucking little girls.

'Eddy was always so go-go-go, always on the move, as if he thought to be PM you had to be Superman. I've found it so relaxing; the office practically runs itself. There are so many people who think they have an answer to every question – even those that haven't been asked!' the PM joked.

'It takes talent to go with the flow, sir. Eddy wasn't the easy-going type, he made his own problems.'

'We have to go, Prof., we have a meeting, then a reception for the German Foreign Minister. Besides, your master doesn't like it when people take up your time!' Colin said.

'You should tell your man to behave, Elena, he's becoming such a tease.'

'Being PM's spoiling him, I guess. You know what they say about power,' Sharon said.

'You guys take it easy now. You know the Prof. hasn't fully recovered, Sharon!' She smiled at his implication and gave it back like a stroke in a fencing match.

'Elena promised to recover you, Prime Minister. So you can tease all you want!'

'Bye, Prof., sorry we have to leave you without protection from this wild woman!'

Sharon and Elena still had their arms around each other's waist when she saw them off and when I heard the engines revving I knew she was waving till they were out of sight. When she returned she was skipping and I thought she was happy they were leaving so we could fuck.

'What's all the excitement, you're looking like you're hoping I'll fuck you upside down.'

'They're getting married.' '*Married?*'

'Yes, he showed her the divorce papers. The wife's not contesting.'

'Doesn't make sense, she wouldn't divorce him when he was lowly Foreign Minister. Why now, when he's the all-powerful PM? They're also Catholic and Catholics don't allow divorce.'

'You know her friend in IT, who gave us the memory sticks and DVDs, and told you about your phone and computer spyware? He hacked into the wife's computer and found a file with photos of her in bed with the First Secretary at the US Embassy. They were roommates at Vassar. When the women saw the pictures they lost the stomach for a fight.'

CHAPTER THIRTY-FOUR

When we got back to the condo I felt well enough to walk the grounds and even wandered up the hill to get clothes and greet Miss Robotham who started crying when she saw the weight I'd lost and how pale I looked. There was also the gauze bandage which I covered with a cheap Panama I bought at M&S. Sharon was going to take the GRE to apply to my old university and I called Moses to tell him we could meet. I was surprised when Delroy came in the same town car and wondered how Eddy thought he could get these boys to betray Moses. Sharon made me lunch of fried dumplings and ackee and saltfish so I ate and took my medicines before I set out. We took a road I'd never been on and was surprised the houses looked older, more individual and with more land than those being constructed by the Chinese. The roads were older too. The grounds were more established, with mature trees and well-tended gardens. Some had royal palms at the gates or lining the long driveways and many had dwarf palms, oranges, Otahite apples and pomegranate trees. There were flame trees along the road and as we went up there were roundabouts with filled with flowers of every colour. A few had big swimming pools and I began to notice apple, peach and pine trees as we got further up. It was also becoming cooler. Delroy knew I didn't like air-conditioning so he left the windows open but now I began to feel as if the AC was on. But what surprised me most was the stillness, the absence of people. There were also no dogs. Then about halfway up I noticed the house Eddy showed me when Rosemary let me know houses weren't the only things I could slide into.

'Stop, Delroy, there's something I want to look at.' I thought what Eddy showed me was paradise but the pictures were taken by amateurs, probably Sharon and Rosemary with mobiles. Nothing in the photos captured the heavenly qualities, the spatial arrangement, conjunction of colours, wholeness of design making it almost impossible to judge the size or age. The doors, windows, lights, fittings were organic extensions of the house itself. And the glass did not look transparent but like a mirror in which you could see all creation. I was thinking I should have accepted it from Eddy before I heard he was planning to kill me. As the thought of him in the hotel and Rosemary bringing me the album with the pictures entered my head, I was becoming so sick with the vision I wanted to move on, 'We can go, Delroy.' I was also afraid of what I'd see nearby, and as we moved I saw it around the corner, squatted below the Cairncross folly like a slave in chains. Elizabeth's description was as if she had been there, shivering at its boarded up mystery but still brave enough to enter and survey. I too was shaking as I looked inside it years ago and saw what I could never remember for a long time. The vast expanse of Elizabeth's father's 'castle' looked empty and I didn't know if there was anyone inside except the ghosts which would haunt it forever. I'd seen John Cairncross at Eddy and Donnie's funerals though the organisers had put him as far away from his daughter as possible. He was supposed to possess vast holdings in several Hollywood studios, grooming teenage starlets of increasingly younger ages, their life stories appearing in the scandal sheets when they entered rehab, were arrested for shoplifting or driving while drunk. But it wasn't the shabby mansion that attracted my attention. Only a few acres of untended gardens were left around it, all the rest of the endless Cairncross lands, extending up the mountain and beyond, were covered with the Christmas trees Sharon told me about. The Chinese had replaced a plantation of sugar cane where slaves were tortured and killed, with trees they exported to the rest of the Caribbean, North and South America. As I gazed at the forest quivering like needles in the wind from below, we passed a few more houses till I heard the sound of a brook. As the sound of water grew louder, and I thought we were about to leave, I saw a house built into a rock jutting into nothingness. Just as my dream house below made my garret and even Eaton Square look like huts, this one surpassed all dwellings I'd ever seen and from its location a believer might think it was heaven.

'We're here, Prof.,' Delroy said and I was surprised when a glass front gate opened and as we drove through revealed Moses' big black Toyota cruiser. There was a spiral staircase with glass steps beyond the cars and Delroy led me up them to another glass door opening onto a dark corridor, at the end of which yet another glass door slid open into a large living room lit by soft spotlights buried like stars in the glass ceiling.

'Welcome home, Prof.,' Moses said.

'Thank you, sir. It was kind of you to find time to see me.'

'The pleasure is mine, Prof. You a important man in our country.'

I watched as the lights grew brighter and thought there was a dimmer switch but when I looked up I saw the roof which looked like green thatch had retracted to let the sunlight in. There were huge glass windows on all sides, through which you could see most of the town down the hill. The furniture was carved wood like those in the round hut resort, glass tables on stainless steel frames, and Scandinavian designed lights backed by mirrors that magnified the light.

'This is a magnificent house, sir. I suppose you relax up here after all the stress downtown.' He smiled but didn't say anything after pointing me to a seat and sitting himself. Delroy brought us a wooden tray with big glasses of rum punch filled with ice. 'You're the first person we're seeing since we started up the hill, sir.'

'You been away, Prof., you don't know our people anymore. This where the children of slave owner move when we start having enough money to move into their old high-class place. You know we have a little difficulty of recent with Eddy – they all take off to Florida, California or London. When they think we behaving again they come back. Only you friend, Stephen, don't move – see their house.' He pointed to the right and I saw the white house on a promontory with columns and a small dome. I was happy Stephen and Elizabeth didn't behave like the others who still acted like aliens after four centuries of occupation.

'All this area belong to your ancestor one time, Prof., right next to the Cairncross property on this side. His grandson was a notorious gambler and womaniser; he love one woman so much he gamble all his land and lose. The woman was Cuban, the husband another Cairncross who gamble and drink rum with him. You grandfather want to get the land back but never have money before they build house here for rich white people of the time. You father is a architect, he buy this rock up here to build a house when he have a money. When he get a little cash he make that house below you see board up now. Him wife control him gambling. Me and him enter a thing, me have a money and connection, me buy land, government make road, provide light and water and you father design the house. Me and me brother, Eddy father, is good friend with you father and him wife. You grandma a nurse when she young, she know how dangerous Aaron is and she come from a good Catholic family who don't think decent people should mix with us ruffian who make money from herb and other bad activity. Aaron was me identical twin, me can't know how sick him is, it surprise me when he do that to Miss Vie, Eddy mother. He think he love you mother and that she love him too. He think is you father holding her back, preventing her from giving him her love. You know what happen.'

I was too ashamed to tell him how recently I found out what happened. For years I'd lived in a fog in which what happened to my parents was wrapped in a glass cocoon, impervious and unbreakable. It was when Eddy's killers shot us and bullets exploded in my head that the glass broke and I saw it all, not like a memory but as if it was happening there and then. I saw my mother taking me to the opening of that resort with round huts by the sea, my father on the platform with Moses and the Governor General, smiling at her and her smiling back, the most beautiful woman who had ever been. In my blue sailor suit, blue socks and white shoes, my hair slicked back, my mother's friends were teasing her about her 'blue angel', her 'handsome little man'. The blue of my costume was of the round water hole and the sea. I could feel the love, pride, the warmth in her hand holding mine. When they took me to my grandmother the old woman was always weeping as she held me, her eyes seeing something in me which made her call me her 'precious little one'. My father developed a distinctive style with glass and mirrors, like this house where we were sitting now. I could see us in the mirror as my mother bathed me, I splashed her with the soapy water and she screamed I was a 'naughty boy'. Aaron was there, I looked at Moses now and felt the sickness as I thought how much he looked like his brother. Suddenly my mother stopped screaming, I stopped splashing and we heard Aaron and my father shouting. I saw my mother's face break up, saw the horror in her eyes as she grabbed me, wrapped me in a big white towel and stuffed me into a closet. In her hurry she slammed the door but it flew open and through the mirror under the overhead light I saw Aaron holding my father's hair and slicing his head off with our big butcher knife with the rough wood handle. When he saw my mother the look in his eyes was beatific as he swung her husband's head like a toy. I could see inside his head, hear in his madness his delusions saying 'at last we can be together!' But my mother grabbed a heavy wooden tray, ran at him screaming, and when it crashed into his face and my father's head flew into a corner near a side table, I saw the incomprehension as he thought himself betrayed and denied, a victim of unrequited love. My mother was going for him again and I saw his hand with the knife thrust out and she crashed forward as he pulled it out, blood gushing from her mouth and nose. He smashed her into another full length mirror, I saw the images of her multiply to infinity, fragmented as the broken glass. Then the look of love came into his eyes again as he gazed at her body, her blood everywhere, eyes wide enough to swallow the world, and he began to cut off her clothes. I wanted to rush out, cover my mother's body, save her from this madman but dark came down and my life was without light till fragments of bullets shone like searchlights into my brain and I saw again the horror which had been.

'Maybe you come out the hospital too soon, Prof. Make I take you back for a check-up, sir.' He was sitting there across from me, looking alarmed, and I was seeing his brother Aaron with the butcher knife crouched over the body of my parents. I'd never felt better in my life but I was sweating in the chill air. It was so cold Moses wore a thick windbreaker. It was like I had malaria, my body wracked with fever heat but feeling cold as the parasites ate the substance from my blood.

'I'm fine, sir, sometimes I get allergic reactions when I get exposed to strange pollen, like up here.' 'I really glad, sir. After all you suffer from my brother, Aaron, and now my nephew, Eddy... I call you up here to give you this house, is the one I want to tell you about in the hospital. Is you father house; you grandma refuse to take it, she say me is a drug dealer and gunman. You see how beautiful the house is, sir. Plenty people want buy it but me say is for one of the family. You know you father get the land cheap, 'cause they think nobody can build on it.'

'I've never seen a more beautiful house, sir; it looks like something out of a dream. Eddy offered me one down the hill, near our old house but I told him I had to talk to Sharon.'

'Nothing to talk about this time, Prof., is you father house.'

'It's still so sudden, sir. I need time to think about it...'

'And talk to Sharon! – I understand, Prof., man like you don't jump to take a thing man offer him. You like you parent and grandma... Delroy!' Delroy came, he was eating a sweetsop he must have picked in the backyard. 'Bring that red box from me car, Delroy.' Delroy brought the big box file, Moses opened it and began to hand me files with my parents' names. I hadn't remembered, my grandmother had changed our name so people wouldn't be reminded of the horror and I never identified with the name she gave me, thinking of myself instead with nicknames from horrid cartoon characters or maniacal dancehall stars. 'You parent leave money, Prof., and me put it in a account with high interest. And the business we start still going, so me put their share in too.'

I looked at the statements and calculated there was enough to buy a nice house in Barnes near the river. I began to fantasize about this wonder house, a perfect wife, a home in an upper-class suburb of London plus money to invest. Then I thought of Sharon.

'Thanks, Moses. This looks fantastic but I need time to think.'

'And talk to Sharon! I know, Prof., but the money is you parent, the same as you own. Take all the time you need – money here in the bank, it won't go nowhere.'

He mentioned my grandmother's house as an afterthought. 'The place use to be choice property in the old days but now the area gone down. Eddy and him Chinese friend start buying up the land cheap; people don't know. You grandma don't leave a will but I take it on myself and tell Eddy the place is yours and me want the best price, now they plan to build big shopping mall and hotel there.'

CHAPTER THIRTY-FIVE

Elena and her 'cousin' the new PM were married not long after my meeting with Moses. She knew I was going back to London to see about publishing my book and insisted on a quick wedding so I could attend. She promised to go to our wedding, wherever it was, even though neither of us had said a word about marrying. When he heard the news the Archbishop sent an envoy to her, one he thought she respected, to beg her not to marry the man, as her 'cousin' was a Catholic and the Church didn't believe in divorce. Because the man was an old friend of her father's people, she sent him back with polite words about this being the twenty-first century. But the Churchman was obstinate, he sent the envoy back to insist and warn her they would be excommunicated. Sharon knew her friend, she insisted on accompanying her to all these sessions, to prevent the man from being physically attacked but she couldn't prevent Elena from sending him back to his Archbishop with a string of our country's famous expletives. But the Archbishop still wasn't satisfied and though the envoy was afraid for his life, he took her the Churchman's message that if they insisted on marrying they should do it low profile, so as not to embarrass the Church and the PM's office. Other friends tried to convince them a high Profile wedding could cost votes, the country had a huge Catholic population and there was sympathy for the ex-wife, since no one explained why she was sacked.

Elena got her friend in Security to hack into computers of the people who organised the wedding of Prince William and planned to make hers the wedding of the century, with a dress more spectacular than Kate Middleton's. It took Sharon to convince her to tone things down and even then she wouldn't agree till the PM promised to upgrade one of Eddy's houses with genuine 'Made in Italy' furniture and a grand ballroom based on one she saw in a brochure on Vienna's palaces. Kate Middleton's designer made her dress, food supplied by British and French caterers and the wedding list was two hundred. Despite concerns about divorce, the Vatican sent the same Cardinal who came to Miss Violet's funeral. The parents of boys abused by priests in a country school had sued the Church and the trial was due to start in a week. This was splashed in all the papers and the PM had to send Eddy's Commando to guard the priests. Frank Walters spoke to the parents, they were offered houses and a million local dollars, the cases were dropped, the priests deported to Ireland and news appeared in *The Chronicle* that the Cardinal had been invited by the Archbishop, they would attend the wedding in the Cathedral, the Churchman eulogizing the couple as prime exemplars of the 'Holy Family'.

Sharon looked divine in her bridesmaid's dress and Elena took me aside, practically ordering me to marry her, *toute suite*. For once Elena looked more like the star in her wedding dress, to which the designer had added parrot feathers as a special touch when she heard it was for a bride from the most beautiful island in the world. Together they looked like twin angels and I wondered where they had come from. The bride was given away by Frank Walters, who I heard was distantly related to her and when I saw them walk up the aisle I thought of lines from Dylan Thomas: *The lips of time leach to the fountain head; / Love drips and gathers, but the fallen blood/ Shall calm her sores.*

We had problems deciding what to give them. Then I remembered I had agate necklaces I'd picked up in Northern Nigeria where I had given a lecture on Barth. The necklaces traditionally worn by the nomadic Fulani women had each bead strung with twine. When he saw them in my room, a friend from Oxford whose family owned part of *Boodles* promised to have them restrung using precious metals and I'd forgotten to collect them. I'd written a paper for him in German when he broke up with his childhood sweetheart and went on a cosmic bender. I called him; he was off the sauce, couriered them and today wearing them Sharon and Helena looked like Fulani princesses. I'd expected something lesser than this but they were so fine the Queen could wear them. They were strung with platinum, the lockets 22 carat gold, each bead capped with fine discs of the metal. Sebastian's people must have spent a fortune but when I offered to pay he told me to go fuck myself, which he said he knew I loved doing!

Elena refused Rosemary an invite, she told her not to come anywhere near the wedding nor the reception in the PM's house near the Governor General's but Rosemary turned up wearing a knock off Versace gown and already smelling of liquor. She couldn't keep her eyes off me and kept giving Sharon dirty looks. She managed to squeeze in to a table next to mine and drank the pink, specially labelled champagne as if it were cola. Then she stood up, walked over to my table and took a piece of spicy chicken from my plate. It seemed she'd gone from loving me for Eddy's money to wanting me because I had Sharon. When Elena saw her she pounded her little fists into the high table, shouted for her friend in Security, and ordered him to dump Rosemary into one of the king-sized bins supplied by the catering services of the PM's Office. Sharon had advised her to invite Rosemary, she said she had no fear I would yield to temptation but Elena insisted no man should be stressed out by exposure to so much skin. When she saw the security heading toward Rosemary, Sharon persuaded them she would talk to her and, after giving her a lady's goody bag, she led her out. The bag contained a litre of *Armagnac,* vintage the year of Elena's birth, a Louis Vuitton bag made for the occasion, a 9 carat gold plated bracelet, a slice of wedding cake and square of extra ripe Roquefort cheese. But though Sharon rescued her from the king-sized bin and gave her presents, Rosemary still called her a 'bitch' before drunkenly stomping away.

CHAPTER THIRTY-SIX

When I told Sharon about Moses she took my laptop and logged on to Alpooz.com, real estate listing site for the whole country. My laptop and phone were now 'clean' – Elena's friend deleted the malware Eddy's people installed. The house that supposedly belonged to my father was listed under a company registered in the British Virgin Islands. She went back some years and showed balance sheets with colossal profits, rent on the house listed as an expense.

'The company belongs to Moses and Cairncross, they set up in the BVI to avoid tax. There's no evidence your father had anything to do with it. Even if he did, the whole scheme was a scam organised by Moses and Cairncross. The land then was practically worthless, its value created by government building roads, putting in water and electricity, and granting planning permission. Your father's role was to design the houses, your mother to landscape. They were idealistic people believing in perfection, you see how beautiful their creations are. They had no business sense and couldn't have known what their crooked partners were doing. Your father was a gambler, thought he could beat the odds but was kept in line by your mother. No money was paid to government, just bribes for officials. I don't know how Moses calculated the money he says was your father's: it was all dubious. That's why your grandmother refused to have anything to do with it. Moses may have been a friend but was also a businessman, politician and crook. '

I had delusions about having money and now I was deflated. My morality was based on the principle it was right to steal from a thief, so I saw nothing wrong in taking Eddy's money. But Sharon and my grandmother apparently thought differently. 'See your grandmother's place – what Moses said about the price was true and that's already gone up. This place belonged to your family for generations. That one you can take.' This was still a lot, though it was now considered downtown.

'Moses told you the high-class development was built before your father's time but look at the date in the land registry. You can see he designed the houses, they have his distinctive style.' I was disappointed Moses had participated in a scheme bordering on apartheid, to let the children of slave owners live apart from descendants of their slaves who made good. That was logical for a man like Cairncross but Moses had dragged himself from below the gutters and still lived among his people. He refused to marry and have children, he feared producing monsters like his brother Aaron or his nephew Eddy. But he had taken in strays, orphans, any child whose parents couldn't afford to bring them up. He treated them better than most parents their blood children and his kids were more loyal than they would to those who gave them birth. My excuse for him was that you couldn't judge great men by the same criteria as pygmies. My father's involvement was due to naivete – he thought he had a wonderful wife and house and thus the perfect life. My judgement of Eddy was similar to that for Moses, had Eddy brought me back to finish what his crazy father started with killing my parents? I don't think so. Maybe he had some pangs of rudimentary conscience, felt sorry for me, knew I had problems from when I was in school here. Maybe he wanted to make amends while getting a book that would boost his image as my earlier book had done for Joseph. Winston had mentioned it was Bloom, my old teacher who recommended me to the publisher for my first book and he had put in a word with Eddy. But when Eddy's spy people reported what I said on my phone, wrote on my computer, who I saw, he considered me disloyal. And for a man with his psychology, disloyalty was a capital offence. At his hotel he'd given me the last chance – leave Sharon and fuck Rosemary who would spy on me, take the nice house he offered and write the crap he wanted. I'd refused and deserved to die.

Before I left we decided to look at the progress the Chinese made since Eddy's death. I'd hoped they'd let up, leave the people in slums where their families had lived forever. But they seemed to have accelerated. They left Moses and his people alone in his estate. We saw they'd repaired the damage done by Eddy's American friends, my father's design was sturdier than that of the towers destroyed by bin Laden and survived the missile strikes. In memory of the late PM's heroism the place was now called THE EDDY HADDAD ESTATE. At other slums, including those in opposition areas, there were brand new, factory-shiny red buses lined up to move the people to their new dormitories. Behind them were TGVs with containers to take their belongings, though their new homes were furnished. All were supplied with cardboard boxes containing loaves, sardines, rice, flour, sugar and other provisions. They were also supplied with orange overalls, though many preferred to wear their rags. Behind the trucks, kept out of sight, were big, shiny bulldozers. Because the Chinese had a civilization of over six thousand years, the bulldozers would not move until the people were out of sight, where they could not see places they called home being flattened. We saw the new road Winston had taken, where the Chinese had completed orderly rows of towers like on the Eddy Haddad Estate, built to my father's design with precision, like termite colonies.

The night before, Elena gave us tickets to a concert where new stars of the dancehall assembly line, including Jayzee, gathered to welcome the new PM, mourn the old one, and weep for their beloved Donnie. These people were much more sophisticated and refined than Lover Man, the Rhino and their gang. Their lyrics and melodies were well crafted, based on positive experiences in the ghetto; they didn't bray homophobic, misogynistic, ultraviolent themes. The PM was growing in confidence, he shouted that relocation of slum dwellers was a progressive masterstroke, guaranteed to make their lives go forward, provide jobs, stability, and a bright future for their children.

'Elena wrote the speech – see how many times he used "guarantee"? When we were kids she bought a Chinese pen "guaranteed for a year" and it broke the same day. I told her what guarantee meant and taught her how to spell it.' What she said made sense – he used phrases from an essay by Amilcar Cabral, assassinated leader of Guinea (Bissau) and Cape Verde, which I'd given Elena when she saw it on my desk and said how much she liked it.

We wanted Bunny to take us around but he'd lost an aunt in the country and had to go for the funeral. So we called up my schoolmate at Avis and he gave us a complimentary car with a full tank. Sharon drove – she knew the way. I'd noticed her eyes cloud over when we saw the repaired towers on the Eddy Haddad Estate and lines of buses waiting for people in other slums, whose homes would be levelled. Now it was my turn and I felt the sting of salt in tears I refused to let go, thinking of my little girl of glass. We parked and just sat looking on my grandmother's house, standing out like a mast on a ship marooned in red earth gouged out by giant bulldozers. The windows and doors were boarded up, I could remember nothing of the time I spent there after my parents were slaughtered, or of my grandmother's lonely, bitter life, as she contemplated betrayal by God. I tried to imagine the big mall and hotels Moses said the Chinese planned for the site, calculating the money he'd give me when he sold it.

We saw a bicycle rider selling papers and bought *The Chronicle* and *Independent*. The headlines said the Rhino, Lion Man and Lover Man had been arrested and extradited to America. The *Independent* wrote that the three dancehall stars were in Lover Man's uptown mansion with five schoolgirls and one schoolboy, fed with jerk pork, drunk with rum punch spiked with Rohypnol. The girls when discovered were confused and unsteady and were allowed to dress in their red tartan uniforms and white blouses, then taken out through the back gate to hospital where they were tested for HIV and treated for the effects of the drugs and sexual assault. They were found with local thousand dollar bills hidden in schoolbooks, pockets and bras. The boy, in khaki uniform and striped purple tie, was unconscious and bled from his ass. He was taken out on a stretcher, covered up. The musicians were handcuffed, shackled at waist and ankles, taken out naked in front of a crowd of people and camerawomen from all the TV stations. All they wore were pink t-shirts from the Sydney Gay Pride March. They were shoved onto the floors of two black Range Rovers, where women Commandos sat with boots on their backs as they sped to the airport. One paper wrote that Lover Man's thighs were like massive tree trunks. The new PM had ordered his Commando to open up and recruit women from the Security Police. The musicians were taken onto a Falcon jet owned by an Air America plane and I was happy these boys had been dealt with but wondered where the PM had got the balls.

Then I thought we'd die of shock when we heard the car radio announce the Commando were looking for Moses. This we could not understand. By the time we got home we heard he'd been captured in a red wig and pink shades; that gunmen gathered from all over to protect him and seventy-six persons were killed. He too was driven straight to the airport. Sharon was so unsteady I told her I'd get take-away food or something from Miss Robotham where I was going to collect my clothes. But she said she'd already prepared my goodbye meal and it would be no trouble getting it ready while I was gone. I knew we had nice rum punch but still asked Miss Robotham to give us her best Rose. I didn't want to rush off after refusing the meal she offered but I told her Sharon was upset and she was very understanding when I said goodbye. We'd have enjoyed the meal of escoveitched fish and rice if it wasn't for the bitter taste left by Moses' extradition. We drank the Rose with the meal – it was good D'Anjou. Then as we drank the rum punch we mellowed enough for Sharon to tell me Elena phoned when I was away.

The musicians met in a house bought by Lover Man in a new Chinese development every Wednesday, for what they called 'Spring Chicken' day. They picked up schoolgirls and boys, gave them money, fed them, gave them over-proof rum and drugs, then raped them. The place was bugged, and Elena's friend in Security gave her the DVD where they boasted they would come over to Government House and do her, since her husband only knew how to 'fuck little girls.' After they shouted this, they called over the drugged schoolchildren to suck them off. We saw YouTube videos of them being shackled. Liquid was pouring from Lover Man's eyes, nose, mouth and, down below, from what looked like a turkey's wattle, between his legs. He had written five songs in homage to his colossal dick, which he titled Gigantic Silo, Enormous Lighthouse and Cylinder Mountain. His ICBM had won the Ucwamb Bolt Award, the dancehall equivalent of the Grammys.

Moses was a different matter. He chose Elena's husband as PM, because he wasn't Eddy, he would do what he was told, even raise his hand for permission if he wanted to go to the head. But Moses didn't like submission and couldn't hide his contempt for Eddy's first cousin. Whatever people said of Eddy he was a *man*. And Eddy was *blood*. He wasn't impressed the man spoke six languages – the word for 'coward' was the same in every language for men who couldn't handle women their own age! It didn't matter that he read thousands of books. Moses had never finished a single one and world leaders listened to him. He didn't consult the PM when he made decisions and Colin and his wife read about them in the papers with the rest of the country. Moses was so shocked when the Commando grabbed him, his remaining hair started falling out on the way to the airport. The PM had started on Elena when she was a schoolgirl and thought she would die from the pain of anal sex. But while she was eleven her spirit was hundreds of years old and, as the years went on, she became even more mature, stronger, while her lover remained the age he was when he started screwing little girls. He might have read thousands of books, including Hegel, Marx, and other thinkers who taught the processes through which the master became a slave and the victim a conqueror.

Elena might have felt pain in her ass but she'd grown balls. Now the three musicians and Moses were having theirs frozen off in CIA jets at forty-thousand feet, with tunes from the Beach Boys blaring on big Realistic speakers. In the bed I tried to comfort Sharon as she wept in my arms.

I wanted us to go in the rental to the airport but didn't want her to drive back alone so I rang Delroy. When she called Elena for me to say goodbye she said she would come with us. I could see Sharon's face twitch; she obviously thought of Range Rovers of Commando and deafening sirens but Elena came in a Lincoln town car with a single bodyguard, a plain Volvo following with women Commandos. We couldn't complain – if you went after people like Moses and the musicians, you had to prepare your firepower in case they tried to fuck you back. Sharon was Elena's best friend, perhaps her only friend but Elena wasn't like us. She knew what power was and didn't operate on likes, dislikes or moral feelings. We could rejoice at execrable musicians being humiliated but were upset at what happened to Moses who we liked a lot, despite what we knew of his methods. But I calculated Elena liked him more than I did; he helped bring her up but when he threatened the man she loved she had as much compassion as an angry tiger. Just as Eddy, who tried to kill me, though I knew he liked me a lot. She wore the *ase oke* from the picture in the condo but this time there were no red beads, just the 22 carat gold necklace with a ruby heart the PM had given her as a wedding present. She used Sharon's Incanto she'd pinched when she left the condo. Luckily Chin called to say he was coming up from Florida and I asked him to bring two bottles from duty free. He brought three and Sharon gave her one. We noticed how she squeezed herself into the corner, leaving us space in case we felt like copping a feel or giving each other tongue. Obviously, being fucked in the ass as a little girl made her a victim of child sex but hadn't affected her common sense.

The forty storey hotel with its rows of blinding glass was complete; the PM had taken us to dinner at the restaurant with the giant sign, CELESTIAL GARDEN OF PERPETUAL PEACE, on the roof. Six girls served us in the ornate 'presidential room', one for water, one for wine, one for meat, one for fish, one for desert, and one to schmooze. We needed shades to protect our eyes from their outfits of dazzling red and yellow Chinese silk. The tasting menu of twenty dishes had animals whose origins I didn't want to know. The prize dish was a sterling silver bowl of shark fin soup, for a thousand five-hundred bills. It was from the Great White and I suppose, on the scale of world history, Great Yellow trumped Great White every time. Outside the glass walls was a garden like a rainforest, brilliantly lit, where frogs, spiders, scorpions, termites and cicadas trilled all night. I thought of Mr Wang as I listened to melodies of Linda Ronstadt, California's Governor and ex-Jesuit, Brown's former squeeze. There were ponds with exotic fish, pits with snakes, cages with wild birds to ensure they were live when cooked. I was becoming reconciled to the melding of good and evil, beauty and decay, love and death. Our PM, Colin Shepherd, had an IQ off the scale, a gift for languages but was a paedophile. So was Socrates, Plato, Aristotle, Alexander and other heroes of our civilisation. Elena was a tragic victim of the horrors but also a survivor. She was generous but capable of unimaginable evil and extravagance. I looked over at Sharon and wondered how she'd managed to escape the duality. I thought of a verse by Heinrich Heine, *'du bist so wie eine rose, so schon und hold und rein',* which translated roughly as *'you are so like a rose, so beautiful, wholesome and pure.'* On the ground floor was a collection of luxury shops and as we passed I noticed the queue outside the Brioni Bespoke Establishment where they measured you for fifteen-thousand dollar Vicuna suits. The Christian Louboutin establishment made shoes from exotic leathers for Chinese women with dreams of status back home. Delroy took a new exit to the airport road and we saw the giant new ALL STAR SHOWROOM with Rollers, Bentleys, Daimlers, Mercedes, Beamers, Porsches, Ferraris, Maseratis and Lamborghinis. This looked like the type of place Chin and Mr Wang might be involved in. A man who won ten million in a casino on Blue Island might be looking for expensive wheels. The Chinese were the new Texans, they believed in BIG. Chin was a real pal. When I recovered from the coma my first call was from him, he was with Mr Wang who wished me well, again inviting me to Macau. Chin asked me to send the bill and when I told him it was already paid, he sent me a first-class ticket to London and ten-thousand pounds.

Just before we got on the airport road we saw what the GUINNESS BOOK OF RECORDS advertised as the biggest poster in the world. It promoted a concert in the National Stadium by Rihanna, Beyoncé and Lady Gaga. I was feeling queasy and wondered why I was upset by Beyonce's legs. She looked hot but I'd never had a hard on or wet dream about doing her and knew it wasn't just because she and Jay-Z made such a good couple.

When I was six I remembered this statuesque maid who frightened shit out of me. One day my grandmother went to the doctor and Elaine led me to her room, lay on her bed, pulled up her skirt, pulled down her knickers and pulled me onto her. She kept screaming for me to 'do it' and as I didn't know what to do I pissed into her. She was so angry she squeezed me where it hurt most, threatening to 'cut it off' if I told my grandmother and my eyes went blind. From that day I felt chill and wet myself whenever I saw her, upsetting my gran, till the old woman sacked her for bringing hemp-smoking men friends into her room at night who burgled our house of silver heirlooms and ancient Chinese crockery. Beyoncé was a wonderful girl, she wasn't a diva, her mother went with her on tour and allegedly slapped her if she thought she was getting out of line. I didn't like swearing on people, and was willing to bet she didn't fuck anyone but Jay-Z. But when I saw her legs I didn't get hard or feel the buzz, just panic; her pins reminded me of that fucking bitch Elaine.

When we got to the airport we were astonished it was complete and while it reminded me of *Star Trek* when I first saw it, Gene Rodenberry couldn't imagine the finished product in the next five-thousand years. The Chinese used architects from all over in their construction and they would buy, borrow or steal to ensure perfection. Of course it was called THE EDDY HADDAD INTERNATIONAL AIRPORT. I took out my trusty camera phone. I thought we would head for Departures and see how brilliant our friends were, compared to the architects of primitive Heathrow Terminal Five. But Delroy headed for an unmarked glass door at the side and opened it for us to enter an ultramodern car park. A host of attendants were waiting and Delroy opened the boot for them to take my luggage after giving a pretty girl my passport. I could smell the fear and wondered how they knew it was Elena who had pulled off the stunt yesterday. In the papers which some of them held, shackled musicians were being dragged butt-naked into Range Rovers with captions crafted from phrases they made famous about 'tearing up young pussy' and 'killing battymen.' The women Commando herding them were in short black skirts showing flashy pins and hints of frilly red knickers, their hands grasping Scorpion machine pistols like giant fountain pens. Then I noticed a smaller headline, saying that top officials from the Security Service had been retired and Elena's friend was now Deputy Director. I looked at her and Sharon with their arms around each other and could see no change, no sign of her new power. When we got into the lounge, I thought she would hang around. But she loved her friend, she wanted her to succeed and gave us space.

'I have something to do, Sher. I'll come back when Prof. has to go.' I could see the film over their eyes but they didn't want to weep. I thought of my little estate girl as I watched her walk away with her visored, black clad bodyguard. Elena had turned her tragedy into power that would shield her while that little one made of glass chewing her nails had no protection and was doomed. They brought us pink champagne from the wedding and tiny patties, jerk pork and chicken cut into bite sized chunks. The glass and steel tables glittered like suns, we could see our reflections in the purple mahoe floors and leather of the chairs was the softest I'd felt. Above, the roof curved like the sky with constellations of the brightest stars. We noticed the stark nervousness of the young people with us.

Then from concealed Bose speakers I heard the most fabulous rendition of Mozart's Laudate Dominum ever. We were in the house one night discussing music we liked best: they liked old soul and Reggae and I told them I liked everything, including classical. I told them the *Laudate* did things for me and Elena hadn't forgotten. I'm sure she got them to put in this Bose set which reproduced the music so accurately I could see the conductor's baton twirling, each musician producing each note on radiant instruments, the composer scrawling the notes, brow furrowed, feeling the horror which made him die at thirty five and be buried in a pauper's grave. I couldn't tell them of the years I wouldn't listen to the piece when I heard it was the favourite of Reinhardt Heydrich, racist, mass-murdering Nazi, ferocious predator of small Jewish boys. Or that I started listening again when I learned fragments from the grenade thrown by the assassin penetrated the Nazi's organs while horsehair from his car's upholstery poisoned his blood.

Sharon and I did everything to hold back the tears, we promised to call and e-mail several times a day and had to refrain from kissing or cuddling as our minders watched us like hawks. When we saw Elena coming I thought how much she looked like a Yoruba princess strolling in an Oba's palace in ancient Ibadan. It was she who lost it when she gave me my passport, hugged me and wept as she told me she would take good care of her friend. I looked at the attendants and couldn't see any decrease in their fear, knowing their vengeful Mistress could shed tears. As I embraced Sharon, trying not to flow over like her, I heard Elena whisper to the two most senior aides to take me right to my seat on the plane.

All the times I left before I felt relief getting away to somewhere more pleasant and secure. But now as I looked back and waved to Sharon weeping in Elena's arms I knew I was leaving home.

CHAPTER THIRTY-SEVEN

At Gatwick I felt like someone from a star ship landing on the planet Zog. I hadn't noticed before how alien these people were, their cold indifference even to each other. I'd felt something for the people in the VIP room at our new airport despite the smell of their fear. I liked Eddy even though I knew what he was and should have hated him for trying to kill me. I respected Moses for what he achieved and was sorry he was humiliated. I had some idea of how many men Donnie killed but loved him for what he did for Elizabeth and the brilliance of his songs. And I loved Elena for being Sharon's best friend, who would keep her from becoming a monster and destroying herself like Aaron, Moses and Eddy. With these people, I handed over my passport, they checked on their machine and imagined them calling the pigs if I even so much as smiled. Long ago I learnt an Englishman would rather you fucked and murdered his grandmother than delay him for his train.

My little place was like the cell where I supposed Moses was now freezing his ass off. I couldn't call Sharon from here – I thought I might crack or she'd feel the horror I was experiencing.

~

I decided to see some of the places I'd dreamed about while on Google Earth and started walking five to ten kilometres along the river, from Barnes and Putney, way up to Richmond, Kingston, Hampton Palace Court and Walton-upon-Thames. One day it snowed heavily and among the flakes I thought I saw my parents smiling and recalled the passage from a book 'which of us has known his mother, which of us has looked into his father's heart...' When I watched Google Earth I always tried to imagine what the places looked like, which people occupied the houses. When I got to the one made of glass between Kingston and Hampton Court, I walked back and forth, trying to see if anyone was in, then I realized I was looking for my parents and the pain came back, the tears inside almost steaming over.

I called Sharon from Barnes Bridge while looking at the blue plaque on a house where Gustav Holst had once lived. He had been a teacher at St Paul's Girls' school and I wondered how an ordinary guy like him could produce such music; if I lived a thousand years I couldn't write stuff of that quality. Now Moses was locked up I wouldn't get the premium I was expecting on my grandma's place. I couldn't afford a house like this. My troubles didn't end with Moses it seemed. My agent said Gutenberg didn't want my book anymore and paused for at least two seconds when I told him it was a bummer having to give their advance back. I never appreciated what agents are for and thought this one took fifteen per cent to save me the trouble of reading contracts or talking to publishers. I disliked him – he wore red socks, braces and grey pinstripe suit like the character played by Michael Douglas in that awful film about

Wall Street by Oliver Stone. There were lawyers and real-estate agents I liked better. I liked him even less when he joked that authors were like children who needed minders. He said Gutenberg had signed a binding contract hoping to advance their business interests and now Eddy was dead they didn't want to upset the new crowd. When he threatened to sue they said he was welcome – sueing cost money and authors were skint. When he sued they said I could keep the advance, I said how thrilled I was, prompting another two second pause while he thought up another polite insult. Articles appeared in the *Guardian* and *Independent* detailing the mercenary attitudes of the publisher's owner, most unwelcome as the Competition Commission was probing his holding company and four others for constituting a cartel in the drinks industry. The publisher decided to settle out of court, offered to pay our costs and give twice the original advance. Then the agent arranged an auction which garnered an even bigger advance due to the publicity surrounding Eddy's killing and violence, the extradition of Moses and the dancehall musicians caused. I calculated how much I had now and what type of place I could afford after selling my garret, spurting in value due to the construction of *Westfield* shopping mall and the regeneration when the BBC moved out of Television Centre.

Sharon called to say she'd heard from my old school, they promised her a full scholarship. I knew Elena would have paid her fees, even offered to buy her a house but she knew her friend would never accept. The Brits were slow and it would take time for Oxford and LSE to make an offer. I was pretty sure they'd say yes but they didn't have the bread to make as good an offer as the Yanks. I told her this but let her know the money I had would buy an even better place if we went to America. To be frank, I wasn't keen about either place now and would be happy wherever, as long as I was with her. Now I was in the twenty-first century I realised the Internet, like Carlsberg beer, reaches places other media can't.

I heard a company connected to Jay-Z and Will Smith had read a resume of my book online and wanted to make a movie. St Martin's also signed a contract to do an American edition. These guys were into music, Jay-Z's company signed several dancehall people. Maybe they wanted to highlight the music and help sell more records. But when I thought about it I began to have misgivings about Smith playing me. He was a big, handsome guy, who would be a babe magnet if not for his wife, Jada. I was a Richard Lester type of guy you could pass in the aisle in Tesco without noticing. Beyoncé couldn't do justice to Sharon: she didn't have her brains and would obliterate the character with her fame. Besides she still reminded me of Elaine who did havoc with my balls. Maybe Sharon should play herself. Eddy wasn't a problem, Forest Whitaker wouldn't even have to wear make up. Although he was getting on in age, James Earl Jones would make a brilliant Moses and his twin. Chewetel Ejiofor was a shoo-in for Winston, he was African, looked intelligent and sensitive and I could imagine him in the ICU in that New York hospital with tubes hanging out of him. Elizabeth was a problem, for a character like her even brilliant filmmakers would try to exploit the sensational. They would want Angelina Jolie, based on her notoriety, history of self-harm and family. They would like to use the myth of her alleged ancestress, supposed to have fucked horses and slaughtered slave lovers. But Elizabeth would not marry a guy like Brad Pitt. She wouldn't adopt a United Nations of Children and wouldn't abide those swollen lips. This was a factual book. From my research the 'White Witch' was not Elizabeth's ancestress, she had an accident with a horse when she was a teenager and couldn't have kids. She developed a habit of sleeping with slaves, usually the most muscular and ill-tempered who battered her after fucking. She didn't kill them all, only those she liked a lot, who fucked her but insisted on remaining with wives, having kids she couldn't.

Sharon called to say Elizabeth had a beautiful baby girl she called Donelle to remind her of her dead lover. She looked in good shape, no one was battering her, and I'm sure the woman beaters were now terrified of Elena's Commando chaining and dragging them out with asses and cocks exposed.

Today is Boat Race day and I decided to watch it from the start at Putney Bridge. I don't know why, I resented those privileged assholes, for whom racing a boat was part of the life society and their rich parents prepared for them before they were born. Their fathers got bonuses in the City, mothers bought prams at Harrods or Peter Jones, their prep schools, Eton, and Oxbridge belonged to them. I thought of how the decks were stacked against Sharon, Elena, my *Lalique* girl, Moses, Eddy, Donnie and all the others, with greater odds of premature death than any other endangered species. Eddie and Donnie were much smarter than David Cameron but they were dead. Moses was smarter than them all, he hadn't even had bootlaces to pull himself out of the gutter but succeeded; now he was freezing his ass off in a maximum security cell in Colorado.

I used to watch these jokers on the river at my old school, when I had the illusion we were headed somewhere. But while their striving was part of their belief in progress, in school, in Profession and life, I always felt I was running from something when I was on the track. The Jesuits preached about sound minds in sound bodies – in some Latin crap I forget – but my own history said this was a fucking lie, that we were all sick as shit. I looked around and couldn't see a single cop in the stifling crowds while at the Notting Hill Carnival where our people went there were so many you had to look for room to breathe. I was becoming so flustered I decided to watch the end of the race instead, and knew a way through Putney Heath and Barnes Common to take me to Mortlake in about fifteen minutes. I found myself resenting the little girls I saw along the way, the same age as the dancehall queen, my *Lalique* girl and Stephen's daughter but protected by the state, society, the law, public opinion, the media, their families. Any man who fucked them prematurely would do long jail time.

I got to Barnes Bridge and was looking at Holst's house again when Sharon called. She was weeping and I thought of the time Miss Vie died, how long it took to get her back. I was anxious but didn't ask her what was wrong right away; I didn't want to rush her. 'Take it easy, baby,' I kept saying, 'you know I'm here for you.' I could hear the mouthfuls of air she was gulping down, the strangled cries she couldn't get out. 'Breathe easy, babe, breathe slowly, in and out, in and out.' But she wept more and I began to panic, thinking maybe they'd killed Elena when they found out she was responsible for kicking out the musicians and sacking the security people who had been leaking stories about her husband.

'I'm here, babe. You be patient now, tell me when you're ready. I can wait all day.' She calmed down and then it was my turn to scream.

'Moses is dead,' she said. 'They said he was smoking in bed and fell asleep. He was burnt to death.'

I wanted to shout but my body had fled again and nothing would come out. Moses and Aaron had asthma and Moses never smoked. I'd often wondered why Eddy's friends never smoked weed in his presence till I found he would pass out or kill them. Aaron's problem was the weed made him feel he was suffocating and fed his paranoid schizophrenia. I'd wondered how long Moses would last in an American prison, away from the people and places he loved. People like the Farnham's, Bushes and Whitney's didn't like secrets he could spill in court. So they must have killed him. Sharon texted me his picture from his cell before he died and he looked like the character Odo in *Star Trek: Deep Space Nine* when the Federation infected his people with the virus that reduced them to rag and stick men and women.

I decided to go back home but didn't want to see these people now I knew Moses was dead, a man I had been sure would outlive me. I would retrace my steps through Barnes across Commons and Heath and hope the crowds had dispersed from the start. Just across from Barnes Tennis Club there's an abandoned cemetery where ancient notables rest in broken tombs. In their day some must have believed black slaves were created by their Master to serve them, while others thought all men were created equal – but not with the same capacity to become good, upstanding and faithful citizens. I thought if I climbed the fence and fell in a tomb no one would hear me scream though they played tennis in plain view and the busy A306 was not far. The graveyard was covered with vegetation as in a civilised rain forest; there were weeds with brilliant pink, blue and yellow bellflowers. I thought if the present government stayed in power long enough they might level this place and build a huge massage parlour. Or if the other lot came back, they would construct a brothel and call it the Cherie Blair Finishing School for Young Ladies.

Since the accident my hair had grown back but in irregular patterns where fragments of the bullets scythed through my scalp. So as not to make people think I was a gang member from LA I wore my cheap M&S made-in-China Panama hat to cover it. But coming back I remembered I'd bought an expensive one in the Harrods Sale. It was reduced from four-hundred pounds to fifty pounds and I was attracted because it was called 'Borsalino', reminding me of the anti-mafia judge blown up by a thousand kilo bomb on his way home in Sicily. A man like that needs remembering. When I tried it on, some upper-class looking cocksucker resembling Rod Liddle said how perfectly it fit, though it perched on my hair like a fucking yarmulke. I'd looked at the guy, tried to appear neutral so he wouldn't see how pissed I was, at his thinking he could patronise me because I clearly couldn't afford to come within ten kilometres of the place for the things they sold at full price.

Now my hair is shaven off it fits perfectly, reminding me of a Graham Greene hero suffering moral meltdown in a steamy tropical hole like Freetown or Port-au-Prince. Greene was a lapsed Catholic like me and we think we're suffused with Original Sin, from which there is no escape. We believe in a God who taught us to worship pain and seek salvation through suffering.

Right now I want to get away from the pain but what I seek is not salvation but oblivion.

I called Sharon again and heard she'd calmed a bit, still crying, but silently.

'I'm coming home, baby,' I said. 'I'm coming to help you bury him.'